He leaned clo[...] to shore up his cour[...] need to talk."

She didn't need to be Perry Mason to see he was about to make some sort of declaration about his feelings, but one Baldwin brother per night was all she could handle. "Sean—" she began, alarmed.

"I'm crazy about you." Hesitantly—nervously—he raised his hand and ran the backs of his fingers down her cheek; her instinct was to shake him off. Over Sean's shoulder, ten feet away by the bar, she saw Mike staring at them, cold fury in his eyes. "I want to get to know you better. I want to take you to dinner tomorrow night."

She fell back on the words she always used when a man she had no interest in tried to hit on her. "I don't know what to say."

"Just think about it."

Trouble

Ann Christopher

Dafina
Books

Kensington Publishing Corp.

http://www.kensingtonbooks.com

To Richard

DAFINA BOOKS are published by

Kensington Publishing Corp.
850 Third Avenue
New York, NY 10022

All Kensington Titles, Imprints, and Distributed Lines are available at special quantity discounts for bulk purchases for sales promotions, premiums, fund-raising, and educational or institutional use. Special book excerpts or customized printings can also be created to fit specific needs. For details, write or phone the office of the Kensington special sales manager: Kensington Publishing Corp., 850 Third Avenue, New York, NY 10022, attn: Special Sales Department, Phone: 1-800-221-2647.

Dafina and the Dafina logo Reg. U.S. Pat. & TM Off.

First Dafina mass market printing: July 2006
10 9 8 7 6 5 4 3 2 1

Printed in the United States of America

She that has a choice has trouble.
—*American proverb*

Chapter 1

"Promise me, Michael."

"Mama, I can't promise I'll smooth things over with Sean. He hates me."

"Your brother doesn't hate you. And I need your help."

Mike Baldwin made a strangled, impatient sound. Irritated, he looked around the crowded, sunny downtown Cincinnati cafe and wondered how to extract himself from this situation. The cafe was packed and noisy, and the very last place on the planet he needed to be.

The jury was still out, and he should be with his client right now, holding her hand like any other criminal defense attorney worth his salt would do. Or he could take a few minutes to sneak back to the office, where the work of about twenty lawyers waited for him. He'd much prefer to eat a quick lunch at his desk, where he could at least open some of his mail, but Mama had called at the last minute, insisting on lunch today.

She stared expectantly at him. The old girl was sharp; her caramel skin and dark, hooded eyes glowed in the bright light from the huge window near their table, and her short salt-and-pepper hair looked glossy. She was as beautiful as ever. "Well?"

Mike tossed down his menu and sighed. "What's this all about?"

She pulled her crisp white napkin from her lap and clutched it with fidgety hands. Worry lines creased her forehead. "I'm worried about Sean."

Mike resisted the urge to snort. Well, of course, she was worried about Sean. His baby brother gave her plenty to worry about. "What's he done now?"

"Nothing. Yet. But we both know law school is going to be really hard for him."

Mike shrugged impatiently. "Everything is really hard for Sean."

She gave him a dark look. "I think he's going to need our—your—help."

Mike felt his jaw tighten. "What Sean needs is to stand up and be a man. To work hard for once in his life. And have you forgotten I helped Sean two years ago, when I hired him to work as a paralegal in my firm? And I helped him by not firing him even though he deserved it. I helped him get into law school. I helped him when I loaned him money to get his car fixed the other week. And I use the term 'loan' loosely. What else do you want?"

"I want you to make up with him. I want you to be brothers. I want my family back. Nothing's been the same since Daddy died."

Mike couldn't let her get away with such a blatant sugarcoating of their family's history. "Nothing's been the same since way before that, and you know it." She caught his gaze and held it while the server delivered their tea. After a minute Mike looked away from her accusatory eyes. Tension shot through his shoulders;

he reached his hand back to rub his neck. "Trust me. The best way I can help Sean right now is to give him some space. School just started. Let's wait a few weeks and see how he does."

Mama smoothed her napkin—now hopelessly wrinkled—and put it back in her lap. "I'm afraid to wait. I've been calling and calling him. He never calls me back. And then, last night, I finally got hold of him. And did he want to talk about school? No! All he could talk about was some woman he met in his class." She leaned forward in her chair, anxiety dripping from her pores like sweat. "And do you know what he said? He thinks he's in love with her!"

Worry finally started to worm its way into Mike's belly. He'd desperately hoped Sean would focus on law school—at least for the first semester—without falling prey to other distractions. Sean couldn't focus on two things at the same time; he could barely focus on one thing at a time. And if he was focused on some new relationship, it was a safe bet he hadn't cracked open a book in days. But who was this woman? Sean liked to have sex as much as the next guy, but what was so special about this one particular girl? Mike's curiosity got the better of him. "Who is she?"

"Oh, I don't know." Mama waved a manicured hand. "He says she's beautiful and sweet and funny. Who cares? All I care about is Sean staying on track and making it through law school."

Mike nodded sympathetically. "I agree. But Sean and I almost killed each other when he worked for me. I can't help you. I'm sorry." He picked up his menu and flipped it open.

"Do it as a favor to me."

Mike heard the tears in her voice and went rigid

with alarm. He dropped the menu and covered her hands with his own. "What is it? Tell me."

Her wet eyes held his. It took her a very long time to speak. Finally, she took a deep breath. "There's a lump."

Mike blinked at her as he struggled to process her words. "A lump?" She nodded and swiped her hand under her eyes. "Whi-"—Mike cleared his throat—"which breast?"

Mama studied the table. "The left one."

"Damn it, Mama!" Mike slammed his palm on the table. People at other tables jumped and stared at him, wide-eyed. He lowered his voice. "I told you a lumpectomy wasn't good enough! I *knew* you needed to get the mastectomy! For God's sake, Mama—"

She held up a hand, silencing him. "Do you think I need a lecture now?"

There was no reproach in her tone, but Mike choked back his panic and clamped his mouth shut, anyway. He had a tendency to be judgmental, and that certainly wouldn't help Mama now. "What did the doctor say?"

Her eyes were dry now, and she showed no signs of emotion, except for her hand, which trembled slightly as she sipped her iced tea. "He says he'll know more after the biopsy tomorrow. But he doesn't like it. And I don't want you to tell Sean anything about it."

Mike's heart sank through the floor. Mama had cancer. Again. He felt all the old fear rushing back. He desperately tried to think of something comforting to say—something meaningful—but nothing came to him. "What can I do?" he said helplessly.

Mama's eyes didn't waiver. "You can make up with your brother. You're all he's got."

"He's got you!"

"For now."

Mike couldn't believe his ears. "Knock it off, Mama! You've got yourself dead and buried already. Why don't you wait and see what the doctor says?"

She smiled gently. "Don't you think I know whether I'm sick or not?"

"Oh, Mama."

She squeezed his hand. "Don't be sorry for me, Michael. I've had a good life. A wonderful marriage, two boys I'm proud of . . ." Mike raised an eyebrow, and she swallowed hard. "I know Sean has had some rough spots. But he's okay now. And *you*." She beamed. "If I could just get you married and settled—with a child or two—I'd be in heaven."

Mike tried to smile. "Who's got time to get married?"

"You'd have more time if you stopped working so hard."

"Someone's got to pay the bills."

Suddenly she scowled. "I just hate what that girl did to you."

Had he missed something? "What girl?"

Mama humphed. "What girl? You know! The one from college!"

He scratched his head, bewildered. Mama had cancer again, and she wanted to talk about some girl he'd known a thousand years ago in college? "Can you be more specific?"

"Michael! Your girlfriend who left you for your roommate."

Oh, *that* girl. Debbie. What was her last name? He couldn't even remember. He hadn't thought about her for years. Technically, she hadn't been his girlfriend, because all they'd done was have sex—like rabbits—his first term at Harvard, when he'd been drunk with the freedom of living on his own. Unfortunately, what he hadn't realized was she was simultaneously screwing one of his roommates. Debbie's overly affectionate nature came to light one Sunday afternoon, when he'd taken an early flight back to school after a weekend at home and stumbled on Debbie and his roommate naked on the floor, engaged in one of the more athletic positions from the *Kama Sutra*.

His heart hadn't been broken. He hadn't cared enough about Debbie for that. Truth be told, he probably wouldn't even have minded if she'd been up-front and announced she wanted to date his roommate. No, what had hurt was the treachery and deceit. The fact that they'd lied right to his face, for quite a while, apparently, and he'd trusted them. Looking back, he'd realized there had been moments when he'd seen them together, and they'd exchanged a look or a smile. He just hadn't paid close enough attention to the signs. One time he'd asked the roommate if something was going on, and the guy had lied. So, of course, when he'd found out the truth, he'd kicked himself for ignoring his gut instincts. In the end, he'd chalked it up to a lesson well learned, forgotten about Debbie, and moved to another dorm room. So why had Mama mentioned the incident now? "What's Debbie got to do with anything?"

Mama made an exasperated sound. "That's why you're not married yet, Michael. You don't trust women."

Mike let out a surprised bark of laughter. "Don't trust women? What are you talking about, Mama? I don't have any problems with women!"

Her smile was gentle and troubled. "You don't even know it, do you? You don't have problems sleeping with women. You have problems letting them in."

Mike's mouth fell open, but before he could begin to

think of a response to *that* bit of psychoanalysis, his beeper, which he'd clipped to his belt, went off. "Uh-oh." He snatched it off and looked at it. "Jury's back. I gotta go." He leaped to his feet and kissed Mama on the cheek. "Sorry."

"You silly boy," she said as he straightened and grabbed his briefcase. "I don't know why you're so excited. I don't think you've ever lost a case."

Mike snorted. "Yeah, well, there's always a first time." He grabbed her hand. "Listen, about the doctor. I don't want you to worry because—"

"I wouldn't have a worry in the world if I knew you were looking out for Sean."

Mike shook his head in disbelief. "You don't miss an opportunity, do you?" She knew just what to say, just the right buttons to push. As if he didn't feel guilty enough that his life and career were on track while Sean always seemed to flounder.

"You have so much, Michael. Would it hurt you to give a little back?"

"I've already given till it hurts," he grumbled.

Mama pressed her lips together. "Give some more, Michael."

He sighed harshly. He'd never been able to say no to his mother, and today, apparently, was no exception. "I'll try. Professor Stallworth is giving a party Friday night for the first-year students. I'll probably see him there."

Her smile was glorious and triumphant. "Good."

Mike watched the jury file in, his stomach in knots. For the moment he'd put Mama and his promise on the back burner. He glanced down at his client, the defendant—

Janet Hawkins, battered wife and accused murderer. A petite brunette with dramatic dark eyes, she was still pretty. The late, unlamented Seth Hawkins had confined his abuse to her limbs and torso because he'd never wanted to damage her face. Who said sociopaths weren't thoughtful people? Janet did look a little green, though. Mike couldn't blame her. He gave her arm a reassuring squeeze.

When the jury was seated, everyone else in the packed courtroom sat down. Mike saw the lights from the TV cameras over in the corner. All three local networks were here. He hated the press having cameras in the courtroom. Too many of the prosecutors turned into Al Pacino when the cameras rolled. In his humble opinion, an attorney's job—his only job—was to do his best for his client. Anyone interested in theatrics should go audition for the local dinner theater.

It worried him that the jury looked so tense. If only he had a sign, he thought as he fidgeted with his pen. Who would take care of her three children if Janet went to jail? Their father—as worthless as he'd been—was now over at Spring Grove Cemetery, in a nice little plot overlooking a duck pond. Who would . . .

Juror number eight, a single white female, aged thirty-two, a nurse anesthetist and condominium owner, looked directly at him for no apparent reason. And smiled.

His stomach lurched. There was his sign: they'd acquitted Janet. It was over. He'd won.

"Has the jury reached a verdict?" the judge said from the bench, snapping him back to attention.

"Yes, Your Honor," said juror number two, the foreperson. He handed the verdict form to the bailiff, who passed it to the judge, who read it. "Not guilty."

Janet gave a choked sob and launched herself into Mike's arms. He hugged her, squeezing his eyes tight shut. *Thank God. Thank God.* "You did it!" Janet cried over and over, her tears wetting his cheek and the collar of his shirt. "You did it! Mike, you did it!"

He opened his eyes in time to see the press closing in around him like jackals. Lights flashed everywhere, and reporters shoved microphones into their faces. He steered Janet out into the hallway, surveying the chaos all around. Reporters called to him, Janet wept, and the prosecutor glowered. Right. Just another day at the office.

But as they wove their way past the press and onto the elevator, his mind shifted back to Sean and his new girlfriend, the distraction. He had no doubt she would be nothing but trouble for Sean. She—whoever she was—had aroused his curiosity.

What kind of woman could she be?

"Dara? Dara! Over here!"

Dara Williams turned around in time to see Monica weave her way toward her through Professor Stallworth's packed great room. Monica waved and smiled. "I made it!"

Dara held her glass of merlot in one hand and pulled her close for a hug with the other. "Late as usual."

Monica's hand went to her head. She'd had her shining light brown hair twisted into African knots since class this afternoon. "How does it look?"

Dara surveyed her critically. Some people thought Monica was unattractive because of her weight problem, but Dara always thought she looked great. Intelligent hazel eyes sparkled from behind her dark-rimmed glasses, and her coral sweater perfectly complemented her light brown skin. "You look beautiful."

Monica dropped her hand and smiled. "Thanks."

They both looked around the room. A pianist played something jazzy on a gleaming black grand piano on one side of the room, and on the other, a fire crackled in a fireplace big enough to drive a car through. People milled around the buffet and two bar areas. Others sat on the overstuffed chairs and sofas artfully arranged into seating areas here and there. Monica whistled. "Professor Stallworth has some house."

"No kidding." Dara discretely nodded her head toward a woman sitting on the hearth, sipping a glass of white wine. "See her? She's with the prosecutor's office." She turned and indicated a man shoveling spaghetti onto an already overloaded plate. "And he's with the U.S. Attorney's—"

Monica's mouth twisted. "Can you turn it off for one second? Can we at least eat dinner before you start in on your plans to conquer the legal world?"

Dara frowned at her. Conquering the legal world was the legacy bequeathed to her, as Monica well knew; Dara's father was a federal judge, and her grandfather had been a prominent civil rights attorney. She'd wanted to be a lawyer since the first time she'd seen her father in court, when she was seven. "The whole point of this party is for law students to get a chance to network with alumni. Don't you want one of them to hire you?"

Monica snatched a piece of bruschetta from a passing server's tray and took a generous bite. "You need to work on being a little more well-rounded," she said out of the side of her mouth.

Dara huffed. "I'm perfectly well-rounded. I read novels. I practice yoga. I cook."

Monica rolled her eyes. "You study. You go to class. You study some more. You talk about getting a good internship. You talk about getting a 3.5 GPA so you'll have a chance of making law review in the spring. Do you ever accidentally think about anything else?"

Dara put her hands on her hips. Monica had a way of making her life's ambitions sound dull, like her biggest goal was to find a way to stop socks from disappearing in the dryer. "I do *not*—"

Monica covered her mouth with her hand and feigned a yawn. "Boring."

Dara had to laugh. "Fine. What do *you* want to talk about?"

Monica finished her snack and gleefully rubbed her hands together. "Where's Sean, and has he asked you out yet?"

"He'll meet us here, and no."

"Because he's going to. It's just a matter of time."

Exasperation crept into Dara's voice. "How many times do I have to tell you, I'm not about to date anyone now." She spied an empty stool by the piano and grabbed Monica's arm to steer her to it.

"But *why?*" Monica asked as she sat down. "He's a law student. He's handsome." She counted off on her fingers. "He's crazy about you. What more do you want?"

Dara looked heavenward. "I want to be a lawyer. That's it."

"I'll never understand you. Men take one look at you and drop at your feet, and all you ever talk about is being a lawyer. It's insane."

"What's wrong with that? My father is a lawyer. It's a noble profession."

"You're practically a virgin! When—"

"Hush!" Dara hissed, horrified. She looked around to make sure no one was within earshot. Reassured, she turned back to glower at Monica. "I'm *not* a virgin! What are you talking about?"

Monica lowered her voice. "You've had sex, what? Twice? One night two years ago?"

Mortified, Dara longed to drop-kick Monica out of the nearest open window. "Yeah . . . so?"

"Dara, Antonio was a rotten jerk. But you need to get over him."

Dara winced. Yeah, he'd been all that and more. Her so-called first love, the guy who'd sworn he loved her, then bragged on the phone to his friends he'd "tagged it" the morning after she slept with him. She could still remember the shock she'd felt when she stepped out of the shower, floating in the afterglow, and heard his laughing voice through the thin walls of his apartment. The incident—two years ago now—had pretty much ended her brief foray into the world of romance. Still, she wasn't pining over him. In fact, she hadn't thought about him in months. "I *am* over him."

"No, you're not. If you're so over him, why don't you ever date anybody? When are you going to make time for a social life?"

Dara waved her hands in exasperation. "Right now my life is about doing well in law school. There's always time for men later."

The first person Sean Baldwin saw when he walked into Professor Stallworth's kitchen was, alas, his brother, Mike, who stood by the counter, studying the food. For a second, he considered backing out of the door and walking around to the front entrance to the house, but then Mike turned around and saw him, and it was too late.

"What's up, man?" Mike cried, smiling broadly. Sean warily took his brother's hand, worried Mike would demand repayment in full for the money he'd loaned him the other week. Generally, Mike was pretty cool about debt forgiveness—why shouldn't he be, with the kind of money he made?—but if he wanted the money tonight, he'd have to be disappointed, because he didn't have it. Mike almost looked like he was genuinely glad to see him. What was that about? "What's going on? How's school so far?"

"Not too bad." Sean shrugged out of his jacket and hung it on top of the towering mound of coats on the coatrack. Actually, "not too bad" was as blatant a lie as he'd ever told. He hated school so far. His stupid professors seemed to pride themselves on the amount of reading they piled on the students every day; school was nothing but a massive pain in the butt.

"What about the reading every night?" Mike watched him closely. "The professors really like to stick it to you first-years."

Obviously, Mike wanted a sign he'd screwed something up already. Well, he wouldn't get one. "Yeah. Nothing I can't handle, though." Hopefully, Mike would drop the whole concerned big brother routine. He didn't feel like an inquisition right now.

"Let me know if you need any help with anything."

Sean snorted. Here it was. The part of the conversation—*every* conversation with Mike had one—where Mike lorded it over him. This time the message was clear; Mike was a high-powered, very successful criminal defense attorney, while Sean was just a first-year grunt who couldn't make it one semester without his brother's help. "I don't need your *help*." Mike winced and Sean was glad. The word came out exactly as he'd meant it to: as if Mike had offered him a free pile of horse manure. Sean snared a shrimp from an iced bowl and dipped it in some cocktail sauce. "Been here long?"

Mike's eyes glittered with anger, but for once he didn't take the bait. He seemed determined to be pleasant. "Nope. Just got here. Before I forget to ask, what about basketball next week?"

Basketball? Actually, that sounded like a good idea. They'd played together in a league for a while, and on court they managed to have fun, probably because there was no opportunity for conversation. "Yeah. Good."

Mike steered him toward the great room, and they found a quiet corner off the main hallway. Sean kept his guard up. Mike apparently had something on his mind. "Mama says you met someone."

Sean couldn't stop his grin; thinking of Dara always made him smile. "Mama's got a big mouth."

"So who is she?"

Sean's grin widened. "Another first-year. She should be here somewhere." He looked over his shoulder into the great room, but with so many people standing around, he couldn't see her. He turned back to Mike. "Wait'll you see her, man. She's beautiful. Sweet, smart."

Mike nodded but looked at Sean like he thought he was insane, as if he'd announced he was leaving immediately for an expedition to Mars. "Sean," he began cautiously.

Sean's back stiffened. Here it came. Whatever it was, he didn't want to hear it. "What?" he snapped.

Mike hesitated. "Don't you think it's a little early in the year to be getting involved with—"

"You think I'm going to mess up school, don't you?" Sean's voice rose, and a woman emerging from the powder room gave him a funny look before she hurried on her way.

"It's not that. I just remember how tough the first year of law school is and—"

"And what? With me being a big screwup, you thought I couldn't handle two things at once? That it?"

Mike's jaw tightened, and he looked away. Sean could almost hear him counting to ten and telling himself to calm down and not lose his temper with his pathetic little brother. Mike turned back to him and said, "Sometimes I get sidetracked myself, and I—"

Sean's lips twisted into a sneer. What a ridiculous idea. Mike getting sidetracked was like the sun falling out of the sky: it just didn't happen. "When did *you* ever get sidetracked? All you ever do is work. I'm not even sure you're human."

Mike's eyes had that familiar angry flash in them. He threw up his hands. "Forget I ever said anything, Sean."

"I will." Sean jammed his hands in his pockets, openly hostile now. He wheeled around and stalked off down the hall to the screen porch, determined to get away from that jerk. Where was Dara?

Mike stared after Sean and shook his head disbelievingly. Why on earth did he promise Mama he'd try to work things out with that maniac? He'd never get past Sean's anger and defensiveness, and he didn't know why he tried. Skirting the crowd, he slipped into the great room and turned toward the buffet table in the corner. Halfway there he stopped dead in his tracks, paralyzed. The most beautiful woman he'd ever seen stood by the piano, not ten feet away from him, talking to another woman.

Who was she?

He felt his mouth fall open, then go dry. She made his heart take off like the horses out of the gate at the Kentucky Derby. He knew he gaped at her like he'd just seen a UFO land in Professor Stallworth's great room, but he didn't care. He felt like he'd never seen a woman before this very moment. She was a little taller than average, with a tiny little waist and curvy hips and long legs. Stunning, lush breasts strained against her white shirt. But her face made his breath stop. Big, beautiful dark eyes; high cheekbones; wide, full lips. When she laughed at something her friend said, he felt his gut clench with need. He needed to be the one to make her laugh and feel the shine of her smile on his face. She was sweetness and light, his reward for hauling his tired butt to the party tonight.

Remembering to breathe suddenly required a supreme effort; her appeal was overwhelming and undeniable. He would have her, he decided, creeping a little closer so he could see her better. There was no question of *if*, only *when*. Not tonight. He knew that. Well, fine. He could be patient. And she was not going to be a little fling, either. A couple of nights with this girl wouldn't do it for him. She was very young, though. Early twenties at the oldest. It didn't matter. If she was over eighteen, and she had to be, or she wouldn't be a law student, then she was his. If he had to make it his life's work to get this woman in his bed, then so be it. He didn't care if she was here with someone, or if she had a boyfriend or was engaged. He probably wouldn't even care if she was married. *Look at me, sweetheart,* he silently told her. *Look at me, look at me.*

Dara had the strangest feeling suddenly; the air in the room had changed. Now it was charged with electricity and the tension of waiting, the way the wind shifts before a storm. For no discernible reason, she turned her head to the right, and her eyes locked into place with *his.* She froze, her smile still on her lips.

This wasn't one of her law school cronies. Oh no. He was, by a factor of about ten, the most attractive man she'd ever seen. Very tall, well over six feet, probably in his early thirties, he had broad shoulders and a narrow waist. He wore an ivory cotton sweater, and the long sleeves emphasized the lean muscles of his arms and chest. His faded jeans were a little baggy, but they couldn't hide his powerful thighs and long legs. His short hair was the blackest coal and thick and wavy. His skin was warm and rich, the color as velvety smooth as coffee ice cream, and he had high cheekbones; a long, straight nose; and full, tantalizing lips, framed by a mustache and the sexiest five o'clock shadow she'd ever seen.

But, God, there was something about his eyes, which were dark, brooding, and framed by thick, expressive brows. They were mischievous, if not downright wicked—as if he knew an amusing secret he'd tell her when he thought the time was right. Dara felt electrified, like she'd tapped into an invisible power source that hummed and vibrated all around her. After a long moment—too long for mere polite interest—his eyes left hers and slid over her white scoop-neck silk T-shirt, which, she suddenly realized, fit snugly across her breasts, to her slim black pants, to her black strappy sandals and brightly painted toenails. He was bold.

She'd give him that. He was not a college boy she could
easily handle. He looked at her as if they were lovers
alone in their bed and she was his to enjoy—to
devour—in his own good time. He seemed unaware of
all the people but, more likely, was aware of the others
but didn't care what they thought of him. His lips
arranged themselves into an admiring, dimpled smile
that was just this side of a leer. Clearly, this man was
headstrong and arrogant. She'd have to take him down
a notch or two—or fifty—if she ever met him.

She'd never felt more exhilarated in her life.

For a moment, she feared she'd smile back at him,
but she managed to purse her lips and raise her chin
with a haughtiness she didn't entirely feel before she
looked away.

He laughed at her.

She knew it was he; the sound was deep, warm, and
unabashed. Lusty. She felt his eyes burning the side
of her face, but she wouldn't—*wouldn't*—look at him
again.

Monica saw him and gaped. "Who is *that*?"

Dara shrugged carelessly even though her heart still
raced. "I have no idea, but he sure is full of himself."
She took Monica's arm and steered her toward the
buffet table. "Let's get something to eat."

On the way they passed Professor Stallworth, their
hostess for the evening. Dara remembered something
she'd wanted to ask. "Professor Stallworth, I heard
you have some slave memorabilia."

"Oh yes." Professor Stallworth signaled one of the
caterers to bring out more food. "I've got quite a col-
lection. Why don't you go on down to see it, and I'll
meet you in a minute. It's in the library at the end of
the hall." She hurried off toward the kitchen.

Monica rolled her eyes at Dara. "Way to go, Dara. I'd rather eat dinner." She picked up a plate and reached for the salad tongs. "I'll see you in a few."

"Later, then," Dara said, working her way through the crowd.

Mike watched her the whole time. He shouldn't have laughed at her, but he couldn't help it. She was a piece of work, all right. So she'd decided to blow him off, had she? Well, it wasn't that easy to get rid of him. And, anyway, she hadn't wanted him to go away. Not really. So he'd just bided his time for a while and gotten himself a drink. And then he saw her turn to go and knew his chance had come. He put his Coke on the edge of the bar and turned to follow her.

He turned down a long hallway leading to another wing of the house. He saw several doorways, but only one room was lit, and he went inside. It was a beautiful library, with hundreds of books on the shelves and cozy leather sofas with lots of pillows. Mike detected a movement from the corner of his eye and glanced in that direction.

And there she was, staring up at him, her eyes wide with surprise.

His heart gave a powerful lurch, and he felt the oddest jolt of recognition, which, of course, was impossible because he knew he'd never seen this glorious angel before tonight. He froze as if he'd stumbled on a rabbit in the woods, afraid to move for fear she'd scurry away. All he could do was stare at her. The second she looked into his eyes at close range, his throat clamped down and wouldn't have let any sound out even if he'd miraculously recovered the use of his brain and been able to think of something to say. So for a second—less than that, really—he, Mike Baldwin,

criminal defense attorney, law firm owner, possessor
of a *Juris Doctor* and a degree in electrical engineering, former Boy Scout and all-state basketball forward,
generally okay guy and quick thinker, simply couldn't
put two coherent words together.

Who could blame him? This girl—surely, she
wasn't much more than that—was spectacular. Her
skin was perfectly smooth, and she had an oval face
with sharp cheekbones and a small, pointy chin. Hair
a brilliant black, long, and softly curled. He couldn't
wait to dive into it and intended to do so at the first
opportunity. But all that was secondary to her sweet
dark eyes and lush, pouty mouth. She returned his
stare; she wasn't shy, this one. And she liked him. He
could tell because she wanted to smile. The ends of
her mouth kept trying to turn up, but she pressed her
lips together to stop them.

Was he still staring?

He shook his head to break her spell. "I followed
you," he blurted, the first thing he could think of
to say.

Chapter 2

Dara vainly tried to gather her wits about her. He was more impressive than he'd been from across the room, if that was even possible. She was tall, but he was much taller, and he didn't walk so much as he prowled, like a sleek black panther that had spied a monkey in the trees and climbed up for a closer look. He vibrated with energy and vitality so magnetic, she half expected to see a blue aura glowing around him.

She opened her mouth and prayed her voice still worked. "I see that."

He grinned sheepishly, ducking his head. "I, uh . . . I hope you don't mind."

"It's too soon to say," she said, laughing. "Do I know you?"

"No." His eyes focused on her mouth and then returned, reluctantly, to her eyes. "Not yet."

Dara's heart continued to gallop like a herd of stampeding cattle. "Was there something you wanted?"

His admiring eyes slid over her face again, lingering on her lips. His thoughts couldn't have been clearer if he'd taken out a full-page ad in the *New York Times*. He wanted *her*. Desperately. And if she gave him the slightest encouragement, she'd find herself at home with him—in his bed—before the hour was out.

"I wanted to find out whether you're as beautiful up close as you are from across the room. You are."

Dara opened her mouth to blast him for using such outrageous flattery on her, but then she realized he was serious. The devilish glint was gone from his eyes now, and he seemed reluctant, almost begrudging, with his compliments. Almost as if he hated to admit how deeply she affected him.

"Do you always accost strange women at parties?" she wondered aloud. Sure, he seemed sincere, but he was probably a habitual flirt. She'd seen this routine before.

He grinned, and Dara wanted to kick herself for asking such a stupid question. This specimen of masculine perfection was clearly not now, nor had he ever been, an accoster. "I didn't think I was accosting you, and I didn't think you were a strange woman," he told her, "but no, I don't."

She was utterly captivated. His eyes glittered with amusement and mischief, and his smile was devastating: wide, dimpled, and boyish, with perfect white teeth gleaming in the light. Was he teasing her? "Do you always stare at women the way you stared at me?" she demanded tartly.

His smile grew even brighter. "As I recall, you did some staring yourself earlier. But, no, I don't usually stare at women."

Dara was grateful for the dim lighting so he couldn't see her burning cheeks. "Have you seen everything you wanted to see?"

"No," he grunted.

Dara felt like he was peeling her clothes off with his

eyes. When his eyes lingered, just for a second, on her breasts, she felt them tighten. "Who are you?" she cried, flustered.

"Mike Baldwin." A distant bell of recognition rang in her mind, but she ignored it. He stepped closer. "I would really like to spend some time alone with you," he said softly. "Let's go somewhere and get some dinner."

Her breath caught; that low murmur of his slid over her like water, as hypnotic as the waves of the ocean. "I came *here* for dinner," she said, knowing this man wouldn't take no, however it was disguised, for an answer.

"But you haven't eaten yet."

"I don't leave parties with men I don't know." Somehow she knew arguing was pointless; he'd disregard her second excuse as he had the first and as he would the tenth. The power of his will felt like a force of nature; saying no to him was like saying no to a tornado. If she had any sense at all, she would leave this man alone right now; she needed to become involved with him like she needed a couple of hits of heroin. He'd be just as addictive and much more trouble. He was older and more experienced, and she was smart enough to know when she was out of her league.

His tone was reasonable but insistent, his face determined. "You can meet me at a restaurant."

She hesitated for a long moment, trying to resist his pull even though she would have loved to have dinner with him. "I can't," she said finally, out of excuses.

His thick brows lowered into a frown of frustration. "Why not? It's not because you don't want to."

She bristled, annoyed he could read her so easily, but didn't bother denying it. "I'm meeting someone here," she said, belatedly remembering Sean. Technically, Sean wasn't her date, but this man didn't need to know that. "I really should get back to the party."

His frown deepened. "You're seeing someone?"

Trapped, Dara said nothing. She didn't want to admit Sean wasn't her date or that she wasn't dating anyone, because then she'd have no reason to refuse Mike's dinner invitation. And she had to refuse because her attraction to this man scared her. So did the ache of longing in the pit of her belly.

"Who is he?" Mike asked sharply.

Was he jealous? Dara fought the ridiculous urge to reassure him. "I'm not sure that's any of your business."

Grudging respect appeared in his eyes. He pressed his lips together for a long moment, clearly outlining his strategy. "So why are you still in here with me?" He looked very serious, as if they were discussing the fate of humanity.

Dara stiffened. She couldn't decide which was worse: his frankness or his arrogance. She had the terrifying thought he could read her mind. "I don't think there's room for you, me, *and* your ego in the room," she said, outraged, "so I'll just leave."

"No!" He looked alarmed, as if she'd announced she was leaving to get married in five minutes. He put his hand on her arm to stop her. She froze, startled by the fact that he'd actually touched her and by the heat of his hand on her bare arm. "Stay with me," he said huskily. His hand slid down her arm and twined her fingers in his firm, warm grip. "Please don't go."

The feeling of his skin on hers sent a jolt of throbbing sensation through her. She was in imminent danger of becoming deeply infatuated with this man; in another ten minutes, she'd be lost. Completely lost.

She'd never been lost before—not really—and the very idea petrified her. But she wouldn't leave. She couldn't. All by themselves, her fingers curled around his hand, and her head nodded yes. The tension immediately disappeared from his face, and he stepped back to the sofa, pulling her down to sit beside him. She tugged her hand away, and he reluctantly released it.

Mike felt equally relieved and stunned. Stunned by his violent reaction to touching her. Relieved because she'd deigned to stay with him. He didn't care if she'd deigned, nor did he care he'd had to beg. She'd humbled him pretty quickly, hadn't she? So what? He'd be happy to beg a little more if she'd stay and let him touch her again. "Thanks for staying." She nodded slowly, trancelike, her wide eyes riveted to his face. She seemed disoriented, as if someone had woken her from a deep sleep. "Why didn't you leave?"

"I don't know," she admitted softly. "I was just asking myself the same thing."

It'd been a mistake to touch her. Now that he'd felt that warm, smooth skin, he was dying to touch the rest of her. He needed to know whether her lips were as soft as her breasts, wanted to feel the warmth of her thighs and her hips, and the leap of her muscles as he trailed his fingers along her belly. And he had the unshakable feeling that waiting to make love to her would be the hardest thing he'd ever done.

But first things first. "What's your name?"

She blinked as if she couldn't quite recall her name. "Dara Williams."

"You're a first-year?"

Some of the tension left her shoulders. Hopefully, she would relax a little. "Yes. Does it show?"

He shook his head. "I know I've never seen you

before, so you must be a first-year." He eyed her speculatively. "How old are you? Twenty-two?"

"Twenty-three." He whistled softly, and she narrowed her eyes at him. "What's that supposed to mean?"

"It means most twenty-three-year-olds I've seen recently are silly and giggly. But not you."

He could practically see her hackles rise. "Maybe you should stop trying to categorize me," she said sourly.

"No can do," he said, grinning. "I'm going to have to put you firmly in at least one category."

She raised her eyebrows. "Which category is that?"

His smile faded. *Women I desperately want to make love to.* "Women I want to get to know much better."

"Oh, really?" She sounded skeptical. "And how many dozens of other women occupy this category with me?"

He stared at her. "None." To his surprise, his voice had gone hoarse.

Their gazes locked and held for an electric moment. "How old are *you*?" she finally asked him.

"I'm thirty-four," he said impatiently. He didn't want to answer *her* questions. He wanted her answering *his* questions. "Where are you from, Dara?"

"Chicago, but I graduated from Michigan last spring."

Michigan. That confirmed his suspicions that this girl was really smart. Good. He wanted someone to share the *New York Times* with over breakfast. "What's your degree in?"

"English literature."

"Interesting. Why aren't you writing novels or teaching creative writing?"

She laughed. "Because I've always had this strange desire to be a lawyer."

Dara's desires. Well, that topic definitely required exploring. "And do you have any other strange desires?" he asked, leaning closer.

She shivered almost imperceptibly, and a delightful flush crept over her cheeks. "None that I'd care to share right now," she said primly.

He could kiss her now, he realized, thrilled. She wanted him to; her glowing face and sparkling eyes told him so. Well, he wanted her begging for his touch. He wanted her to be as sure as he was. He would never force her into anything. "What kind of lawyer do you want to be, Dara?"

Dara rolled her eyes. "Why don't you just give me a written questionnaire to fill out? Maybe that would be easier."

He laughed. "I'm a pretty good criminal attorney, Dara. When I ask questions, I expect you to answer them, or else I'll have to treat you like a hostile witness."

"And how is that?"

"It isn't pretty."

She threw her head back and laughed, a throaty, sensual laugh—the most exciting sound he'd ever heard. "What was the question again?"

His eyes found her smiling lips and remained there for a long beat. When would he find out what she tasted like? When could he touch his mouth to those sweet lips? What would it feel like to have her mouth moving—opening—beneath his? She looked at him expectantly. Darn it! What had he asked her? "What, ah, what kind of lawyer do you want to be?"

"I'm not sure. My father is a federal judge in Chicago. But I have an interest in criminal law. Maybe employment law."

"What about your mother?"

"She's a nurse."

"Brothers and sisters?"

"None."

"No brothers and sisters? You're spoiled, then."

Mischief glimmered in her eyes. "I'm an angel. As long as I get what I want when I want it."

Mike didn't believe her for a minute. This girl was fiery, and he'd bet his last dollar she had a temper to match his. But there *was* something angelic about her. Something sweet that attracted him like a hummingbird to an open bottle of juice. "You have the face of an angel. But I think you'd drive a man crazy."

This seemed to surprise her, as if she'd never considered that possibility before. Didn't she realize the inherent power her beauty gave her over men? "Good crazy or bad crazy?"

He cocked his head and considered. "Both."

"Well then, maybe you should run while you've got the chance."

Run? Maybe he should. He was just getting to a place where his firm could turn a profit, and he really didn't need any distractions from work right now. And this girl was a walking distraction; she'd probably be a walking obsession, if he let her. But he wouldn't. "I'm not going anywhere, sweetheart," he murmured.

She froze, her wide eyes unwavering on his face. Half a smile drifted across her lips. She very clearly didn't know what to make of him. "You're not too bright, then, are you?"

He roared with laughter, delighted. He was going to have fun with her. "Did anyone ever tell you you've got a smart mouth?"

Dara beamed, as if this was the highest compliment

he could have paid her. "You wouldn't be the first," she said. "Anyone ever tell you you're arrogant and nosy?"

He laughed again. "I was right about you. I knew when I first saw you that you would never be boring."

"When you first saw me?" she said faintly. "Was that before or after you undressed me with your eyes?"

There was just no predicting her, was there? She liked to have all the cards out on the table. Well, so did he. Even so, he hesitated before answering because he didn't want to scare her away. "Don't ask me a question unless you're ready to hear my answer," he warned softly. When she didn't say anything, he took her wary silence as permission to speak freely and to touch her again. He raised his hand and very gently and slowly ran his fingers down the side of her face, from her temple to her chin, then ran his thumb around her dewy bottom lip. She gasped, trembling slightly. Her lids fluttered, as if she wanted to close her eyes and give herself over to the moment. "When I undressed you with my eyes and saw how you looked back at me, I wished I could take you home and make love to you."

Suddenly, she went rigid and gaped at him as if he'd suggested she might enjoy a career as a prostitute. With a horrible, sinking feeling, he realized he'd made a gross miscalculation.

She sprang to her feet and glared down at him, furious. "*That's* something you'll never know!"

Mike stood up, silently cursing his own idiocy. He'd just shot himself in the foot. Well, he'd come on a little strong, but he had no intention of backpedaling now. She might as well know it all. He wanted her and fully intended to have her, sooner rather than later. They'd have to deal with it. "Dara—"

They heard a light tap on the door, and then Sean appeared. "You in there, Dara?"

Mike's frustration nearly blinded him. He'd forgotten all about the party and his brother. What did that knucklehead want with Dara right now? "What's up, man?" he said coolly, hoping Sean would take the hint and get out of there as soon as possible.

Without bothering to look at Mike, Sean went straight for Dara and folded her into a bear hug. "You look beautiful!"

Dara stiffened and stepped out of his arms almost immediately. "Hey, Sean," she said, clearly flustered. "Where did you come from?"

"Andrea sent me down to tell you she's sorry for taking so long."

Mike felt alarmed and irritated by the sight of Sean touching Dara. A terrible, heavy feeling grew in his belly, but he couldn't bring himself to think about what it might mean. "You . . . you know Dara?" he asked Sean casually.

"I told you about Dara, man," said Sean, giving Mike a significant look.

Mike forced himself to take a good look at his brother. Sean's feet barely touched the ground; he glowed like a sixteen-year-old with his first car. "*This* is the woman you told me about?" He wanted to suspend time at that moment, before Sean answered, because he didn't want to know. Not really. Because if Sean had had this woman, or thought he was in love with this woman, then he, Mike, could never have her. Sean barely tolerated him now as it was. If he made a move on Sean's woman, Sean would hate him forever. And if Sean hated him, he couldn't repair their relationship.

It was simple, really: he couldn't have Dara and

keep his promise to his mother. He had to choose: he could heal his family, or he could go after Dara. He couldn't do both.

"Right," Sean told him, looking at him as if he were Bozo the Clown.

Mike sucked in a strangled breath and focused on not howling with frustrated fury, no easy feat when he felt like his guts had just been ripped from his abdomen.

"How do you two know each other?" Dara interjected.

"Sean's my brother," Mike told her, staring at her surprised face while his mind frantically tried to remember exactly what Sean had said about his relationship with her. Hadn't he said they were already involved? Was this woman sleeping with Sean? He couldn't make himself believe it. It just didn't make any sense. It was like staring at the Statue of Liberty and having someone try to convince him it was the Eiffel Tower. He'd thought she felt the attraction between them as strongly as he had, but maybe he'd imagined it. Was this beautiful girl sleeping with his brother—in love with his brother? Had Sean touched that silky skin, run his fingers through that shining hair, and kneaded those breasts and that butt? Had Dara moaned for him? Cried out his name? Scratched his back? The bile rose in his throat, and he thought he might vomit.

But, of course, whether Dara was sleeping with Sean or not was a moot point. What mattered was the way *Sean* felt about *her*. He was obviously crazy about her, and he would never—*never*—forgive Mike if he took one look in her direction. All Sean needed was another reason to hate him.

Sean looked first at Mike, then Dara. He seemed

bewildered. "Uh . . . Weren't you two talking in here? I thought you'd have introduced yourselves."

Dara's stricken gaze flew to Mike's face and he flashed her a silent warning to keep quiet. The last thing he needed was for her to tell Sean they'd been flirting, although, of course, if she was involved with Sean, she wouldn't volunteer that information. "We introduced ourselves, but I guess neither of us made the connection to you, man," he told Sean.

Sean nodded, satisfied. "Did you two eat yet? I'm starving."

"No," Dara said weakly.

"Let's go." Sean put a light hand at the small of her back and guided her to the door. Dara hesitated and turned her head halfway, as if she wanted to look back over her shoulder at Mike. But then she put her nose in the air and marched out of the room with Sean.

And Mike stared after them, seething and sorely tempted to rip Sean's arm from its socket as a punishment for touching Dara.

Back in the living room, Dara's jangled nerves wouldn't let her chitchat with anyone, nor could she eat a bite of dinner. Her heart simply wouldn't return to its normal rhythm. Worse, no matter where she went in the room, she felt Mike's accusing gaze following her. She didn't want to look at him, but she couldn't help it; her eyes seemed to find him, the way a compass needle always finds north. He was furious and, as near as she could tell, hurt. She felt guilty for flirting with Mike when she knew very well Sean cared for her.

She was anxious and fidgety, like she'd drunk too much Mountain Dew or taken too much cold medicine. Mike *Baldwin*, he'd said. He'd had her hormones in such an uproar, his name hadn't clicked. This man was Sean's brother. They *did* look somewhat alike, now that she thought about it. Their skin color was roughly the same, and their hair, although Mike's was shorter. But Sean was always open and cheerful. Mike's expression was darker and more intense.

She watched as Mike walked to the buffet table, and an attractive woman—she had no idea who she was, but she hated her on sight—followed him and struck up a conversation. They were too far away for Dara to hear what they said, although Mike didn't seem particularly engaged. *Darn him!* He had her so agitated, she could barely sit still. She'd never encountered a man who was as handsome, virile, or intense. Nor had anyone ever stared at her with such absolute focus. Did he realize what he did to her? Did he have the faintest idea how lethally attractive he was?

Clearly, he'd done something to her body— something indescribable and terrifying, but delicious. His light, fresh cologne lingered in her senses, and so did the timbre of his voice. He'd said he wanted to make love to her. And now here she was, fantasizing about sex with a man she'd known a grand total of thirty minutes.

The whole episode with Antonio had apparently taught her nothing about men, she thought, disgusted. Casual sex was not something she'd even consider, so Mike was not the man for her, and it was a darn good thing she'd realized it now. He was arrogant and overbearing, and sex was all he wanted. He'd admitted as much. *Well, good riddance.* She felt like she'd narrowly escaped disaster, as if she'd caught the last helicopter out of Saigon. Because Mike Baldwin would consume her. It was all or nothing with him, and he would insist on all. If she let him, he would fill up her every waking thought, the way he filled up every room he entered. If he set his mind to it, he wouldn't be satisfied until he knew and understood every part of her. He would read her thoughts and get inside her mind. And if she let him make love to her, he would take her places she'd never dreamed of, teach her things about her own body she didn't know. And if he decided he wanted them, which, of course, he would not, he wouldn't be happy until he possessed her heart and her soul.

She could never let that happen. Law school was her purpose in life. That was it. She wouldn't let anything stand in her way. Especially a man like Mike Baldwin. Vivid memories of that semester with Antonio flew through her mind: her stunned disbelief and over-whelming feelings of betrayal; the abrupt end of their sexual relationship; the destruction of the friendship she'd thought was solid as a rock; the end of her ro-mantic dreams, silly though they were. And she remembered the aftermath—how she'd become de-pressed, lost weight, skipped classes, and darn near flunked her finals that term. So the year she turned twenty-one, her biggest lesson hadn't come from school; Antonio had taught her that a romantic rela-tionship, good, bad or otherwise, was simply not something she could juggle along with school.

And she wouldn't soon forget it.

She and Sean found seats on one of the sofas. "You seem distracted," he told her. Dara was disturbingly aware of his eyes, hopeful and intent, on hers. There were times, like now, when he watched her so closely, she felt like he was her Secret Service detail and she was the president.

She couldn't help but compare Sean to Mike, and she wondered how siblings could be so different. Sean's skin was about the shade of caramel, and his beautiful black hair was wavy and would probably have been curly if it wasn't so short. He was tall, around six feet, and athletic. Unlike Mike, Sean's face was clean shaven. Mike was taller and a little fairer than Sean, but that wasn't really it. Mike had the confidence and grace of a cat, and seemed to have a feline disregard for his surroundings and what others wanted. Sean was no clod, of course, but he didn't have that same self-assurance. Most of all, she'd bet Mike was a person who decided what he wanted from life and didn't stop until he got it. But what about Sean? He was no Mike, but he *was* attractive, and she was only human. She'd noticed his broad shoulders, his tight butt, and his disarming smile. But she needed to spend all of her time studying, not playing footsie with classmates.

"I think I'm getting a little tired," she lied.

"You're not leaving now are you?" he said, groaning.

"Not yet." She watched Mike shake his simpering little friend and stride to the bar for a drink. "Tell me about your brother."

Sean rolled his eyes. Clearly, Mike was not his favorite topic. "Well, he has his own criminal law practice—"

"You were a paralegal for him, right?"

"Right. He handles all kinds of felonies."

"He's not dating anyone?"

Sean shrugged impatiently. "No one special. He's always been pretty focused on his work." He raised his eyebrow at her. "Why?"

She suddenly couldn't look him in the eye and

fussed with lint on her pants. "Just wondering. He seems pretty arrogant."

"You have no idea," he told her, laughing.

"Are you close?"

His smile faded and disappeared. "Used to be." She was dying to know what problems they'd had, but Sean fell silent, and she didn't feel comfortable asking. Suddenly, he smiled, and she saw that shy, puppy dog look in his eyes. He leaned closer and took a deep breath, as if to shore up his courage. "We need to talk."

She didn't need to be Perry Mason to see he was about to make some sort of declaration about his feelings, but one Baldwin brother per night was all she could handle. "Sean—" she began, alarmed.

"I'm crazy about you." Hesitantly—nervously—he raised his hand and ran the backs of his fingers down her cheek; her instinct was to shake him off. Over Sean's shoulder, ten feet away by the bar, she saw Mike staring at them, cold fury in his eyes. "I want to get to know you better. I want to take you to dinner tomorrow night."

She fell back on the words she always used when a man she had no interest in tried to hit on her. "I don't know what to say."

"Just think about it."

Unwillingly, her eyes flitted to Mike's again. He stared at them, rigid and unmoving. Clearly, he was jealous; he probably thought something was going on with her and Sean. She felt his unhappiness as if it were her own. And in that moment, she wanted to tell Sean no way, that she could never care for him. But then she looked back at Sean, saw the absolute adoration in his eyes and realized she couldn't tell him no.

Not now, not in public. She would let him down gently, tomorrow. "Okay."

From across the room, Mike nursed his Coke, watched Sean and Dara in a frustrated rage, and bided his time. He knew he should leave before he said or did something he'd regret—other than throwing himself at his brother's girlfriend, of course—but he couldn't take his eyes off them. Maybe if he stared at them together long enough, it would start to sink in.

Had Dara been toying with him? Laughing at him, making a fool of him when all the time she'd known he was Sean's brother? He didn't think so. Maybe his ego was way out of hand, but he still felt like he knew a little bit about women. He knew when a woman responded to him, and Dara had. So what did that mean? That she was just a slut who didn't care how many men she slept with? Didn't even care if they were brothers? That didn't seem right, either. She didn't seem like the free and easy type.

Without thinking, Mike followed Dara when she went to the bar. He slipped behind her and waited while she ordered a glass of merlot. When she turned around and saw him, she froze abruptly in her tracks. The wine sloshed out of the glass, spilling over her fingers. He'd had no idea what he wanted to say, but then his mouth opened, and the words came out. "Busy little thing, aren't you?" he murmured, looking around to make sure no one overheard them.

Her eyes widened with outrage. "Excuse me?"

Suddenly, it was imperative he hurt this woman and make her suffer the way he suffered. He couldn't have her—Sean had gotten to her first—and he needed to punish her. Very deliberately, he looked her up and down, letting his eyes linger on the delectable breasts he would never touch and the lips he would never taste. "Well, there's me, there's Sean . . . anyone else?"

She flinched. "You . . . you think I sleep around?" Her voice sounded strangled.

The obvious pain in her eyes was strangely satisfying. He shrugged as if the matter held only a passing interest for him. "Don't you?"

"No." For a long moment, she just stared at him, and in the dim lighting, he could have sworn he saw tears shimmer in her eyes. But then she collected herself, and her face hardened into stone. "Get away from me."

The harshness in her voice smacked him like a slap across the face. Never in his life had he talked this way to a woman—not even to Debbie—and suddenly, he felt ashamed. His lips twisted into a crooked smile, and he bent from the waist in a mocking little bow. Then he turned and walked away, leaving her staring after him.

Determined to leave before he said or did anything worse, he stalked through the crowd to the foyer, ignoring a couple of people who spoke to him along the way. Forget this night, this party, and his brother. Forget Dara. Forget his jacket, wherever he'd laid it. He could buy another one. He reached for the door.

"You leaving?"

Cursing to himself, Mike turned and saw Sean. He struggled to keep his turmoil off his face. "Yeah. Long night."

Just then, Dara materialized from around the corner and marched toward the door. Something about the rigid set of her shoulders and unyielding line of her mouth reminded Mike of an armored tank. She fished in her purse, head down, and almost ran directly into

Sean. Sean caught her by the shoulders, and she looked up, startled. "You're not leaving, are you?"

She nodded, pulling her keys from her purse. "It's getting late, and I'm a little tired."

Sean reached up a solicitous hand to touch her chin, but she shrank away from him. "You do look a little strange." He dropped his hand. "Are you getting sick?"

"No," she said tightly. "Just tired."

Sean looked at Mike. "Well, I'm glad you two got to meet. What did you think of her, man?"

Mike's eyes flickered to Dara, then back to Sean. Above all else, he did not want Sean to get hurt. He forced the edges of his mouth up into a lopsided smile. "She's really something."

Sean nodded, pleased. He turned back to Dara. "Let me walk you out."

"Aren't you taking her home?" Mike choked back the bile in his throat at the very thought, but he had to know. Had to.

Finally, Dara looked him in the face. A wild light glittered in her eyes. For several long seconds, she stared at him with absolute revulsion, as if he were a moldy substance she'd discovered growing on top of the leftovers in her fridge. She was furious; that much was obvious. If she'd had a knife, she'd have filleted him like a trout. And there was something else in her big baby browns, something that looked suspiciously like hurt. But then she abruptly turned to Sean and smiled at him, a glorious, breathtaking smile that felt like a knife directly to Mike's gut. She slipped her arm through Sean's, and he stared dazedly but worshipfully down at her. "Let's go." Her voice had dropped to a sexy murmur. She turned and led Sean through the door.

Mike, sick with misery and fury, could only follow them down the long walk to the street. The night breeze felt cool and crisp, a refreshing change from the crowded air inside the house, but he barely noticed. His entire being focused on Dara's hand touching Sean. Then Dara whispered something in Sean's ear, and they both laughed. Mike clenched his fists at his sides and resisted the urge to smash his hand through the windshield of an SUV parked at the curb.

It was apparently Dara's SUV; Sean walked her around to the door. Mike started past the sickening little lovebirds, on his way to his car. Dara glanced up, her glittering eyes bright and hard. "Good night," she said sweetly.

Mike grunted something—he had no idea what—in response and continued on his way. Dara's clear voice rang through the night air behind him. "Dinner tomorrow?" Sean laughed and said something Mike couldn't hear. A little voice told him to just walk the twenty or so more steps to his car and get away from her, but something made him slow down and look over his shoulder. And he saw Dara step into Sean's arms, wrap her hands around his neck, and pull his face down to hers.

Chapter 3

The violent slam of Mike's car door jarred Dara to her senses. What on earth was she doing? Alarmed, she turned her head the second before Sean's lips touched hers. Sean groaned disapprovingly and tightened his arms around her, pulling her closer. Dara heard the squeal of tires as Mike's car shot out of its parking space and hurtled down the street, like a felon trying to escape the police on one of those cop shows. Somehow she wedged her arms between herself and Sean and put her palms on his chest. "Sean, I-I'm sorry. I can't do this."

Sean's arms slid away from her waist, and comprehension appeared in his eyes. "Am I going too fast for you? I didn't mean—"

"No." She shook her head and tried to smile. "I know you're going to think I'm a complete fruitcake. But I-I just realized that we should be friends. That's all I can really deal with right now."

Hurt and bewilderment flashed across his face. "But I thought . . ."

Yeah, she knew what he'd thought. That she was interested in him, that she wanted a relationship—

a sexual relationship—with him. And, of course, the only reason he thought those things was because she'd been so infuriated and hurt by Mike's little innuendo, she'd lashed out at Mike by trying to make him jealous with Sean. So Mike thought she was a slut, did he? Well, she knew just how to punish him. And the agonized fury she'd seen in his eyes when she flirted with Sean was the perfect balm for her wounded feelings. The only problem was, Sean was an innocent party, and she had no right to drag him into the cross fire. She thought of Sean as more like a brother. Nothing more. "I know," she said quickly. "And I'm really sorry I gave you the wrong impression. But I just . . . Can we be friends, Sean?"

His eyes held hers for a long minute, searching, clearly trying to make sense of her sudden about-face. "Yeah," he said finally, ruefully, "we can be friends—"

"Good."

"For now."

She tried unsuccessfully not to frown. "What do you mean?"

The intensity of his stare made her a little uncomfortable. He seemed to realize it and smiled a reserved but warm smile full of dreams and expectations. "I can hope, can't I?"

Dara's heart fell. She could see what he was doing: holding out hope that he could woo her with friendship and gradually change her mind about the course of their relationship. What he didn't realize, and what she wouldn't tell him right now, was she really wasn't attracted to him, and probably never would be. She smiled gently to soften her words. "I wish you wouldn't."

The shining light in his eyes died abruptly, and he looked away. A long, awkward moment passed. Sean shoved his hands in his jacket pocket; Dara studied her shoes. The night air had grown cool around them, and Dara suddenly longed to go home for a nice hot bubble bath with her gardenia bath foam and a glass of Riesling. She needed something—anything—to help her come down from the state of agitation she'd been in since she first saw Mike. As much as she tried to focus on Sean and letting him down gently, Mike was still with her, hovering around her thoughts, demanding her attention. She shivered a little—from the chill or from thoughts of Mike?—and waited.

Finally, Sean looked back at her, all emotions safely shuttered. "See you Monday in civil procedure?"

She smiled, the weight of a thousand elephants lifted from her shoulders. "See you then."

Dara rounded the corner and ran down the hall of the law school, cursing fate with each step. She'd spent two sleepless nights fretting about Mike Baldwin; to her horror, she seemed to be constitutionally unable to think of anything else. And then, finally, around dawn this morning, she'd fallen asleep, only to sleep through the alarm. So now, for the first time in her law school career, she was late and unprepared for a class.

She tried to sneak into the amphitheater-shaped classroom, but the door creaked. To her horror, the person writing on the board was clearly not white-haired Professor Appleton, but someone who looked, from behind at least, as he wrote on the board, suspiciously like Mike Baldwin.

Mike knew it was Dara even before he put the chalk on the rail, turned away from the board, and saw her skulking to a seat in the back row, like a fox sneaking into a henhouse for a few eggs. He'd spent the whole weekend thinking about her and picturing her kissing Sean. And then, this morning, he'd been so engrossed during his jog, he'd run an extra mile and a half before he'd realized what he was doing. Now his knees were killing him, and it was all her fault.

He swiped his hands together, creating a cloud of dust. He just couldn't make sense of the whole situation. He'd been so certain she felt their attraction as strongly as he did, but then Sean had come in and blown his little fantasy all to pieces. And what had happened to his instincts about people? Any woman dumb enough to get involved with Sean was clearly not someone he should think about twice. And now here she was again, and all of his feelings came churning to the surface. Her waltzing into class twenty minutes late pissed him off, but so had the strange thud of disappointment he'd felt when he'd thought she wasn't coming at all.

He hated it when people were late or skipped a class. In his book, if you did one or the other, you were either lazy or stupid, possibly both. Dara obviously didn't appreciate the importance of working hard and making the most of her education. Not surprising, really, since her father—he'd taken the liberty of doing a search on her father on the Internet late last night, when he couldn't sleep—was a federal judge and before that had been an extremely successful attorney in Chicago. The man had obviously spoiled Dara and raised her to believe she was a beautiful princess who could float through life on the basis of her looks alone. She'd probably never done a hard day's work in her life.

"Ms. Williams!" he intoned as she tiptoed to a chair

in the very last row, which was so far away, it probably had a different zip code. "I'm so glad you could join us."

The edges of her lips went up into a strained smile, but anger glinted in her eyes. "I'm so sorry I'm late." Her voice dripped with honey. "It won't happen again." She eased into a chair.

"Come down front." He waved at the first few rows, which were dotted with empty seats. "Plenty of room down here." For some inexplicable reason, he wanted her close, where he could get a better look at her. She gave him another tight-lipped smile, clearly embarrassed, then marched down the steps and slid into a seat. Satisfied, Mike turned back to the board and picked up the chalk again.

"Where's Professor Appleton?" he heard Dara whisper to her neighbor.

His grip tightened on the chalk until it snapped in two. Did she think he couldn't hear her? Or maybe she thought he'd forgotten about her already. "Are you volunteering to discuss the *Erie* doctrine with me, Ms. Williams?"

"No," she said, sounding resigned, "I wasn't volunteering." Her classmates, grateful his attention wasn't focused on them, tittered.

Mike swung around and raised his eyebrows at her in a direct challenge. She was gutsy. He'd known that since the second he'd laid eyes on her. "Do I need to call on you, then?"

"I really wish you wouldn't." Her classmates laughed.

He clenched his teeth. He knew he was being a childish jerk, but he didn't care. This was what she'd reduced him to. He folded his arms and leaned against the lectern. "Are you passing?"

She glared at him for a long moment. The look she gave him could best be described as unadulterated hatred with generous sprinklings of malice and spite. "Yes."

Well, there. She'd said it, and he had his little victory. He waited for the surge of satisfaction he'd expected, but it never came. All he felt was disappointment. About everything. "I'm sorry to hear that," he said sincerely. "I'm sure it would have been interesting." He turned away at last and saw the other students watching him curiously. Great. By the end of the day, there'd be rumors he was cracking up. He looked at the class roster and randomly selected a name. "Mr. Whittington?" A pimply-faced student in the front row raised his hand, and Mike smiled at him. "Let's talk about the *Erie* doctrine."

"You heading to the library?" Sean asked Dara in the crowded hall after class.

She stared at Sean, glad he'd made the overture to at least try to remain friends with her. All weekend—well, during the parts of the weekend she hadn't obsessed about Mike—she'd worried that Sean would completely write her off and give her the cold shoulder, which she would hate. So she really did need to try to nurture their fragile friendship. But for now she felt so unsettled. She didn't know whether to confront Mike or not. "Yeah," she said. "No. In a minute. I'll meet you up there."

Dara watched Sean go, and her mind immediately shifted back to Mike. *Mike, Mike, Mike, Mike, Mike.* She was sick of it. If she was smart, she would just forget the entire classroom incident and pretend he didn't exist or, better yet, that a massive sinkhole had appeared from nowhere and swallowed him alive. He'd been nasty to her, with his ugly little innuendo, and he clearly thought she was a slut. Plus, he'd gleefully embarrassed her today in front of her classmates. But he'd also been warm, funny, charming, and exciting. Which was the real Mike?

When her feet began to walk, they led her back to the classroom. She swung open the door and marched inside. Alone now, Mike lounged against one of the desks in the top row by the door. His knowing, moody eyes didn't seem at all surprised to see her. They studied each other in silence. This was the first time she'd seen him in the light of day; his eyes were lighter than she'd thought, his hair blacker. His eyes, in fact, were a gorgeous shade of light brown—amber, wasn't it?—like the smooth, rich honey sold in the gourmet aisle at the market. He wore a stunning dark suit with a white shirt and gray tie. Oh, he was beautiful. She was woman enough to admit it. Too bad he ruined it every time he opened his stupid mouth.

"Ditched Sean already?" he said finally.

"Nothing better to do today than terrorize poor first-year students?" she snapped.

He shrugged and shoved his hands in his pants pockets. "I fill in sometimes with some of the classes. Professor Appleton had minor surgery today. He'll be back tomorrow. And for the record," he continued blandly, "I only terrorize students who are twenty minutes late for class. I hope you don't make a habit of *that*."

For some reason, the unexpected note of concern in

his voice touched her. "I don't. I overslept, and I didn't have a chance to review my notes before class."

He snorted with absolute disbelief. "Right. Late night with my brother, I presume."

White-hot anger flooded her. She forgot he was her teacher for the day and that she therefore shouldn't antagonize him. "Listen, you self-important jerk," she hissed, aware students could arrive any moment for the next class. "I know you don't like me—"

Mike's eyes bulged nearly out of his head. Clearly furious, he advanced on her, crowding her space, but she stood her ground.

"But you have no right to embarrass me in front of my friends, and you have *no right*"—she realized she was waving her arms like a chimpanzee and dropped them to her sides—"to talk to me like that!"

"Well, since you brought it up," he spat, leaning down until his face was just inches from hers, "I'll tell you *exactly* what I think of you! I think you're lazy and undisciplined, and I wonder how you graduated from Michigan and got yourself into law school when you can't even get out of bed on time! And I think my brother can do much better than you. He deserves someone who doesn't throw herself at strange men every chance she gets! *That's* what I think of you!"

"I . . . you. . ." she sputtered, speechless with rage. Finally, she recovered her voice. "I didn't throw myself at you!" she screeched. "And not that it's any of your business, but your brother and I are just friends! Ask him if you don't believe me!"

That seemed to take him by surprise. He snapped his mouth shut and dropped his hands to his sides, clenching and unclenching his fists. His expression was intent and strained, almost as if he was struggling with himself about something. Finally, he shrugged carelessly and looked away. "If Sean had his way, he'd be a lot more than just friends with you." He looked back at her with expressionless eyes. "And it doesn't matter to me, anyway."

For a long moment, she stared at him, desperately searching for some glimmer of the warmth and charm he'd shown her the other night, but there was none. Quite obviously, he wanted nothing to do with her. Stung beyond words, she choked up and turned away so he wouldn't see how upset she was. Why did he hate her so much? And why did she care? "What's this?" he said behind her, sounding bewildered. "Cat got your tongue?"

She refused to look at him again. "You're wrong about me," she said quietly as she brushed past him, heading for the door. From the corner of her eye, she saw him open his mouth to say something—she almost had the idea he wanted to call her back—but suddenly the door swung open, and Professor Stallworth walked briskly into the classroom. "Mike!" she cried. "I was hoping you were still here. And Dara, too. Now I can kill two birds with one stone! I've found the most promising criminal law student to be your intern for the semester, Mike," she beamed. "She's bright, hardworking, and enthusiastic. You'll *love* her."

Dara could see they didn't need her. "I'll just leave you two to talk in private."

"For your public service internship," Professor Stallworth announced to Dara as if she'd won a cruise around the world, "I've assigned you to work with Mike at his firm."

Dara nearly stumbled. "But . . . I requested the public defender's office." She was horrified; she'd rather defend the free speech rights of the Ku Klux Klan than work for Mike Baldwin.

Professor Stallworth looked stupefied. "You don't work for city council if there's a job available at the White House, Dara."

"But—"

"It looks like Dara really had her heart set on working in the PD's office," Mike interjected smoothly. "Why don't you go ahead and place her there and give me another intern?"

Professor Stallworth whirled on him, her face pinched with irritation. "Because I have already awarded those internships to other students, and because *you* insisted you wanted the best student to work for you, and *Dara* is the best student," she snapped. "She's done an excellent job here so far, and she was in the top five percent of her class at Michigan. What more do you want?"

Mike shot Dara a look of absolute surprise and disbelief. But to her relief, he said nothing.

Hearing no further opposition, Professor Stallworth clapped her hands together. "It's all settled, then!" she boomed, turning to Dara. "Mike is the best criminal defense attorney in the city. This is the opportunity of a lifetime. Am I being clear?" She gave Dara a chilling smile.

Dara swallowed hard. "Crystal. When do I start?"

"I'll let Mike handle those details." Professor Stallworth swept out of the room.

"You've certainly got her fooled," Mike muttered as the door clicked shut.

Dara turned on him in a fresh fury. "Why didn't you tell her you wanted someone else?"

His sardonic grin was back, although it didn't quite

reach his eyes. "Why would I do that and deprive myself the pleasure of firing you when you screw up?"

"You won't fire me!" she shrieked, too angry to care who heard her. "I'm going to be the best intern you ever had!" She stiffened her back and raised her chin, determined now that, if nothing else, he would respect her work ethic and legal skills.

He held her unflinching gaze for a long time before he smirked at her. "I really doubt that."

How she hated him. "Who do you think you are?" she shrieked.

His sarcasm was gone now, replaced by a grim resignation. "I'm your new boss."

"Are you going to sulk all night?" Sean asked. He watched as Dara stirred her coffee again, then clanked the spoon down onto the saucer. They sat in the coffeehouse across from the law school, where they'd gone after Sean invited her to dinner at a Chinese place. They'd each paid for their own meal. While she'd been glad Sean still wanted to spend time with her, she had no intention of muddying the waters by behaving as if this was a date.

"I can't believe I have to work for your brother for three months!" Dara picked up her spoon, realized she'd already stirred her coffee thirty-six times or so, and slammed it back down again. "He's going to make my life a misery for three months!"

Sean chuckled, to her further irritation. Why was he laughing? For some reason, her abiding hatred of his brother seemed to amuse him no end. "Why are you so upset?" he asked her. "He's not all that bad."

She shook her head in amazement. "I'll bet he's a tyrant in the office."

"I lived to tell the story." He smothered a grin. "Barely."

"If only you were still going to be there," she said beseechingly. "It wouldn't be so bad if you were there with me."

"Not a chance. My days as a paralegal are over. I'll be at the ACLU if you need me."

Dara sat sullenly for a few more minutes, her arms crossed over her chest. Sean seemed to know now was a good time to keep his mouth shut. Finally, she relented. "Sorry I'm being such a wet blanket. I don't want to waste one more thought on your brother tonight."

"Good."

Her plan, when the evening began, had been to wolf down her dinner and dash home to study for the rest of the evening. But then something funny happened. Over fried rice, steamed dumplings, and her glass of zinfandel, she'd realized she had fun with Sean. He made her laugh. He stared at her as if she were the most fascinating creature on the planet. And what a flattering switch that was from the virulent contempt she'd seen in Mike's eyes after class. Mike. Why was he on her mind again? She smiled at Sean. "I'm glad you suggested dinner."

He grinned like he'd discovered a chest full of pirate's gold buried in his backyard. "Me, too."

That look of absolute adoration reappeared in Sean's eyes, to Dara's chagrin. He wasn't still thinking he could get her to change her mind about their relation-ship, was he? She had no intentions of sending him any mixed signals or leading him on in any way; the last thing she wanted was to hurt him when he'd been nothing but wonderful to her. So she picked up her wine glass in a toast. "To new friends."

Sean blinked once, and his smile dimmed infinitesimally. But then he picked up his water glass and clinked it with hers. "To new friends."

To her horror, Dara's heart pounded as she arrived at Mike's office on Monday morning, but she told herself it was just first-day jitters. She'd made up her mind to be the best law clerk in the history of law clerks so he could never fire her. How could he fire her, anyway? It was an unpaid internship, for God's sake! She was a glorified volunteer. Sure, Mike's low opinion of her hurt. But what he thought of her was his problem, not hers. And she wouldn't let anything—not her budding friendship with Sean, nor her former attraction to Mike—distract her from her studies. Law school was the most important thing—the only important thing—in her life.

Laura Hartman, an attractive, middle-aged blonde who was Mike's secretary, greeted her at the door of Mike's office, which occupied a rehabbed brownstone downtown. Dara was startled when she saw it. Did Mike own the building, then? Was he doing so well at such an early age? "I'm glad I came in early." Laura said as she waved her inside. "I wasn't expecting you for another twenty minutes." Dara gave an inner smirk of satisfaction. So the jerk thought she was lazy and undisciplined, did he? Well, she planned to be twenty minutes early for everything from now on.

The office, Dara noted without comment, was sunny and open, understated and beautiful. Heavy leaded glass with beveled edges cut in intricate patterns framed the massive oak door that stood at the top of several steps leading up from the sidewalk. Inside was a large foyer with a round mahogany table centered on a Persian rug and adorned with a beautiful arrangement of burgundy silk hydrangeas. A gracefully curved staircase led to the offices upstairs. The waiting area had overstuffed chairs in dark greens and blues, and the mahogany woodwork everywhere was simple but elegant. Well, Mike had good taste, she decided begrudgingly. Big deal. All that proved was he'd had the sense to hire a decent real estate agent and decorator.

Laura showed her the small law library, the kitchen, Mike's office upstairs, and the small office next to Mike's that was to be Dara's. They passed a conference room with a television and VCR. The last office, barely a broom closet, belonged to Jamal. Dara furrowed her brow. "Who's Jamal?"

"You'll see." Laura grinned as if Dara was about to be the recipient of a very amusing practical joke.

Back in the foyer, they ran into Amira Baxter, the receptionist. Young, dark skinned, with short, natural hair and a dazzling smile, Amira, Dara quickly discovered, was the despotic gatekeeper who screened calls from would-be clients and decided who could speak with Mike and who couldn't. "I'm at the university," Amira said as she shook Dara's hand. "I take classes at night so I can keep working during the day. I have a two-year-old son."

"Nice to meet you," Dara replied automatically, her mind shifting again to Mike. She tried her best not to be impressed with him, but she was. How could she not be? He already owned his own firm, with three full-time employees, and he was only thirty-four. That certainly helped explain why he was so cocky. He probably thought he was God's gift to the legal profession, their own local version of Thurgood Marshall. Cocky or not, he was obviously very bright and no stranger to hard work.

Dara had avoided asking for as long as she could, but she was dying to know. She cleared her throat and turned to Laura. "Where, uh . . . where is Mike?"

Laura looked at her in surprise. "I thought he told you. He's in trial today. Armed robbery. I'm not sure how long it'll last."

Relief swamped her. She was scheduled to work at the office every morning from eight to ten, so the chances were good she wouldn't see him today. It was just as well. She planned on ignoring him as much as possible anyway, and now she wouldn't have to make the effort. Laura walked her back to her new office and pointed her to a stack of transcripts on her desk. A note from Mike sat on top, with handwriting in slashes and swirls of blue ink, as strong and bold as his personality. Dara picked it up. "He says he wants me to read these trial transcripts for any signs of error by the defendant's attorney," she told Laura.

Laura nodded. "I'll leave you to it, then. Call me if you need anything."

Dara settled in and the morning flew by while she scribbled notes on a legal pad. When she remembered the time, at five till ten, she felt vaguely disappointed. It was time to leave for class. She really wouldn't see Mike today. Big deal. What was she missing except another opportunity to be abused? Anyway, she'd be back tomorrow, and any insults he had for her would surely keep till then.

But Dara didn't see Mike the next day, or the next day, or the next, and after the second day her pride kept her from asking about him again. But his presence was everywhere. "Would you look at this?" Laura muttered one morning when Dara passed her desk on the way to the kitchen. Laura showed her a thick stack of typed papers with Mike's handwriting scrawled all over it.

"What is it?"

"It's a brief we need to file tomorrow. Mike edited the whole thing last night at home. It's over sixty pages. Doesn't he ever sleep?" Dara was impressed. It took her hours to read sixty pages of legal text, and she was no dummy. "And look at this." Laura waved two micro-cassettes. "He dictated two other motions in other cases. I don't know how I'm going to get all of this done. How am I supposed to keep up with him? He needs to hire another secretary."

"You want some cheese with that whine, Laura?" called Amira from her post at the front desk, and they all laughed. But privately, Dara felt sorry for Laura, a mere mortal, after all. How could she keep up with someone who worked as hard as Mike? Just then the phone rang. "Mike Baldwin's office," Amira said into her headset. "Hey, Mike . . . nothing. Just talking to Laura and Dara."

Dara's ears pricked up. Mike was calling from court to check in. He'd probably want to talk to her, see how she was doing, and ask if she had any questions about the transcripts.

"Uh-huh," Amira said, jotting notes on her message pad. "Okay. Okay. Got it. Okay. I'll get her. Hold on." Dara cleared her throat, started toward the phone on the end table in the waiting area, and waited for Amira to transfer Mike to her. She reached for the phone, but then she heard Amira speaking again. "Mike's on line two for you, Laura." Laura went back to her desk, and Dara snatched her hand away from the phone as if it had turned into a spinning table saw.

Dara strolled back to the front desk and tried to look nonchalant. "Did, uh, did Mike say anything about me?" she asked Amira casually, despite her heart's pounding. Surely there was something. A message. A word of encouragement. An acknowledgment. Something. Anything.

Amira looked up from her notes. "Nope. Do you need him?" She reached a hand out to the phone. "I can get him back—"

"No," Dara said quickly. "It was nothing." Suddenly, her mood turned foul, and she stalked back upstairs to her office, without getting the coffee she'd come down for. So he didn't want to talk to her. It didn't matter; she really didn't need anything. But why did she feel . . . neglected? Was he avoiding her?

Every day she pored over the transcripts, leaving her desk only to go to the ladies' room or the kitchen for coffee. By the end of the week, she'd drafted a memo summarizing what she'd found. She wanted to give it to Mike before she left the office Friday morning. But Laura, swamped just with Mike's work, couldn't finish typing the memo for her before Dara left for class on Friday morning. Since one of her afternoon classes was canceled, Dara went back to the office in the late afternoon to make sure it got done. She'd just settled into her chair and booted up her computer when she heard Mike's voice booming in her doorway. "What are you doing here?" he demanded, clearly alarmed.

Chapter 4

Mike promptly forgot about his mission of going downstairs for a little coffee. He was astonished to see Dara here at this time of day; she should have been gone hours ago. He'd have been less surprised to see Jimmy Hoffa sitting behind her desk. It was bad enough he thought of her constantly. Now here she was, turning up at the office at unauthorized times—times when he shouldn't have to see her at all.

He'd spent the last several days reliving their confrontation in the classroom. Try though he did, he couldn't understand what had happened to him that day. Never before in his life had he embarrassed a student in class. Worse, it had infuriated him when Dara hadn't backed down when they'd argued. In his experience, people were generally a little intimidated by him, because of his size if nothing else. But Dara clearly wasn't. So he'd taunted and needled her and hadn't been happy until he'd made her speechless. Finally, he'd shut her up. Her rage thrilled him. It told him he got to her like she got to him. But then there'd been that strange moment when she'd looked away, and he thought he'd made her cry. And suddenly, he'd felt lower than a garden slug. And just as suddenly, she'd pulled herself together, and he'd felt overwhelming relief and . . . admiration because she had too much pride to let him see her upset. Admiration. What was that about?

And what about her claim that she and Sean were only friends? Could it be true? They sure didn't look like friends the other night, when she'd pulled him into her arms, although, come to think of it, he hadn't actually seen them kiss. It didn't matter, anyway. The point was Sean cared about her—regardless of what she thought about Sean—and Sean would never forgive him if he went after his dream woman. Period.

So why couldn't he think of something else besides Dara for more than thirty seconds? She took his emotions through more ups and downs than a ride through the streets of San Francisco. Well, it was going to stop right now. He was absolutely determined to get through her internship without interacting with her in any meaningful way. He couldn't stand to look at her, and he planned to do it as little as possible. If only she would cooperate.

She frowned up at him. "I work here. Or did you forget?"

He watched her for a long moment. Oh, he'd like to forget her all right. Forget his uncontrollable attraction to her. Forget the searing pain that sliced through his chest every time he thought of Sean touching her or making a move on her. What did she care, anyway, if he never talked to her again? She'd made her contempt for him painfully obvious on more than one occasion. But her eyes were locked with his, and she was doing it again: giving him that arrogant look of hers, calling him on the carpet, and demanding an explanation. As if *she* were the boss and *he* were the employee. Unbelievable. "I haven't forgotten," he said coolly.

She pressed her lips together. Now she seemed frustrated. She reached for her pen. "How's the trial going?"

"What I meant," he said, ignoring her question completely, "was what are you doing here *now*?"

She waved her hand impatiently. "One of my classes was canceled, so I came back to make sure Laura finished my memo and got it to you."

He had no idea what she was talking about. "I didn't ask you to do a memo."

"I know, but I thought it would be helpful."

"Thanks," he said begrudgingly, and a smug little smile flitted across her mouth. Well, she'd won that point. He'd expected sloth and laziness from her, not this kind of professionalism.

"How's the trial going?" she repeated.

He stared at her. Why was she determined to be pleasant? Was it because she knew how much it freaked him out? He had piles of work waiting for him on his desk, but suddenly, he couldn't leave. He stepped into her office, then sprawled in the chair across from her desk. "Our client was acquitted this afternoon."

"That's wonderful!" she cried. "You must be thrilled."

He watched her suspiciously. "Not really." He shrugged. "He'll probably be robbing another gas station next week. It's his calling."

Her mouth fell open. "You mean he really did do it?"

She was naive, he realized. Give her another minute and she'd be confessing she still believed in the Easter Bunny. "Of course, he did it. Don't tell me you thought criminal defense attorneys only represented people who didn't commit crimes."

She blinked. "Well, no, I didn't think that. I've just never heard anyone be so blunt about it before."

"My job—*our* job—is to make sure our clients get the full protections they're entitled to under the legal system. It's not our job to represent only innocent people."

"But what if this guy holds up another gas station next week and this time he kills someone? How would you feel then?"

He asked himself that same question a thousand times a day. "Terrible," he said somberly. "But I'd remind myself I took an oath to represent my clients zealously, and it was the jury, or the judge, not me, that decided to let him go."

"So criminal defense attorneys are like prostitutes or mercenaries," she said, and he threw back his head and laughed. "You'll represent any murderer or rapist or child molester who has the money to pay you."

There was nothing she wouldn't say. He liked that. "I do have some standards. I *don't* represent people accused of rape or child molestation. I don't have the stomach for that."

"But murder!"

"Usually, my clients have some excuse, like self-defense, or that it was a crime of passion, something the jury may understand. Anyway," he continued, "I thought this was the kind of work you want to do."

She frowned. "I don't know. You have to be really passionate about something to be as good at it as you are, and I'm not sure I have the nerves for this."

Had she just complimented him? He must have gaped at her, because suddenly, she looked away and began to compulsively straighten the files on her desk. Was she flustered? "I also do a little bit of personal injury work. In fact, I have a big case that's set for trial in a couple of months. Our client is a thirty-three-year-old man who was hit by an eighteen-wheeler while he was driving home from work. Now he's a quadriplegic—"

"Oh no!"

"And he's had a huge loss of income, plus crazy medical bills for the rest of his life. He's married with three small children."

"Oh, God. That's so awful! Why doesn't the truck company just settle? It's not going to come off very well in front of a jury."

He gave her a wry smile. "I've been asking myself that same question for three years."

"Three years! You've been working on the case that long?"

"Yeah."

"How much would you settle for?"

"Three or four million."

Her mouth dropped open. "That's a whole lot of money, Mike."

He stared at her. "Yeah, well, I'll ask you what I'm planning to ask the jury. Would you give up your ability to care for yourself—even to scratch your own nose when it itches—and to run around in the grass with your kids for three or four million?"

Grudging respect gleamed in her eyes. "You're good. How long have you been out on your own?"

Strangely, he found himself wanting to tell her all about himself and the firm he'd worked so hard to build. "When my father died a few years ago, he left me and Sean a little money. So I decided it was time to leave Hopewell Standish and strike out on my own."

Her eyes gleamed brighter. "So now you're your own boss. It must be wonderful."

He had to fight the urge to puff out his chest and grin idiotically. "Usually it is. But the problem is I've traded the steady salary I had at Hopewell Standish—and it was a big one—for financial uncertainty. So now I do a lot of nail biting."

She smiled knowingly, as if she knew some fabulous

secret about the future of his little firm. "I'm not worried. And you know what they say, No guts, no glory."

"Do you know something I don't know?" he asked, intrigued by her obvious confidence in him.

Flustered suddenly, she looked away. "No, of course not," she said, shaking her head. Her gaze darted to his face and away again. "I'm sure you'll work very hard and do what you need to do."

Was she telling him she believed in him? And if she did believe in him, why? He would kill for the answers, but one look at her now closed face told him her lips were sealed on the topic. "How is everyone treating you?" he asked after a long moment.

She raised her gaze back to his. "Very well. But who's this mysterious Jamal?"

"Jamal is my indentured servant."

She grimaced. "Isn't that what I am?"

"No. As my law school intern, you're one half step higher on the totem pole than Jamal. He's seventeen. He got into a little trouble, and I represented him several months ago, after he tried to steal a car. After that, he came to work for me while he gets his GED at night. So now he does all kinds of things around here. He files documents at the courthouse, tracks down witnesses, goes to court with me, changes lightbulbs, gets lunch. You name it, he does it."

Dara looked horrified, as if he'd told her he'd hired Jeffrey Dahmer. "So you hired him—just like that?"

"Just like that."

"And you trust him?"

"Look, Dara. He's grown up with a single working mom and four younger brothers. He's had no male role models in his life. No one was around to make him get his butt out of bed and get to school. So now I do it."

"How's he doing on the GED?"

"He did great on the practice test."

"I think that was him," she cried, pointing over his shoulder toward the door.

Mike twisted around in his chair. "Jamal!" he bellowed. "Jamal! Get in here, man!"

Dara raised her eyebrows at him. "*This* is how you teach him how to behave in the office?"

Mike winked at her, then turned again as Jamal rushed in. Dark skinned, with short hair; tall; lanky; wearing a white shirt, tie, and dark pants; and carrying a stack of papers, Jamal was clearly in the middle of something and did not want to be interrupted. "You told me to make these copies, man," he complained before he saw Dara and froze, his mouth dropping open.

Mike struggled not to laugh at Jamal's stupefaction. Dara could certainly make a first impression. "Jamal, this is Dara," he told him. "She's our intern for the next few months. Be nice to her. Show her around. Help her out."

Jamal took her all in with one sweeping glance. Then suddenly he broke into a grin as he came around to Dara's side of the desk to shake her hand. "You're *beautiful*," he told her.

"Man, get your hands off her," Mike snapped before Dara could respond. "And don't try any of your sorry moves on her, either. I've already warned her about you."

Jamal showed no signs of ever releasing Dara's hand. "I can pull more little shorties than you any day of the week, Pops," he said to Mike over his shoulder, and Dara laughed.

"Get out," said Mike, annoyed now, his eyes on Dara's hand still wrapped in Jamal's. It pissed him off that Jamal could touch her and he couldn't. "You got those copies finished yet?"

Jamal looked back at Dara and jerked his thumb at Mike. "You see what we're dealing with? I'm outta here."

Dara laughed as Jamal left. "When do you two take your act on the road?"

For the life of him, Mike couldn't think of anything to say. Why was she being pleasant to him all of the sudden? He didn't know how to act. He felt like Steve Irwin circling a sleeping crocodile, trying to decide the best approach. "Well," he said after a long pause, getting to his feet. "I should let you get back to work." He didn't want to go. He wanted to see her laugh again. He wanted—

"Here you are!" Sean materialized outside Dara's office door and walked in to shake Mike's hand. Mike stiffened, then recovered enough to take Sean's hand. Sean settled on the edge of Dara's desk as if he owned the place. "I heard about the acquittal, man," he told Mike over his shoulder. "Congratulations."

"Thanks." Mike felt the bile rising in his throat. Sean had obviously come to collect Dara for their little evening together. Is this what "friends" did these days? Spend Friday nights together? He realized his hands were balled up in fists and shoved them in his pockets.

"What, ah, what are you doing here?" Dara asked Sean. Mike heard the hitch in her voice and his gaze flew to her face. She didn't look at him, but she fidgeted a little in her seat. She seemed uncomfortable.

Sean smiled down at her. "I thought we could go to dinner, if you're finished here."

Mike couldn't bring himself to look either one of them in the face. He needed to get out of here. "I'll see you two later."

"What about basketball next week?" Sean called after him.

Basketball was the very last thing on Mike's mind, but he and Sean had had fun the other day when they played. They should probably keep doing it because it helped heal their relationship. "Yeah," he told Sean. "I'll call you."

He stalked out.

Dara watched Mike go, feeling rattled. She really needed to work on getting used to his physical presence. He was such a huge creature. So tall, so broad-shouldered, so disturbingly . . . masculine. The room seemed to shrink when he came and grow when he left. And the energy felt different—more charged—when Mike was there. It was like having a tiger come and go.

And his commitment to helping others surprised her. Not just with Jamal, but with his other clients, too. She'd thought reputable attorneys, like Mike, the ones with expensive suits and nice offices, somehow sniffed out the thugs and assorted lowlifes and only represented the wrongfully accused. The Truly Innocent. But Mike wanted to make the legal system available to everyone. Who knew?

"Dara," Sean sang. She started and he waggled his fingers at her. "Hell-o-o! Anybody home?" As usual his dimpled smile was contagious and she couldn't help but laugh. "You ready? I'm starving."

"Not yet. I need to finish this memo."

"By the way," Sean said as he settled into the chair Mike had just vacated. "What was going on with you two when I walked in?"

"What do you mean?"

"You were talking like normal people." He grinned. "If you don't watch out I'm going to start thinking you actually like him."

"Ummm," was all she could say, her face flushing for no apparent reason.

* * *

Jamal wandered into Mike's office at the end of the day, or what passed for the end of the day for all normal human beings, a group to which Mike Baldwin clearly did not belong. Mike, it seemed to Jamal, got a second wind around six or six-thirty, and worked until God knew when, only to go home and work some more. It was Jamal's firm belief that eight hours a day, minus half an hour—well, forty-five minutes, to be honest— for lunch was more than enough time to devote to the pursuit of justice.

Mike looked up from the open file on his desk long enough to spare him a glance. "What's up, man?" he said distractedly.

Jamal wondered what could be so interesting that Mike would devote nearly every evening to work. When did he ever get any action? A brother like Mike was a shorty magnet. Owned a business, a house, a new black SUV. And that was only the icing. Women would sleep with Mike on the basis of his looks alone—they tripped all over themselves trying to catch his eye. He'd seen it time and time again. And Mike hardly noticed. "I'm out," Jamal told him. "You coming?"

"Not yet," Mike muttered. "I've got a deposition tomorrow."

Jamal collapsed in one of Mike's chairs. He was dying of curiosity about what was going on with Mike and Dara. Mike hadn't liked it when he'd held Dara's hand earlier. Why? Something was definitely up and he wanted to get to the bottom of it. He liked to think of himself as a submarine captain. Every now and then you needed to send up your periscope and see what you could see. "What's up with Dara?" he asked Mike. "I don't know when I've seen a girl that fine."

Mike bent his head low as he jotted some notes on his legal pad. "Ummm," he grunted.

Jamal knew he was onto something. Mike had a perfect memory—he hardly ever took notes because he remembered everything. Now here he was, scribbling like he'd discovered the cure for cancer and needed to write it down before he forgot it. "'Ummm?'" Jamal cried. "Man, that girl is beautiful, and you know it!"

Mike's lips tightened. "She's all right, I guess." He did not look up.

"'All right?'" Jamal cackled. This was too funny for words. This clown actually wanted to debate whether Dara was beautiful or not. The next thing he knew Mike'd be arguing about whether Michael Jackson had ever had a nose job. It was time to move in for the kill. "If I was a little older I'd try to get me a piece of that. You tagged her yet?"

It was a tense moment. Mike slowly looked up from his work, his eyebrows a forbidding line running over his eyes, which were now so dark they were almost black. Jamal thought he saw a muscle clenching in his jaw. "Don't talk about Dara that way," Mike said in that softly dangerous voice Jamal had, fortunately, heard directed at him only once or twice before.

My work here is done. Jamal nonchalantly stood up and shrugged. He knew everything he needed to know and more; it was time to get out of Dodge before Mike lunged across the desk at him. "Whatever, pops." He turned and strode out, grinning from ear to ear as soon as his back was turned to Mike's still glowering face. *Oh, yeah.* Mike wanted Dara and he wanted her bad.

This was going to be fun.

What on earth happened? Dara could swear that Mike really was ignoring her. No—it was worse than that. He didn't want to be anywhere near her. Didn't even want to be in the same room with her.

Reassured by their polite conversation on Friday, she smiled at him when she passed his office first thing Monday morning. "Good morning, Mike." He sat at his desk, typing on his computer. She took a good look at his office for the first time; he'd never invited her into his precious inner sanctum. His sleek glass desk sat in front of bookshelves, which contained, along with the requisite books, several beautiful African sculptures, mostly animals. His leather chair was tall and black, but the other chairs and the sofa were a muted black and tan pattern. African masks, paintings, and mirrors hung on the walls. The office was sophisticated and light and airy and elegant. She loved it.

He glanced up at her, and his gaze quickly slid from the top of her hair to her navy silk dress and down to her pumps. His jaw tightened, and his attention immediately shifted back to the computer screen. "How are you?"

"Good." She lingered in his doorway, taking off her jacket. She felt a little strange standing out in the hall, but for some reason, she didn't feel like he wanted her in his office. "How was your weekend?"

This time he didn't even bother to glance at her. "Fine." He typed a few more words, then seemed to remember his manners. "How was yours?" Without waiting for her answer, he bent his head and flipped through some papers on his desk.

"Good." She loitered for a minute, puzzled. Hadn't they broken the ice on Friday? "I had some thoughts about the transcripts I've been reading. Maybe if you have a minute, we—"

He started typing again and apparently couldn't spare her another glance. "Maybe later. I'm pretty busy."

So that was it, of course. He was obviously very busy right now. It had nothing to do with her. "Oh, sure. I'll come back later." She turned to go, nearly bumping into Jamal.

"What's up, Dara?" he said amiably as he turned into Mike's office.

"Hey, Jamal." She veered around him and went into her own office.

"What's up, man?" she heard Jamal say to Mike as she hung up her jacket and purse and settled at her desk. Dara paused and listened. "Did you see the game yesterday?" said Mike, his tone animated, his voice muted only slightly by the wall. She sat, trying to read transcripts, her blood doing a slow boil, while Jamal and Mike discussed the football game for ten minutes or so. So much for Mike being "pretty busy."

When Jamal finally left, she found her pad and pen, and marched back to Mike's office to ask him about the transcripts. No way was she going to let him blow her off like that. She found him standing by his desk, putting on his jacket, briefcase in hand. He looked unpleasantly surprised to see her, as if he'd looked up to discover a skunk headed his way. "What's up?" he asked her, glancing at his watch like Donald Trump, too busy to give her the time of day.

Dara resisted the urge to punch him in the face. "Remember?" she said, trying to remain pleasant. "I wanted to ask you about the transcripts?"

"Right," he said. "Let's do it tomorrow. I've got court." He gave her the briefest hint of a smile, then left, leaving her standing alone in the middle of his office.

"Right. Tomorrow." She felt like an idiot, but maybe she was being too sensitive. Mike was a professional, and he would want to help his intern with any work related issues. Tomorrow she'd catch him at a better time, and she was sure he'd be more receptive. But when she poked her head in his office the next day, she found him in the middle of a phone call. "Sorry," he mouthed.

"No problem," she said, smiling, determined not to take it personally. He was busy. That was all. She would try again later in the morning. But half an hour later, he e-mailed her to say he wanted another memo. Flabbergasted, she read the e-mail, then reread it. Sitting at her desk, she could hear Mike, still in his office right next to hers. What was that? A hundred steps? Thirty feet? And he couldn't even come to her office to talk to her directly?

Every day was the same. When she was nearby, he stayed in his office, with his head bent low over his paperwork, or on the phone. He communicated with her only through Laura or via e-mails or memos. She couldn't get him to talk to her, or even to look at her. He wouldn't stay in a room with her. She was *not* imagining it. And it drove her crazy.

". . . And the national security advisor was on *Meet the Press* yesterday. She said that—," Mike was telling Laura one Monday morning, when Dara came into the kitchen to get her coffee. As soon as he saw Dara, he stopped talking, his train of thought derailed.

"Good morning," Dara chirped, looking as fresh and beautiful as a summer rainbow in her violet silk dress.

"Good morning." Laura smiled warmly at her.

"Hey," said Mike in Dara's general direction. *Great.* Here she was again. He avoided her whenever possible, and lately, he'd also tried not to look directly at her. Childish, maybe, but it couldn't hurt. He had to do something to get on top of his physical attraction, and not looking too closely at her seemed as good a place as any to start. That way he wouldn't see her in the morning, looking good enough to eat, then spend the rest of the day fantasizing about her, like he'd done the other day, when she'd worn some dark knit dress that had clung to her butt in a way he longed to do.

This had set him to wondering what kind of underwear she must be wearing. Ultimately, he'd concluded there were only two choices: no panties at all or thongs, both equally unsettling. He couldn't picture her going without underwear, so he'd figured she wore thongs, but he'd immediately started wondering whether they were black, white, cotton, lacy. The possibilities were mind-boggling, and infinitely more fascinating than the hearing he'd been preparing for. When all was said and done, he'd only billed about half an hour that morning, a pace that would have him filing for bankruptcy within the month.

No, it was better not to look directly at Dara. But not looking at her didn't help with his other major problem, which was smelling her. She wore some subtle, floral perfume that was, he was sure, supposed to be as innocent as a fluffy white kitten. Unfortunately, on Dara, it made him think of making love to her in a field of flowers until she begged for mercy.

Dara poured herself a cup of coffee. "I saw that interview," she told him. "I still don't think the administration knows what it wants to do about Iraq. I'm not sure how much longer they can go on. . . ."

Mike stared at her, stupefied. What on God's green earth was she doing? Did this woman have not even the most basic understanding of the unspoken rules whereby the two of them could peacefully coexist here at work? Rule number one: don't show up in outfits that make Mike's eyes pop out of his head. Rule number two: never try to engage Mike directly in conversation. Use e-mails, Laura, notes, faxes, and messenger pigeons, for all he cared, anything to avoid direct interaction with each other. Rule number three: *never* discuss current events in a well-informed and thoughtful manner, thereby highlighting your intelligence, which he found as sexy as her body.

It was all so unfair. He'd been minding his own business, working hard, earning a little money, enjoying mindless sex with a variety of beautiful women, each one exciting and lovely in her own way, but one roughly equivalent to any other. And then *bam!* God dumped a clear standout right into his lap—someone clearly smarter, sexier, and prettier than anyone else he'd seen since . . . well, since. . . Had he ever met anyone like Dara?

But he couldn't have her. Could never have her, because Sean wanted her. But he still had to see her every day, and she taunted him with her sweetness and unavailability, a constant thorn in his side. What was a man supposed to do?

And now she stood there like Henry Kissinger, analyzing world events. Give her another minute and she'd be outlining a plan for Palestinian statehood and lasting peace in the region. Heck, maybe the president should invite *Dara* to Camp David.

But the joke was on him, wasn't it? God was having a good belly laugh at his expense. Because Dara wasn't his and would never be his. His stomach churned until he wondered if he wouldn't shortly reexperience the oatmeal he'd had for breakfast. He just couldn't stand it; he couldn't look at her another minute. "Excuse me," he interjected, glancing at his watch. Dara trailed off and looked at him expectantly. He focused his gaze on some vague point to the left of Dara's eyes. "I just realized what time it is. I'm going to be late." He turned and sped on his way.

Dara stared, openmouthed, after him. There he went again! What had she done wrong?

A week passed, and then another. On Tuesday and Wednesday of her fourth week in the office, she told herself the same thing over and over—*it doesn't matter*—until it became a mantra. But it *did* matter. By Thursday she was sulking, and on Friday she was in a solid funk. Why was Mike doing this to her? Why had he banished her to Siberia when everyone else could soak up the warmth of his attention? Why did he hate her? Just because of a passing attraction they'd had? She'd never been jealous before, but now she resented the words and smiles and looks he gave to everyone else. Every time she heard his laughter, she got angrier and angrier. The morning she saw him talking to the FedEx man and asking about the man's children by name, she fantasized about deleting all his client files from the office computer network. Maybe *then* he'd look her in the face.

Her foul mood carried over into the weekend. She didn't even feel like going to the movies Saturday night with Sean and Monica. She was a little snappish when Sean called to invite her, and when he hung up, her guilty conscience told her to call and apologize, but she didn't feel like doing that, either. She'd make it up to him on Monday. But she woke up in the middle of the night with a raging fever and aching joints, and she stayed in bed all day Sunday. Ironic, wasn't it? Now her physical condition matched her mood: foul.

Sunday evening she got tired of being in bed, so she shuffled into the living room and parked on the plush denim sofa to burrow into the pillows and wallow in her misery. After a while she hauled herself into the kitchen to crack open a can of chicken noodle soup and make some toast, but when she pulled the steaming bowl out of the microwave, her stomach heaved in protest. She dumped the soup down the kitchen sink and poured a glass of orange juice instead.

As she resettled on the sofa, snuggling down under her ultra-soft cashmere throw—an apartment-warming present from her parents—the cordless phone on the coffee table rang. She stared at it indifferently for several rings—why couldn't she just die in peace?—then snatched it up. "Hello?" she snuffled.

"What's wrong with you?" said Monica.

Dara dabbled her clammy forehead with a wet washcloth and shivered. "I have the flu or something."

"Oh, God. Need anything?"

"No."

"Good. You won't believe what happened last night. Sean and I went to Club Destiny after the movie. You know, the place where all the athletes hang out. Guess who's the owner's wife?"

Dara fluffed her pillow, then flopped down and tunneled back under the covers. "Monica, my temperature is 102. I wouldn't care if you saw Oprah at the club last night."

"Alicia Carey from high school, only she's Alicia Johnson now. Her husband is Mark Johnson. Used to play for the Falcons. Anyway, you should see her. She's dripping with diamonds. Drives a Benz bigger than my apartment. She asked all about you and said to tell you hi."

Dara vaguely remembered the woman. "Fascinating. Can I go back to sleep now?"

"No. Here's the unbelievable part. I saw in the paper this morning that there was a shooting at the club last night, after we left. Some guy was killed in the back room. Mass hysteria. The police came and closed the place down."

"Good Lord. Thank God you and Sean were already gone."

"No kidding. I can't wait to see who they arrest for this. There must have been three hundred witnesses."

Eventually, Monica let her go, and Dara went back to sleep. She was no better Monday morning and called the office to tell Mike she had the flu, as if he'd notice she wasn't there since he ignored her, anyway, but Laura said he was in court. "Take care of yourself," Laura told her. "I'll tell Mike you won't be in. And don't come rushing back tomorrow if you're not ready."

Dara hung up and snorted at the image of Laura informing Mike she wouldn't be in. *Dara? Dara who? Does she still work here? What's she been up to?*

Mike wouldn't care if she called in sick for the rest of her internship or was abducted by aliens or disappeared into the witness protection program.

By Tuesday morning, the fever had broken, but she felt so weak, a trip to the kitchen exhausted her. "Don't worry about a thing," said Laura when Dara called the office. "We'll see you tomorrow." By early evening she felt restless and decided to get some fresh air. She showered and dressed for the first time in days and drove to the office to see if Mike had put anything on her desk while she'd been sick. She let herself into the darkened brownstone with her key and went upstairs. The silence and complete lack of bustle was strange. When had the office ever been this quiet and peaceful? She crossed the threshold into her office and froze. There was a movement by the window. Someone was in her office—sitting in her chair, staring out the window. She saw the black silhouette of a man against the light filtering in from the window. Alarmed, she fumbled for the lights and flipped the switch.

It was Mike, looking as surprised to see her as she was to see him. "Mike!" she cried, her hand at her throat. "You nearly scared me to death!"

He'd loosened his tie and rolled his shirtsleeves up, revealing muscular brown forearms. He wasn't in a good mood; his brows were lowered across his eyes, and his mouth was a tight, grim line.

She braced herself.

Chapter 5

Mike stared at Dara, unpleasantly surprised to see her. She'd caught him at what was, quite possibly, the lowest point in his life: skulking in her office in the dark, trying to get a whiff of her perfume from her chair, wondering when he'd see her again. He'd thought seeing her every day was the worst thing that could happen to him, but now he knew there was something worse: *not* seeing her every day. He was furious with her for getting sick and putting him through this. And he was furious with himself for being such a ridiculous sap. "Where have you been?" he asked quietly, his temper on a hair trigger.

Her eyebrows flew up in surprise. "I've had the flu."

He'd known that, of course. Her flushed face and bright eyes confirmed it for him now. She'd been sick, darn her. "Why didn't you call to tell me?"

She looked baffled and nervous. She shifted back and forth on her feet, then ran her hand through her hair. "I did call. First thing Monday morning. Didn't Laura tell you?"

His frown deepened. "Why didn't you ask for *me*?" So he could have heard her voice and known she was really okay. He'd worried like she'd had a confirmed case of Ebola. He was disgusted with himself.

She was absolutely bewildered. "I-I *did* ask for you, but you were already in court. I don't understand what the problem is."

"The problem," he said, frantically scanning his brain for some reasonable excuse for his behavior so he wouldn't sound like the raving lunatic he really was, "is that I expect *you* to tell *me* when you're not going to be in the office. You should have paged me."

"Did I miss a deadline or forget something that needed to be done while I was gone?"

"That's not the point," he snapped. "The point is you were supposed to be here."

"I was sick!"

"I expected to see you here," he said, as if that should explain everything. He knew he needed to cool it, but he just couldn't seem to rein himself in where Dara was concerned.

She rubbed her temples as if her head was throbbing, and then she exploded. "You expected to see me here?" she screeched. "That's pretty funny, considering you've gone out of your way to ignore me for weeks!"

"What are you talking about?" he said, stunned, his body tense and alert. He leapt to his feet and stalked around the desk to glower in her face. Had she really noticed he'd been avoiding her? And here he thought he'd been very discreet this whole time.

"What am I talking about?" she cried. "You haven't said two words to me in weeks, and now you're acting like it matters whether I'm in the office or not? What a joke! Well, I'm not a potted palm to be forgotten in the corner of your office! Isn't this supposed to be an internship? Did you forget about that? Is this your idea of teaching? And how dare you pretend to care whether I'm in the office or not! I guess I should have dragged my feverish, half-dead self into the office so you wouldn't miss a day of ignoring me!" She gestured wildly, her arms waving a staccato beat in time to her words. Her eyebrows, normally two butterflies poised for flight, had come crashing down around her eyes. She was wild and out of control, a maniac.

He was mesmerized; he watched her with silent fascination, infuriated. Who did she think she was, this woman, to challenge him in his own office? Mike stared down at her in utter disbelief. She stood toe-to-toe with him, and he just couldn't believe her guts; she didn't care if he was bigger, older, or her boss. She'd made up her mind to cut him down to size, and, by God, she wouldn't be satisfied until she did. How on earth did Sean handle her? The thing that really stuck in his craw was she was right. He'd been so busy ignoring her, he'd failed miserably in his job as her teacher. "I don't want you here!" he roared. "Do you get that?"

Dara flinched but stood her ground and raised her chin. "I know you don't like me, but I don't deserve this! Why are you so moody with me?" She was obviously hurt now, beseeching.

Well, of course, he was moody. Why shouldn't he be when he had to pretend, day after day, he had no sexual interest in the one woman on the planet he wanted? At this point, they should all just be grateful he hadn't lapsed into a homicidal depression and taken a loaded rifle to work. He shook his head and ran a hand through his hair. "You can't work here," he said, talking as much to himself as to her, well aware he hadn't answered her questions.

"God!" she cried petulantly, stomping her foot. Then she seemed to realize she needed to get control of herself and took a deep breath. "Mike," she said reasonably, "things would work fine if you'd give me a chance."

He looked heavenward for a long moment. "You never wanted to work here in the first place, Dara," he reminded her. "Are you telling me you're willing to work with me now?"

She looked sad suddenly. Was her lip quivering? "I am telling you," she said softly, "that I am trying to be a professional and make the best of an awkward situation." She wrapped her arms around her sides, hugging herself, and he realized her face was glistening. She was sweating. Maybe she was still feverish. And her eyes were still bright, but were those tears? He hadn't made her cry, had he? Suddenly he felt terrible. What kind of jerk badgered a sick woman?

"I would prefer to work with someone who can stand to be in the same room with me for more than three seconds at a time," she told him, "but since I've been assigned to you, I'll just have to do the best I can."

His face twisted and he snorted in disbelief. He couldn't ever remember being so frustrated before, so hamstrung. How could she be so unbelievably blind? Didn't she know how much he still wanted her? Didn't she feel any attraction—anything for him? Apparently not. And God how it hurt.

She stared at him, waiting. He took a deep breath to pull himself together. "I don't want to get you in trouble with Stallworth," he managed to say calmly, as if the matter didn't interest him at all. "Stay if you want to stay."

Her head tilted to the side and her brow crinkled;

clearly she was trying to figure him out. For one second—one long, horrible second—he thought maybe she'd quit her internship just to get away from him. And he didn't want her to go. But then she nodded, once, and he discovered his lungs could draw complete breaths again. He turned toward the door and she stepped aside to let him pass.

He couldn't go on like this—ignoring her and sending e-mails and not looking at her. He wasn't in fifth grade. He was a grown man and he needed to act like one. Even if it killed him. He looked over his shoulder at her. "I don't think I'll be able to work with you, Dara. But I'll try." He felt like he was consenting, against his better judgment, to work with a known terrorist. She nodded eagerly. Tomorrow. He would start over with her tomorrow.

Dara ran into Mike in the kitchen getting coffee the next morning. Wary, she faced him and his eyes locked with hers. What sort of a mood was he in? He looked sane enough for the moment—even though he stared at her so strangely—but was he Dr. Jeckyll or Mr. Hyde today? She drew a deep breath and prayed for the best. "Good morning, Mike."

The beginnings of a smile softened his mouth and eyes. "Welcome back," he said quietly. His voice, when he spoke quietly like that, had a husky, intimate quality that slid right under her skin and shivered up her spine. Her heart began a slow drumbeat for no discernible reason. And why was it so hot in here all the sudden? "How are you feeling?"

When he focused on her, she felt like the only

person in the world. Every last coherent thought in her brain scattered. "I—," she faltered.

"Dara?" he said, looking concerned. He stepped closer and touched her arm. "Are you okay?"

She had absolutely no idea what he'd just said. "I-I'm fine," she stammered idiotically.

The tension left his face, and that wide, lazy smile crept across it. "Good. Because you've got a ton of work to do. Meet me in my office in an hour."

He walked out of the kitchen, and she stared after him, her heart still thundering uncontrollably.

Mike was on the phone when Dara knocked on his open door, but he waved her to one of the chairs across from his desk. "I'm sorry I can't help you," he told the caller, scribbling idly on a legal pad. "I'm just way too busy right now." He watched her cross her legs and rolled his eyes impatiently at the speaker. "It's not a matter of money. I know you could pay the retainer." He sighed and listened again. "If you'd like to hold on, my secretary can give you the names of some other criminal attorneys in the city. Okay. Hold on." He transferred the call to Laura, then turned to Dara. "Sorry."

She leaned forward in her chair, excited. "What was all that about?"

He waved his hand dismissively. "There was some shooting at a club over the weekend, and the club's owner's been arrested. He's at the justice center. He wanted me to represent him."

Dara's eyes flew open wide. "That club shooting? You were his one phone call?"

"Yeah. Waste of fifty cents."

"Why?" she cried, flabbergasted. "What kind of

self-respecting lawyer with bills to pay turns away a wealthy client?"

"There's more to it than money, and I didn't really want the case."

"Why not?" she persisted. "A nice juicy murder case. What could be more fun?"

He laughed. "Only a first-year law student could think of a murder case as 'fun.'" He leaned back and propped his feet on his desk. "For one thing, he talked to the police." He narrowed his eyes and wagged a finger at her. "Never let a client talk to the police. Also, one of his employees is apparently giving him an alibi, which I don't trust because he signs her paychecks. He's talked to the press, so the case is even more high profile than it would already be with a local celebrity. I hate high-profile cases."

She raised her eyebrows. "Anything else?"

"Yeah. I didn't like him," he said flatly. "He was arrogant."

"I see." She nodded gravely. "And what with you being arrogant enough for two or three people, that could create problems."

"Exactly." He couldn't help but laugh at her little dig.

"But still. What's your retainer?"

"For murder? I dunno. Twenty thousand or so," he said, shrugging carelessly. She gaped at him, and he wondered again if he hadn't made a terrible mistake by refusing the case. The firm was doing okay— pretty well, in fact—but being in business for yourself was always a risky proposition. Johnson could have written his retainer check without missing a beat. Still, his gut screamed at him that Johnson was bad news, and he tried to always listen to his gut. "Dara, Dara, Dara. It's not all about money. And a thug gets

thrown in jail every 2.5 minutes, so there'll be someone else to pay my exorbitant fees. Anyway," he
continued as he swung his feet down and opened the
file on his desk, "if the firm hits hard times, I'll just
save on expenses by firing my legal intern."

"You don't pay me," she replied tartly.

"Ah. Jamal, then. Are you going to do any work
today, or were you planning to interrogate me further?"

She brandished her pen and legal pad. "At your
service."

"This is awful." He tossed an opinion letter she'd
written, now covered with red ink from his pen,
across his desk to her. Actually, *awful* was too strong
a word. She was bright and a very good writer. But
her legal reasoning needed work. "We'll talk about
it later, after you've had the chance to read my comments." She looked up long enough to shoot him a
blistering stare, as if she wanted to hurl the memo at
his face. "Don't tell me you can't take a little constructive criticism?" he asked innocently.

Dara smiled sourly. "Of course, I can," she said
through her teeth.

Mike tried hard not to laugh at her. She looked like
a kid trying to pretend she liked her cough medicine
as she choked it down. "There's something else. I
don't know if you remember that personal injury case
I told you about. Our client was hit by a truck, and
now he's a quadriplegic."

"I do remember. It's such an awful story."

He slid a thick transcript across the desk to her. "I
need you to summarize the defendant truck driver's
testimony from his deposition. I need to start preparing for my cross-examination. The trial's coming up
soon. You can help me with the questions."

Clearly thrilled, she gave him a dazzling smile. "Sure." She picked up the transcript and flipped through it. "I heard you did other work besides the criminal stuff, and I . . ." She looked up and saw him watching her. She trailed off and blinked at him.

Mike realized he was staring and hastily looked away to rummage through some papers on his desk. Oh no. She'd caught him staring at her. Again. But how was he supposed to think straight when a girl this beautiful talked to him? When she'd smiled at him just now—like he'd discovered a way to make stiletto heels so they didn't hurt women's feet—he'd felt like a god. Like he was seeing brilliant colors for the first time, after a lifetime of nothing but black and white. "Well," he said, his voice husky now, still rifling papers. "I'm not paying you to sit around in my office."

She rose to her feet. At the door she stopped and turned back to him. "Mike?"

He didn't look at her again, but her plaintive tone said it all. She was afraid she'd done or said something wrong. "Chop-chop," he said, grabbing his phone as if to make an urgent call. "Time is money." Dara gave him a small smile and left. And as soon as she turned the corner, he heaved a huge sigh of relief and put the phone back down.

Dara had just settled back at her desk when Laura buzzed her to say Alicia Johnson was in the lobby to see her. Alicia was the friend Monica had seen at the club—the alleged murderer's wife! What on earth could she want? Startled, Dara stood up again and spoke into the intercom. "I'll be right down."

Alicia, her tense shoulders squared, paced in the waiting area. Petite, pretty, brown-skinned, she looked chic in her black leather suit and her engagement ring, which, as Dara could see as she walked down the stairs, was the size of Rhode Island. She threw herself into Dara's arms. "It's so good to see you! Have you heard?"

"Yes." Dara led her to the sofa, and they sat.

"Dara, Mike won't represent him." Alicia's eyes swam in unshed tears, and her nostrils and lips quivered.

"I know. He's, uh, very busy," said Dara, feeling guilty about the lie.

"But we need him. Monica told me you work for him. Please talk to him for me, Dara."

Dara was horrified. "I can't. I just started here myself. I don't have any clout with him and—"

Alicia gripped her arm like a drowning woman holding onto a life preserver. For such a small person, she had a surprisingly strong grip. "Mark didn't do it. We have two children at home, and I'm pregnant. Please, Dara." She pressed a tissue to her mouth and whimpered back her sobs.

Without a word, Dara nodded and stood up. What else could she do? She slowly made the long walk up the stairs and crept into Mike's office, cursing her softheartedness every step of the way. But who could refuse a crying pregnant woman?

Mike sat at his desk, writing on his legal pad. When he looked up and saw her, his eyes widened with concern. "What's up?"

She swallowed hard. She hated asking him for such an enormous favor, especially when they were just beginning to have a thaw in their relations. Maybe he'd be so angry, he'd go back to ignoring her. "Mark Johnson's wife is here. Turns out she's a friend of mine from high school. She begged me to talk you into representing him."

He folded his arms across his chest, but his lips curled with amusement. "You gotta be kidding me."

"Yes, well, couldn't you just consider it a personal favor?"

He snorted. "Picking up coffee for someone is a personal favor. Driving someone to the airport is a personal favor. Taking a murder case because your legal intern wants you to goes above and beyond a personal favor, don't you think?"

"If you'd just—"

"No," he said firmly, looking back at his work.

Now she was irritated. She marched up to his desk, planted her hands on his papers, and leaned down until she was in his face. "I'm really tired of you dismissing me by looking at your papers, like I'm invisible." She smiled tightly.

Mike glared up at her from under his thick eyebrows. "You're like a dog with a bone. Are you always this much trouble to your employers, or is it me?"

Dara ignored that. "She's pregnant."

"Well, that's just great." He threw down his pen and sprang up from his chair to pace. His long, restless strides carried him back and forth in front of the windows. "I don't want this case. Something's going on that we don't know about. Something's not right."

Dara was glad to see he wasn't the ogre she'd thought. At least he had some feelings, even if he reserved them for high school dropouts and pregnant women. Stepping in front of him, she put her hand on his arm. "Please, Mike."

Mike stared down at Dara, frozen with indecision. He'd had no intentions of taking the case. Not for twenty thousand, not for fifty. Mark Johnson was a liar, and the poor sucker who wound up representing him would inevitably be sorry. But something in Dara's face stopped him; she looked so hopeful, so confident he could save Johnson. In fact, he felt like he could do anything with her looking at him like that. A harsh sigh escaped his lips. He'd always thought his mother was the only woman in the world he couldn't refuse. Apparently, he'd been wrong. "How can I say no?" he said, resigned.

"Thank you." Her face lit up like the Vegas Strip, and he was strangely moved. Was this how she always looked at Sean? He felt his jaw tense and shoved that disturbing idea far away. "Don't thank me yet," he said gruffly. "I want twenty-five for the retainer." He glanced at his watch. "I suppose she wants me to drop everything else I need to do to be at the arraignment this afternoon to bail his butt out of jail."

"Probably," she said as she headed to the door.

"Meet Jamal here at two-thirty." Dara froze, then threw her hand over her heart as if the very idea of tagging along was too good to be true. He had the strange thought that the look of excitement on Dara's face, more than any retainer Johnson might pay, was his reward for taking the case. A ridiculous, unstoppable grin split his face. "You don't want to miss any of the fun, do you?"

"Of course not," she cried, beaming as if he'd just insisted she split the lotto jackpot with him.

"Good. Because if I have to work my butt off on this case, you can be sure you will, too."

Dara met Jamal back at the office at two-thirty. In lieu of a greeting, he looked her up and down, eyeing her critically. "You're not wearing *that*, are you?" He said it as if she'd shown up in a bikini. Startled, Dara surveyed her simple black knit dress with three-quarter-length sleeves and knee-length skirt and pumps. The outfit, as far as she was concerned, was perfectly acceptable for school and work, although, come to think of it, Mike had looked at her rather strangely the other day when she'd worn it. She frowned. "What's wrong with this?"

"Mike said he left a message on your machine for you to change," Jamal said sternly.

Obviously, Mike, and, therefore, Jamal, took the issue of her attire very seriously. "Well," she said, thoroughly irritated now, "I haven't been home to check my messages. Why didn't he tell me this morning?"

"He said he forgot to mention it before you left for school. He's not gonna like this."

"Oh, for God's sake!" she snapped, annoyed beyond all reason. Why did everyone speak of Mike in the reverential tones normally reserved for God? Was she the only person on the planet who didn't obey his every utterance without question? "I'll wear what I want to wear. Let's go."

They quickly walked the eight blocks to the justice center and, after they passed through the metal detectors, met Mike by the elevators. He took one look at Dara and, without bothering to greet either of them, turned on Jamal. "What's this?" he said, jerking his thumb at Dara.

Dara's blood pressure went through the roof. "*This?*" she cried. "Well, *this* has ears, and *this* doesn't appreciate being talked about as if *this* isn't here!"

Mike turned to her at last and drew a deep breath, apparently trying to collect himself. "Dara," he said, with a preternatural serenity, "I think it would be best if you changed your clothes."

"There's no time for that now," she said impatiently. "Let's go before we're late."

"Dara," he said, putting a hand on her shoulder, the edge creeping back into his voice, "I really think you should change. We can wait for you."

She shrugged his hand off. "I'm fine," she snapped. "I can handle myself. Let's go." She turned her back on him and pressed the up button on the elevator. Mike shook his head in amazement, stole one last incredulous look at Jamal, as if to make sure he hadn't imagined the whole incident, and then followed Dara onto the elevator. He shook his head and muttered something—whatever it was didn't sound very flattering—under his breath.

They arrived on the floor where the violent offenders, like their client, were housed. While Mike went to the information desk to fill out a sign-in form, a guard unlocked a door for Dara and Jamal and took them into a visiting area with long, cafeteria-style tables with attached benches. Several inmates in striped jumpsuits sat here and there at the tables, talking in quiet, urgent tones with various harassed-looking attorneys, all of whom were male.

Inside the adjoining glass-enclosed holding pen, other inmates loitered, waiting to come into the visiting area to talk with their attorneys. Dara was startled to see the prisoners could move freely around both rooms. She'd somehow expected to see them in their cells or at least shackled to the floor. The inmates with their attorneys spared her a quick glance, then resumed their conversations, ignoring her; the inmates in the holding pen, having nothing better to do, gawked. The second she stepped into their view, on the other side of the glass, the stunned looks spread like wildfire. No one bothered to be discreet; every prisoner ogled her with openmouthed fascination. After several seconds of surprised but appreciative silence, they started to murmur, point, and laugh until her ears burned. She worriedly looked around for the guards and saw them sitting, disinterested, at a desk across the room from her. She couldn't believe it. What did people pay taxes for? Was it too much to expect those stupid guards to actually guard something while they were on duty?

"Come on." Jamal, as uncomfortable with the attention as she was, took her arm and led her to a black pleather sofa, where she sat with as much dignity as she could muster, even though she was still in plain view of the prisoners. Things quickly got worse. An inmate came right up to the glass and sauntered past, looking her up and down like she was one of the elephants in an enclosure at the zoo. Very quickly, a loose procession of gapers formed and paraded by like jackals waiting for their turn at the carcass.

And then, when Dara thought things couldn't possibly get any worse, an inmate in the visiting room with them stood from his bench and came over after his attorney left, but before the guard could come collect him. Tall, burly, with short, twisted braids and enough gold flashing on his teeth to make a lovely bracelet, he wore a black eye patch over his left eye, the one thing that could make him look more menacing than he already did. He had probably murdered people before breakfast at least once a week. "Whassup, sweet thang?"

Dara, fighting the panic rising in her throat, deigned to look up at him. "Hello," she said coolly.

He snickered, then reached out a ham-sized hand to touch her hair. She jumped to her feet and slapped his hand away, panic choking off her breath. "Don't touch me!"

"I betchoo ain't had none a' this in a while," he taunted, grabbing part of his own anatomy, "otherwise, you wouldn't be so uptight. Why don't you come in the other room with me and let me work that pretty little . . ." He trailed off, leaving his romantic proposal unfinished, his eyes fixed on a point just behind her, and she knew Mike had arrived.

His face was black with rage. He slid a protective hand around her shoulder, and she shrank against his side, aware of his broad, powerful chest, and grateful for his strength. He squeezed her reassuringly. He seemed worried and studied her face intently for a long moment. Then he turned a withering eye toward the inmate. "Whassup, Mike?" the man said, with reluctant respect, though his eye remained cold and flat.

"Terrell," Mike replied in a soft but menacing voice. He was the only man in the room who approached Terrell's height. He looked more than furious enough to cut Terrell down to size; his anger shimmered around him the way heat shimmers on the desert floor.

"She witchoo?" Terrell asked warily, looking at Dara's hand still clutched in Mike's.

"She's with me," Mike said, his voice louder now so everyone in the room could hear. "And I'm sure I won't ever hear you or anyone else here talk to her like that again." He gave Terrell a grim, tight-lipped smile that made the "or else" unnecessary.

"No problem, man." Terrell raised his hands and backed away from Dara as if she'd turned radioactive.

"You shoulda said something sooner." A guard came, took his arm, and led him back into the holding area.

Mike turned back to Dara, eyes narrowed. The warm concern had vanished, and he looked like he wanted to kill her. And it wouldn't be a quick, merciful death, either. She winced and stepped out of his grasp, eyes on the floor.

"Let's go," Mike barked, turning on his heels to lead them to a small table in the corner. As Dara walked through the room, she again felt the prisoners staring at her, but this time, to her tremendous relief, they watched her with a newfound respect.

Mark Johnson, alleged murderer and former NFL player, was escorted to their table a minute later by one of the guards. He was huge, taller even than Mike, and outweighed him by at least forty pounds. He was bald, with a mustache and goatee and pierced ears on both sides. Multiple tattoos ran up and down his arms, and his hands were at least twice the size of hers, his fingers like Polish sausages. He was attractive, in a thuggish sort of way, and his body was certainly something, although he was far too bulky for Dara's tastes. His neck was like a log of firewood.

She strongly disliked him on sight.

She remembered the Alicia she'd known in high school—sheltered, sweet, a little spoiled—and tried to reconcile her with her husband, this menacing giant from the streets with the checkered past. Why would Alicia have married him? Maybe Alicia thought the love of a good woman would help him walk the straight and narrow.

Dara doubted anything would make this man walk the straight and narrow.

She already knew from the paper that Johnson's

partner, Dante Morgan, the murder victim, was a childhood friend of Johnson's—she took that to mean lackey—who had partnered with him in the club. But she needed to know more, so she'd taken a few minutes at the law library to research Johnson on the Internet. Thirty-six now, he'd retired from his position as wide receiver for the Falcons, where he'd had an extraordinary career, two years ago, after a knee injury.

He'd played college football after being recruited from a high school in one of the most gang-infested areas of Los Angeles. Every few years, apparently, he had a run-in with the law: constant fighting in college, a conviction and thirty-day sentence for weapons possession, and rumors—twice—that he'd raped women while on the road with the team. And rumors he'd paid hefty settlements to shut the women up.

"Thanks for taking my case, man," Johnson said to Mike after the introductions were made and they'd seated themselves around the table.

"Don't thank me. Thank Dara," said Mike.

"Thanks, sweetheart," Johnson told her, with a wink and a smile. His voice had deepened into the Barry White/Lou Rawls range. His eyes slithered appreciatively over her face, lingering on her lips, then down the front of her dress and back up again.

Dara managed a brittle smile. The idiot was actually smirking at her. Apparently, he was arrogant—or stupid—enough to think she'd be so impressed by his money that she'd overlook the minor issue of his being arrested for murder. "Don't mention it." She turned to Mike, waiting for him to begin the interview.

Mike watched Johnson leer at Dara and seethed. He didn't like the way Johnson looked at her, not one little bit. Plenty of women went for the professional athlete types, with their big bucks and fast cars. Maybe Dara was one of them. Not that it was his problem. Dara could—and probably did—sleep with whomever she wanted to. But he still didn't like Johnson undressing her with his eyes. Jerking his briefcase open, he scrounged around inside for a pen. It took him longer than usual to organize his thoughts. "Dara, would you mind taking notes for me?" he finally barked.

"Of course not," she replied earnestly.

"Tell us what happened," Mike told Johnson.

Johnson shrugged, and his eyes widened into an innocent baby look, which Mike didn't believe for one second. "I don't know. Someone shot my partner at the club the other night. Now they blame me for it, but I didn't do it."

"Where did it happen?"

"In the storage closet."

"Where were you at the time?"

"In my office."

"Can anyone vouch for you?"

"My hostess, Desiree Campbell."

"Anyone else?"

"No."

"What were you doing?"

"Talking about seating at the tables."

"Why do the police think you did it?"

Johnson hesitated for several beats. "Because I found him. And because we, uh, had a few words earlier in the evening."

Mike struggled to keep his face blank. "About?"

Johnson stiffened. His jaw tightened until his face looked like a block of granite. "I don't like the way he keeps the books."

Mike watched him for a long moment—a very long moment—in silence. He could see where this was going: Johnson was the innocent victim here, a man who had—alas!—had the misfortune of coincidentally arguing with Morgan the night he'd been killed by someone else. "I suppose there are dozens of witnesses to the argument."

Johnson slowly nodded his huge head.

This punk did it. Johnson was a cool liar and probably a decent poker player, but Mike didn't believe him for a minute. But maybe there were some extenuating circumstances. Something he could work with, some way he could piece together a defense. Dara—Johnson!—was counting on him. "You know," Mike said idly, doodling on his pad, "juries tend to understand crimes of passion. Say, for example, you and Morgan had an argument, and it escalated. Maybe a punch was thrown, things got out of hand. It wouldn't be the end of the world." He looked up and waited.

Johnson growled. "I said I didn't do it."

Mike's jaw tensed. *And I'm Nelson Mandela.* "Do you have a gun at the club?"

"Yeah, but it was in the safe."

"Security videos?"

"Not for that part of the club. Police took 'em."

Mike shot to his feet and started jamming his things back into his briefcase. This conversation was going nowhere fast, and he had plenty of stuff to do back at the office. "Here's what'll happen. The prosecutor will read the charges against you, and the judge will ask how you plead. I'll say not guilty. Then I'll ask for bail. The prosecutor will oppose bail because you're wealthy and could flee to anywhere in the world. I'll say you won't flee, because of your family. The judge will grant bail, but it'll be high. I'm guessing between a quarter and half a million, and you'll have to come up with twenty percent and surrender your passport. You'll be home by dinner. Any questions?"

Johnson seemed impressed. "Yeah. Can you fast-track my trial or something? I need to get my name cleared, and I need to get my club back open."

"Once the grand jury returns the indictment, I'll see what I can do."

"Can they nail me for this, man?"

Mike rubbed his hand across the back of his neck and assessed the evidence. His own personal opinion about Johnson's guilt notwithstanding, they were actually in decent shape. "No witnesses to the shooting. You have an alibi. No weapon that we know of. Sounds like their case is mostly circumstantial, although we need to see what the forensics reports say. If your alibi holds up, I'd say you've got a fighting chance." Jamal and Dara also stood, preparing to leave. "Your wife brought a suit for you to wear," said Mike, looking back at Johnson. "One last thing," he said, and Johnson looked up in surprise at the sudden sharpness in his voice. "I have just one rule: any client who lies to me gets fired." Mike wheeled around and, without waiting for Johnson's reaction, led Dara and Jamal to the courthouse, where things went exactly as he'd said they would.

Mike snuck Jamal and Dara out the back door of the courthouse to avoid the press of reporters out front, then led them on a forced march back to the office. They had to break into a slow trot to keep up with his long, angry strides, but he was barely aware of them. He just couldn't understand Dara, and worse, he couldn't understand his own reactions to her.

Initially, he'd wanted to wring her neck for not listening to him about the dress. Dara's stubbornness was actually beautiful in its purity. It was like a force of nature. Obstinacy was to Dara what the instinct to hunt was to a T. rex. The girl obviously needed a good spanking. That was her problem—one of her problems—in a nutshell. She was an only child, and her parents had allowed her to run wild. She thought she could do anything she wanted, with no regard for the consequences.

He'd been almost gleeful at the thought of the inmates ogling her. He couldn't wait for them to teach her a little lesson in humility. He'd given her ten—no, five—minutes with the inmates before she ran crying from the room. They'd make her wish she'd never been born, he'd thought. But then his prediction had come true, and he'd wanted to punch every one of those punks for embarrassing her. Worse, he'd wanted to kill Terrell when he'd looked up and seen him touching Dara's face. And then when he'd seen Johnson eyeing her, well . . .

It had to stop. Dara wasn't his problem. If she wanted to embarrass herself in front of a bunch of inmates, why was it any concern of his? And why should it matter to him if she returned Johnson's interest? Why couldn't he distance himself from her? "Can I see you in my office for a minute?" Mike said curtly to her when they got back to the office. They needed to get a few things settled, pronto. If nothing else, he was determined for her to respect his authority in the office.

"Uh-oh," Jamal said, snickering, before he scurried off to the relative safety of his own office.

"Great," Dara muttered, rolling her eyes.

Mike skewered her with his gaze. After a long moment, she marched up the stairs, stalked into his office, and threw herself down on his sofa. Furious, Mike slammed the door behind her.

Chapter 6

He frowned down at her, and she frowned mulishly up at him. "I think what we've got here is failure to communicate."

"Wonderful," she snapped. "Now you're quoting *Cool Hand Luke.*"

He reined his temper in, hard. "You see," he continued as if she hadn't spoken, "when I tell you to do something related to work, I expect you to do it."

"The way I dress has nothing to do with work," she said indignantly.

"It does when we go to the justice center," he snarled.

She shifted uncomfortably. "I appreciate your concern, but I'm a grown woman. A few stares and comments from a bunch of thugs won't kill me."

He snorted and shoved his hands in his pockets, calling on reserves of patience he hadn't even known he possessed. "Dara, do you think it's possible you don't know everything about everything at the ripe old age of twenty-three?" She opened her mouth to respond, but he waved her off. "In that room were men accused of everything from murder to spousal abuse to robbery to rape. A lot of them were sprung on bail this afternoon, the same as Johnson. They saw you were with me. They could find you again if they wanted to. Do you think maybe you shouldn't have done anything to draw any undue attention to yourself?"

Her unflinching gaze wavered for the first time. "I wasn't trying to draw undue attention to myself." She blinked several times, then swallowed hard. "This is the same dress I wear to school and church. There's nothing wrong with it! Why should I change just because some stupid prisoners—"

Something inside Mike snapped. Was she really that naive? Didn't she realize she wielded her sexuality as carelessly as a toddler wields a loaded gun? "Don't you get it?" he yelled, waving his arms like an air traffic controller. "It doesn't matter whether you were trying or not! Do you need me to draw you a picture? It's not the *dress*, Dara! It's the body!" Mike froze. What had he just said? Disgusted with himself, he turned, yanked the door open, and stalked off.

Agitated, Dara stared after Mike for a long minute. What on earth had he meant with that comment about her body? Surely, he hadn't meant it was her fault— for being so beautiful—that the inmates had reacted that way toward her. She was attractive, sure, but many women were more beautiful than she was. Did Mike mean she drove men to distraction? Did she drive *him* to distraction? She wandered thoughtfully back to her office and surveyed the pile of work on her desk. There were more transcripts to read, or maybe she should start with the . . .

"Still standing, I see." Jamal chuckled from the doorway, then sauntered over and collapsed in a chair.

"Your boss has a terrible temper," she snapped as she sank into her own chair.

"It sounded to me like you gave as good as you got."

Her gaze shot to his face. He smiled warmly at her, as if she'd single-handedly slain the dragon and freed the kingdom. "Great. Everybody heard."

"You got it."

"He makes me so mad, I could just scream!" She collapsed her head into her hands.

"I want to tell you something." He leaned forward in his chair like he was about to divulge the secret to eternal youth. "Listen up. This is important."

"Hit me."

"The thing about Mike you need to understand is he's all heart." She opened her mouth to argue the point, but he waved her off. "I know he's cocky, and he can be a bully—"

"*Can* be a bully?" she cried, incredulous. "He *is* a bully."

Jamal tilted his head and reconsidered. "Okay. He *is* a bully."

"Thank you."

"But the point is I know he would do anything for me. He would give me his last dollar if he thought I needed it."

Dara was in no mood to hear him sing the praises of the mighty Mike Baldwin. "That's beautiful," she said, drumming her fingers on the desk. "What's it got to do with me?"

"He would do anything for you, too, Dara. He was only looking out for you today. Just because you don't like the way he says something doesn't mean you shouldn't listen to what he's saying."

This whole stupid discussion was a waste of time, and she had work to do. She picked up her pen. "Listen, Jamal," she said. "I really appreciate what you're trying to do here, but don't bother. Mike doesn't like me. The only reason I'm here is because my professor forced me on him."

Jamal looked stunned and disbelieving. "Mike doesn't like you?" He studied her face intently for a second, as if he were solving a complicated mathematical theorem, then snorted. "What are you talking about?"

There was no use arguing the point with him. "You don't know the whole story." She flipped open a volume of the *Federal Reporter* to the case she needed. "Trust me. He doesn't like me."

Jamal twisted his mouth into a wry grin. "*You* trust *me*. I may not know the whole story, but I know Mike well enough to know he likes you *just fine*."

There was a hidden meaning behind the last two words, but she was too drained to decipher it. "Well, anyway," she said, "I'll be sure to mention to Mike that you think so highly of his advice."

He sprang to his feet. "You do that and you're a dead woman."

Dara laughed, but Jamal regarded her with speculative eyes. "You dating Sean?"

"No." She was surprised to receive this much attention from Jamal, who was usually too busy with his own work to notice her. "Why do you ask?"

"But he's asked you, hasn't he?"

Flustered, she fidgeted in her seat. "We're just friends."

"Yeah. Good." Jamal nodded thoughtfully, then turned to go, pausing to smile at her before he left. Dara realized she'd made a new and valuable friend. Well, maybe the afternoon hadn't been a complete waste, after all. She sat at her desk for a few more moments and heard Mike moving around next door. Before she could think better of it, she got up and slowly, painfully, made her way into his office. He replaced one of the books on the bookshelf closest to his desk. Then he turned and watched her for a long minute, eyebrows raised.

She leaned against the door frame and folded her arms across her chest. "How alarmed should I be that you and Terrell are on a first-name basis?"

Mike smiled, and the tension between them was broken. "He's practically family. I represented him a couple of years ago on drug possession charges, but he was convicted."

"Oh, my God," she gasped, throwing her hand across her heart. "Am I to understand the great Mike Baldwin has lost a case?"

He smiled indulgently. "Shocking, I know. Don't worry, though. It doesn't happen that often. It wasn't my fault, anyway. I didn't know he'd tried to intimidate one of the witnesses before the trial, and when the jury found out about it, I think it turned against him. Plus, then he faced an obstruction charge."

"Did . . . did you just say there was something you didn't know? Let me sit down."

"Very funny," he said, but he grinned.

She decided to say it quickly, before she lost her nerve. She hated apologizing. "I, uh . . . I didn't think it would be that bad at the justice center."

He gave her a knowing look as he sank back into his chair, then flipped through some papers on his desk. "Ummm," he said, without looking at her. "That's interesting because I thought I told you it would be bad if you wore that dress. Actually, I think they would have treated you the same way no matter what you wore. But you still should've listened to me."

"I'm sorry for blowing up at you."

"You should be."

"Oh, all right!" she cried, wondering why she'd thought, even for one misguided moment, she could talk to him like a reasonable human being. "If you weren't such an overbearing bully, maybe I would have listened to you!"

His eyes glittered at her, and she could see that she amused and irritated him. "Anyone ever tell you you've got a smart mouth?" Immediately, his expression became pained, as if he was afraid he'd said too much.

She froze. He'd asked that exact question at the party, and it caught her off guard. She'd tried to put the night they met out of her mind and had presumed he'd done the same.

"Dara?" called Sean from the hallway. "Where are you?"

She hesitated for a moment, but whatever spell had been woven between them was broken the instant they heard Sean's voice. Mike looked away from her.

"Dara?"

"In here," Dara said. Mike's shoulders tightened as if she'd flipped a switch. Did he tense every time Sean appeared, or did she just imagine it?

"What are you doing in here?" Sean asked her as he came in.

Mike's lips affected a smile, but the gesture came nowhere near his eyes. "We were just talking about what happened today, man. You really should keep a closer eye on Dara. She almost caused a riot at the justice center." His gaze flickered to Dara, then back to Sean.

"I'm outta here. "You two lock up when you leave." He rose from his chair and vanished down the hall.

Sean turned to Dara, a bemused expression on his face. "What was that all about?"

Dara took a minute to get her thoughts together. It seemed like she couldn't have even the simplest inter-action with Mike without becoming flustered and agitated. Her heart raced, and her adrenaline flowed as if an unleashed wolf had entered the room, and she stayed that way until she was no longer in Mike's pres-ence. Now that he was gone, she could breathe normally again. She twisted the ends of her hair, realized what she was doing, and stopped. "Nothing. Just ignore him."

After the disaster at the justice center, Jamal took Dara under his wing. He introduced her to the court-house and showed her where the clerk's office was and how to file pleadings. He taught her the ins and outs of the firm's computer system and fixed the copy machine for her when it jammed, complaining the whole time about how annoying she was because she always needed him to save her butt. Soon they were bickering like siblings. "You're taking pretty good care of me," she said to him one day, when he stopped by her office to see if he could bring lunch for her when he came back from the courthouse.

"Don't get excited." He scowled. "This doesn't mean I want you for my baby's mama or anything."

One day she poked her head in his office to discover him poring over his GED textbooks. "Whatcha doing?"

"Waiting for a bus," he said, without bothering to look up at her. She'd long since learned to ignore his perpetual crabbiness and had come to think of him as the firm mascot—Baldwin & Co.'s own personal Oscar the Grouch, a thousand times grumpier than the original. But before she could think of a comeback, Mike, coffee mug in hand, strolled by on his way to the kitchen. "You two planning a revolt?" Mike asked.

"Jamal was just telling me how much he loves to study."

"I'll tell you what," Jamal said to Dara. "It's a good thing you're cute because you sure ain't funny." Dara smacked him on the arm. "Ouch!" he yowled. "Can I get workers' comp for this abuse?"

"Don't let him fool you, Dara," Mike interjected. "I talk to his teacher every week, and she says he's the hardest-working student she's got. Never misses a class."

"Looks like I need to sue you *and* the teacher for violating my privacy rights," Jamal huffed.

A laughing Mike continued on his way to the kitchen. "Where'd you get the idea you had any rights around here?"

Dara loved to watch the two of them together. It quickly dawned on her that Jamal and Mike had a complicated and intricate relationship, like square-dancing partners, and they both knew the steps. They'd both pretend they barely tolerated the other, when really they'd kill or be killed for each other.

The other thing she quickly discovered was Jamal was extremely bright. One day, when she'd gone into the conference room to review her notes before she left for class, she'd seen Jamal's books spread all over the table—and an open notebook. Glancing furtively around to make sure no one saw her, she snatched up the notebook, which was opened to a draft essay written in Jamal's microscopic but neat hand, and saw it was about life in a gang. After a moment she sank into a chair to get comfortable; she didn't care whether Jamal caught her nosing around in his things or not. The essay was bleak and honest and horrifying. And astonishingly good.

"What the hell are you doing?" Jamal cried when he returned and found her.

"I'm reading your story," she said, unrepentant. "It's amazing."

Jamal's frown creased his forehead and pulled his lips into a tight line. He snatched the notebook from her. "Why don't you keep your hands off my stuff?"

"Your story is really wonderful. You should submit it to some magazines and—"

"Oh, really?" he said. "You think the fellas round the way want me to go around publishing stories about how they run the neighborhood?" He cocked his head as if considering the idea. "Yeah. Good thought. I'm sure they wouldn't care if I wrote about the shootings and whatnot."

She hadn't thought of that. "Well . . . you could change the names and—"

"Drop it, Dara," he barked. The chill in his eyes, and the bravado, the fear underneath, shut her up. What was it like for this boy who wanted to make a new life for himself in the same old neighborhood with the same old problems? "Do you see any of your old . . . friends at home?"

"Yeah." His jaw clenched as he shoved his books into his backpack.

"Do they try to get you involved with . . . things again?"

Jamal's entire body tightened, and the scornful look he shot her actually made her flinch. It actually made her feel guilty for the sheltered life she'd lived with her two parents in their nice brick house in the suburbs, where the worst thing that happened was a drunk driver occasionally knocking down a mailbox. "No, Dara. They were cool once I gave 'em my freakin' letter of resignation."

The next morning Jamal ran into Dara in the hall near the reception area. "I didn't mean to be a punk," he mumbled. He knew he'd overreacted, even if she had had her nose all in his business. But what did she expect? Even if he'd wanted to explain, which he didn't, she couldn't possibly understand. It'd be easier for her to understand what life was like on Pluto.

Dara tossed her head and waved her hand dismissively. "Oh, you know. I can be a little nosy sometimes."

Right. Just like *Titanic* had a little problem with icebergs. "I noticed."

"Well, anyway," she said earnestly. "You should really think about what I said about having your work published, Jamal."

Jamal shook his head, amazed. She had guts. He'd give her that. "Don't you ever give up?"

"No."

She was like a dog with a bone. Mike didn't have anything on her in the stubborn department. They deserved each other. He watched her for a long moment, unsure what to do or say, then looked down at his shoes. He was half afraid if he told her no, she'd arrange a sit-in or form a picket line or start a petition drive or something. Finally, he looked her in the eye. "I'll think about it. But I ain't makin' any promises. Okay?" He wheeled around and took off down the hallway.

"Okay," Dara said to Jamal's back. She'd won! Only when he was safely gone did she clap her hands together in excitement, then look to the ceiling. "Thank you, God," she whispered, turning toward the steps. She'd taken only one step in that direction when she passed the fax machine, which was hidden behind a cubicle screen, and saw Mike studying her with a bemused expression. Obviously, he'd heard her entire conversation with Jamal.

"Thank *you*, Dara," he told her, a warm half smile on his lips.

He looked as if he wanted to say something else, but she felt suddenly and unaccountably shy. Worse, her heart seemed to skip every other beat. She managed a small smile before she scurried away like a silly, scared mouse. She felt his eyes burning holes in her back.

Mike hung up the phone and rubbed the back of his neck to relieve some of the tension permanently lodged there. He glanced at his watch and realized it was just after six. Wait a minute. Was Jamal still here? He got up and stalked out into the corridor outside Dara's office. "Jamal!" he bellowed down the hall. "Jamal!" Dara, who'd started spending more and more time back at the office after classes—he had no idea why—sat at her computer and looked up at him. Just then, Jamal poked his head around the screen that hid the copy machine. "What are you still doing here, man?" Mike asked him. "You're going to be late for class!"

"Well, you told me to finish making these copies before I left," Jamal hollered back.

Mike shook his head in exasperation. "You don't

have the sense God gave a goat! I didn't mean for you to be late for class!" He heaved a long-suffering sigh. He didn't like for Jamal to be on the street waiting for a bus after dark. "I'll take you. Get your stuff and meet me at the front door."

Dara had begun packing up her backpack to go home, but she looked up and smiled as Mike came into her office. Lately, Mike realized, he'd developed the extremely annoying habit of seeking Dara out before she left for the night. It was like something was left unfinished if he didn't see her that one last time each day. "That boy's going to be the death of me." He shrugged into his jacket.

Dara cocked her head and studied him, her brow knit in concentration. Mike could almost hear the wheels spinning in her sharp little mind. "You don't want Jamal on the street at night, do you?"

"I was heading that way, anyway," he stammered, astounded at her insight.

She shook her head firmly, clearly rejecting his explanation as nonsense. "You live fifteen minutes in the other direction."

Mike stared at her, too shocked to speak. He ducked his head and rubbed his hand over the back of his neck. What kind of Jedi mind trick was this? Every day this girl found new ways to mess with his head. And why was she looking at him so strangely? As if she actually respected him. Liked him. "It's no big deal," he muttered.

She came around to the front of her desk and looked up into his face. Her eyes were warm and unwavering. "It *is* a big deal," she said softly. "And when he makes something of his life, it'll be because you believed he could. Jamal is dedicated, hardworking, and smart, and no one would ever have realized it if *you* hadn't taken an interest in him. *You* volunteered to be his mentor. *You* stay in touch with his teacher. *You* drive him to class. It *is* a big deal."

He could only stare at her in slack-jawed astonishment. For the life of him, he couldn't think of anything to say. How was it she could understand him so well on this issue and still not have the slightest idea he was fighting a losing battle to control his attraction to her?

She must have realized she'd been staring at him, because her face flushed suddenly. "Well, anyway." Her eyes lowered, leaving her lashes spread upon her face like a bird's feathers. "Good night." She swept past, and Mike pivoted and stared, openmouthed, after her.

Sean and Dara walked around Cincinnati Fountain Square after dinner. The sun had set, and spotlights lit the water as it streamed from the sculpted woman's outstretched hands, misting them with a fine spray. Sean felt happier than he'd been in a long time. "We've known each other for a little while now," he solemnly told her, "so I feel I can ask you a personal question."

"What is it?"

"*The Godfather* or *The Godfather: Part II*?"

She blinked at him. "Excuse me?"

"Best movie of all time. Which one?"

"*Gone with the Wind*," she said, laughing.

He grimaced. "Well, you're off to a bad start. John Coltrane or Miles Davis?"

"Miles Davis, of course."

"Interesting. Dinner and a movie or a party with friends?"

"Chinese takeout and a DVD at home."

"You're about as boring as my brother," he snorted. "Chocolate or vanilla?"

"Butter pecan."

"I wouldn't have taken you for a butter pecan girl," he said thoughtfully.

"I'm full of surprises."

"I had a great time," he told her, putting his hand on the small of her back as they walked down the sidewalk toward their cars. Actually, he'd had a fantastic time. Dara had stared at him with those sweet eyes while they'd talked, laughed at all the right places when he'd told her stories, and made him laugh when she'd told stories of her own. He was crazy about her. No. He was half in love with her, probably more than half if he really thought about it. And it seemed like she was warming up to him even though she'd told him she didn't think they should date. They studied together and ate lots of their meals together. True, Monica was with them most of the time, but still. Dara wouldn't spend so much time with him if she didn't think their relationship had romantic potential, would she?

"Yeah." She stopped walking and put her hand on his arm, smiling up at him. "Me, too."

His eyes slid to her lush lips, and he took half a step closer to her, wondering if he should risk giving her a kiss.

"But next time we'll have to make sure Monica can come with us," she told him, dropping her arm and continuing on her way. "Things are always so much more fun when she's around, don't you think?"

His heart crashed through the ground. And as he stared after her—she'd started chattering happily about the chocolate cake she'd had for dessert—it occurred to him that despite all the progress he'd thought he'd made with her, Dara still thought of him as just a friend.

And maybe she always would.

Mark Johnson was a pimp.

That was the only explanation for the suit he wore when Dara and Mike went to Club Destiny to interview him again. She and Mike knocked on the locked door of the club, located in an old warehouse in one of the rehabilitated areas downtown, and Johnson opened it for them, wearing a getup that was clearly not regulation Brooks Brothers. "Come on in." Johnson stepped back and bowed, waving them in with his hand, a king opening the gate to his kingdom.

Dara stepped over the threshold and gaped at him. This, obviously, was his business attire. The brown pin-striped suit—if you could call it pin-striped since the stripes were over a quarter of an inch thick—was clearly of the finest wool and custom made; no off-the-rack suit would ever fit Johnson's bulky chest and arms. But the lapels reached to his shoulders, and Dara couldn't count how many buttons marched down the front of the jacket. Five? Six? Eight? What self-respecting designer or tailor would have anything to do with such a monstrosity? He'd also added his earrings—diamond studs in each ear, well over five carats each—and several sparkling rings. There were only two possible conclusions she could make: either Johnson was going to a costume party, or he was a pimp.

Mike shut the door behind them and exchanged pleasantries with Johnson. Dara stared at Mike appreciatively. He wore a subdued but elegant gray suit with a blindingly white shirt and yellow tie. He looked tasteful and classy, but not as if he had tried too hard or spent hours of the day planning and preening in front of the mirror. Actually, he looked wonderful. She jerked her mind away from that thought. She wasn't here to judge a fashion contest! She tried to listen to the threads of their conversation.

"Why don't you show us around?" Mike asked Johnson.

"Sure." Johnson led them into the huge main room of the club, and Dara gaped again. She felt as if she'd stepped into a tacky Turkish harem. Sheer scarves in garish oranges and pinks swooped from the corners of the ceiling and back up again. The walls were lavishly tiled and depicted scenes of orgies with women, with breasts the size of watermelons, and pashas, who all bore a striking resemblance to Johnson, with noticeable bulges in their pants. Dozens of seating areas dotted the room, with overstuffed chairs and booths and banquettes. Pillows, intricately woven with sparkling gold thread, graced every conceivable free space. A huge dance floor stood at one end of the room, while a thirty-foot bar, with a massive, ornate mirror hanging behind it, occupied the other.

Dara had never seen anything so horrifyingly gaudy in her entire life. She made the mistake of looking at Mike to check his reaction. He caught her gaze with wide eyes and eyebrows raised about half an inch above center; he obviously agreed with her assessment completely. Dara struggled not to laugh. Johnson threw his arms wide, clearly proud. "What do you think?"

Mike looked around slowly. "It's really something."

Dara nodded. "You don't see a place like this every day."

Johnson smiled broadly. His eyes lingered on Dara's face. "I'm glad you like it." His tone was warm and intimate and clearly meant for Dara alone.

Mike cleared his throat. "Show us where the shooting happened," he said sharply. Dara looked at him, surprised by the new edge in his voice. Any amusement she'd seen on his face ten seconds ago had vanished, and his jaw now seemed tight. He did not look at her. Johnson led them out of the main area and down a long hallway with several side doors, all of which were closed. At the end of the hallway, almost to the back exit, he opened a door on the right and turned into it. He flicked on the light.

Mike edged past him into the storeroom, and Dara followed. It was large, with floor to ceiling shelves jammed with all sorts of paper and cleaning products. Dara had wondered how anyone could possibly have shot someone in there without getting spattered by blood, but now she realized there was more than enough space for such a thing to happen. Someone had died a violent death in there. She shivered.

After walking slowly around the room, Mike took out his digital camera and started taking pictures from every angle. He was entirely absorbed. She watched him, engrossed, and Johnson watched her. "Would you like to come to the kitchen for somethin' to drink?" He smiled.

Dara frowned. Every smile was a smirk with Johnson, every step a strut. He managed to make asking about a drink sound like an invitation to engage in a sexual act right there in the storeroom. Mike looked up from his camera. "I need Dara to stay with me," he snapped, eyes narrowed.

Johnson's face darkened perceptibly. He'd been

leaning negligently against the door frame, but at Mike's words, he stood up to his full height. "Is there a problem, man?"

Mike glared at him. "Dara's going to take some measurements." He turned to her. "Where's your tape measure?"

She'd forgotten all about her appointed task. "I left it in my purse on one of the tables. I'll get it." She scurried back to the main area. Johnson followed her for some reason; she'd bet her very last dollar his eyes stayed on her hips and butt as she walked. She found her purse, ignoring him as he came to stand beside her.

"I like you, Dara." He nodded slowly. His eyes were half closed, heavy lidded with admiration. "I wanna take you to dinner sometime."

She rummaged in her purse so she did not have to look at him. "I'd love to have dinner with you and Alicia."

His lips curled. "Alicia's pretty busy with the kids. I was thinkin' jus' you and me."

Now Dara did look at him, outraged. She raised her chin and crossed her arms over her chest. "Let me see if I've got this straight." She kept her voice icy. "You think I'm stupid enough to sleep with the married husband of a pregnant friend of mine. A man indicted for murder. Is that right?"

To her surprise, Johnson threw back his head and laughed as if he was at a Richard Pryor concert. "That's why I like you! You don't take no stuff!"

"What have I ever done to make you think that I'm that stupid?" She had half a mind to demand an apology.

His eyes gleamed. He leaned closer. "Let's just say I think you're smart enough to know a good opportunity when you see it." Johnson held out his left arm

and pulled his sleeve back to flash his watch at her.
The thing was huge—with a thick gold band that
probably weighed five pounds or more. The entire
face glittered with diamonds the size of beans. The
whole thing was so hopelessly glittery, there was no
chance anyone could actually look at it and tell what
time it was, but of course, telling time with such a
watch was hardly the point. Johnson smirked at her. "I
like to take care of my women."

Dara had to laugh. This whole situation was so
ridiculous. You'd think someone facing a murder rap
would have better things on his mind than seducing
women. But Johnson *was* charming, in a bizarre sort
of way. Was he a murderer? Mike thought so. But
shouldn't he have a horn or a tail or an evil gleam in
his eyes—something that signified to the rest of the
world what he was? "So if I sleep with you, I get a
gaudy piece of jewelry."

Johnson nodded, clearly pleased she finally understood the full implications of his offer. "Exactly."

Dara looked heavenward. "Oh . . . so you think I'm
a prostitute."

Johnson shrugged. "Call it what you want."

Dara laughed again. "Well, as charming as this
offer is, I think maybe we better keep our relationship
professional."

"Well," said Johnson good-naturedly, taking no offense, "you never know till you ask."

"Dara!"

Dara jumped and whirled around. A scowling Mike
stood at the doorway, with his hands on his hips; he'd
probably heard most—if not all—of her conversation with Johnson. "Are you going to help me, or were
you planning to flirt with Mark all day?"

Dara sputtered for a second, furious. "I was not—"

But Mike had already spun around on his heels and disappeared back down the hall. After a second they heard a door slam. She and Johnson stared at each other. Johnson let out a low whistle. "Is your boss always this jealous?"

Dara felt her face flush. She hastily looked away and fished the tape measure out of her purse. "He's not jealous. He's just overbearing."

"I know jealous when I see it," Johnson insisted. Dara just shook her head violently. Johnson threw his hands up. "Whatever you say."

Before they left the club, Mike and Dara sat down at one of the tables for a few minutes to ask Johnson some more questions about the night of the murder. Mike was in a terrible mood, which he couldn't seem to shake. He should never have brought Dara with him. Of course, he'd known Johnson would lapse into his Billy Dee Williams routine with her. What was wrong with the man? Didn't he have enough problems in his life without trying to contaminate Dara's life, too? Couldn't he see Dara was ten thousand times too good for the likes of him? Sure, Dara had shot him down, and rightfully so. But did she have to be so nice about it? Why couldn't she have slapped his face or something? And why couldn't she turn down her sex appeal a notch or two or fifty? He was sick and tired of every man she met dropping to his knees within thirty seconds of meeting her.

But the worst thing about the whole afternoon was that his jealousy was so painfully obvious, he couldn't ignore it. He was jealous of Johnson, Sean, and any other man who could openly tell Dara about his attraction to her. He was the only man on the planet, apparently, who was not free to act on his feelings. Mike turned to Johnson. "Did Morgan argue with anyone else besides you that night?"

"Yeah." Johnson leaned back in his chair and stretched his legs out in front of him. "I been meanin' to tell you. I seen him arguin' with some other guy. Couple hours before he was shot."

Mike perked up. "Someone else? Where?"

"Out here. Some brotha with a black leather jacket and a mustache. Dude waved his hand in Dante's face."

Mike's radar kicked in. He didn't believe Johnson for a minute. This was the kind of information someone arrested for murder would immediately scream from the rooftops. An innocent man wouldn't wait one hour before he mentioned it to his lawyer. Plus, none of the other people they'd interviewed so far had mentioned seeing this other argument. Still, he had to play along. "Do you know who this guy is? Or anyone that knows him?"

"No. I never seen him before."

Mike closed his file and slid it into his briefcase. "Let's go, Dara." Mike helped her with her chair, and they walked to the door, with Johnson trailing behind. "We'll be in touch." Mike extended his hand to Johnson.

Johnson shook it distractedly. His eyes were glued to Dara's face. Again. "See you soon." He winked at Dara. Dara scowled at him and stalked out. But it didn't matter. The damage had been done. Mike still wanted to smash Johnson's face like an empty soda can.

Dara drove her car through the dark downtown streets, compulsively clicking her automatic door locks every several blocks or so. After reviewing

Jamal's essays for him, she'd forgotten to give his notebook back before he left the office this afternoon. He'd need it tonight at his GED class, so she'd decided to drop it off at his apartment. It had seemed like a perfectly reasonable plan until she got to Jamal's neighborhood.

She would've never dreamed there was a place in Cincinnati, within ten miles of her own sheltered world, that felt so scary, but here it was. She drove down the narrow streets, past smashed streetlights, trash blowing across the street like urban tumbleweeds, and the rusted shell of a car parked by the curb. On every corner stood groups of people, mostly men, with bulky jackets and sweatshirt hoods pulled low over their eyes. They all watched her suspiciously as she drove by, as if they knew she didn't belong here.

Finally, she found Jamal's apartment building, an old brownstone with crumbling steps and looping, swirling white graffiti climbing the walls like kudzu. Miraculously, there was a free parking space in front of the building. She parked and climbed out, squeezing her way past yet another group of menacing men. Too bad she didn't have any of Mike's business cards to pass out. Surely, everyone in this group kept a criminal attorney on retainer. Dara reached for the buzzer outside the front door, but it had been smashed—why on earth would anyone smash the buzzer?—beyond recognition, and at any rate, the door was ajar. Inside the stench of urine and trash and God alone knew what else almost knocked her to her knees. And Jamal lived here?

She climbed the steps to the second floor and knocked on his door. She heard someone on the other side mumbling and then a loud "What the . . . ?"

before Jamal yanked the door open. "What the hell are you doing here, Dara?"

"I-I'm returning your notebook," she stammered, surprised by his alarm and, beneath the surface, his shame. "I know you need it for class."

He snatched it from her, then jerked her arm and marched her back down the steps and outside. She tried to yank her arm free, but he didn't let go. "Don't ever come here alone, Dara," he hissed. "This ain't the suburbs. Wait till Mike hears about this."

They'd reached the driver's side of her car, and she snatched her arm away. "Fine!" Apparently, no good deed went unpunished around here. "But don't you dare tattle on me to Mike!" But Jamal just shook his head darkly, and she knew that he would tell Mike and that her goose was cooked.

"What's this I hear?" Mike stormed into Dara's office first thing the next morning, slamming the door behind him. "You went to Jamal's neighborhood at night by yourself? Are you out of your mind?" His heart beat crazily, as it had ever since Jamal told him what Dara had done. Just last week a fourteen-year-old girl was sexually assaulted in an abandoned building across the street from Jamal's. Didn't Dara read the papers?

But there was more to his anger than that. The enormous power she had over him enraged him. He tried to do his absolute best to forget about her, and then she went and did something thoughtless and stupid that petrified him. And that left him with the painful realization that he couldn't forget her.

She'd been sitting at the computer, typing a memo, but now she swiveled around in her chair. "Look." She folded her arms across her chest, and her expression turned mulish. "Jamal has already made me swear never to go there again. It's a dead issue." She turned back to her keyboard.

Mike was livid. He wanted to grab her by the collar and shake her until her eyes rolled back in her head. "Don't you understand, Dara?" He stalked to her side of the desk and turned her chair around to face him. "What if something had happened to you?" He squatted until he was at her eye level and put his hands on the arms of her chair, trapping her.

Chapter 7

Dara's entire body jerked, as if she'd been riding in a speeding car when suddenly somebody slammed on the brakes. At this distance, Mike's strength and power—his raw masculinity—hit her like a punch to the gut. And all at once, it was clear in his wild eyes, the throbbing of the pulse in his forehead, and the tension in his jaw. He was alarmed. She . . . mattered to him.

Stunned, Dara watched him for a long moment. Suddenly, she felt ashamed of herself, both for going in the first place and taking an unnecessary risk, and for being petulant with him. She couldn't seem to look away. His eyes, as clear as two prisms on a chandelier, were astonishing. With his anger, they had turned a darker brown, but she could see flecks of gold and green in them. A person—a woman—could very easily get lost in those eyes. And then the unthinkable happened, and her gaze slipped to his full lips. The set of his mouth was harsh and cruel, but some primitive instinct told her his lips, on hers, would feel . . .

"You promise me?" Mike murmured in a husky, urgent voice. "You promise me you'll never do that again?" Dara looked up from his lips, swallowed hard, and nodded. He studied her for a moment longer and then, satisfied, rose slowly to his feet and strode out of her office.

And she wondered when her heartbeat would ever slow back down.

The amount of work needed to prepare a defense in a murder trial was unbelievable, Dara quickly discovered. Mike made endless lists of witnesses to interview, legal issues to research, motions to write, documents and records to review. "Can you handle it?" Mike asked, handing her yet another list of research issues, during one of their weekly strategy meetings with Jamal in the conference room.

Dara leaned across the table, took the list, blinked, and swallowed hard. Her gaze flickered to Jamal, who gave her a ghost of a supportive smile, then back to the list. *For goodness sake!* Did Mike think she was a machine? Had he forgotten her real job was as a full-time law student? That she might actually need a little time to study when she wasn't spending forty hours a week in the office? But a secret part of her felt thrilled because Mike treated her like a professional, and she never wanted him to regret giving her a chance. She smiled brightly. "Of course, I can."

"Good." His gaze, intense as Game Seven of the NBA finals, had been on her the whole time. She felt him watching her, examining what she'd said, then tossing it aside to consider what she hadn't said, what she really meant. Somehow she resisted the urge to squirm in her chair. He was testing her. And even if she killed herself in the process, she would earn his respect.

Because she respected—admired—him so desperately.

As hard as she worked, Mike worked ten times harder. He never stopped or slowed down. And he had a photographic memory, or something darn close to it. He was, quite simply, brilliant.

When he was unexpectedly called to court on another matter, he sent Dara and Jamal to interview Desiree Campbell, the hostess who provided Johnson's alibi, without him rather than cancel the appointment altogether.

Dara was as excited as a kid on her first pony ride, but nervous. This was the most important task Mike had given her to date. "Are you sure you trust me with this?" She paced around his office. "I've never interviewed a witness before. What if I screw it up?"

Mike's lips curled with amusement as he packed up his briefcase to head to court. "Why do you think I'm sending Jamal along?" She grimaced. "Just kidding," he said quickly, sliding his arms into his suit jacket. "You'll conduct the interview. Don't worry about screwing anything up. She's a friendly witness, so she won't give you a hard time." He studied her for a long moment. "You're not nervous, are you?" he asked her, a faint, mocking little smile on his lips.

His amusement galled her no end. "Of course not," she said haughtily.

"Good." Admiration gleamed in his eyes. "Break a leg. I'll see you back here later."

Dara and Jamal drove to Desiree's apartment, a sleek affair in one of the new high-rises on the river. Dara looked around at the plush carpets and mirrors and glass in the lobby in silent wonder. How could Desiree afford this? What was Johnson paying her, for God's sake? How much could a woman earn for saying "this way to your table" a hundred times a night?

"Come on in." Desiree let them into an apartment that was all sparkling windows and glass and black lacquer and brass. Slick, like the woman herself, but tasteless. Desiree, twenty-something, beautiful, tall, shapely, with eyes a mossy green that didn't match her dark brown skin and what seemed to be a million tiny braids tumbling in curled cascades to her waist, wore jeans with a teeny black T-shirt. Her braless breasts strained against the shirt to the point that Dara wondered whether Desiree could expand her chest enough to sneeze, should the need arise. Dara was dying to see what Jamal thought of this walking wet dream, but she didn't dare look at him now.

"Mark was with me that night," Desiree said, without prelude, when they settled onto the sofa.

"Where were you?" Dara asked her.

"In Mark's office, goin' over the seating arrangement."

"How long were you there?"

Desiree thought for a moment. "Twenty minutes or so."

"Then what happened?"

"We went back out to the main room together."

Dara saw Desiree look at Jamal in a frankly assessing, sexual way. When Desiree's eyes lingered on Jamal's crotch, Dara could only gape. Then Desiree threw her shoulders back and rubbed the small of her back, like she was stretching, her eyes on Jamal the whole time. Her breasts saluted Jamal, and his eyes nearly popped out of his head. Dara was outraged. She had to stop herself from slapping her hands over Jamal's eyes to shield him from this exhibitionist. "Did you see or hear anyone at that end of the hall?" she barked.

Desiree's gaze shot back to Dara. "No."

"Did you hear Mark's argument with his partner?"

"No." Desiree snuck a glance at her watch, then at her hands.

Dara watched Desiree study her bloodred talons, which were studded with various diamondoids and seemed to be at least three inches long. The woman looked like Edward Scissorhands. Dara wondered what her full story was; she had the feeling Desiree danced around the truth and left out as many details as she revealed.

Desiree pressed Dara's arm when they rose to leave. "Will your boss take care of Mark?"

"Mike always does the best he can," Dara replied, surprised by Desiree's obvious concern. She waited until they'd walked back to the car before she turned to Jamal. "What do you think?"

He looked starstruck. "I think I need a cold shower."

"Try to focus for a minute, will you?"

"I think Johnson's doing her. How else could she afford to live in *that* crib with *those* clothes unless she had a sugar daddy?"

"Get out!" she cried, but the idea took hold. Of course, that was it, she decided as she slid into the driver's seat and started the car. Desiree certainly was attractive, in a slutty, come-screw-my-brains-out-right-now sort of way. Apparently, that blatant sexuality appealed to some men. Go figure.

Mike looked up from his work as Dara and Jamal strode back into his office. He'd finished up at court just a few minutes ago and had been waiting impatiently for them to return. "Johnson's doing Desiree,"

Jamal announced. He threw himself into a chair and stretched out his long legs. "You should have seen her, man. Titties out to here and—"

"Hey!" Dara perched on the edge of the sofa. "Can you two save the locker-room part of the conversation for later?"

Jamal wouldn't let it go. "Do you think they were hers?"

"Of course, they were hers," Dara snorted. "She paid for them. Along with her fake eyes, fake hair, and fake nails."

"You're crazy! I—"

"Children, children," Mike said, and the bickering trailed off. Watching these two together was funnier than a *Seinfeld* marathon. He sat on the other end of the sofa from Dara. "Give me the bottom line. Do we have a credible alibi or not?"

Dara and Jamal looked at each other for a long moment, weighing and considering. "I think she'll be fine," said Dara, "but I have the feeling she didn't tell us everything."

"Well, that's something, anyway." Mike smiled with pleasure and relief. And as he held Dara's gaze for a long beat, she smiled at him like she'd just won an Olympic gold medal. Suddenly, Mike couldn't tear his eyes away. She really was amazing. He worked her hard, and she never complained, although he knew she must be exhausted. He couldn't believe he'd ever thought she was lazy; between work and school, she worked every bit as hard as he did. She never gave up, never backed down, and never said die. She surprised him every day. Her commitment—to school, to work, and to Jamal—was a constant source of wonder to him. And he was in trouble. Because his attraction to her grew exponentially as the days passed. And it was getting harder to convince himself it was purely physical.

The moment stretched. Dara suddenly looked a little . . . breathless. Worse, he felt Jamal's eyes on him, sharp and amused. Mike cleared his throat. "Well," he said hoarsely, "you two need to go do some work and make me some money while I'm still young."

One day, when Dara and Mike sat on his sofa, discussing one of her memoranda, Laura buzzed him to say he had an important call. "Mike?" a voice said curtly when he picked up. "It's Miller."

Sam Miller was a detective from District One, which covered, among other neighborhoods, the cesspool Jamal called home. Mike had gotten to know him pretty well over the years and respected him for his fairness. Even so, a frisson of alarm edged up his spine, and he shot Dara a worried look. "Everything okay?"

"No," Miller said. "I got the call on another case last night around one. A robbery down the block from Jamal's building. We were canvassing the area and saw Jamal on the corner with a bunch of his so-called friends. They were all drunk."

"Oh no," Mike said, his stomach lurching violently. His brain automatically ran through the list of charges the police could bring against Jamal for this infraction, any one of which would land him back in the juvenile facility: breaking curfew, underage drinking, public drunkenness, spending time with other felons. The list went on and on. "Did you take them in?"

"No, but you owe me one. I gave them a warning, and they scattered without any problem."

Mike's relief overwhelmed him. It took a moment before he could speak. "I won't forget this, Sam."

Dara had been watching and listening, her eyes wide with concern. "What is it?" she asked when he hung up.

Mike struggled hard to keep his temper in check, when what he really wanted to do was march down to Jamal's office and wring his scrawny neck for being so stupid. "That was Sam Miller, one of my friends on the force. He had to break up a bunch of punks loitering and drinking on the street last night. Jamal was with them. He was drunk."

"Oh no," she cried. "What about his probation?"

"Luckily, Miller just gave them a warning, and they went home without any problems." He shot to his feet and paced back and forth, agitated. What should he do? His mind raced with possibilities. Too bad Jamal was too big for corporal punishment. Should he call his mother? Dock his pay? He could . . .

Dara stood in front of him and put her hand on his arm. "I'm not trying to excuse him," she said calmly, "but you know that teenagers drink all the time and—"

He looked at her as if she'd announced plans to join the Aryan Nations. "Come on, Dara! If Miller had arrested him, he'd be on his way to juvenile detention, no matter how much I begged the judge! And what do you think the guards and the other inmates would do to him there?"

"I know it was stupid," she said reasonably, "but it's normal teenage behavior. If you come down too hard on him, you'll drive him away, and who knows what'll happen then?"

Maybe she was right, but he was still petrified when he thought of the odds against Jamal ever leading a safe and productive life, or even reaching the age of eighteen in nine months. He tried his best to help Jamal, but what could he really do? Could he really come between Jamal and his birthright and his "friends" and his own self-destructive behavior? He couldn't choke back his fear; maybe, despite all he'd done to try to give Jamal a brighter future, it wouldn't be enough to save him from his fate.

"He's not invincible," he told Dara. "He's got to do everything he can to stay out of trouble because trouble will find him, anyway." He collapsed on the sofa, and his head slumped in his hands.

"Mike," she said reproachfully. "Didn't you ever drink with your friends? Sow any wild oats? It's usually harmless. I'm not saying you should let him off the hook, but keep it in perspective."

He jerked his head up. "I rarely drink. I don't approve of teenagers drinking. Do you?"

She rolled her eyes. "Of course. The great Mike Baldwin doesn't approve of drinking, and woe to those—"

"'The great Mike Baldwin?'" he said, surprised. "What's that about?"

She narrowed her eyes at him. "Isn't that how you think of yourself? It's how you act."

He blinked several times. "You really think I'm a pompous jerk, don't you?"

She gave him a wry smile. "I hate to tell you this, but most of us are mere mortals. We're not going to live up to your impeccable standards every second of every day. Sorry."

Mike gaped at her. "Is there a point anywhere in my future?"

"The point is you're the only positive thing in his life, and he needs you." She sat beside him on the sofa. "Don't come down too hard on him," she murmured, leaning closer. "You're not his father. I'll bet he's had a pretty good scare thrown into him already."

Mike lifted his face from his hands. "What would you do?" He was, much to his own surprise, anxious to hear her opinion. She and Jamal had become pretty friendly, and she was closer to Jamal's age than he was.

She thought for a moment. "Don't you have a hearing in juvenile court later in the week? Why don't you take him to lockup with you when you meet with the client? That'll give him something to think about. But don't make a big production out of it."

He hung his head again and rubbed his temples. "I'll think about it."

"Don't worry, Mike," she said softly. "Don't worry." The way she said his name was an endearment. Her voice, soothing, husky, and sweet, slid through him, and his eyes drifted shut. She was so close. He wanted to lay his head in her lap, soak up her comfort, and let her share some of the worrying about Jamal. He needed her. Did she do this with Sean, too? For once he didn't care. As long as she did it with him.

And then she stroked the back of his neck. Her hand felt soft, warm, and smooth—her touch firm and confident. And his whole body went up in flames. He wanted to crush her supple form to his, to taste her sweet lips, to lose himself inside her body, to feel her convulse around him. Just as suddenly, Sean's face flashed before his eyes, and he stiffened. He jerked his head out of his hands and stared at her. He'd forgotten—for one second—that Sean also wanted Dara.

"Don't," he growled, leaping to his feet.

She snatched her hand back and stared up at him. Bewilderment flashed through her eyes, followed quickly by hurt. "I-I'm sorry." She jumped up and fled from his office. And he wanted to snatch her back and beg her to touch him again.

Jamal found Dara in her office later. "Mike says I should thank you for saving my butt."

Dara had heard their discussion earlier, and while it wasn't the fifteen-round bout she'd feared, Mike had still yelled. Quite a bit. What would it have sounded like if she hadn't "saved" Jamal? She was gratified and ridiculously pleased that Mike—strong, opinionated, arrogant, and determined—had bothered to listen to anything she'd said. "What happened?"

Jamal grimaced. "He's docking my pay for two weeks and giving me a bunch of boring work."

She kept her face neutral. "You think that's unfair?"

He broke into a grin that was as wicked as ever. "Nah. Not when you consider the stuff I've gotten away with that Mike doesn't know anything about."

Dara wasn't amused. "I don't really think doing things that could get your probation revoked is a laughing matter."

"I screwed up." His smile faded. "I won't do it again."

His eyes didn't waver, and Dara believed him. Just as she'd thought, he wouldn't want to disappoint Mike again. "Good."

"What I want to know is, what have you done to Mike? He doesn't listen to anyone."

"We just talked."

"Ummm." Jamal turned to go but stopped to look back at her, a wry smile on his face. "I just hope you use your powers for good and don't go over to the dark side."

Dara had no idea when it happened, or how, but one day she came to the bizarre realization she couldn't stay away from the office. "You're never around anymore," Monica complained during one of the rare afternoons when Dara joined her and Sean at their usual table in the library.

"That's not true," said Dara. But it was true. She'd long ago discovered the small conference room at work was an excellent place for reading for class. She could spread her books and notes and study guides all over the large table and leave them there, undisturbed, when she left to do her work for Mike. One day she'd come back to the office to resume her reading and studying, then the next, until it dawned on her she returned to the office every afternoon after class. She usually stayed until six or seven, long past the point when everyone else but Mike had gone home.

"Dara's kicked us to the curb," Sean interjected. "Guess she thinks she doesn't need our help with con law anymore. We'll see how she does come finals."

"You've got some nerve." Dara tapped him on the hand with her blue highlighter. "You barely even go to classes anymore. What are *your* grades going to look like?" As soon as the words came out of her mouth, Dara's guilty conscience squirmed to life. She'd skipped

a couple—well, okay, three or four—classes herself
lately so she could dash back to the office and work on
the Johnson case. She would have to stop doing that because it would catch up with her come finals, if Mike
didn't realize what she was doing and kill her first.

"Ouch!" Monica sniggered, then they shushed each
other and went back to their reading.

But Dara had discovered something better than her
study group: Mike. His unlikely career as Dara's personal legal tutor began one morning, when she drove
into the office early to study a little before she began
her work. The office was quiet and dark, and she made
some coffee and settled in with her study manuals.

"Aaargh!" she cried after fifteen minutes of frustration. She nearly jumped out of her skin when Mike,
alarmed, appeared from nowhere and poked his head
in her office. She felt a disturbing jolt of pleasure.
She'd hardly seen him the last couple of days because
he'd been at court. Frequently, he was the first person
she saw in the morning and the last person she saw at
night. "Hi," she said breathlessly.

When he saw she was okay, he raised one sardonic
eyebrow at her. "Problem?"

She swallowed her frustration. The last thing she
needed at this particular moment was more of his sarcasm about how she was destined to flunk out of
school because of her laziness and other faults of
which he'd previously accused her. "No," she said
stiffly. "Nothing I can't handle."

He took a cautious step into her office and leaned
over her desk to see what she was doing. "Ah," he said
when he saw the textbook. "Civ Pro. Very tricky. Can
I help with anything?"

His face was bland now and, if she didn't know any

better, sincere. But still, he'd probably laugh at her questions, which would only make her feel dumber than she already did. He was like Lucy to her Charlie Brown, claiming she could trust him only so he could yank the football away at the last second and make her look ridiculous. This was, after all, the man who, not so long ago, had made it his life's work to ignore her. Anyway, she'd figure it all out by herself if she gave it a few more minutes. She didn't need his help. Even if she did fear and loathe civil procedure like the bubonic plague. "No, thanks."

His face softened. "I hate to think of you struggling when I could help."

She narrowed her eyes at him. How like him to brag about his own skills while making her feel stupid. She wasn't *struggling*. "I can manage," she said sourly.

Stung, he nodded and retreated. "Suit yourself." He shrugged as he left.

But after another day of reading about Rule Fifteen and all its attendant nuances, she'd have paid Satan himself for a one-on-one study session. With feet of lead, she walked to Mike's office and, hearing him on the phone, lingered in the hallway. How much crow would he make her eat?

"What's up?" Mike said when he hung up, his expression neutral.

"I was wondering if, uh," she floundered. "If you had some time—"

"Need a little help with civil procedure?" he said graciously, with not a hint of sarcasm.

"Yes," she said, brightening. "But if it's a bad time, I can—"

He smiled and waved her off. "Pull up a chair," he said. "Pick my brain."

And she did, for nearly an hour. If he had other pressing business, he didn't mention it, and he patiently answered her endless questions. He didn't seem to think she was dumb at all. "You worry too much," Mike finally said, laughing. "You know this stuff cold."

"Do you really think so?" She had a pathetic but overwhelming need for his praise and admiration. Apparently, she wasn't too proud to fish for them.

"Dara," he said, serious now, "I'd bet my last dollar you're going to get all As on your finals."

She grinned idiotically, more pleased with herself than if she'd won the Nobel Peace Prize. Mike was the smartest person she knew, bar none. His encouragement felt like the greatest gift she could possibly receive.

From then on, she went to him whenever she had a question, and he always dropped everything to help her. She could hardly believe the same Mike who was so cocky and judgmental was such a patient and supportive teacher, but he was. She'd never spent much time analyzing her feelings, but it occurred, even to her, that maybe the real reason she spent so much time in the office was because that was where Mike was. There were times when she thought she actually liked him—liked him very much, in fact—but that idea was too perplexing and alarming to explore.

Chapter 8

"So how's con law going?" Mike asked Dara one night when he poked his head in the conference room, where she was studying. The lamp on the corner table gave a soothing glow—a welcome change from the usual glare of the fluorescent overhead lights. "Have you got it all figured out?" They'd established a routine of sorts: after everyone else left for the night, he would find her, and they'd talk. He would pretend he hadn't looked for her, like he'd stumbled upon her accidentally, and she would act surprised, as if she hadn't known he'd come.

"Almost." She smiled up at him. "Thanks to all your help."

His heart gave a hard thump whenever she smiled at him like that; he was astonished—he was always astonished—by her beauty and sweetness. He could almost let himself believe she was glad to see him. When she relaxed, like now, he hardly knew what to do. Half the time he felt like a kid seeing Christmas lights for the first time; she was that dazzling. "Am I going to have to carry you the whole semester? You want me to take your finals for you, too?"

"Would you?" They both laughed, and he sat in the chair across from her. "How are you coming with your cross-examination?" she asked him.

He was prepping for a burglary trial next week, but he didn't want to talk about it now. He waved his hand to dismiss the topic. "I've had enough of that for the night."

"You know," she said, still smiling, "you haven't threatened to fire me today. Yesterday, either. Does this mean anything, or will you just fire me tomorrow?" She sifted her fingers through her hair in that ancient, infinitely seductive gesture of a woman who is sexually aware of—attracted to—a man.

Mike's blood began to heat. Was she *flirting* with him? Or was this just garden-variety teasing? He loved it when she teased him; there was something deliciously intimate about it. "The night's still young. I could just do it now and get it over with."

"I wish you wouldn't." She watched him for a long moment, and he raised his eyebrows in a silent question. "Tell me something. When do you eat and sleep? You're always here in the office. Don't you have a life? I mean . . . I'm sure you do, but it's like my parents having sex: I know it happens, but there's never any evidence of it."

"I manage," he told her when he'd stopped laughing. "I usually leave here by eight-thirty or so, and I eat when I get home." Her gaze glided over his chest—he'd loosened his tie and undone the top two buttons on his shirt hours ago—lingering on the hollow between his collarbones. Then it slid down his arms. But she seemed to catch herself and realize what she was doing, and her gaze flew back to his face. And then she flushed.

Mike was surprised she'd looked at him in such a

frankly assessing way. Sure, he was in pretty good shape, and he was used to women staring at him, but this was different. This was Dara. "Dara?" He'd sacrifice his first-born child to know what she was thinking. "What is it?"

Flustered, she smiled much too brightly. "Eat what? Microwave popcorn?"

"Whatever I cook up."

Her jaw dropped in amazement. "You cook?"

He grinned at her. "There's no end to my talents, Dara. You'll realize that one day."

"There's no beginning to your modesty," she said sourly.

"What about you? You've been keeping some late hours here yourself." Actually, Dara was in the office almost as much as he was, and he couldn't figure out why. Looking a gift horse in the mouth was never a good idea, but he needed to know. Why didn't she study at the library or her apartment—somewhere with Sean? Was the coffee better here? Was her chair more comfortable here? Did she prefer fluorescent lights? Or could it be . . . He almost didn't want to let himself think the thought. Could it be her studying here had anything to do with *him*? Yeah, probably. Where else could she find a free legal tutor?

"Oh, I don't know." For some reason, she wouldn't look at him now. She was suddenly completely absorbed with straightening her papers. "I like to study here. It's quiet."

She was lying. Well, maybe not lying, exactly, but she wasn't telling him the whole truth. He might regret it later, especially if she decided to stop spending so much time here, but for now he had to know. "Why don't you study with Sean?"

"Oh, I do," she said quickly, "but sometimes we have to get on him about talking too much. And sometimes I just like to study by myself."

Well, of course, there was nothing more to it than that, he thought dejectedly. "So what do you do for fun when you're not here or at school?" There was so much about Dara he was dying to know. Come to think of it, he was dying to know everything about her. But he'd made it a point never to ask her anything too personal. It wouldn't be right. Hobbies were a safe area, though.

"Well, I read a lot. And I like to bake."

"It doesn't look like you eat too much of what you make."

"Unfortunately, I like to eat what I bake a little too much. But luckily, I also exercise."

"Ummm." He couldn't help smirking. Of course, she exercised; the girl's body was darn near perfect. Slim but wonderfully curvy, with great muscle tone in her arms and legs. He'd kill to see her abs. Well, he'd kill to see a couple other selected areas first, and then he'd kill to see her abs. He'd bet they were toned but still rounded and feminine. One of his recurring fantasies was of burying his face—his tongue—in her belly button while he slid his fingers down to her . . .

"'Ummm?'" she said tartly, frowning. "Was there some comment you'd like to make?"

Somehow Mike managed to subdue his wicked smile, leaving his lips to quiver. He was treading on dangerous ground here, but so what? "Let's just say I had, ah, already concluded you take pretty good care of yourself."

Her eyes widened with surprise. "W-well, anyway," she stammered, "I practice yoga every day."

"Yoga?" The image made his heart race. He'd stumbled past a yoga class at the gym once when he was on his way to lift weights, and he'd seen what those incredibly supple women could do with their bodies. Suddenly, his mind seethed with endless possibilities, each more lurid than the one before. Dara in a form-fitting black yoga outfit, with the top part like a bathing suit, and hip-hugging pants that could be peeled away like the skin of a grape. Dara bending and stretching, spreading her legs wide into some fantastic position, her breasts pushed together and upward with each movement. Dara breathing hard, a light sheen of sweat glistening on her . . .

"What do you do with yourself when you're not here?"

What? Did she say something? Violently, he jerked his mind back to the present and rewound her question through his brain. "Well, I, uh . . . I play in a basketball league," he said after a minute. "I read a lot. I see a lot of movies. And I like to travel."

"Where was your last trip?"

"I went to Paris over the summer."

"Paris! How was it? I've never been."

"Amazing."

"So is it true it's the most romantic city on earth?"

His smile faded a little. "I wouldn't know. I went by myself."

"By yourself!" she cried. "Why didn't you go with one of your friends or a girlfriend?"

"Well," he said, laughing, "Paris isn't exactly a place you go to with the fellas. And I didn't have anyone I wanted to take with me, so I went by myself."

She looked flabbergasted, like he'd told her he'd walked to Paris. "Why aren't you—"

Mike knew what she was thinking even though she hadn't finished her question. "Why aren't I married yet?"

She watched him intently now, with the strangest look on her face, a new tension in her shoulders. "Let me guess," she said flippantly. "You're not the marrying type? You like to play the field?"

His guard went up, as it inevitably did whenever he and marriage were mentioned in the same sentence. Dara was teasing him again, but her casual tone didn't match her eyes, which were strained and intense. Clearly, she didn't think his marital status was a laughing matter. But why? Why should she care whether he ever got married or not? "I'm not the marrying type." Her face fell in horror, as if he'd said he wasn't the showering type. "At least, not right now," he continued. "Right now I need to work on building the firm."

Dara stared at him, unblinking. "Well, in the meantime I'm sure you have your choice of women."

He snorted. His choice of women. What a ridiculous thought. That was the one thing he didn't have. "I *don't* have my choice of women, Dara," he said darkly. Suddenly, he felt like smashing his fist through the wall. "I have a few women I can have sex with."

"Well," she said faintly, "don't keep me in suspense. What would you want in a wife if that mythical day ever came?"

He didn't hesitate. "Someone who's smart and funny, but sweet. Someone who's independent and strong. With attitude."

"And beautiful."

He shrugged. "Beautiful wouldn't hurt. But looks aren't everything."

"Are you dating anyone right now?"

He stared at her, astonished at the direction the conversation had taken. Why was she suddenly so concerned about his personal life? Did she still feel the attraction between them as strongly as he did? Was she willing to act on it? "Why do you ask?" he said carefully, tensing, his heart racing. If she gave him a sign—the slightest sign she was interested in him—he knew he would climb across the table and pull her into his arms. He would gladly give his car, the shirt off his back, and probably his right arm, if only he could touch her now. "What's it matter to you?"

Dara went rigid. Just like that she froze—a deer caught in the headlights, poised to flee. "I . . . of course, it doesn't matter to me," she said suddenly. She laughed nervously, as if she couldn't quite get over the absurdity of the idea. "What would give you a crazy idea like that?"

Stunned, Mike's face fell, and he slumped back in his chair. What a fool he was. The way he wanted this girl ate away at his guts like battery acid, and she didn't feel a thing for him and never would. It was all a hallucination—her wistfulness, the softness in her eyes when she looked at him, the way she smiled at him sometimes—none of it really existed, and he was a fool for thinking it did. "Right," he growled.

"Mike . . . " She reached a hand out to him.

He stood abruptly and stalked toward the door. His own office—the place he loved as much as he loved his home—had closed in on him like a tomb, and he had to get away from here—from *her*. She was bad for him, this girl. She would bring him to his knees if he wasn't careful—if she hadn't already.

"It's late, and you need to go home," he barked, without bothering to look at her again. Why was she here, anyway? Why was she always here, where he couldn't get away from her? How was he supposed to go on like this without losing his mind? He stomped out, slamming the door behind him.

Dara replayed the scene over and over again. Had she dreamed it, or had she and Mike really enjoyed each other's company and talked like friends? She hadn't said anything to Mike that she wouldn't have said to any of her other male friends. And yet, with little warning, he'd become angry with her—so angry he couldn't stand to be in the same room with her. Why couldn't she have a simple discussion with him without feeling like she was tiptoeing through a minefield without a map? She felt shocked and disoriented, like she'd been laughing and playing on a sunny beach when suddenly, with no warning, a hurricane had hit, blackening the sky and drenching her with rain. And she had no idea why.

Certainly, there had been times in the past when she'd openly and, yes, gleefully defied him, but not tonight. Tonight she'd been pleasant and charming. And so had he. The more she thought about it, the angrier she became with herself for even caring about Mike Baldwin and his dark moods. Who was he, anyway? Her boss for a stupid, non-paying legal internship. When her tour of duty was over, she probably wouldn't ever see him again.

When she got to work the next day, she went straight to her office and put her head down. She didn't trust herself. After a while, when she thought the coast was clear, she crept downstairs to the kitchen for some coffee. She was almost back to her office, congratulating herself on her impeccable timing, when Mike came out of his office and started at the sight of her. "Dara," he said calmly. "How are you? I didn't hear you come in."

Mike's face was smooth and bland, so he was apparently Mike the Charming today instead of Mike the Sullen and Moody. Was he for real? Was it actually normal in the parallel universe he lived in for people to get angry for no reason and leave midconversation, then act like everything was just fine? Had she stumbled into the freaking Twilight Zone? She wanted to keep the peace. Really she did. But she couldn't stop herself from narrowing her eyes at him. "Mike," she said coolly, then edged past him into her office. His bewildered expression gave her some small measure of satisfaction, but not enough to make up for her restless night. He was such a stupid jerk.

But then, not half an hour later, she ran into him—literally ran into him—in the small closet they used for storing office supplies. She'd been so busy daydreaming about him, she opened the closet door and ran directly into him. As the heavy door swung shut behind her, his arms wrapped around her waist in a steel grip. Then he swung her to the side and let her go. "Whoa!" He dropped his hands. "Watch where you're going!"

Dara took a hasty step back and, flustered, shifted on her feet. "Sorry." Her shoe tapped something on the floor, and she looked down to see an aluminum bucket half filled with sloshing water. Immediately, she looked up and saw a dinner plate–sized patch of discolored ceiling directly over the bucket. "What's this?"

"The roof," he said, shrugging. "It leaks. And all this rain isn't helping."

"Oh." She edged around it and kept her eyes on the floor. She felt like she was trapped in a cave with a polar bear; Mike took up every inch of the small space, and the air seemed unusually close. Suddenly she felt breathless. She felt his eyes on her face, studying her intently. Why did he always stare at her like that? Panic set in; she couldn't think with his eyes boring holes in her. She had to get out of here—away from Mike—and she had to do it now. Unfortunately, he stood right in her way. She brushed past him to reach the legal pads on the shelf, then turned to leave—to flee—but his voice, chilly now, stopped her.

"Dara," he said, "if you have a problem with me, why don't you just say so?"

Of all the things he might have said to her at this point in their relationship, such as it was, this was clearly the most ridiculously hypocritical. "'Just say so?'" she jeered, astonished he had the audacity to say such a thing after the way he'd treated her last night. "Is that what *you* do when you have a problem with someone?"

He nodded. "That's what I try to do, yes."

She saw from his puzzled expression he had no idea what she was talking about. In fact, he seemed to think *she* was the one with the problem. God, she wanted to kill him. If being direct was indeed his policy, then it was yet another rule he applied to the rest of the Western world but not to her. Another example of his separate and unequal treatment. She humphed. "That's funny, because you obviously have a problem with *me*, but you've never given me the courtesy of discussing it."

A wave of understanding crossed Mike's face, but then he blinked several times and gave her a bland stare. But there was something. His eyes were too wary and alert all of the sudden, his posture too rigid. She'd hit a nerve and was treading on sensitive ground. He knew exactly what she meant, even if he had no intention of admitting it. "Who says I have a problem with you?"

"Do you think I'm an idiot?" she yelled, the last remnants of her patience lying in shreds at her feet. "You treated everyone in the office better than you treated me for weeks after I started here. And then, last night, we were having a friendly conversation like normal people do, and all of the sudden you got angry and left. Why? I didn't say anything inappropriate or hurtful to you." Mike's face grew darker by the second, his brows sinking lower and lower above his eyes until his frown engulfed his entire face, but she didn't care. "What have I ever done for you to hate me so much?"

His eyes were narrow slits of rage now, and he shook his head as if he couldn't believe her abject stupidity. She flew into a fresh fury. He always looked at her like there was some vital piece of information she needed to know, if only she wasn't so hopelessly blind and stupid. "And I am *so* sick of you always looking at me like you think I'm the dumbest person on the planet! What is it you think I'm too stupid to get, Mike?"

He'd towered over her in the small space, his anger beating down on her like the midday desert sun. But suddenly he turned away, refusing to look at her. She knew whatever he said next wouldn't be the truth, or at least not the whole truth. "I *knew* we couldn't work together," he shouted, looking back at her at last. "There is no way this will ever work!"

He was back to that again? "Why not? I've been a professional! I've tried to work with you! I've done everything I can think of to be your friend, and I—"

"*Friend*?" Mike spat, as if the very word left a disgusting taste in his mouth. He looked insulted, as if she'd slapped his face. "You think I want to be your *friend*?"

Deeply wounded, Dara staggered back a step. Her hand went to her stomach as if to recover from a blow. Well, now she knew. The illusion of friendship she'd had over the past few weeks had been just that. An illusion. He hated her now as much as he ever had. God, how it hurt.

Tears stung the backs of her eyes. She had to get out of here before she humiliated herself. But first she'd see how much she could hurt him back. "You know what?" Unshed tears made her voice raspy, and she cleared her throat. "I don't care whether we're friends or not. I don't care whether you like me or not. All I want you to do is treat me with the same courtesy you treat all your other employees. We're stuck with each other for the rest of my internship. So if it's that hard for you to deal with me, then that's your prob—"

"Why, you little . . . ," Mike grunted, and his hand shot out and grabbed her upper arm, jerking her against him. His fingers burned her flesh through her shirt, and Dara gasped and struggled to breathe. Her anger evaporated as if it had never existed, replaced with an explosive excitement and yearning. His body, hard and wanting, pressed against hers; he yanked her around and into his arms, pulling her firmly against him. Her mind spun like a gyroscope, full of raging thoughts and feelings. His body felt like granite. The sensation was almost like hugging one of the marble pillars in front of her parents' house, except that his body was unspeakably warm and vibrant and had wonderful hollows and ridges that fit so well to her own.

He held her gaze; his eyes still glittered darkly, but with desire now, not anger. Unthinking, she lifted her face and parted her lips as raw lust roared through her. She'd never wanted anything as much as she wanted to taste his lips and feel his hands all over her body. She could feel the warmth of Mike's breath, see the heat in his eyes. His scent—fresh, clean, too faint to be cologne, too delicious to be soap, maybe a combination of factors that defied analysis—flooded her senses. God, she wanted him.

Mike studied her face for a long moment. Then he pulled her closer, with a low growl. *Yes*, Dara's mind— and body—screamed. *Yes. Finally*. But before his lips reached hers, he tensed and raised his head to look at her again. He squeezed his eyes shut and took a shuddering breath, and Dara realized, with a horrible sinking feeling, he'd remembered Sean, even if she hadn't, and was struggling with his self-control. Finally, he shoved her away, then glared at her as if she'd clubbed a baby seal to death instead of almost kissing him.

Disappointment, bitter and overwhelming, hurtled through her. "No," she protested weakly as he brushed past her and ripped the closet door open. Within seconds he'd retreated into his office, and the slamming of his door reverberated through Dara's body. Her arms, where he'd touched her, still tingled, but the rest of her body felt cold and empty.

After she took a few deep breaths to calm down her racing heart, she scurried out of the closet, half afraid she'd see Mike again. She didn't. Inside the relative safety of her own office, she sank into her chair and picked up her pen, but her hands trembled too violently for her to write anything—not that her jumbled thoughts would have let her work now, anyway.

She desperately wanted to understand what had happened. How many times had she caught Mike staring at her? How many times had she wondered why he hated her so much? But had it been hate? The only thing she knew for sure was Mike wanted her. And she'd only be lying to herself if she pretended she didn't want him.

She was embarrassed and astonished by her reaction. One touch—a rough one at that!—and her entire body had gone up in flames like a California forest during a wildfire. She'd never felt such mindless and overwhelming desire before; if Mike had kissed her, she'd probably still be in the closet with him, begging him to make love to her.

But Mike had pushed her away, and rightly so. Getting involved with him was courting disaster, and she knew it. Luckily, he'd kept his head. Still, she felt disappointed that she hadn't kissed him after all. She absently ran her fingertips over her lips and wondered what his kiss would have felt like.

She was so engrossed, she didn't see the shadow fall over her desk.

"Dara?" sang Sean. "You look like you're in a trance."

She jumped as if he'd fired a shot. "Hi." She couldn't force her lips to turn all the way up into a smile. Sean's sudden appearances at the office always unnerved her; he was intruding on a part of her life where he didn't belong. "What are you doing here?" She nervously watched him come closer and perch on the edge of her desk. Just then she heard Mike's door open, and she prayed he'd go downstairs—anywhere else but her office. But he came to her.

He'd been pacing back and forth in his office, trying to compose himself, when what he really wanted to do was to smash everything in his path. His blood boiled with heat, frustration, and anger. Why had he done it? What had made him grab Dara like that? As if it hadn't been torture enough to work alongside her for months without touching her. At least then, he'd been blissfully ignorant of how perfect she felt in his arms. At least then, he hadn't known how delightfully her body shivered to life under his fingers. Well, he knew all that now, didn't he? Knew how her eyes closed with passion as she waited for his kiss, knew how eager her supple body could be. And now he'd be taunted by this one single memory forever.

Dara. He wanted to touch her, to taste her, to know every part of her, and she wanted him, too. She'd claimed she wanted his friendship, but her body—her flushed face, her harsh breathing, her tilted head—gave her away. There was a savage satisfaction in that. It would have to be enough. But it wasn't.

Mike stalked back and forth relentlessly in front of the window, seeing nothing, furious with Dara for doing this to him. For making his gut twist in knots and his breath stop and his groin tighten to the point of agony. And he was angry with her for not getting it. He knew he should be relieved she still didn't understand the depth of his feelings for her, but for some reason her continued blindness enraged him. How could she be so bright when it came to work and school and Jamal's problems, and so clueless when it came to him?

Finally, he threw himself onto the sofa and pinched

the bridge of his nose between his fingers. *Help me, God, please.* He needed strength to avoid Dara, to do the right thing and not pursue his brother's "friend." And he needed to apologize to her. If nothing else, she was currently his employee, and he couldn't go around grabbing employees and almost groping them in broom closets.

After a few minutes, he recovered enough to walk to her office. "Dara, I . . . ," he began as he came into the room, not bothering to knock or to notice Sean already there until he was nearly to her desk. He had a glimpse of Sean leaning over her—she looked miserable—before she heard him and jerked away from Sean.

Mike recoiled as if he'd turned the corner and seen a grizzly bear. He felt muscles flexing uncontrollably in his temple and jaw. For one minute a red haze of bloodlust fogged his brain. What was going on here? Why was Sean always here if they weren't involved? Because they were friends? If so, they were the friendliest friends he'd ever seen. "Sean," he said hoarsely, fixing his eyes on Sean so he wouldn't have to look at Dara. "What brings you here?"

"Yes," Dara said to Sean, "you didn't say."

Sean turned his loving gaze back to her. "I thought we could get some dinner."

Mike snuck a glance at her to gauge her reaction to this proposal. Her eyes looked feverishly bright, and her smile was fixed and vacant. "We're supposed to meet Monica at the library tonight, Sean, remember?" she asked pointedly, her eyes darting to Mike and immediately back to Sean. "We were going to order a pizza. We need to work on our study outlines."

Sean waved a hand dismissively. "Friday nights are for fun. We can work tomorrow."

Dara shook her head firmly. "We need to work tonight *and* tomorrow."

Mike had had enough. He felt like his head would explode. Sean sat there talking with Dara, touching Dara's face, and would probably take Dara to dinner, and God knew what else after that. All things Sean had every right to do, and he did not. The crushing weight of his envy pressed down on his chest until he almost couldn't breathe. Maybe he couldn't have Dara, but he sure didn't have to stand by and watch her with his brother. "You two don't need me for this," he said, his voice ragged. He walked to the door.

"Wait, man," called Sean. "About your Black Lawyers Association awards banquet."

Mike turned back around and tried to keep his face blank. "Right. I bought a table for the firm. I'm expecting you and Dara and the staff to come."

"I know. But it's next weekend, and I'm going to go visit the fellas in Chevy Chase."

"But, Sean," Dara said, clearly alarmed, "next weekend is when we take the practice exams and have the professors score them. Do you think you should miss that? It's like a dry run for finals."

Sean shrugged. "I can take some practice tests on my own time. It's no big deal."

Mike had that familiar uneasy feeling. This was how it always went with Sean. At first, he'd be gung ho about school or work or whatever, then he'd begin to slack off and ignore his responsibilities, and then . . . "Are you taking care of business like you should, man?" he asked Sean quietly.

Sean bristled, then glared at him in an open challenge. "I think I can handle it." Sean turned away from Mike. "But there's no reason Dara can't still go and—"

"Because you're welcome to come here and study. If there's anything I can help with, you know I'm glad to—"

"No." Sean swelled up until he looked like a gorilla about to pound his chest and battle the alpha male for supremacy. His face went rigid with defiance, and he held Mike's eye for a long, charged moment. Finally, he smiled crookedly. "Thanks."

Mike resisted the urge to shake Sean and ask what the heck was wrong with him. This was the story of Sean's life in a nutshell: he'd cut off his nose to spite his face every single time. He'd rather flunk out of law school than ask Mike for help, or accept it when it was offered. Well, fine. So be it.

"Can Dara go with you?" Sean asked him. "She can sit at the table."

"Oh, I don't think I'll go," she said quickly, her voice sounding strained. "This way I'll have more time to study."

"You study too much as it is, Dara," Sean told her. "You should get out and have a little fun."

"I don't think so." Her voice was firm. "Anyway, I'd feel a little funny going by myself."

"Mike could take you or just meet you there."

Mike didn't say anything, but his eyes flew to Dara's face. She looked panicked, suddenly, as if Sean had suggested Ted Bundy escort her to the dinner. "You probably shouldn't speak for him," she said hastily. "What if he already has a date?"

"You don't mind, do you?" Sean asked Mike.

Mike felt sick and thrilled. Here, beautifully gift wrapped for him, like a present on Christmas morning, was a legitimate and innocent reason for him to spend time with Dara away from the office. But, of course, his feelings for Dara were anything but innocent. And only a rotten, scheming, lying bastard would agree to such a dangerous proposal.

"No." Mike looked directly into Dara's stricken eyes for the first time since he came into her office. "I don't mind at all."

Dara's eyes lowered, but, if possible, the flush in her face grew even brighter. "Well," she said faintly, "I guess that's settled." Suddenly, she leapt to her feet, her eyes on the floor. "Excuse me." She edged around Sean and sidestepped Mike. "I just need to . . . bathroom." Once out in the hall, she hurried away, her fading footsteps sounding as if she had broken into a run.

The second she was gone, Mike turned to Sean and asked the question he'd been dying to ask for months. "So what's going on with you and Dara?"

"Nothing." Sean maintained his perch on the edge of Dara's desk but turned around to face Mike. He smiled ruefully. "But not for lack of trying."

As if some invisible switch somewhere had been flipped, Mike's breathing evened out, and his lungs felt less constricted. So they really were just friends. Well, thank God for small favors. But there was still the issue of Sean wanting Dara. "Are you still trying, Sean?"

"Got to, man." Sean held his gaze, and Mike felt Sean's abject misery as clearly as if it were his own. And he understood that even though Sean knew his feelings were unrequited, he still dreamt of Dara, still held out hope, as hopeless as he had to know it was. "Can you blame me?"

The question was a roundhouse kick directly to Mike's heart. He, better than anyone else on the planet, understood Dara's allure; he understood it all too well. He felt his lips thin. "No. I can't blame you."

Sean stood up, shoved his hands in his pockets, and went to look out the window. "Hey. Before I forget to ask, what's up with Mama? I haven't talked to her in a while."

Any empathy Mike had felt for Sean instantly vanished. He talked to Mama daily to see how she was handling the chemotherapy, so he knew she still hadn't told Sean she was sick. But he'd assumed Sean at least called her every now and then; he should've known better. What kind of son was this jerk, anyway? "Yeah, well, why don't you pick up your phone once a year or so and call?"

Sean bristled. "I've been meaning to. I've been a little busy with school, if you hadn't noticed."

Mike snorted. Busy? Sean didn't know the meaning of the word. Dara—now she was busy: busy working forty hours a week, busy going to class, busy studying. And *he* was busy working forty hours a week on the Johnson case and fifty hours a week on all his other cases. Sean busy? What a laugh riot. Sean was so busy with school, he had time to take the weekend off, skip his practice finals, and fly to the coast for a fun-filled weekend with his buddies. The pathetic part was Sean actually believed the crap he spouted. "You've got time to make a five-minute phone call to your mother to see how she's doing," he snarled.

Sean winced and shot Mike a look designed to kill. "I'm outta here."

Eventually, Dara stopped hiding in the bathroom and snuck back to her desk. Once there she sank into her chair, propped her elbows on her desk, and buried her face in her hands. She was still violently aroused. The tips of her breasts hurt, and there was a gnawing ache high up between her thighs. The urge to rub herself was almost impossible to ignore. For a few awful minutes in the powder room, she'd actually thought about masturbating just to get her feverish body to cool down a little. Thankfully, she'd resisted that temptation. She massaged her temples—as if *that* would really help. "Oh, God," she moaned.

"Dara."

She shot to her feet. Mike, his fists shoved deep into his pockets, shoulders rigid, eyes hooded, stood right in front of her desk. She hadn't even heard him.

Chapter 9

"I shouldn't have grabbed you," Mike said, without preamble and without looking at her. "It won't happen again."

Undone, she could only stare, openmouthed, at him. Even now, she wanted to taste him, to climb across her desk and into his arms, to wrap herself around him, rub herself against him. God, she wanted him. Was he sorry, then? He glanced up at her, his eyes hopeless and flat, as he went back to his office. And suddenly everything—everything—made sense to her.

How could she have been so blind? It was there in the slump of Mike's shoulders and the throbbing of his jaw and the despair in his eyes. He was miserable. His unhappiness permeated every muscle in his body, every hair on his head. She wondered how on earth she'd ever been foolish enough to think he hated her. No, he *wanted* her. And it was killing him.

"What's wrong, Sean?" Dara asked him again.

They sat at their usual table at the library, but Sean couldn't concentrate and couldn't stop shifting restlessly back and forth in his seat. He couldn't remember when he'd last been this edgy. "It's nothing," he told her. "I'm having a little trouble with the job."

"I thought you loved the ACLU."

He shrugged, eyes on his open torts book. "I did. I do. But my boss is a jerk, and we had some words yesterday." He had the worst luck in the world when it came to bosses; he'd never found one he could work with, including his own brother. Keeping a job for longer than four or five months was always tricky when there were so many jerks in the world. His manager at the bookstore in college had complained he'd called in sick too often. Well, he'd been sick. Sure, there were one or two days when he'd partied a little too hard the night before, but what boss of college kids didn't expect a little absenteeism? He'd quit that job pretty quickly. Who wanted to work somewhere where you had to show up when you were sick? None of his other employers over the years had ever been any better. His current boss was a hugely respected attorney who was nationally known for his work in the area of free speech rights. But he was still a jerk. "He's been giving me these stupid research assignments," Sean said, embarrassed to have to tell Dara about the extent of his problem. "So I asked him about it, and he said he hasn't been impressed with my work product."

Dara rubbed his shoulder sympathetically. "Oh no. So did you ask him what the specific problems were?"

Sean looked at her in surprise. "Hell, no. Why would I do that? My work has been good. This guy just doesn't like me."

Her eyes widened into what looked like alarm, as if he'd confided his secret career goal was to run off and join the circus. "What did you say to him?"

Sean was unapologetic. "I told him I'm doing my best and we have different styles and I'm not certain I can change my style to suit his."

Dara gaped at him for a long moment, clearly at a loss for words. "But Sean," she stammered, recovering, "maybe he just wanted to give you a little constructive criticism. Mike does that with my work all the time. I don't like it, but he's usually right."

Sean shook his head. "Screw him. I think I'll see if Stallworth can put me somewhere else."

Her voice rose in alarm. "But you really wanted to work at the ACLU, Sean. You can't throw away the opportunity to do work that matters to you just because you don't like your boss."

He shook his head again. "I've had it with the ACLU. I need a fresh start somewhere else."

Dara blinked at him as if he were some unidentified species of mammal she desperately needed to classify. The silence lengthened and became awkward. It killed Sean that Dara didn't understand him any better than this. Clearly, she was judging him, and he was coming up short. "What happened to you last night?" she asked quietly. "I thought you were going to meet us here."

He'd decided at the last minute to watch the game at the apartment of one of their classmates. Sure, he should have called her, but he hadn't wanted to hear another lecture about the importance of studying. And he had the alarming idea she hadn't even noticed— or cared—when he didn't show up last night. He waved his hand. "Don't worry. It's all under control."

"I wish I had your self-confidence. Finals will be here before we know it. And if I skipped class as much as you do, I'd be in a panic."

Sean scowled. "I'm sick of school, Dara. The grind is really starting to get to me."

"You don't need to tell *me* about it. Between classes and the reading—"

"That's not what I mean," he said impatiently. "School isn't what I expected." That was a mild understatement, but he didn't think Dara would understand if he told her the truth, which was he hated law school with every fiber of his being. The reading was boring and endless, the classes were stupid, and he'd met lichen with more personality than most of the professors.

She stared at him again, obviously bewildered. "You're probably just a little burned out, Sean," she said encouragingly. "The trip to D.C. will do you good."

"I don't know," he muttered. "The amount of work and reading every night is killing me."

Her mouth fell open. "It's *law school*, Sean, not a walk in the park."

He snorted. "Now you sound like my brother. By the way, what's he been up to? We've been getting along pretty well lately, but now it's like he's disappeared off the face of the earth. I've called him a couple of times, but he never calls back. And I thought he acted a little strange yesterday."

Dara got a funny look on her face. "Um, I don't know. He's pretty busy, but he seems fine to me." Suddenly, she slammed her books closed and started shoving them in her backpack. "It's late. I really need to go. You okay?"

He swallowed his disappointment that she was leaving. "Yeah," he lied. "I'm okay."

Mike stalked relentlessly back and forth in the brownstone's foyer. It was seven-thirty Monday morning, and he was the only one there so far. Weak sunlight streamed in through the slats of the open wooden blinds, making the room a warm, peaceful haven at this time of day, but he didn't notice. With every step, he felt himself become more agitated, like a teapot right before the boil. Dara would be here any second. And he was waiting for her—had been since seven. It wasn't cool to accost the poor girl the second she arrived at the office, but at this point he was too far gone to care about social niceties.

He'd barely survived the weekend. Saturdays and Sundays were getting harder and harder because he couldn't stand to go two days without seeing Dara. In fact, what used to be the best part of the week now felt like a forty-eight-hour punishment. If he kept on like this, he'd have to institute a mandatory weekend work-day just so he could get his fix of her. This weekend was especially unbearable because he kept remembering how she'd felt in his arms, how she'd turned her face up to his, how she'd seemed to vibrate with passion. Now he knew one undeniable fact: Dara wanted him. Of course, that one fact didn't do him one bit of good, but it gave him a fierce feeling of satisfaction.

And a strange sort of hope.

He stopped pacing long enough to glance at his watch. Seven thirty-one. Aaargh! Was she even coming? When would she get here? Soon? God, he hoped so. He couldn't possibly get any work done until she arrived. His unfailing discipline had failed. Nothing on earth felt as important as seeing Dara. Still, he hated to completely waste his time. Maybe he should make some coffee. He'd taken two steps toward the kitchen when he heard the jingle of keys outside the front door. She was here! He wanted to fling the door open and jerk her into his arms. Instead, he turned and sprinted up the steps to his office. He felt idiotic, like a love-struck schoolboy riding his bicycle past a girl's house to see if she was home.

But Dara didn't need to know that.

Dara's heart thundered as she gingerly let herself into the office and shut the door behind her. Everything had changed, and she couldn't deny it. She was dying to see Mike. She was terrified to see Mike. He was already here. She smelled the faintest traces of his cool, clean scent by the receptionist's desk as she walked toward the stairs. And, God help her, her breasts tightened and swelled when she passed his office. Breathless, she called good morning to him and continued on her way, not bothering to stop. But she saw, out of the corner of her eye, that he wore another dark suit and sat behind his desk.

Had he always been this handsome? Well, yes, of course, he had. But how had she ignored that fact for so long? Because he'd irritated her? He wasn't so irritating now. It was, in fact, worse than that. She hadn't seen him for two days. She'd missed him. She looked up from turning on her computer to see him at her door. "Hi," she squeaked nervously.

Mike leaned carelessly against her door frame, as cool and unruffled as ever. "How was your weekend?"

It was an innocent enough question, except that his eyes were so focused and intent—so unwavering— that Dara felt her cheeks burning. He *was* glad to see her. Joy exploded in her chest. "Good." She couldn't seem to look him directly in the eye for very long, nor could she stop her fidgety hands from compulsively straightening the already neat piles of papers on her desk. "Well, boring. Uneventful." She knocked over the cup that held her pens and, embarrassed, snatched it back up. Finally, she folded her hands on her desk and clutched them hard to stop herself from knocking anything else over. "How was yours?" She cautiously raised her eyes to his, only to discover him staring at her lips with such heat, she could almost feel him running his thumb along her bottom lip, touching his tongue to her mouth.

He seemed to realize he was staring. He hastily looked away. "Fine." He rubbed the back of his neck. "I was here most of the time." He may have said something else, but Dara didn't hear it, because she focused on his hands. Why hadn't she ever noticed how long and strong his fingers were before? And his hair. Look how thick and wavy it was! Was it silky or coarse? She would gladly give everything she owned for the chance to run her fingers through it.

What on earth was she doing? She snapped herself out of her reverie to find him still watching her with glittering eyes. "I am, uh, going to need you this week, Dara." She thought her mind was playing tricks on her, because she heard a husky sensuality in his voice, which made her wonder what, exactly, he needed her for, but his face remained neutral. "I got the still prints from the videos at Johnson's club. I need you to look through them and see if you can find the mystery man Johnson saw arguing with Morgan. Then maybe we can show the picture to some of the other witnesses and see if anyone knows who he is. Maybe hire an investigator to try to find him."

She wet her lips. "Of course."

His gaze strayed to her mouth and stayed there for a long beat. "Good," he said faintly. And he paused to give her a long, charged look before he turned to go, leaving her to wonder how long she could stand the sexual tension, which felt so intense the air throbbed with it.

* * *

The next day Mike called Dara into his office to ask her how she was doing on her review of the pictures of the crowd the night Morgan was shot. He was glad to have a legitimate excuse to talk to her. She was like heroin to him now; the more he saw her, the more he *needed* to see her.

"I'm about halfway through the stack," she told him. "It's very slow going. The pictures are grainy and dark. But I'll finish them this week."

"Well, don't kill yourself with it. We've got plenty of other, more productive stuff to do. I think he's lying."

She looked personally offended. "Why are you so cynical? I believed him. I think finding this guy could be the key to our whole defense."

"Dara." He leaned his elbows on his desk. "First of all, there probably is no other guy. Second, do you think if there is some other guy, he'll just confess to the murder the second we find him—assuming, of course, we *can* find him?"

Dara crossed her hands over her chest and set her jaw. Concession did not appear to be an option. "I think this is crucial. And I think there *is* a guy." Mike threw his head back and roared with laughter, which only seemed to irritate her further. "Is something funny?" she snapped.

She was funny, all right. He'd have more luck trying to convince the moon not to come out tonight than he would changing Dara's mind. "Are you always this stubborn?"

Dara smiled slowly. "Only when I think I'm right— about ninety-eight percent of the time."

"Well, anyone who likes to argue as much as you do

is a born lawyer. I can see why you're not writing novels or teaching creative writing." Dara gaped at him for a long moment before she jerked her eyes away and fidgeted with her pen. Mike let her squirm, but she wouldn't look at him; her face flushed, and she looked flustered. He had no idea what he hoped to accomplish by reminding her of the night they met. He wasn't trying to tease her; that much he knew. His feelings about her were much too troubling for that. Maybe it was just that he was desperate to know whether she remembered that night and the connection they'd had, as brief as it had been.

He skated on thin ice with her. Every day the popping and cracking sounds of the breaking ice got louder, but still, he skated right toward the edge. Nothing good could come of his attraction to Dara; Sean would never forgive him if he went after her. But he couldn't stop wanting her.

He reined himself in, hard. "You should get back to work, Dara," he said brusquely.

"Let's get some lunch." She smiled nervously, her eyes intent.

Mike gaped at her. Was this some kind of cruel joke? Or was this another one of her irritating offers of friendship? Did she not realize he had about as much business spending time with her as an alcoholic did going in a liquor store? Could it be that she just wanted to spend more time with him? "Lunch?" he said stupidly.

Her smile faded a little. "Yes. Lunch. A tasty midday meal. Maybe you've heard of it."

He laughed, but his instinct for self-preservation, as weak as it had become, kicked in. "I, ah," he said, sobering, "I have a lot of work to do. I better not."

For just a second, he thought he could see a glimmer of disappointment in her eyes, but then she smiled brightly. "Okay." Slowly, as if she were a mastodon trying to make her way across the tar pit, she got to her feet and left, pausing once to glance back over her shoulder at him.

Mike stared after her. They spent way too much time together as it was, and he really needed to wean himself from her, to prepare for that horrible and inevitable day when her internship ended and she left his life forever. He'd absolutely done the right thing by refusing her lunch invitation. And that would be his cold comfort during the long twenty-four hours before he saw her again.

"What's wrong with you, Michael?"

Mike stared at his mother. She really was unbelievable. Here she was, recovering from her surgery, sick from chemotherapy, and she wanted to talk about what was wrong with *him*. *She* looked awful. She sat on the overstuffed ivory chintz sofa in her elegant living room like the queen of England receiving visitors for tea. The only concessions to her illness, as far as he could tell, were that she'd tucked her feet underneath her and put a cashmere throw over her lap. There really was no point to his wondering why she didn't just keep her pajamas on and stay in bed to rest a little, like any other person who'd recently had a mastectomy. That would be like asking why the leaves insisted on falling from the trees every autumn. But her face—her eyes—gave her away. They were red and a little swollen, with huge dark circles underneath. Her skin, always so warm and vibrant, looked dull, as if it had a layer of dust over it.

She was sick, no matter how much she wanted to pretend otherwise.

He leaned back in the chair opposite her and crossed his legs. "Nothing."

Her lips tightened until they nearly disappeared. "Don't make me come over there. *Something* is wrong with you."

Mike snorted. Yes, *something* was. *Something* weighed on his mind every second of every day, more so than even his worries about his cancer-stricken mother. *Something* attracted, infuriated, dazzled, and frustrated him more than anything he'd ever encountered. *Something* had him in the grip of an obsession he couldn't seem to shake, and if he wasn't careful, *something* would drive him insane and then to an early grave. "It's nothing."

Mama smiled. "So now there's an 'it.' A second ago there was nothing."

He uncrossed his legs and leaned his hands on his knees, looking down at the floor. He was exhausted—much too tired for this interrogation. He was tired of pretending the situation was manageable. He was tired of trying to keep his hands to himself. He was tired of thinking about Sean and Dara spending so much time together. He was tired of the ache in the pit of his belly whenever he thought of her. He was . . . tired. He raised his eyes to Mama. "What do you want from me?" he asked quietly. He felt like Napoleon at Waterloo, Custer at Little Bighorn: utterly defeated. "What is it you want?"

Her smile evaporated. "Is she special?"

Mike hung his head again. He should have known she'd figure it out. "Yes."

"Is she married?"

Mike heaved himself to his feet and shuffled over to the window and brushed aside the heavy drapes. It was dark, but he had no idea what time it was. He stared out and saw nothing. "She may as well be."

"Come here, Michael." He turned, and she stretched out her arms to him. He clutched her hands—they were warm and soft, the same as always—and gingerly sat next to her. She rubbed his cheek. "You'll get through this, sweetheart." Her eyes were proud.

"I don't think I will, Mama."

She put her other hand on his face and pulled him down to kiss his cheek. He smelled the faint fragrance of her face cream—lily of the valley, not the fragrance Dara wore. "You will. There's no doubt about it. You'll do the right thing, and you'll get through it. You always do."

Mike stiffened. The right thing. The story of his life. Well, this once, he didn't want to do the right thing, and he'd almost reached the point where he didn't care what the consequences were.

"How are things with you and Sean?" Mama asked hopefully.

Couldn't be worse. He routinely fantasized about doing his brother some violent bodily harm as retribution for his close relationship with Dara. Staying in the same room with him was darn near impossible. So was looking him in the face. Plus, Sean would apparently rather flunk out of law school than deign to accept help from him. "Fine." He managed a crooked smile. "Good."

Mama beamed at him. "I knew I could count on you."

And Mike quickly looked away, feeling worse than ever.

* * *

At home that night Dara sat right down at her desk, with her magnifying glass, to continue looking through the photos for the mystery man. Her life's goal had changed. Now it wasn't enough to be a good law student. Now she had to prove to Mike she'd make a good lawyer and investigator. And if she dropped dead from exhaustion in the meantime, well, that was a small price to pay. Of course, she had reading she really needed to finish before tomorrow, but that could wait. She was so engrossed in her work, she didn't think of Sean at all, and when the phone rang, she let the answering machine pick it up. "Dara?" Sean said plaintively. "Are you there? Pick up."

She lowered the magnifying glass to feel a moment's guilt. Sean called all the time, just to check in with her. Normally, she thought it was a sweet, albeit slightly annoying, habit, because she usually didn't have much to say, having spent most of the day with him at school. But tonight she was busy, and she'd have to talk to Sean later. She tuned out his voice as he left a message.

An hour or so later, she stumbled onto a couple of photos that showed a man with a dark leather jacket and mustache, just like Johnson had said. He stood near the bar, talking to a woman, in one picture and sat laughing at a table in another. She didn't see any photos of him near Morgan, much less arguing with Morgan, but still. It was a start. She'd show them to Mike first thing in the morning.

But the morning seemed a long way off. Maybe Mike was working on the case himself right now, from home. He often worked late into the night. Wouldn't he want to know what she'd found? Maybe she should call him. Now. She flopped onto her bed on her belly, legs in the air, and dialed his number.

"Hello?" he said after the second ring. Her heart thundered. His voice had a mellow, late at night, slightly sleepy sound that was the sexiest thing she'd ever heard. But he also sounded a little strange, a little . . . sad. She heard voices in the background, then music.

"Hi." She felt nervous now. It was pretty late, after all, and maybe he had company. "Am I catching you at a bad time?"

"No!" She heard a rustle, and then the faint noises she'd heard were abruptly silent. He'd probably been watching TV in bed. "I'm not doing anything. What's up?"

Her body tingled with awareness. There was something so intimate about talking on the phone late at night. Suddenly, she remembered she hadn't introduced herself. "It's Dara."

"Dara," he said, sounding exasperated and amused, "did you think there was some chance I wouldn't recognize your voice?" She barely heard him. Her mind—entirely without her consent—had conjured up the image of her lying in bed, watching TV with him. He probably had a huge bed, with soft, warm flannel sheets for the cold autumn nights. Not that they would need the sheets to keep warm. What did he sleep in? Pajamas? More interesting was the thought of him wearing bottoms only, with the hard, muscular slabs of his chest and arms rippling. Most tantalizing was the thought of him sleeping nude. Why hide perfection like that under pajamas?

Horror slammed through her. What was she thinking? "I-I've been looking through the pictures," she stammered, deciding it was best to stick to the reason for her call. "I think I found our mystery man."

"Great!" he said. "Good work! I'll look at them first thing."

"Um, Mike?" She hesitated to bring up anything personal with him, but she couldn't help wondering what was wrong. And she'd never sleep unless she knew.

"Um, yes?"

"Is everything okay? You sounded a little funny when you answered the phone."

He didn't answer for so long, she started to wonder whether he'd dozed off. "Everything's great."

His voice suddenly sounded so cheerful, it was actually creepy. "I don't believe you."

She heard a harsh sigh. "Something's going on, but it'll be fine. Don't worry."

Dara sat up and pulled her knees to her chest. It seemed terribly important, suddenly, for Mike to confide in her. She needed to know he thought of her as someone he could turn to if he ever needed anything. At least, she could listen. "I'm a worrier, Mike. Did you know that?"

"Dara—"

"And if you don't tell me what's wrong, I won't get any sleep tonight. Is that what you want?"

"My mother is . . . sick," he finally said.

Her heart fell. "I hope it's not . . . serious."

"It is. Very serious. She's had a recurrence of breast cancer—"

"Oh no!"

"And a mastectomy. Her chemotherapy is making her a little sick. The prognosis is good, but I just hate to see her suffer. I wish she didn't have to go through this pain—and the fear."

Dara didn't know what to say. She hadn't had the faintest idea anything so serious had happened. Mike was so strong; nothing ever seemed to faze him. "Sean hasn't said anything."

"Sean doesn't know. Mama wants him to focus on school right now."

To her surprise, she felt irritated with Mrs. Baldwin—a woman she'd never even met—for burdening Mike with her illness and then making him take a vow of silence. Was Mike supposed to bear the weight of the world all alone? "And how are *you*?"

"Me?" She heard astonishment in his voice. "I'm fine."

She felt a vast warmth in her heart for this man. He was so strong. There was nothing he couldn't handle. But he wasn't *fine*. Did he even realize that? Did he give himself permission to be scared or tired or worried? "Mike," she said softly. "Don't you ever get tired of doing it all by yourself? Worrying about Jamal and your mother and your brother and your clients? Everything is not your responsibility, you know. And it's okay to be a little scared. Who wouldn't be with their mother sick?"

His breathing sounded ragged. "God, Dara."

She heard a catch in his throat that hadn't been there a minute ago. Did anything she'd said make any sense to him? Or did he think she was an idiot? "I-I'm sorry," she said quickly. "I don't know what's gotten into—"

"I do get . . . tired." His voice was very soft, as if he couldn't stand the possibility someone might overhear him confessing to a weakness.

"Is the great Mike Baldwin admitting he's human?"

He laughed a little. "Don't tell anyone."

She'd made him laugh. She felt as powerful as a sorceress. Nothing she'd ever accomplished in her life seemed as important as what she'd just done. "I think your mother is very lucky to have a son she can lean on. I think she's the luckiest mother in the world." She heard the surprised hiss of Mike's breath, but he didn't say anything. She was way out on a limb now. She may as well go ahead and saw it all the way off. "And I think I'm lucky you think enough of me to confide in me."

"Dara." His voice was terribly husky now. "I . . . thank you. And . . . about the dinner on Saturday—"

She knew what he was thinking: that they couldn't go together. Of course, he was right. There was already so much sexual tension between them, the air seethed with it. Why light a match near an open powder keg? If she had any sense whatsoever, she would graciously agree, and that would be the end of the matter. "What time should I meet you there?" she asked him.

There was a long, pregnant pause. "Six-thirty."

"Here they are," she crowed the next morning, waving the pictures as she waltzed into Mike's office. She'd decided the best thing to do was to act normal, as if they hadn't had that wonderfully intimate conversation last night. "The answer to all our problems. No need to thank me." She plopped into the chair across from his desk and smiled smugly.

Mike, in his shirtsleeves, eyebrows raised, leaned forward in his chair and snatched them from her. "You sure have been doing a lot of yakking about these pictures."

"You'll see," she sang, with supreme confidence.

"Ummm." He bent his head low as he flipped through them. "Hey. These are pretty interesting." And then he looked up from the pictures, and his wide, boyish smile disarmed her completely. "Good work, Dara," he said warmly.

Dara's heart skidded to a stop. And as Mike held her gaze for one long moment, she understood, with absolute certainty, that she was crazy about this man. And he felt the same. He'd never hated her. After a moment their smiles dimmed, leaving them to stare at each other with raw heat. Dara realized she was breathless, almost panting. At last Mike looked away, rubbing his forehead with a hand that looked a little unsteady, and resumed flipping through the stack.

"Did you," he said, his voice low and a little shaky, "did you, ah, find any pictures with close-ups of his face?"

"Ah yes," she said, trying to force her mind back to the topic at hand. "There was one about halfway down. No, not that one." She leaned across the desk but couldn't see with the pictures upside down. "Wait." She walked around his desk to stand alongside his chair. "Let me see." Leaning over his shoulder, she felt him tense and realized, with some embarrassment, she'd brushed her hair against his face. Although he could easily have slid his chair away from her, he didn't. Instead, Mike leaned forward until his face was mere inches from hers, if that. Close enough for her to feel the moist, warm air from his breath feather her cheek. Within kissing range.

Chapter 10

"I think that, uh, this is the one," Dara murmured, not daring to turn her head to look at his face. She glanced down instead to discover, with further embarrassment, her white silk blouse gaping open as she leaned over the desk. He could probably see the tops of her breasts and her lacy black bra. Had he noticed? She couldn't tell, but beside her, he'd gone absolutely still, and his breathing seemed faster, harsher. God, what was this power he had over her—to make her dizzy with lust without ever even touching her? It would be so easy to reach out and touch his hard, chiseled cheek, or to slide into his lap, or to press her breasts to his face. So easy. "This is the one." She handed him the picture and, as gracefully as she could manage, straightened and went around to the other side—the safe side—of the desk.

Mike's glittering gaze on her face was unwavering and starkly hungry. His eyes slowly slid away from hers and down over her breasts, her belly, her hips, her thighs. She could almost feel him peeling—ripping—away her clothes, piece by piece. Her nipples had hardened long ago, and he could probably see them through the thin silk of her blouse. His eyes lingered on her loins, which now throbbed so hard, she couldn't stop herself from squeezing her thighs together. When she did, the jolt of pleasure that shot through her—and the need—caused her to inhale slightly, almost imperceptibly.

His gaze jerked back to her face. He stared unblinkingly at her, a ravenous cheetah in the seconds before he chases down and devours his prey.

"Dara." He stood up and started around the desk for her. She felt his desire pulsing over her body like the beat of a drum. She wanted to wrap herself around him, taste him, and pull every inch of his body inside herself.

But then his desk phone rang, and she jumped half a mile in the air, completely jarred back to her senses. What was she doing? Oh, God, what was she doing? She'd wanted Antonio, too, and look where that'd gotten her. No, that wasn't true. What she'd felt for Antonio was a millionth of the way she felt about Mike; her passion—her *need*—for Mike was overwhelming. And terrifying.

And she would not give in to it.

"You . . . your phone," she said weakly.

A slight frown creased his forehead; he seemed bewildered, as if he'd never heard a phone ring before. Three rings. Four. Mike stood frozen, staring at her, ignoring it. "What are we going to do about this, Dara?"

The phone rang two more times, then stopped. Dara felt petrified, although her mind continued to race. She knew exactly what he meant. What were they going to do about the undeniable, overwhelming, and unwelcome attraction between them? She also knew what she wanted to do: run to him, throw her arms around him, touch him everywhere she could reach, beg him to take her home and make love to her for the rest of the day and night. And for as long after that as he would have her. Worse, she wanted to tell him how much she cared about and admired him.

But what she wanted to do and what she would do were two completely different things.

"Nothing," she whispered.

Mike's jaw tightened, and an invisible shade lowered over his eyes, blocking out the warmth and longing she'd just seen. He clenched his hands, and he shoved them violently into his pants pockets, then nodded once, curtly.

And Dara, relieved but strangely disappointed, turned and slowly went back to her own office.

Mike watched her go, then walked unsteadily over to his sofa, where he collapsed and put his head in his hands. When he touched his face, he realized, with no real surprise, he was sweating a little. He was in agony—a feverish agony of lust for Dara. What had made her lean over him like that? It was the worst torture in the world. The scent of her shampoo, the floral scent of her skin—what flower did she smell like?— all soaked through him, the way water soaks through a dry sponge. When she was that close, he went mindless with need for her.

And when she'd bent over the desk, and he'd seen the velvety tops of her lush breasts straining against her bra, he'd had to clench his fists in his lap to keep from reaching for her. He could understand now why people claimed an irresistible impulse made them do crazy things; his urge to swipe everything off his desk with his arm, throw Dara across the sleek glass, and make love to her had been almost undeniable.

What kind of man was he? He didn't care if she'd slept with his brother; he didn't care if she'd slept with a hundred other men. He wanted her. And it was getting harder and harder for him to care about Sean's feelings. Maybe Sean was in love with her, but she obviously didn't feel the same, or else she wouldn't spend so much time there at the office with him. She wouldn't be almost kissing him in storage closets and calling him at ten-thirty at night, comforting him, and looking at him with glowing eyes.

He'd always thought he was a good man, a moral man, a spiritual man. He tried to do what he thought God wanted him to do. Well, God probably didn't want him sleeping with his brother's dream woman. He'd always been quick to judge other people, to decide what was right or wrong, black or white. He didn't believe in gray. But he was running out of self-control, and if he spent much more time with Dara, if the opportunity presented itself again, if she turned her face up to his again, he wouldn't be able to stop himself from touching her. From having her.

Maybe she wasn't quite ready to acknowledge what was between them; he couldn't blame her. He'd prefer not to acknowledge it himself. He needed to focus on the firm and putting it firmly in the black. His financial success depended entirely on his staying focused and keeping his eyes on the prize. And he had the nagging feeling that as much as he obsessed over Dara now, it would be worse if they actually had a relationship.

But he didn't think they could ignore it much longer, no matter what she'd told him just now.

Was God testing him? Pushing him beyond his limits and showing him everything he'd believed himself to be was wrong? Was that why Dara was here, tempting him every day? If this was a test, he was almost willing to concede defeat and stop the agony. He needed some peace.

He burrowed his face in his hands again and willed

Dara's scent to leave his nostrils and his painful erection to recede so he could get back to work.

"Hello, stranger," said Sean when he called Dara that night at bedtime. He slumped on his unmade bed—why make a bed when you were only going to mess it up again?—with his stomach in knots. Lately, she'd stopped answering when he called. She hardly studied with him anymore. He couldn't stand it. She'd started to pull away from him, and he felt like he was coming unglued.

"Hey. It hasn't been that long, has it?"

The enthusiasm in her voice was underwhelming. She sounded like she'd received a call from the IRS. "It feels like it. Is everything okay? You've been a little distant this week."

"Ummm. I don't know," she told him. "I've got a lot on my mind, I guess."

"Like what?"

"Oh, this and that. Nothing much," she said softly.

Why wouldn't she ever open up to him and let him in, just a little? Sean wondered miserably. There were days when he felt like she could take him or leave him, that he could disappear off the face of the earth and she wouldn't even notice. Every time he saw her, she'd slipped a little farther away from him, was a little more aloof, a little more disinterested. As much as he needed this trip to D.C.—this break from the torture that was law school—he was petrified that when he got back, she would be completely out of his life.

If he didn't know better, he'd almost think she was dating someone. It was one thing to deal with her lack of romantic interest in him. He didn't know how he would handle it on that inevitable day when she became involved with someone else, and he had to stand by and watch helplessly. What kind of man would she fall for? And what did that man have that he didn't?

It was an otherwise quiet Friday in the office when the Johnson case imploded.

Desiree Campbell arrived for her appointment with Dara and Mike. Mike was very anxious to meet the most important witness for Johnson's defense. Unfortunately, he was still on a conference call for another case, so Dara went down to the reception area to greet Desiree by herself. "Thanks for coming," she told her. She found it impossible not to stare at the woman's micromini and four-inch stiletto heels—marvels of modern engineering. Dara was no expert, but she knew at some point Mike would have to tell Desiree to tone it down for the trial, which was not, after all, the MTV Video Music Awards. "Mike's anxious to meet you."

Desiree inflated like one of those puffer fish they always show on *Animal Planet,* clearly proud to be part of the action. "How's it goin'? Does Mr. Baldwin think he's gonna get Mark off?" Before Dara could answer, the heavy front door opened behind them, and they turned to see Alicia Johnson arrive. Dara was not expecting her and felt slightly alarmed to be confronted with both Johnson's wife and his presumed mistress. Even so, she smiled warmly at Alicia, who wore low-slung leather pants and a tight knit top that clung to her rounded, though still small, belly.

"Dara!" Alicia launched herself into Dara's arms. "I should have called first, but I was downtown, anyway, and I wanted to see how the case is coming and so . . ." She trailed off when she saw Desiree, but then she smiled. "Desiree!" She threw out her arms to hug the woman.

Desiree slowly pulled away from Alicia, her eyes glued to the woman's stomach. "Are you . . . are you pregnant?" she gasped.

"That's right." Alicia contentedly rubbed her belly. "We haven't seen you since the club was closed. I'm almost five months."

Dara saw Desiree flinch slightly, as if she'd received a mild shock from an electrical outlet. "Mark must be happy," Desiree said faintly.

"He is." Alicia beamed. "This is the one good thing that's happened to us lately."

Mike strode down the stairs. "Ladies, how are you? I'm Mike Baldwin." He extended his hand to Desiree. Desiree lifted her arm as though it were made of lead and shook Mike's hand. "Are you okay?" Mike shot a bewildered glance in Dara's direction before returning his attention to Desiree. "You look a little . . . ill."

That was the understatement of the year. Desiree now looked strangely grim, like she'd just been told her entire family had been killed in a house fire or something. Desiree raised her hand to her temple and rubbed it. "I am feelin' a little sick." Her eyes turned watery. "I think I need to reschedule, if you don't mind."

"Of course not," Mike said graciously.

Alicia touched Desiree's arm, and Desiree jumped away. "I can drive you home."

Desiree blinked back her tears. "No! I-I mean, don't worry. I'll be fine."

"I'll walk you out." Alicia trailed after her.

Mike watched the women leave together and tried to tamp down his rising alarm. Johnson's whole defense rode on Desiree, and there she was, acting like a fruitcake. "That went well," he muttered.

Dara threw up her hands. "That was so weird. Desiree was fine two minutes ago."

"What made her sick?"

"Seeing Alicia was pregnant," she said grimly.

"Great." He jammed his fists into his pockets. "That's
just great." He'd known all along Johnson was a lying
punk, hadn't he? Mike hated it when he ignored his gut
instinct, and it came back to bite him in the rear. He
stared after Desiree as if he could still see her. No class.
She was a tramp. Tight clothes, too much—way too
much—make-up, no bra. Breasts with implants that jig-
gled like water balloons. "Well, I think Jamal was right,"
he said thoughtfully. "Johnson wouldn't keep a woman
like that around unless he was sleeping with her."

The smallest of frowns wrinkled Dara's smooth
forehead. "'A woman like that'?"

Mike shot her a bemused look. There was something
in her tone he'd never heard before. If he didn't know
better, he'd think she was jealous of Desiree, but Dara
was too sensible to feel insecure over any woman, especially a trashy one. "Everything about Desiree
screams, 'Come do me.'"

Dara made a strangled sound. Her features twisted
until she was unrecognizable, and her eyes glittered
like shards of broken glass. "Well, if she's your type,
I'm sure she'd be yours for the taking, once the dust
settles." Her words erupted like lava from a volcano.
"She'll be needing another sugar daddy."

Mike gaped at her, too shocked to respond. She
turned to flounce off to her office, but he sprang to
life. Enraged, he grabbed her arm and whirled her
back around. She tried to yank free, but he jerked her
arm again, and she froze. Why did she have to push
him beyond his limits every single time he was with
her? Why was he cursed with her?

Suddenly, he was so sick of Dara, he wanted to vomit. He was sick of her mixed messages and her longing glances and her offers of friendship when she had to know he was obsessed with her. "Is that what you want?" he barked. She seemed paralyzed; he wasn't certain she was still breathing. He tightened his grip on her arm, threatening to cut off her circulation, but she didn't seem to notice. "Is that what you want?"

She'd gone absolutely still, her eyes wide with astonishment. Finally, she recovered herself and moved her head half an inch to the right. She meant no. Mollified, his hand still high on her arm, he pulled her closer, ignoring her cry of surprise. She turned away from him, half in profile, but he leaned down to speak in her ear. "Do you think I don't know what you want?" he taunted, letting his lips graze her ear. She whimpered, shifting restlessly on her feet, pressing her face a little closer to him. "Do you think I don't see how you look at me, Dara?"

She turned to look him fully in the face, and her gaze slipped to his lips. "Don't—"

"Answer me." Her gaze shot back to his, and she vehemently shook her head. Disgusted, he shoved her away as he released her. "You little coward." She winced, then turned and ran up the steps as if the Headless Horseman rode for her, sword raised. Mike watched her go, still agitated, but satisfied. Dara wouldn't be happy until she destroyed his last little fingerhold on sanity. But at least, she'd admitted she didn't want him with another woman. That was something. Wasn't it?

They didn't have to wait long for the other shoe to drop on the Johnson case. Desiree came back within the hour, charging through the front door, almost running into Dara, who was putting on her coat to leave for class. "Desiree!"

The woman shook with rage and sobbed hysterically, her eye make-up running all over her face. "I'm not lying for that punk no mo'!" Desiree screeched. Dara choked back her rising alarm and grabbed her by the arm, steering her past the reception area, where Amira sat at her post, with shocked eyes that threatened to swallow her entire face, and upstairs into her office, where she shut the door. Desiree sobbed and cursed the entire time. "He cain't do this to me! Does he think I'm a fool? Does he think I'm a lay down and take this mess? He done messed with the wrong woman!"

Desiree talked almost entirely to herself, and Dara gripped her arms and shook her so she'd focus. "What happened, Desiree?"

Desiree growled with fury. "That punk's been sleepin' wit his wife this whole time! *The whole time!* She's pregnant, Dara! He ain't never gonna leave her!" Her veneer of sophistication and class was gone. The streets still pulsed through Desiree, and she was too distraught to hide it.

Dara wanted to roar with frustration. All of Mike's hard work—and hers, for that matter—was about to be wasted. She wondered if Mike would ever forgive her. "You've been having an affair with Mark Johnson," she said, stating the obvious. "For how long?"

"For a year!" Desiree spat. "I been spreadin' my legs for that jerk for a year!"

"And he said he would leave Alicia," Dara prompted. Behind her, she detected a movement and turned to see Mike slip into the office, shutting the door quietly behind him. His eyes, dark and alarmed, took in the scene, but he didn't say anything, and Desiree seemed not to notice him.

"When I seen him just now, he said he just screwed her one time, and now she pregnant. That liar still claims he's gonna leave her. How she don't understand him, how they marriage ain't workin', how he was staying there for the kids. He said they didn't even sleep in the same bed no mo'." She laughed hysterically. "Well, if they ain't sleepin' together, how she get pregnant? Huh? I may be stupid, but I ain't that stupid!"

Stealing a glance at Mike's horrified face, Dara pulled Desiree over to a chair and pressed her into it, then sat in the chair next to it. "What does this have to do with the case?"

Desiree looked at Dara as if Dara's face had turned purple. "It means I wasn't wit him when Dante got shot, like he said." Dara gasped and looked at Mike, whose clenched jaw now pulsed with anger. He shook his head in disbelief but kept quiet.

"What happened?" Dara asked calmly.

Desiree snorted. "After he argued wit Dante that night, I seen he was upset, and I was scairt what he might do. So I pulled him back to the office wit me and tried to calm him down. Then he wanted me to go down on him, so I did. Then he told me to go back out front, and he was still mad. When I was leaving, he was openin' the safe. Next thing I knew, Dante got shot, and Mark was tellin' me to cover for him. Then the police came."

"What was in the safe?"

"The gun."

Dara shook her head. "The police have already tested that gun. It isn't the murder weapon."

Again Desiree gave Dara a look of withering contempt.

"He got another gun. One that ain't registered. He got it off the street. *That's* the one he shot Dante wit."

Of course, there was another gun. Thugs like Johnson probably collected guns like other people collected DVDs. "Where is this gun now?"

Desiree shrugged. "Dunno. I don't know how many shootins he got on that gun. Police would love to get they hands on it."

"But"—Dara struggled to collect her racing thoughts— "but what about the other man—the one Johnson saw arguing with Morgan? The one in the pictures?"

Desiree stared at her. "Mark made that up to give you somethin' to work wit."

Dara slumped back in her chair and covered her face with her hands. What had she done? She'd convinced Mike to take this case when it was nothing but a can of worms, as he'd known it would be. Everything had depended on Desiree, and now they had nothing. As if he knew what she was thinking, Mike squeezed her shoulder, and she gratefully covered his hand with hers. "Will you go to the police?" Mike asked Desiree.

"I dunno." Desiree shrugged and dried her eyes with a bedraggled tissue. "He pay my bills, you know? I done lied to the police already for him. Now maybe they throw me in jail wit him."

"The prosecutor might cut you a deal if you testify against Johnson."

She hauled herself to her feet, moving slowly and deliberately, as if she were under six feet of water. "I cain't think about this now. I got to go."

Dara and Mike walked her to the front door and closed it behind her. Dara felt unwillingly sorry for this woman. Maybe Desiree had gotten what she deserved for being stupid enough to sleep with a married man.

But she still felt sorry for her. Dara turned and looked at Mike.

"Don't worry, sweetheart," he told her. His face softened, and the ugliness of their last conversation vanished. "A woman like Desiree has a knack for landing on her feet."

Dara knew he was right; she trusted his judgment absolutely. "But what about Alicia?" she wondered. "Two kids already, with one on the way, and married to a man who keeps women on the side and is probably a murderer, too. What about her?" Mike opened his mouth, but before he could say anything, the front door banged open. Mark Johnson, dressed in a track-suit and athletic shoes, his face thunderous, his head lowered, and his shoulders stiff, charged in.

"Have you seen Desiree?" he asked warily.

Mike's face hardened into concrete. "My office." He turned on his heels to lead the way. "Right now."

The three of them marched stiffly up the stairs. Mike shut his office door behind them, then sat behind his desk, while Dara and Johnson sat in the chairs across from him. Wordlessly, Mike reached into his drawer and pulled out the three-ring binder containing the firm's checks. They watched while Mike cut a check and held it out to Johnson. Johnson took it. "What's this?"

"I'm returning your retainer," said Mike, through clenched teeth, "since I'm quitting."

"Why?" Johnson demanded, aghast.

"Because you lied to me, and I told you the one thing I won't tolerate from my clients is a lie."

Johnson's temples throbbed so violently, he looked like he would burst a blood vessel. "What are you talking about?"

"You lied about your alibi, and you planned to have

me put Desiree on the stand, knowing she'd lie," Mike said calmly. "If a client lies to me, then all bets are off."

"You believe her lies?" Johnson waved his arms wildly. "She's pissed off, and she's trying to get back at me. But I was with her when Dante got shot."

Mike's level gaze never wavered. "No, you weren't."

Johnson apparently decided to take another tack. "Look, man," he wheedled. "Let me talk to her. I'll bring her around. Tomorrow this whole thing'll blow over."

Dara saw that Mike's hands shook, and for a moment she actually feared he'd lunge across the desk at Johnson. "I don't know what you're suggesting." Mike shoved his chair away from his desk as he shot to his feet. The chair slammed into the bookshelves, and the bric-a-brac rattled dangerously. "But I'm an officer of the court, and I won't call a witness to testify if I think she'll lie. This conversation is over."

Johnson jumped up and stalked around the desk to stand in front of Mike. "You can't just quit on me before the trial. The judge won't let you screw me like this," he cried.

Mike's voice, hard and menacing, sent a chill up Dara's spine, and she prayed she'd never hear him use that tone with her. "If you don't agree I can withdraw, then I'll file a motion with the court. But either way, you better find yourself another lawyer, because I'm finished with you."

Johnson raised his hand to jab two fingers in Mike's face. "Who do you think you are, you little punk?" He was beyond fury, the cords in his neck straining, eyes threatening to bulge out of his head. His raw power and hatred terrified Dara, but Mike didn't flinch. "Do you know who I am?"

"Get out," Mike spat.

Johnson held his gaze for a long moment. "I'm gonna kill you for this," he said quietly, then abruptly turned and strode from the office without another word.

Dara rushed around to Mike's side of the desk. Was he scared? He didn't look scared. He looked . . . pissed. His entire body vibrated with anger. And was he furious with her for dragging him into the case in the first place? "Mike, I—"

"Dara." He sounded tired. He ran his hand through his hair. "Aren't you late for class?"

"Yes, but—"

"Dara." He braced his palms on his desk and leaned down, as if the effort to deal with her was too much right now. "Let's just call it a day. You and I had words. I fired a client and won't get paid for thousands of dollars worth of work." From his top drawer, he grabbed a stack of papers and waved them at her before throwing them back in the drawer. "I don't know how I'm going to pay all these bills. My life has been threatened. Johnson could be getting his gun right now. This could be my last ten minutes on earth. I'd rather not spend them arguing with you."

Her gut tightened with alarm until she saw the sardonic gleam in his eyes and realized he was teasing her. He wasn't scared of Johnson in the least. Well, she was scared enough for both of them. Johnson would just as soon kill Mike as look at him. "Don't joke! You know Johnson's a thug! He's already served time. Maybe you should get a restraining order. Maybe—"

Mike hung his head down again and muttered under his breath. "Dara," he said tightly when he raised his eyes, "I swear to God, you're the bane of my existence. You're like my own personal plague of locusts. One of these days, you're going to drive me right out of my mind."

She didn't care about his barbs and insults. She only wanted him safe. "Promise me you'll call the police."

He straightened. "If you promise to go away and leave me alone for the rest of the day, I'll call one of my friends on the force."

"Good." She rubbed her stomach and felt her fear ease back, allowing her to breathe again. "I really don't want anything to happen to you. If you'll call the police, I'll be able to sleep tonight."

He looked sharply at her, but then, after a long moment, gave her a lopsided smile. "To hear you tell it, if you break a fingernail, you can't sleep at night." He watched her—he looked very intent—and waited.

She did not return his smile. "The only thing that disturbs my sleep these days is *you*."

Mike gaped at her, clearly too shocked for words. Dara held his surprised gaze for several long beats and fought the urge to throw herself in his arms. And then, when the need to touch him became overwhelming and she couldn't stand the heat in his eyes, she forced herself to turn and walk away.

"So what's up with you and Sean?" Monica whispered the second she and Dara settled at their usual table in the library, after taking their practice exams. "He's been moping around like a sick puppy. He keeps asking me what's going on with you."

Dara's mouth fell open in surprise. "First of all, there is no me and Sean. Second, what makes him think anything's going on?"

"Cut the crap, Dara. You know as well as I do, Sean still likes you. Why do you think he spends so much time with you?"

"Because we're friends! There's nothing more to it

than that." Dara nervously smoothed her hair behind her ear, wondering for the millionth time if she wasn't somehow leading Sean on by spending so much time with him when she knew both that he probably still cared for her and that she would never care for him. "And Sean knows it."

Monica's lips thinned with disapproval. "He may know it, but he hasn't *accepted* it. You need to cut him loose so he can get on with his life."

"'Cut him loose?'" Agitated, Dara flapped her arms. "Please explain how I can cut him loose when he's not mine! We've never even kissed!"

Monica snorted. "Yeah. I still don't get that. I don't see why you never gave Sean any play."

Dara impatiently eyed her stack of books, wondering how much longer she'd be forced to defend her friendship with Sean when she had four lifetimes' worth of reading to do this afternoon. "I'm not attracted to him. And that will never change."

"Maybe it's because you're practically still a virgin," Monica suggested helpfully. "Maybe you should give it a little more time to see if you can warm up to him. He's such a sweet guy, Dara."

"For God's sake!" Dara cried. "Are you saying I should sleep with him to see if *sex* would make me more attracted to him?"

"No," Monica said, laughing. "I'm saying maybe you don't know much about passion."

Dara thought of Mike—how she couldn't think straight when he was within a twenty-foot radius of her—and her body immediately began to tingle in all her secret, hidden places. "Monica. You'll have to trust me on this. I know about passion."

Understanding dawned on Monica's face. Her eyes narrowed. "Enter Mike Baldwin."

"I . . . no! That's not it!" Dara looked away. Well, that was it, but she wasn't about to admit it to Monica. Anyway, just because she was attracted to Mike—oh, all right, cared about Mike—was no reason to act on it. "I don't know how many more times I have to tell you I'm focusing on school now. And I am not going to sleep with either of the Baldwin brothers, or anyone else, for that matter. Okay? Can we study now?"

Monica stared sadly at her, as if she thought Dara was the most tragically misguided person on the planet. "How long are you going to hide from life, Dara?" she asked quietly.

Dara gaped at her, too stunned by the question to think of an answer.

The ballroom looked beautiful, with candlelit tables draped with white tablecloths. The centerpieces were fragrant confections of yellow and orange roses with greens and berries, not that Dara really noticed. She'd just arrived and stood in the lobby area, searching for Mike, wondering if she should go ahead and check her velvet cloak or wait for him. She glanced at the nearby faces, her stomach churning with an unbearable excitement. All the men seemed to be staring at her with appreciative eyes, but she only cared about one man: the one who wasn't there yet. What would he think when he saw her?

She knew she looked great. She wore a black knit silk sheath, simple almost to the point of severity, except it clung to her curves like a second skin. The dress had a portrait neckline and was off the shoulder, with long, straight sleeves, a slim skirt that skimmed the floor, and slits on both sides that showed startling glimpses of her bare legs and ankle-strap sandals. Her hair was in a high, loose ponytail. Shimmering crystal chandelier earrings dangled from her ears.

Dara didn't bother asking herself what she was doing dressing for a man she'd sworn she would not get involved with; some questions were better left unanswered. She stepped around a huge potted palm, and then she saw him, standing with Jamal, turning this way and that, clearly looking for her. Finally, he saw her, and across the space of ten feet, their gazes locked and they both froze. Mike's mouth fell open. After several seconds, he wove his way through the crowd to her, leaving Jamal behind without a word.

Dara waited for him to come, stunned speechless to be in the presence of such a striking man. All she could do was stare. He wore a classically cut double-breasted black tuxedo that hugged his broad shoulders and tapered to his narrow waist as if it'd been sewn for him this afternoon. His silvery gray bow tie was elegant and beautiful. He looked fantastic, like a model who'd escaped from the pages of some overpriced fashion magazine. Looking at him was almost too much for her eyes; surely, God would smite her dead for beholding such beauty. When he stopped in front of her, she realized he smelled delectable, just-showered fresh. She wanted to bury her lips in his neck.

Mike's sparkling eyes were dark—nearly black—and smoldering now. His gaze skated over her, taking its time, performing a silent inventory. Her hair, face, shoulders, breasts, hips, legs, shoes, breasts again. He saw—and approved of—every part of her. She felt deliciously feminine under his hungry gaze—and helplessly out of control. His stare turned her body into an unknown entity. One with a heart that thundered erratically, lungs that couldn't fill all the way, breasts that swelled and ached to be rubbed and sucked, loins that grew wet and hot and throbbed violently. She was terrified that if he touched her, she would ignite like Atlanta during Sherman's march to the sea.

She was terrified he wouldn't touch her.

His gaze shot back to her face. He tried to smile, but it wouldn't come. "Another black dress, I see," he said hoarsely. Somehow he made it sound like the most lavish compliment she'd ever received; the stark hunger in his eyes communicated everything she needed to know.

"Yes." Dara's eyes never left his face; they were soft and seductive and filled with a woman's secrets. She smiled. Mike stared at her, realizing his brain had gone dead. No, that wasn't entirely true, because he could still see and smell and feel. She was gloriously beautiful. Her skin, her huge dark eyes, and her shiny black hair—they all glowed. And her scent, delicate though it was, went right through him, wrapping his mind in a thrilling fog. Control continued to evade him. Some vague, distant corner of his brain whispered that he was staring like he was a twelve-year-old boy at a pool party at the Playboy Mansion and should stop, but he ignored it.

His gaze slipped again. Her breasts. Oh, God, her breasts. He could see the upper third of them—maybe more—over the neckline of her dress. They looked so soft and smooth, such a warm, velvety brown. And her hips, flaring away from that tiny little waist he knew he could wrap his hands around. Womanly hips, hips he wanted to hold, to anchor her while she rode him and . . .

She took a step closer, and her dress shifted. His attention moved abruptly to the mile-high slits in her dress. Look at those legs. They just went on and on and on. But wait. Was she wearing panty hose? No, he saw. Her legs were bare all the way up to her . . .

He ran a shaky hand through his hair. He felt like a toddler in a department store, not allowed to touch the forbidden—but infinitely alluring—crystal and china. Since he was absolutely incapable of thinking of anything coherent to say, he reached out and took her soft velvet wrap from her and turned toward the coat-check counter, which was right there, to check it for her.

Jamal materialized from somewhere; he'd forgotten all about him. "You're hurtin' me!" he cried, looking Dara over with the frank appraisal of a man, albeit a young one. "Look at you!"

Mike frowned, still watching Dara. Absently, he found his place at the end of the line. Dara laughed, looking very pleased with herself and very alluring. "Do I look okay?" she asked Jamal. Mike seethed. Jamal looked at Dara exactly the way a cat looked at a mouse before he pounced, not that he thought Jamal would do any pouncing. Jamal took Dara's hands and held her at arm's length to study her more closely. "You look good enough to eat, Dara." His voice dropped an octave, registering husky appreciation.

Something twisted in Mike's gut. He impatiently waited for his turn, then shoved the cloak at the attendant. He did not wait for his ticket. He stalked back from the counter and stood between Dara and Jamal, nudging Jamal out of the way. "Scram, junior," he said testily. "Go find someone your own age to play with."

Jamal chortled. "Dara *is* my own age."

Mike's mouth sagged; Dara's eyes widened. *Thanks a lot, Jamal!* Everyone already knew he was eleven years older than Dara. The last thing he needed was for Jamal to remind her of that fact. Pretty soon she'd start thinking of him, Mike, as some kind of father figure or something, and wouldn't that be just great. "No, she's not," Mike growled.

"Well, she's closer to *my* age than she is to *yours*," Jamal noted triumphantly.

"Sean wanted me to come with Dara to keep young hounds like you away," Mike told Jamal, bristling openly now. Without a conscious thought, he moved closer to Dara, as if to shield her from Jamal's nonsense.

Jamal's eyes glimmered with mischief. "Yeah." He studied Mike's possessive and protective stance at Dara's side. "But who's going to keep *you* away?" He turned and went to the bar in the corner, laughing all the way.

The dinner and speeches seemed endless. Dara stared listlessly at her plate: chicken, mixed vegetables, rice. It might as well have been two shoes and a brick. She couldn't possibly eat.

Trapped at the long head table that faced the other tables, Mike watched Dara the entire time; she doubted he even blinked. And she watched him. Saw him lift his glass of red wine to his mouth and imagined a drop on his lips, longed to run her tongue along his . . .

"Why don't you give Mike a break?" Jamal whispered beside her, startling her out of her daydream. He stared intently at her, as if she were a complex mathematical theorem he intended to solve.

"Wha—what are you talking about?"

"Don't mess with me." He speared a bite of chicken and shoved it in his mouth. "You're practically making him sick. Ever since you came, he's been grouchy. You've got him walking around like there's a big black thundercloud hanging over his head. He screwed up some dates with some depositions last week. I don't know if he's eating, and he practically lives at the office. You're driving him crazy, Dara."

She fidgeted with her earrings, then realized what she was doing and shoved her hands in her lap. "I . . . he . . . ," she stammered. "He practically lives at the office because he works too hard."

Jamal looked at her as if she'd sprouted wings and a tail. "He never worked this hard before," he said flatly.

"What's any of that got to do with me?"

"Dara," he said impatiently, "don't play dumb with me. *I've* seen the way he looks at you. I'm sure *you've* seen the way he looks at you. He wants you."

She smoothed her hair uncomfortably, embarrassed to be discussing her personal life with a teenager, but not embarrassed enough to stop. From the front of the room, she saw Mike watching them with interest. Wouldn't he be thrilled to know she was discussing his personal life with Jamal? "Well," she said, "maybe that's all it is. He'll probably forget all about me as soon as I finish my internship." She was fishing, of course. But she desperately needed Jamal to reassure her and say she wasn't imagining it all and Mike really did care for her.

Jamal rolled his eyes. "Dara," he said, "you're the sorriest judge of character I've ever seen. You think Sean's a great guy, and you think Mike will forget about you. You need to wake up."

"What's wrong with Sean?"

He snorted. "The fact you have to ask that question only proves my point. Why would you spend so much time with Sean when you could have Mike? Who chooses cubic zirconias when they're giving away diamonds?"

Now she was irritated. "So Sean's a C.Z.?"

"Yeah, you could say that."

"How do you know all this, anyway? Did Mike say something to you?"

"Of course not. *I* know people, Dara. You don't need a high school diploma to read people. I've seen you and Mike together. You want to be with him as much as he wants you. You just can't figure out how to get there from here." He slid to his feet, tossed his napkin on his chair, and headed for the men's room.

She twisted around in her seat and started to call after him—she'd follow him into the men's room if she needed to—but she felt Mike's intense eyes on her, his brows raised quizzically. He could probably tell they'd been talking about him. She shrugged helplessly and looked away.

After dinner Mike and several other prominent attorneys in the city were duly recognized for their work with the poor. Dara watched while Mike walked stiffly to the podium to receive his plaque. She almost laughed at the expression of extreme discomfort on his face. She knew he hated attention like this. Still, she was proud of him.

The second the presentations were over, he rocketed back to his table, his gold-plated plaque in hand, like a laser-guided missile. He sat at the only empty place, on the other side of Amira and her date, watching Dara to the exclusion of everyone else. Dara knew they were out in public, and she should be discrete. But she couldn't look away from him. She would trade anything, do anything, give anything if only she could kiss him tonight. His obvious hunger for her only made her want him more. He stared at her with eyes so hot and intense, she almost felt feverish. Already she was soaking wet and could feel her terrible aching need for him high up between her thighs. When she could no longer resist the urge to squirm, she excused herself and headed to the bathroom.

Mike watched her go, seething and aroused. He kept his napkin tucked into his lap and prayed the fire alarm wouldn't go off and force him to stand up and reveal the bulging front of his pants. How had she done this to him? How could that one girl worm her way under his skin and into his blood and his dreams and his every waking thought? Why couldn't he think about something else besides Dara for one lousy second out of sixty? Why did he want—no, crave—her so much? To the point where his skin felt like it was on fire. To the point where the idea of having sex with someone else had become inconceivable. To the point where he almost felt like his life would never be complete unless he could possess her.

What was so special about Dara? Sure, she was beautiful, but every woman he was with was beautiful. Why couldn't he isolate the source of her powerful allure, then root it out forever?

"Mike?"

When would he have his life back? He didn't have time for this nonsense. He had a firm to run, cases to work, clients to bill. To accomplish his goals, he needed a clear, thinking brain free of clutter and distractions— something he couldn't seem to maintain when Dara was anywhere in the vicinity. Take the Johnson case. She'd talked him into it even though he'd known Johnson was trouble; he'd taken the case because he couldn't stand to tell her no. Then he'd worked hundreds of hours on it before he'd had to quit and return the retainer. And those were hundreds of hours he could have been working on *paying* cases.

"Mike?"

So now he was out $25K and had no real idea how he would earn it back anytime soon. And the scary part was he'd been more concerned with making sure Dara didn't feel guilty about the whole incident than he had been with figuring out how he'd pay bills next month. What was that about? And why . . .

"Mike!"

Mike jerked and looked up to find Jamal looking at him from across the table, with a knowing little smirk on his face. "Did you say something?"

"Yeah. Congratulations." Jamal smiled broadly. "You deserve the award."

Mike grinned and tried to tear his mind away from Dara. "Thanks, man. But you're still not getting that raise you asked about."

Jamal shook his head sadly. "Didn't anyone tell you slavery was abolished about a hundred years ago?"

"It was closer to a 150 years ago, you ignoramus." Mike sipped his ice water. "If you'd study a little harder, you'd know that."

"If you didn't work me like a slave, I'd have time to study harder."

"When you pass the GED in two weeks, we'll talk about a raise. But not before."

"When I pass the GED, I'm outta your little sweatshop operation."

"If you think someone else'll hire your sorry butt, then good riddance."

Jamal snorted.

Mike stood and dropped his napkin in his chair. "You ready? Let's go."

Jamal frowned. "What about Dara? Aren't you gonna wait till she gets back and tell her good-bye?"

Mike didn't care for Jamal's disapproving tone. And he had no intentions of getting anywhere near that siren in the black dress again tonight. He planned to avoid the rocks at all costs, and he considered himself lucky he'd made it this far into the evening unscathed. "*You* tell her," he said. "I'm gonna give our ticket to the valet. I'll meet you in the lobby."

Forty-five minutes later Dara, still in her dress, stood in front of her bathroom sink, staring at herself in the mirror, waiting and agitated. She had no idea what she was waiting for. She was agitated because her body was on fire for Mike, and the only relief she could envision was to go ahead and sleep with him and get him out of her system. Except she had an awful, unshakable feeling that nothing would get him out of her system, least of all actually making love to him.

Slowly, she fished the bobby pins out of her hair until it fell down around her shoulders. Her reflection in the mirror was unrecognizable: feverishly bright eyes, flushed face, heaving breasts. Was this her? Certainly, it wasn't the Dara she'd ever known before.

All in all, it was a good thing Mike had left the dinner without saying good-bye to her. What could they possibly say to each other? He'd told her he had no time for romance, and she was devoted to law school. He was her boss and Sean's brother. He'd never made a declaration of love, or anything even close. Come to think of it, they barely even got along. Why on earth would she consider sleeping with him?

But, God, why couldn't she stop wanting to?

Well, she couldn't stare at her reflection all night. It was past time for bed, and her toes, still strapped into her slinky stilettos, had started to protest. She walked into her bedroom and perched on the edge of her queen-sized bed to take off her shoes, but before she could undo the first tiny buckle, she heard a quiet knock on her door. Suddenly, she realized exactly what she'd been waiting for.

She opened the front door and saw Mike standing there, with glittering eyes, his color high. His bow tie dangled on either side of his collar, and he'd undone the first couple of buttons on his shirt to reveal the top of his snowy undershirt. Without offering any greeting, he rudely brushed by her, hands shoved deep in his pockets, then turned to face her as she shut the door again. Their gazes locked, and when Dara felt the depth of his rage—at her—she staggered back a few steps until she hit the door.

Chapter 11

This was a Mike she'd never seen before. She'd seen him angry and irritated, and all the permutations in between. But this was different; this was a Mike teetering on the edge of his control, with one foot already off the precipice. A dangerous Mike who clearly thought she'd committed some heinous offense and was here to demand justice, if not extract revenge. Her knees began to tremble; each breath she managed to take into her constricted lungs felt like a major victory.

"I asked you the other day," he began, voice and body vibrating with anger. "Do you remember? I said, 'What are we going to do about this, Dara?' Remember that?"

Some primitive instinct told her not to answer, that answering would only enrage him further. She didn't dare blink or move a muscle. His gaze raked over her, lingering on her mouth, then her breasts. Just like that, her nipples and her sex tightened and swelled painfully.

His cruel mouth twisted. "And you said, 'Nothing.' Is this ringing a bell, Dara?" As if he didn't trust himself within arm's length of her, he moved away in the small foyer, stopping and turning back to face her from a distance of about six feet. "You stood there and you told me, 'Nothing,' like we could just ignore it." He made a harsh sound that was half laugh, half bark. "Well, that was like saying we could ignore it if a hydrogen bomb went off in the backyard."

He pulled one of his hands out of his pocket and shoved it through his hair before he rammed it back in. The movement drew her attention, and she gasped helplessly. The front of his pants bulged hugely. He was every bit as aroused as she was.

Of course, he'd followed her gaze. He snorted. "That's right, Dara," he said, his voice rising dangerously. "I want you so much, I can't even see straight. I can't sleep, I can't eat, and I can't work. And I can't stay away from you."

"Oh, God," Dara whispered, panting now. Frozen, her back still glued to the door, she closed her eyes so she could block out his sensuous mouth and broad shoulders, so she would no longer see the evidence of the way his body strained for her. But closing her eyes did not stop the lurid images from dancing through her brain: Mike naked and in her arms, the two of them tangled together in her bed, Mike inside her, thrusting and pounding, finally easing the painful ache lodged between her thighs whenever she thought of him.

"So I am asking you again, and I want you to give me a real answer this time." Lured by his voice, which sounded calmer now, Dara opened her eyes, only to find his face contorted as if he were in pain. For one panicked second, she thought she should jerk open the front door and run away before he spoke again—before the verbal blow fell—but he remained rooted to his spot, and she knew he would never physically hurt her. A fine sheen of perspiration covered his face, and his chest heaved as if he had run up twelve flights of stairs. "I don't want any more of your nonsense, and I don't want you to look at me like you don't know what I'm talking about. I want you to tell me what we are going to do about this!" His voice rose at the end, cracking through the foyer like a rifle shot.

Dara understood then: he was leaving it entirely up to her. He was older, more experienced, and her boss; he'd made up his mind he would let her decide whether they should become involved. And she knew that, as much as he might want her, if she told him no now, he would leave and that would be the end of the matter.

But she did not want him to leave.

The thought of Mike touching her was terrifying, but the thought of him leaving was infinitely worse. And so, stomach quivering, heart racing, breasts swollen and aching, sex pulsing and wet, Dara peeled herself away from the door. Slowly, as if in a daze, she crept toward Mike. His eyes widened with surprise. If possible, his breathing became even harsher, more pronounced. She stopped directly in front of him, where the scalding heat from his body radiated over her in waves. She looked up into his strained, intent eyes, then moved half a step closer, so that her entire body pressed along his, breasts to chest, belly to groin, thigh to thigh.

Mike stiffened, panting, but didn't move.

His body felt strange and new, but also familiar and comfortable. Thrilling. She planted her hands on his sides beneath his jacket and slid them up his chest, where his heart thundered under her fingertips. Her lips found the hollow in his neck beneath his jawbone and nuzzled him, soaking up his delicious, just-showered scent. Mike gasped. Finally, she reached up to stroke his hard, rough jaw. His eyes drifted closed, and his face twisted again, but this time she did not think he was in pain. She raised her face, pulled him down, and slowly, painstakingly, fitted her lips to his.

Once, twice, she brushed her mouth over his. Still, he didn't move, although she could feel his enormous power, as if something deep within him strained to get free. But when she touched her tongue to his lips, he sprang to life, crying out. His passion unleashed now, he frantically pulled her into his crushing embrace, too feverish to be gentle. A large hand closed over her sensitive nape, anchoring her, pulling her closer. His mouth—hot, wet, and demanding—slanted over hers, insisting on complete surrender. She gave it. She parted her lips and greedily tasted him, savoring the flavor of the merlot in his mouth. Her hands went to the back of his neck, then into the coarse silk of his hair. Tormented, she pressed her body against his until they were molded together like two parts of a whole. She couldn't get close enough—nowhere near close enough.

Mike's frenzied hands roamed her body, his fingers first twining in her hair, then massaging her bare shoulders, then dipping to the small of her back and lower still. He cupped her, his hands strong and insistent. Finally, he tore his lips away from hers. "You feel so good, angel." His hot breath in her ear made her pant. "I want you so much."

"I want you. *I want you.*"

He gripped her butt and, lifting her on her toes, insistently rubbed his raging erection against her sex. His hard, demanding body found the place at the top of her thighs that answered his touch and begged for more. "Mike." The tension within her grew until she thought she'd explode and shower to the floor in a thousand shimmering pieces. "I need you, Mike. Please. *Please*." The ache felt unbearable now. The only cure was for Mike to impale her, hard. And if he wanted her to beg, she would happily do so. "*Please*."

He backed her against the wall and stooped to press his lips to the valley between her breasts, his hands squeezing them from the sides. "Oh, God," she cried. His hot breath heated her dress until it singed her skin. His mouth found her nipple and bit gently, sending an excruciating jolt of pleasure directly to her sex. "Oh, God." Her arms tightened around his neck, holding his head in place.

He stood up abruptly and kissed her again, deeply and ruthlessly. *His skin,* she thought dazedly. She had to feel his skin on hers. She slid her hands over his granite shoulders and beneath the heavy silk of his jacket, pushing it down his arms and out of her way, but his shirt, crisp with starch, blocked her. Dara had never been so frustrated. She wanted to rip his shirt open down the front and hear the satisfying skitter of his buttons on her floor. She jerked the undershirt down, clearing a patch of smooth brown skin. Quickly, she pressed her mouth and tongue to it. Oh, but his skin was sweet. Smooth and warm and delicious and unbearably sweet.

He made a noise that was half groan, half choking laugh, as she slid her open mouth up the side of his neck to his ear and nipped. "You were made for me, Dara." His hand found hers and fitted it to the hard, hot, heavy ridge in the front of his pants. "Do you see what you do to me?"

Eagerly, she gripped and rubbed him, desperate to explore. She slid her palm down and up his length; he stiffened, gasping. She raised her dazed eyes to look at him. A fine sheen of perspiration shone on his strained face and a wondrous sense of power ran through her. *She'd* done this to him. She rubbed him again, and he groaned. "Do you like that?"

Suddenly, he seemed to reach his limit; his body went rigid. "Don't!" He roughly grabbed both her hands and slammed them over her head, pinning them to the wall. His eyes glinted dangerously. She didn't like being interrupted, but on the other hand, his power and strength—his domination—thrilled her. Still, she thrashed beneath him, testing him, trying to break away. "Let me go!"

His grip on her wrists tightened. Holding her now with just one of his hands, his other hand slid down her side to her thigh, finding the slit in her dress. His fingers glided under her dress and up the inside of her thigh to the edge of her panties, then stopped. Dara froze and waited. A strangled sound came from her throat. "*Please.*"

He stooped until they were face-to-face, close enough for her to see the primitive and merciless gleam in his eyes. "You like torture? Is that it?" His fingers inched under her panties. Dara panted, unbearably excited and desperate for him to stroke her. His fingers skimmed her flesh—just barely. She whimpered. The touch was excruciatingly intimate, but not enough. She struggled to breathe and wondered vaguely if she'd start to hyperventilate. "Do *you* like *that*?" he asked softly. She couldn't speak. The pleasure he gave her was incomprehensible.

His fingers touched her again, firmer now. She

writhed beneath him. "I asked you a question, Dara." His glittering eyes held hers. They were all she could see. His thumb found the center of her very existence and rubbed it, circling. "Do you like that?"

"Yes!"

"Should I stop?"

The tension grew and grew. She pumped her hips, following where he led. "Please, Mike—"

"Should I stop?"

"No! I . . ."

She shattered, crying out his name over and over again. Agonizing pleasure pierced her womb, exploding. He quickly freed her hands and caught her around the waist before she could collapse in a puddle on the floor. He held her close until she caught her breath. Finally, he pulled away a little to look down at her. His eyes were intent, and he did not smile. "Did you like that, angel?"

She stared at him, too stunned to speak. She tried to smile, but her mouth wouldn't cooperate. She nodded. His lips turned up a little at the edges, and he leaned down to kiss her, gently now. Incredibly, the tension in her belly began to build again, and she pressed her soft sex, still pulsing and soaking wet, against his rigid arousal. His hands found her butt again and held tight, grinding against her. "Dara." His hoarse voice whispered in her ear, driving her wild. "I need to come inside you." His tongue traced the curve of her ear, and she cried out. "Please, *please*, sweetheart. Let me make love to you."

Dara found herself nodding. She pulled his face down again for another deep, urgent kiss. Mike increased the pressure on her butt until he lifted her off her feet. The deep slits in her dress let her wrap her legs tightly around his waist, never breaking the kiss. Mike took the opportunity to run his hands up and down her bare thighs before he swung her around and effortlessly carried her into her bedroom. He lowered her to the bed, murmuring incomprehensibly. When he let her go, she scooted back against the pillows and watched as he swiftly unbuttoned his shirt, his glittering gaze glued to hers. He pulled his shirt off; the undershirt quickly followed.

Dara let herself stare. Smooth, broad, sculpted shoulders tapered to the hard slabs of his chest. Every well-defined muscle of his belly rippled as he planted his hands on either side of her and leaned over her. She put her hands on his face and leaned up for his kiss. His hands found the zipper to her dress between her shoulder blades and eased it down. The sound startled her, reminding her of another dress, another zipper, another man.

Let me make love to you, Dara.

She shoved the voice far away and tightened her arms around Mike's neck, pulling him down onto the bed, on top of her. "I need you, angel," he whispered. "I need you so much."

I need you, Dara.

Mike's weight pressed her deep into the mattress. His hands reached up to ease the now-open dress away from her shoulders, and she wriggled a little to help him. The dress slid to her waist. "Ahhh, Dara." Mike buried his mouth between the cups of her black strapless bra. "Dara."

Dara.

She went rigid; her eyes flew open. Mike stilled immediately and raised his head to look at her with unfocused eyes. "What is it, sweetheart? Did I hurt you?"

Dara pulled away from him—he seemed to have a hard time letting her go—and sat up. She was still panting with desire, but suddenly her blood turned cold. Once, long ago, there'd been another man, another night, and another morning after. And there had been pain and betrayal and broken promises.

And Mike hadn't even made her any promises.

She turned to him helplessly. He waited, his concerned eyes wide. "Tell me, sweetheart. What is it?"

"I . . . I can't," she whispered, embarrassed. "I'm so sorry! I . . . I didn't mean to lead you on! But I'm not ready for this."

Mike's face remained strained, but he took a deep breath, and she felt him very firmly leash the passion he'd let run free moments ago. He cupped her cheek and pressed a lingering kiss to her temple. Then he pulled her close, and she laid her head on his chest. "It's okay, angel," he said soothingly. "I understand. Shhh."

Dara clung to him; she didn't ever want him to let her go. She prayed he didn't hate her now. At the very least, he was probably very sorry he'd let himself get so aroused by a silly, inexperienced girl who couldn't decide what she wanted. "I'm sorry, Mike," she said again. "God, I do want you."

His arms tightened, and he rocked her. "Don't apologize. Shhh."

And he held her like that for a long time.

After a while Dara fell asleep, and Mike forced himself to let her go, climb out of her warm bed, dress, and go home. When he got there—the car must have driven itself, because he had no recollection of the drive—he shrugged out of his jacket, tossed his keys on the foyer table, and stalked into the living room, where he threw himself down on the sofa. He didn't bother turning on any of the lights. His stomach was one big knot of frustration, and his groin felt like it would explode—literally explode, not the pleasurable kind—any second. Every part of his body and soul was in agony.

Glancing around the room, he saw the outlines of the beautiful furniture he'd picked out. Leather pieces, mahogany, colors and patterns he'd pored over. He remembered how excited he'd been two years ago, when he bought the house, how he'd saved and budgeted, how he'd lovingly restored the hardwood floors and painted the walls and fixed drips and chips and cracks. He thought of how he loved it here. How he loved his practice, how proud he'd been of himself for all he'd accomplished and all he had.

He'd trade everything for a night with Dara.

Panic roiled around in his belly along with the lust. He'd let things go too far; he felt trapped and had no visible means of escape. He cared for her—deeply. There was no getting around it, no acting like he didn't, no wishing it away, no ignoring it, no pretending it was just lust. Not anymore. He admired her will and determination, her pride and strength. She made him laugh, comforted him, and infuriated him. And when he touched her—oh, God. His groin tightened even further at the thought. He shouldn't have let things go so far tonight, of course, but he'd been greedy. When would he ever have the chance to touch her again? And Dara's feverish response to him had driven him to the brink of insanity.

Dara was a complication he didn't need and didn't want.

Had he ever wanted another woman? He couldn't

remember. He doubted he'd ever want another woman now. He shifted uncomfortably; his tuxedo pants strained across his crotch, threatening to make him a eunuch. He could still smell her musky scent on the tips of his fingers, which certainly didn't help matters any. Eventually, he'd have to force himself to wash his hands—maybe in a week or so. Briefly, he considered going into the bathroom to finish himself off, just to get a little relief, but that would be about as satisfying as eating a nice Spam casserole after having a bite of filet mignon.

He remembered the sweetness of her mouth moving under his, how tightly she'd held him, her look of dazed ecstasy and surprise when she'd climaxed. Had she ever come like that before? Somehow he didn't think so. He felt an overwhelming satisfaction. No one else could love her like he could.

Leaning forward on the sofa, he rested his elbows on his knees, put his head in his hands, and squeezed his temples until he saw stars. Would he stop thinking about Dara if he crushed his own head in his hands? Probably not.

Thank God, she'd come to her senses; he certainly wouldn't have. And what a disaster it would have been if he'd stayed. He would never have been able to leave in the morning and pretend nothing happened. Nor would he have been satisfied with his one night with her. Ten thousand nights with that kind of pleasure would never be enough.

But pleasure wasn't a good enough reason to use Dara like that. He knew if he made love to her, he would inevitably hurt her. She was young and inexperienced. She would probably think she'd fallen in love with him. And even though he cared for her, he couldn't return feelings like that, nor could he offer her a commitment of any kind. He had no room in his life for Dara. He was committed to work, and to Sean.

And he'd never be able to break his brother's heart and tell him he'd made love to Dara.

The thought of Sean's horrified face was ice water in his veins. Sean would never forgive him. Not now, not in five years, not in twenty. And he couldn't throw away his relationship with his brother, strained though it was. He wouldn't do it to Sean, and he wouldn't do it to his mother.

Well, he might as well go to bed. He heaved himself to his feet—he felt like he'd just finished the Ironman Triathlon—and started up the steps when the phone on the hall table rang, startling him.

He stared at it suspiciously. Something told him not to answer, but he couldn't do it. "Hello?" he barked when he snatched it up.

"What's up, man?"

Sean! Mike's heart lurched to a stop, and he almost dropped the phone. What did he want? He thought wildly that Dara must have called him in Washington and told him what happened, but he didn't think she'd do that. Anyway, why would she feel the need to call Sean and confess? Both she and Sean had said their relationship was platonic. And he believed them.

Didn't he?

"Hey, Sean." He clutched a chair for support. "What's going on? You still in D.C.?" He slumped into the chair and braced himself.

Sean paced in front of the window in his hotel room, pulling back the sheer panel on one side. He could just make out the Capitol dome in the distance. "Yeah. How, uh . . . how was the dinner?"

"Good."

Sean realized he was pacing and stopped, dropping into the chair by the window. Immediately, his right leg started to jiggle, an annoying habit he thought he'd conquered years ago. He pressed down on it with his hand. He couldn't remember when he'd last felt this edgy. Every muscle in his body was clenched tight. "Did Dara get home okay?" He felt like the biggest loser on the planet—obsessed over a woman who'd never even kissed him. It galled him no end to have to call his older brother to find out if he knew where Dara was, but he was desperate. It'd been a mistake to come to D.C. in the first place. All he could think about was Dara and how he could possibly get her to just give him a chance.

"Yeah." Mike sounded surprised. "She went home a while ago."

Sean's leg started shaking again, harder than before. This time he didn't even bother to try to stop it. "Are you sure she got inside okay?"

"Yes," Mike said tightly. "What's going on?"

"Nothing," Sean said, embarrassed. "I called a couple of times to check in. She didn't answer."

Mike didn't say anything for a long time. "She's probably in the shower, man."

There was a new, funny quality to his voice, like he'd selected his words very carefully. Sean snorted. Right. Well, she'd been in the shower for a good hour or more, because he'd called several times. He didn't know what to do. "I don't know what to do about Dara—"

"Sean," Mike said hoarsely, "I don't feel comfortable—"

"I love her, man." Sean's voice broke. "And I don't

know what to do. She won't give me the time of day. And lately, I almost have the feeling there's someone else." He didn't know why he'd made the confession, especially to Mike, of all people. Mike thought he was a loser. Maybe he hoped Mike would have some advice, some insight that would help. He knew Dara; she spent more time at the office with Mike than she did with him. And he'd felt a little closer to Mike lately. Whatever the reason, there was still that part of him he'd never been completely able to tamp down— the part that thought his older brother could help him solve his problems. Mike didn't answer him. Was he even still there? What was going on? "Hello?"

"I don't think there's anyone else, Sean," Mike said faintly. "I'm sure everything's fine."

"You're probably right."

"Anyway, isn't she picking you up from the airport tomorrow?"

"No. Mama is." He walked to the minibar and opened it, surveying the choices. Peanuts, candy bars, juice, vodka, gin, scotch. "I'll let you go."

"Sean," Mike said carefully, "you're doing okay, aren't you?"

Sean froze. "Of course, I'm okay," he snapped. "What do you take me for?"

"Okay, well . . . Have a safe trip."

"Right." He reached for the scotch, distracted now. God, he needed a drink.

Mike hung up feeling like he'd been kneed in the stomach. *I don't think there's anyone else.* Had those words actually come out of his mouth? What kind of lying, backstabbing jerk had he become? Because those were the exact words his college roommate had said to him when he'd confided he suspected Debbie was cheating on him. And his roommate had shrugged thoughtfully and said, "I don't think there's anyone else." Just like that. So believable. "I don't think there's anyone else." Only he'd come to find out, *he* was the one who'd been doing Debbie the whole time.

So now here he was stabbing Sean in the back the way he'd been stabbed in the back. Did anyone anywhere tell the truth anymore? Was there a trustworthy person anywhere on the planet? Certainly, it wasn't him. God, he hated himself.

He swore it would never happen again.

But the panic remained, along with a little voice that kept telling him over and over again, *It's too late*.

Mike, portable disk player in hand, stepped out his front door onto the porch and started to stretch for his jog. It was the kind of late fall day he normally loved: crisp and clear, the sky a brilliant blue, almost too bright to look at. But today the weather mocked him. This was a day for lovers to walk in the park, then come home and sip hot chocolate and make love in front of a crackling fire. He and Dara weren't lovers and never would be.

He hadn't slept a wink. Then he'd gone to the early services at church, like always. But ever since he'd met Dara, church had lost all of its soothing, healing qualities. So now he thought he'd try a run, not that he expected that to help, either. But he had to do something, and he might as well try to burn off a little of his edginess and sexual tension. And maybe, if he ran really hard, he could go thirty seconds or so without seeing Dara's face.

An SUV pulled into his driveway, and he straightened

from his lunge to watch it, with only a passing curiosity. He didn't much care who it was. But he realized with a jolt it was Dara. She got out and slowly came toward him. One look at the dark circles under her eyes told him she hadn't slept, either. She stopped short, looking shy, and smiled. "I should've called first."

"No. It's okay. Are you . . . How are you today?"

She flushed prettily, then looked away. After a moment she looked back at him, a satisfied, sensual half smile on her sweet lips. "I'm good."

He grinned idiotically, enormously pleased with himself. "Good."

A flash of heat, hotter than ever, pulsed between them, and his heart contracted, hard. Then the panic rose in his throat. He quickly looked away, his smile dying.

"It's beautiful here, Mike." She turned away, making a show of looking at the house and yard. "When on earth do you find time to take care of the yard?"

"On the weekends. It's pretty relaxing to cut the grass, actually. It helps me unwind."

"Off for a jog?" She smiled nervously.

"Yeah. I usually run every day. It helps me clear my mind." He snorted and felt his jaw flex. That was a lie. His mind hadn't been clear for weeks, and unless he ran to Seattle and back, his mind wouldn't be clear today, either. "It used to help me clear my mind, anyway. But you probably didn't come to talk about the yard or my exercise routine."

Why had she come? Having her here was exquisite torture, partly because his body reacted so violently to her presence. He was like Pavlov's dog at this point; he caught sight of her, and his mouth began to water, his blood to heat. But mostly, it was upsetting because here was where he wanted her. Watching TV with him in the great room, eating at the kitchen table, sleeping snuggled up to him in the big king-sized bed with the new down comforter he'd bought for the winter. Having her here reminded him of all the things he wanted that he shouldn't want and would never have. And suddenly, he was furious with her for turning his life upside down and for turning him into a man he didn't recognize: someone who would betray his brother in a heartbeat.

Interwoven with all that was the panic, the anxiety. He was afraid to hear what she would say, afraid of what he would say back to her. Worse, was afraid she would leave and terrified he would beg her to stay.

"I thought we could talk if you have a minute."

He nodded silently, swallowed his fear, and slowly turned to lead her into the house.

Dara took everything in with appreciative eyes as they walked through the foyer. She saw a beautiful rug—Indian, maybe—and a table with a lamp and mirror, and then a great room with two overstuffed brown sofas and several chairs and end tables and an entertainment armoire. The house was immaculate and masculine but lovely. She sat on the end of one of the sofas, and he sat at the other end, both trying to maintain a neutral safe distance. Mike stared intently at her.

She'd changed her mind; it was as simple as that. Last night, as much as she'd wanted to make love to him, she'd pushed Mike away. In the early morning hours, after he left—she'd grown cold without his body heat and had woken to find him gone—she'd realized what she'd done: she'd punished Mike for Antonio's betrayal. She'd assumed Mike would make love to her, then do something terrible to break her heart, just like Antonio had done.

In the cold light of day, it all seemed so ridiculous! She was a woman now, not that starry-eyed little girl. And she knew what she wanted: Mike. She cared for him, and he cared every bit as much for her. She knew it. She didn't need him to pledge undying love; she could see how he felt every time he looked at her. Mike would never hurt her. Never. So she'd come back to work things out and take a chance with him.

"I'm sorry about last night," she said. "You must think I'm so ridiculous."

His face softened. "I don't think anything like that, Dara."

She'd never felt more terrified, more exposed. Never in her life had she made the first move with a man. Complicating matters enormously was the fact that the warmth of his gaze made it nearly impossible to speak. She swallowed convulsively. "About last night. I was wondering . . . Could we try again?"

His mouth twisted into that pained look she'd seen before. "Try again?" he asked conversationally, as if she'd said she would like to try bowling again.

Fear crept up her spine. He was acting so strangely; his gaze was on the floor, on his hands clenched on his thighs, the window, everywhere but on her. That brick wall was there again, the one he put up to hide his real feelings from her. She could feel it. "Yes," she said faintly.

It took him a very long time to speak. "Why should we try again?"

"'Why?'" she cried, horrified. Why was he playing dumb with her? Wasn't it he who had kissed her senseless last night? She might have been inexperienced, but she wasn't stupid. She knew the chemistry between them was extraordinary. "Do you need to ask?"

"Dara," he said, a warning in his voice. "I hope you weren't thinking we would . . . get involved with each other."

"You don't think we should . . . get involved?" The very idea was incomprehensible to her. Surely, that was not what he meant.

He wouldn't look her in the face. "No."

Hysteria crept into her voice. "Why not?"

He sprang to his feet and turned his back to her, his shoulders rigid as he shoved his hands into his pockets. "Because."

"Because why?" she demanded of his back.

"Because." He still did not face her. "We don't have any kind of a future together."

She was tired of talking to his back. "Why not?" She jumped up and grabbed his sleeve, forcing him to face her, then dropped her hand immediately when she saw the glittering anger in his eyes. "Why did you come last night?"

He snorted. "I thought it was obvious."

"Because you wanted me?"

Mike gave her a sardonic little smile that didn't engage his eyes. "'Want?'" He said it as if he'd never heard the word before. "*Want?*' I *want* a rare steak for dinner. I *want* a hot shower at the end of a long day. The way I lust after you is something else again. But why not? I'm not immune. You're beautiful. You're sexy. Who wouldn't want you? But I'll get over it."

Her vision faded, and for one second she wondered if she might faint. Surely, she wasn't hearing these words come out of his mouth—that he wanted her the same as any other beautiful woman he may have stumbled across in his travels. "You . . . you'll get over it?"

"Yes." He took his hands out of his pockets and clenched them into fists at his side. "I'm a big boy. I know I can't always have everything I want. It'll be better when you finish your internship, and I don't have to see you every day. And I'm sure I'll meet someone new soon enough."

Dara stood there, stunned, trying to make sense of what she believed in her heart to be true and what she heard. Mike's tone was light and cavalier, but she couldn't reconcile it with the strain on his face. And still he avoided her eyes. "That's it, then?" Somehow she remained upright even though her legs wanted to give out. "You want me, but we can't be together, and you'll forget me as soon as I'm gone and you meet someone else? That's it?"

His eyes were lowered now, studying his shoes. "That's it," he said, his voice nearly inaudible.

"But *why*?" she cried. "You haven't given me a reason! Tell me why."

He shrugged carelessly, and in that moment she hated him. "You want a reason? Pick one: Sean would kill me, I don't want a relationship right now, and I would wind up hurting you. Is that good enough? Is that what you want to hear?"

She should have known when she'd been humiliated enough for one day, but she couldn't let the matter drop without hearing him speak the words. "Are you saying," she said as calmly as she could when her throat was constricted with rising panic, "that you don't feel anything else for me?"

He had his back to her again, and his voice was husky now. "Don't make me say things to hurt you, Dara."

Probably good advice, but she still needed to hear it from his mouth. "You tell me," she cried, "because I don't believe a word you've said to me today." She noted, with detached surprise, that the hand she reached up to brush a tear from her cheek was shaking. Then she dropped her hand and stared at him, waiting.

Chapter 12

Mike's frustrated fury collected in the back of his throat, a bile threatening to choke him at any moment. He'd waited and waited for this moment; Dara wanted to be with him. And he wanted to pull her into his arms and forget about Sean. He didn't care what promises he'd made to his sick mother. So what kind of man did that make him? What kind of brother? What kind of son?

But he couldn't force back the panic. It was worse than ever. The bottom line was that—whatever the reason, and he didn't *know* the real reason—he couldn't be with Dara. He just couldn't.

Finally, he forced himself to turn and look at her. She had her chin up, but her lips trembled, and tears shimmered in her eyes. She did not meet his eyes. He wanted to throw himself at her feet, to beg her to forgive him, to take a chance with him. But he felt paralyzed. He had to get over Dara and make sure Dara got over him. He had to get her out of here and make sure she never gave him a second thought. He watched her, waiting. Finally, she raised her teary eyes to his. "Dara." She seemed to brace herself. "I just want to screw you."

She flinched as if he'd spit on her. Then she slapped him—hard—across the face. He blinked several times. Of course, he'd deserved that. He was a lying jerk, and just hours after he'd gotten home from church. He was surprised lightning didn't strike him dead on the spot, because he'd denied his one greatest truth: he wanted Dara, wanted to be with her. He might as well deny he loved his mother, or that he loved God. But he had to do it. He resisted the urge to rub his throbbing jaw. She packed quite a wallop, but the physical pain was nothing—*nothing*—compared to seeing the hatred and pain in her sweet eyes.

She straightened her spine and raised her chin with the modicum of dignity he'd left her. "You're a liar. And a coward."

On Wednesday, Jamal sauntered into Dara's office while she edited a memorandum. She glanced up at him, then quickly lowered her head as if she was terribly busy and couldn't spare the time to talk. Jamal did not take the hint. "Well, well, well." He collapsed into one of her chairs, propped his feet on her desk, and crossed his ankles. "Look who's here."

She didn't care for his mocking tone. Not today. Most likely, he'd come to ask her about Mike, a subject she couldn't bear. She decided to play dumb. "What are you talking about?" Her eyes were wide and innocent. "I've been here all week." Well, she'd been present in the building but had spent an inordinate amount of time in the powder room, the supply room, and the kitchen, the three places she was least likely to see Mike.

Jamal huffed. "Cut the innocent act. Amelia Earhart is easier to find than you are."

"What do you want?" she snapped, all pretense of civility gone now.

He leaned forward in his chair, watching her intently. "Did anything happen with you and Mike Saturday, after you dropped me off?"

Dara scowled. Why did Jamal have to bother her? Couldn't he see how miserable she was? It was all she could do to come into the office and risk seeing Mike. Why did Jamal always poke and prod her, trying to push her buttons? And why did he have his feet on her desk? She stood and pushed his feet down. "What are you talking about?"

"Don't waste my time with the denials, Dara." He carefully replaced his feet on the desk. "You and Mike were staring at each other all night. I expected you to leave together before dinner."

"Why don't you ever bother Mike with your little opinions and theories?" Her voice rose to a screech. "Why can't you leave me alone?"

"Dara." Jamal lowered his feet and leaned toward her, serious now. "You gotta understand Mike. He feels guilty. Not just about you."

"What do you mean?"

"I mean he's older than Sean. Smarter. Better looking. He's always been successful. Probably always will be. Sean's a screwup." Dara sputtered a protest on Sean's behalf, but Jamal waved her off. "Right now Sean has a chance to make something of himself, and Mike won't do anything to mess that up. No matter how much he may want to."

She pressed her hands to her eyes for a long moment and choked back the grapefruit-sized lump in her throat. She wanted so much to believe him. "Jamal."

She let her hands drop to the desk. "All Mike wants is to sleep with me. He's made that painfully clear."

He shook his head and roared with laughter. "You're just like Oedipus."

"Oedipus?" she cried. "You're comparing my life to a Greek tragedy?"

"Yeah. You got eyes, but you can't see what's right in front of you."

"What are you talking about?"

"Don't be such a stupid idiot, Dara." His smile was gone now. "Mike's so in love with you, he can't think straight."

If only that were true! "I think it's just about sex for him," she persisted.

"Dara," said Jamal, exasperated now, "Mike can have sex with whoever he wants. I've seen plenty of women throw themselves at him. Damn. They basically get one look at him and start taking their panties off."

She grimaced. "Thanks for the image."

"Why would he be this unhappy if it was just about sex? Why would he risk breaking his brother's heart if it was just about sex?"

Jamal made some sense, but still. "How do you know?"

"I told you before. I know people."

"I think there's more to it than that," she said, shaking her head. "I don't know what, but there's something else besides Sean."

Jamal frowned thoughtfully. "I don't know about that. All I know is that Mike hasn't been himself ever since you came. And that tells me this is about a whole lot more than sex."

She held his gaze for a long moment. She had no idea why, but it meant the world that Jamal thought she was good enough for Mike. Jamal's faith gave her courage somehow. She smiled at him. "Oedipus, huh?"

"Oedipus."

"Aren't you a high-school dropout?"

He laughed. "I was there the day they taught *Oedipus Rex.*"

"Right."

He looked at his watch and sprang to his feet. "It's time for me to go." His smile was tender. "Don't worry, Dara. You'll get it all figured out." She nodded, her throat constricted with excitement that what Jamal said was true and with fear that it wasn't. At the door he turned back. "We still on for tomorrow night? You were going to help me with my poems."

"I wouldn't miss it."

Dara's luck finally ran out. For days she'd successfully eluded Mike at the office, although maybe "eluded" wasn't the right word when the person you were avoiding also avoided you. Mike had reverted to his earlier habit of staying out of the office when she was there and communicating with her only through Laura or e-mails or notes.

Her crushed feelings of Sunday had, by Thursday, turned to rage. She wanted to rip him to pieces, then feed his body through the office shredder, bit by bloody bit. How dare he smash her heart like that? Did he think she couldn't see the way he looked at her? Or remember how tenderly he'd touched her? Did he think he'd cleverly hidden his real feelings?

So, her anger simmering beneath the surface, threatening to erupt like a volcano with no prior warning, she kept to herself, in her office with the door closed. No need to court disaster. But when she got to the office Thursday evening to help Jamal, Mike, jacket and briefcase in hand, stood in the foyer outside the reception area, his mouth a round O of surprise, clearly startled to see her.

A detached coolness fell over her, and she nodded politely. "Mike." She started past him toward the stairs. She fought the urge to run away from him, hating her body's weakness where he was concerned. She wanted to curse him, scream at him, and scratch his eyes out. She wanted to throw herself into his arms, beg him to touch her, to make love to her.

"How are you, Dara?" His expression was penetrating and concerned.

Did the arrogant jerk think she was suicidal just because he'd rejected her? "Fine." She climbed the first few steps and did not slow down; she needed to reach the safety of her office before she crumbled completely.

"What are you doing here?" he said to her back.

She paused for half a second to look over her shoulder. "I'm helping Jamal with his writing tonight." She had to get away from him; her life depended on it. It hurt too much to look at him.

"Dara!" She heard the urgency in his voice and stopped, her jaw clenched with anger. "Maybe we should talk."

Oh, really? So he could explain in greater detail exactly how little she meant to him? No way. She faced him with eyes as vacant and expressionless as an owl's. "I don't think so," she said politely, as if refusing a refill on her soda. He flinched. Somehow she held his gaze and reveled in the raw pain she saw in his eyes. "I think we've said it all." And as she continued up the stairs, she felt the small satisfaction of seeing a look of absolute misery fall across his features before her own unhappiness engulfed her and she fled to her office.

She settled in and sat idly at her desk, waiting for Jamal. Suddenly, she heard hurried feet outside her door and, alarmed, jumped up in time to see Sean rush in. He looked terrible; his eyes were bloodshot and puffy, and the tip of his nose was red. "Thank God, you're here." He grabbed her and tightened his arms around her, clinging for dear life. "I need you."

"Sean, what is it? Tell me."

"It's my mother." He collapsed in one of her chairs. "She's got breast cancer. Again."

Dara perched on the edge of the other chair and gathered her thoughts. Of course, Sean had no idea she already knew about his mother, and she would never betray Mike's confidence. "Oh, God."

He took her hand, and she gave it a reassuring squeeze. "She's already had a mastectomy and started chemotherapy." His voice cracked, and he turned away, sniffling loudly; clearly, he was just this side of a major meltdown. "She didn't even tell me."

Dara swallowed her mild irritation. Apparently, Halley's Comet was a more frequent occurrence than Sean's visits—and calls—to his own mother, who lived right here in Cincinnati. "She probably didn't want to worry you, what with law school just starting."

"She told Mike," he said bitterly. "She always turns to Mike."

Incredulous, Dara could only stare. "Now is not the time for sibling rivalry, Sean." Something in her reproachful tone caught his attention, and he flinched, then hung his head. "How is she feeling? What's her prognosis? What can you do to help her now that you know?"

Sean shrugged helplessly. "I-I don't know. I was so upset, I didn't really hear her. She left and said she'd call me later." His head dropped into his hands. "Oh, God, what am I going to do if Mama dies?"

Poor Sean. She might have felt more sympathy for him, but he obviously felt plenty sorry enough for himself right now. No wonder his mother hadn't told him sooner. What help could he possibly be to her when he was so busy wallowing in self-pity? Immediately, she felt terrible. How could she judge Sean? Everyone handled grief in his or her own way. She knelt in front of his chair and rubbed his thigh. "It'll be okay, Sean. Everything will be okay."

He pulled her into his arms and clung to her. She held him tightly, wrapping her hands around his shoulders. "It's okay. It's okay."

"What's going on here?" Mike's curt voice lashed through the silence; she and Sean jumped and let each other go. Sitting back on her haunches, Dara warily watched Mike, who stood rigidly by the door, his fists on his hips. His hard, glittering eyes flickered back and forth between her and Sean before they settled on Dara. She stood up.

"Mama's got cancer again." Sean's face was calm and deathly quiet, but his eyes looked wild and terrified. "She's had her surgery already. But you already knew that." Dara suddenly had an image of a younger Sean, scared and needing comfort and reassurance from his older brother. She felt his unhappiness and his bottomless need and resisted the urge to put her arms back around him. Now was the time for Mike to offer Sean a comforting word or a hug—the time for a big brother to protect his younger brother. Only Mike had the power to help Sean at this moment.

Mike clearly did not feel her compassion for Sean. Dara took one look at his unyielding face, and her heart sank. He clenched and unclenched his fists at his sides. His body quivered with restrained anger, and for a minute Dara feared he'd unleash it. "Yeah, I knew. And if you called or went to see her more than once every three months, you'd have known it, too."

Sean winced, then looked away. Furious, Dara stood in front of Sean, blocking him from Mike's glare, a lioness protecting her cub. "If that's all you've got to say," she said, her chin raised, "then I wish you'd leave, because I need a minute with Sean."

His face contorting with a bottomless black anger, Mike wheeled around and stalked out.

Jamal rushed up the steps toward the conference room. Dara was probably already there, and he didn't want to keep her waiting. He heard angry voices when he reached the landing—Dara's and Mike's, by the sound of things—and then a door slam. Well, it was no surprise things weren't going so great between them; they'd both had grim faces all week, like they'd been given only a month to live.

His footsteps slowed outside Mike's office. The door was shut. Normally, he'd tell Mike good night, but maybe he shouldn't this time. Why walk right into a hornet's nest? Before he could decide what to do, he heard a thunderous crash inside. Without bothering to knock, he threw the door open, raced inside, and took in the scene. Mike, face twisted and eyes wild, stood behind his desk, panting like he'd just run up ten flights of stairs. There was nothing on the desk—no papers, files, phone, books, or pens. Nothing. To the far side of the desk were the missing items, heaped in a pile on the floor. Papers and files littered the carpet, and the phone beeped a protest at being unceremoniously dumped.

Ain't this something. Mike had swiped everything off his desk. Mike—*Mike*—had had a fight with Dara, and now he was out of control. Frozen with astonishment, Jamal stood there for a long moment. It took Mike a while to realize he was standing in the doorway. Finally, he looked at him. The expression in Mike's eyes was as dangerous as a loaded assault rifle. "What the hell do you want?"

Jamal resisted the urge to scurry away. He stepped inside the office and shut the door behind him. "Listen, Pops—"

Mike's entire body seemed to vibrate with anger. He stared at him with open hostility. "Now is not the time, Jamal." It was a command for Jamal to get out.

"Mike."

Mike stalked around the mess on the floor, kicking the phone as he passed, and went to the window, staring out. Jamal heard a sharp hiss as Mike drew a deep breath. "What do you want?"

"You can't keep up like this, man," Jamal told him quietly.

"I'm fine."

"Bull." Mike's shoulders tightened, but he didn't say anything and didn't turn to look at him. "Y-you gotta work things out with Dara, man," Jamal stammered.

"I am *not* having this discussion with you." Mike's voice cracked through the air like a lightning strike.

Jamal shook his head in disbelief. How the heck did he get himself into situations like this—trying to talk sense into people? "Dara belongs with you. You know it and I know it."

"Yeah, well, she's in there"—he violently jerked his

thumb in the direction of Dara's office—"all hugged up with Sean."

"She doesn't want *Sean*," Jamal cried, incredulous that Mike could entertain such a thought.

Mike spun away from the window and strode back to his desk, without looking at Jamal. He sat down at the computer station and started typing on the keyboard. "My personal life is not up for discussion, and I have work to do." A muscle throbbed in the side of his jaw.

Scared as he was, Jamal was not about to let this go. This felt like the single most important conversation of his life. "How many chances do you think you're gonna get? You think there's someone else as special as Dara waiting out there for you?" Mike stopped typing and stared at the computer. Jamal waited, but when Mike didn't answer him, he snorted with disgust. "So that's it? You're just gonna be a . . . a . . . martyr because your brother wants her, too? Is that all you got?"

Without warning, Mike's arm flew out, and he swiped the keyboard to the floor with another crash. He shot to his feet, eyes flashing with rage. His face twisted until he looked like a gargoyle. "What do you want from me, Jamal?" he roared.

"I want you to work things out with Dara."

"I can't!"

Resigned, Jamal shook his head. He stared at Mike. "Then you're one stupid punk." Mike's jaw dropped as Jamal turned and walked out.

After Sean left, Dara went to the conference room to sulk, vaguely aware of the faint sounds of Mike and Jamal yelling at each other down the hall. They were probably discussing her, but she was too drained to bother to eavesdrop. Eventually, the voices trailed off, and Jamal came in a few minutes later. He took one look at her murderous face and stopped dead. "You're not about to kill anyone, are you?"

She thought that over for a minute. "I can only say I'm not about to kill *you*."

"Mike looked like he was off to torture some small animals when he left a few minutes ago." Jamal sank into a chair across the table from her. "But I suppose that was just a strange coincidence."

She gave him a grim smile. "That's how he always looks with me."

He raised his eyebrows at her. "He looks that way because he's in love with you, and he doesn't know what to do about it."

She didn't know when it'd happened that she started confiding in a seventeen-year-old high-school dropout, but for some reason, she needed to tell Jamal about Sean. "I don't want to talk about Mike. I'm worried about Sean. He just found out his mother's sick. And he's having a tough time with school and his job."

"So what else is new?"

She looked at him with surprise. "You don't like Sean, do you?"

"I like Sean fine," he said, shrugging. "But he's a screwup. He doesn't know what to do with himself. He'll take whatever's good in his life and mess it up. Plus, he's weak."

Again, she felt the irrational need to defend Sean. He wasn't so bad. A little misguided, sure, but not a lost cause. "How do you know all this? The two of you didn't work together that long before Sean started law school."

"Yeah, but it was long enough. Sean screwed up

everything Mike gave him to do. Usually, he was late. A lot of times he didn't come in at all." Jamal bristled at the memory. "It pissed me off, too. Me and Laura and Amira. Why should we work so hard when Sean got to mess around? And how do you think Mike felt? He worked harder than all the rest of us put together."

She couldn't let Sean go undefended. "I'm sure he did the best he could, Jamal. Not everyone's as smart as Mike. And we don't all work as hard as he does."

"When have you ever known Sean to work on anything?"

"You're funny," she said, irritated now. "I'm sure people have called *you* a screwup before."

As she'd expected, Jamal took no offense. "Hell, yeah. But I live in the 'hood, with just my mama and four brothers. We all had different daddies, and none of 'em paid the rent. People sell drugs and get shot outside my apartment. I never had a chance until Mike gave me one. How many chances has *Sean* had? He had two parents who were there for him. He grew up in the suburbs and went to a good high school. His parents paid for college, and his brother gave him a job and got him into law school. What's his excuse for screwing up school and his job? That he didn't make the track team in high school?"

Dara was speechless. Could Jamal be right? She shook her head to clear it of all thoughts of the Baldwin brothers. "Hey—before I forget to ask—how're you getting home?"

Jamal rummaged around in his backpack, extracting a pen and a binder. "Ice'll come and get me."

"Good," she said, opening her notebook. "Let's work."

And work they did, stopping around nine-thirty. She

made several suggestions for his poems and gave him the names of some magazines she thought he should submit his work to. Then she helped with his English assignments from class. They'd just decided to call it a night when Jamal's cell phone rang. He picked it up and flipped it open. "'Sup?" Dara watched him listen, then frown. "Damn, man. What am I supposed to do now?" He looked up at her and rolled his eyes. "Aiight. I'll holla atcha." He hung up.

"What was that all about?" Dara asked him.

"Ice can't pick me up for another hour." He settled back in his chair. "I'll hafta wait."

"That's ridiculous." Dara snapped the cap back on her pen. "Grab your stuff. I'll take you."

He threw his hands up. "Oh no," he said adamantly, as if she'd suggested she'd be happy to take him on a walking tour of the Sahara Desert. "We've been through this before. You don't belong nowhere near my neighborhood. Mike'll have my butt."

Her guilty conscience flickered to life. She'd promised Mike she wouldn't go to Jamal's neighborhood again. Of course, things were different this time. "Don't be silly. You'll be with me. I won't get out of the car. The ramp to the highway is right around the corner. What could happen?"

Jamal wavered; she could tell he didn't want to sit around the office for another hour. "Well . . . You can drop me off at the convenience store on the corner. I'll walk from there."

Dara had started yawning by the time she stopped her SUV at the red light at the intersection down the street from the convenience store. The place was well lit and bustling with activity. People came and went, calling to each other, laughing, and joking. Hip-hop music blasted so loudly from nearby cars, she felt the vibrations from the oversized speakers. Several teenage girls—she'd swear they looked to be only twelve or thirteen—loitered about with infants in strollers and small children in tow. What time was it, anyway? Why weren't all those children at home in bed?

Longing for her own cozy bed set in; she felt exhausted and anxious. A hot bath—with lots of bubbles—would help relieve some of the tension in her neck and shoulders. And maybe a small glass of merlot before bed would help her unwind a little. Anything to keep her problems with the Baldwin brothers off her mind. Tired of waiting for the light to change, she turned to Jamal. "Good work tonight. I can't believe how good your writing is. You have a career there if you want it." The light changed, and she started to maneuver the SUV through the intersection.

Jamal snorted as he unbuckled his seat belt. "I think I'd better pass the GED first."

"It's next week. Are you—"

And that was all she had time to say before a late-model sedan ran the red light and plowed into the passenger side of her SUV, spinning it around.

Mike stepped out of the shower and toweled himself dry, then rummaged through one of his drawers for sweatpants. He pulled them on, then threw himself on the bed to watch a little TV. After he'd made one full circuit of flipping channels, he tossed the remote aside in disgust. Five hundred channels and nothing to watch.

He prowled downstairs to the kitchen, rubbing his shoulders as he went. They felt like they'd been encased in concrete, and nothing helped to relieve the tension. Not running, not hot showers, nothing. Sex would probably help, and he briefly considered calling someone—Lisa or Nicole or someone—to come over. They were willing, with no questions asked. Straight sex with no emotions would give him a little relief, for a while, anyway. But what fun would that be?

The fridge was fully stocked, and he leaned down to find a snack. Cheese and crackers? Yogurt? A bowl of cereal? Ice cream? Nothing looked appetizing, and all food tasted like dust to him these days. It was just as well. He wasn't really hungry, anyway. He stepped around the island with its granite countertop and went through the French doors onto the dark deck. The cold air smacked him across the face and made the gooseflesh rise on his bare chest and back, but he didn't care. Anything that might help clear his mind was fine by him. The only problem was nothing cleared his mind. Not anymore.

Dara hated him. He'd wanted to talk to her tonight, to apologize, to try to make her understand, to make sure she was okay, and she'd blown him off. He didn't know how he'd expected her to act, but cool detachment sure wasn't it. She'd looked right through him like he was nothing. He'd seen sharks show more emotion than she'd shown tonight. It was all his own fault, he knew. It was a matter of choosing between his brother and Dara, and he couldn't choose her. So now she would punish him because she hated him. Worse, she was indifferent to him.

He'd made his bed. He just didn't want to lie in it.

He sat on the edge of one of his Adirondack chairs,

debating whether he should go inside before he developed frostbite, not that he'd care if he did. This, then, was his nightly ritual. Come home, more work, run, shower, no snack, no sex, roam the house. Eventually, he'd make his way up to his bed—surely the loneliest place on the face of the earth—and pretend to fall asleep for several hours. Then, when he finally did fall asleep, he'd dream about Dara and wake up more frustrated and tired than ever.

There was no plan, no grand design. For the first time in his life, he was flying by the seat of his pants. One day at a time was all he could manage. One day at a time for a few more weeks, until her internship ended. One day at a time, until he didn't have to see her every day. He refused to think about whether he'd ever see her again after that. . . .

The ringing phone inside the kitchen intruded on his thoughts. It was pretty late. Who could it be? Probably some client had been arrested and wanted him to arrange for bail. He stepped back inside and picked up the phone. "Hello?"

"Mike? It's Miller."

A frisson of worry passed through him; the last time he'd called, it was to say Jamal had been drinking on the corner. "What's up, Sam?"

"I . . . there's been a car accident near Jamal's apartment," Miller told him. "It's pretty bad." Mike's heart skidded to a stop. "Apparently, your intern drove him home. . . ."

Mike's legs nearly gave out, and he clutched the countertop for support. His breath left his lungs in a single whoosh, and he couldn't expand his chest enough to form any words. *Not Dara!* his mind screamed. *Not*

Dara, not Dara, not Dara. There was no room for any other coherent thought in his brain.

"Jamal's at the hospital with a head injury. He wasn't buckled."

"But . . . Dara?" The name stuck in his throat.

"She's okay."

Dara was okay! Mike felt a wave of relief and joy so fierce, he was nearly blinded by it. It was a minute before the worry began. Jamal was hurt. He'd already started sprinting through the house toward the steps; he needed to find a shirt and get to the hospital as soon as possible.

Dara sat by Jamal's bed and watched him sleep. He had a small, bandaged cut on his forehead but otherwise looked the same as ever. God, she was tired. What time was it? She looked blearily around. They were in the emergency room, in one of those little areas delineated by sliding curtains, which shield the beds for privacy. Miscellaneous monitors and other mysterious medical gadgets lined the one wall she could see. An IV pump hummed quietly, and she held Jamal's right hand, which had the corresponding needle and tubes taped to it.

His fingers moved, and her gaze shot to his face. His eyes fluttered open, and he regarded her groggily. "Dara?" he said faintly, as if the effort to speak was too much. His grip on her hand tightened.

"Yes?" she said anxiously. Was he in pain? Did he need anything? Should she call the doctor?

"Why don't you look where the heck you're goin' next time?"

"Wha-what?" she sputtered. "It wasn't my fault that drunk idiot plowed into us!"

"Um-hmm." His eyes closed, and the edges of his lips curled. "I want the name of your insurance agent."

She leaned down to press a kiss on the uninjured side of his forehead. "Remind me to kick your rear when you get out of here. You'll be fine. A minor concussion is all. Your mom'll be here any second."

"You okay?"

"Yeah," she said, smiling. "I'm fine."

"I just got one question for you," he said very seriously, fingering the bandage.

"What is it?"

"Am I still pretty?"

When Jamal went back to sleep, Dara slipped out through the curtains and slumped on one of the uncomfortable pleather chairs on the outskirts of the waiting area, wondering what she should do. She would wait until Jamal's mother arrived, of course, before she left. But how would she get home? Her SUV was totaled; maybe she should call a rental company.

Mike could take you home.

Dara ignored the niggling little voice and fished around in her purse for her cell phone. Why on earth would she think about Mike now? Sure, she'd given his number to the police. He'd want to know about Jamal, and she imagined he'd come to the hospital right away to see him. But that had nothing to do with *her*. In fact, she planned to be long gone before he arrived.

You need Mike.

Agitated, she found her phone and shot to her feet, pacing. She didn't *need* Mike. Sure, she'd never been in a car accident before, and she'd never been as terrified as she'd been tonight, when she'd heard the thunderous crash, the scraping and grinding of metal against metal, Jamal's scream. But she was fine. And Jamal was fine. Her stomach lurched crazily as she remembered the horrible thunk of Jamal's head hitting the window and the sound of the glass cracking, the blood . . .

She shoved the images aside, looked down at her phone, and tried unsuccessfully to flip it open. Her hands . . . Why were her hands shaking? With a choked sob, she shook the phone again and again. A nurse with a patient's chart gripped to her chest did a double take as she hurried past. Why wouldn't the stupid phone open? Why couldn't she . . .

"Dara."

Dara froze and looked up, letting her hand drop to her side. Mike stood right in front of her, face strained, eyes wild with worry. For one paralyzed second, she just stared at him, but then he threw his arms open and reached for her. With a cry, she flung herself at him. His arms closed around her so brutally, she thought he might break some of her ribs, but she didn't care. She needed him. He cupped the back of her head and pressed it to his chest. She clung to him, listening to the erratic thundering of his heart.

"Dara!" He pulled far enough away to look down at her face. "Dara! I was so scared! I thought . . ." He broke off, and she felt him shudder. The shakes overcame her, and Mike pressed her back against his chest. "Shhh." He smoothed her hair back from her forehead and cheeks, cooing at her.

Quickly, she pulled herself together and, embarrassed now, tried to pull away. His arms tightened around her waist. "You're okay," he murmured, his eyes locked with hers, oblivious to the hubbub of the hospital all around them. "You're okay." His face twisted, screwing itself up. "I was so scared when they told me there'd been an accident. God, I was scared."

His face was a jumble of dark emotions she'd never seen before. She stilled. "Mike?"

He stared at her so intently, he seemed not to hear her. Then his strong, warm hands stroked her face, and he leaned down and pressed fevered kisses on her forehead and both eyes. Without hesitating, he lowered his face and kissed her mouth. For half a second she froze. And then she forgot she'd been angry with him and, whimpering, kissed him back.

Suddenly, she came to her senses and pulled away; she couldn't meet his hot, anxious gaze. Had she really just kissed him? After he'd told her all he wanted was to screw her? Had anything really changed between them? Of course, he was worried about her now, when she could have been hurt. But what about half an hour from now? How long before he pushed her away again?

He kept a firm grip on her hand. "I want to see Jamal for a minute. Then I'm taking you home."

"I don't think—," she began weakly.

His face tightened. "Don't argue with me."

He towed her behind him to Jamal's partition, where he held the curtain aside for her and followed her through. Jamal now sat up in bed, sipping something from a Styrofoam cup with a bent straw. "What's up, Pops? Your girl here tried to kill me."

Mike, beaming, shook his hand. "Who hasn't?"

Jamal tapped his forehead and winked. "Luckily, my head is much harder than she thought."

"Thank God for that."

"Can I get workers' comp for this? Dara was driving me home from work." Jamal's expression was hopeful.

"Nope. Sorry." Mike turned a dark stare on Dara. "And that's something we need to talk about, since I distinctly remember you promising me you'd never go to Jamal's neighborhood again."

Oh no. She'd been afraid he would mention that. "Alone," she said coolly, as if her heart wasn't pounding ten miles a minute. "I said I'd never go there *alone*."

Jamal narrowed his eyes at her in warning, then turned to Mike. "Yeah, why don't you go on and take Dara home. You two got a lot to talk about."

Mike's intent eyes returned to her face. "Good idea." His tone was quiet but absolutely final.

Dara broke into a fine sweat.

Dara tried to unlock her apartment door, but some combination of post-traumatic stress disorder and anger at both herself and Mike made her hands shake. She fumbled with the lock once or twice; then Mike gently took the keys from her and opened the door, with hands steadier than a brain surgeon's. He quickly followed her inside, making it impossible for her to do what she really wanted to do, which was slam the door in his face.

He was a jerk, but she was an idiot. Who else but an idiot would kiss someone—desperately need someone—mere days after receiving a blow like the one Mike had given her? He couldn't have been any clearer—or cruder, for that matter. He wanted to screw her, period. No feelings were involved, or so he said. It didn't really matter.

He'd sliced her heart from her chest, and he needed to get out of her apartment. She whirled to face him.

"Dara," he said quietly, "I want to talk to you."

"Now isn't a good time," she told him, trying to keep her face blank. "I'm really tired, and I still need to call my insurance agent—"

His jaw tightened. "This can't wait."

"It'll have to." Dara felt a stab of pain in her heart every time she looked at him. She kept remembering how he'd shoved her away the other day, when she'd reached out to him. She couldn't stand to look at his face another minute. "Please leave now." Very carefully, she turned her back to him and hung her jacket in the hall closet. "Thank you for bringing me home, but I'm fine. I don't need you, and I really need some time alone."

Hurt flashed across his face for one brief second. Then he recaptured his usual bland expression. "I think I'll stick around and make sure you're okay."

She laughed a bitter, ugly laugh. Hysteria was right around the corner. She watched the scene unfold as if she were in the audience and some other Dara and Mike were the actors onstage. Mike stiffened and waited, his eyes growing wider and darker. "You're going above and beyond the call, don't you think? For someone who only wants to sleep with me, I mean." Round, fat tears ran unchecked down her face. Annoyed by her own show of emotion, she swiped her hand across her cheek.

He shrank away from her as if she'd waved a loaded gun in his face. "Don't do this, Dara."

"Do what?" Her voice rose an octave. "Remind you of what you said?"

"Dara, please—" Strain crossed his face. Even so,

he was the epitome of calm and reason, and that enraged her.

She couldn't stop herself now. "Why bother to talk, anyway? My internship ends pretty soon, and you can go ahead and forget all about me, like you plan to do."

His face contorted with rage, and his feet widened into a fighting stance.

Then he exploded.

Chapter 13

Mike slammed his hand on the hall table. The basket of keys and her goldfish bowl jumped and wobbled dangerously. "Damn it, Dara! What do you want?"

His rage thrilled her. She was so sick of his aloofness and his pretending, so sick of the indifferent mask he wore with her. She wanted him enraged. "I want you to tell me the truth, you lying jerk!" she screeched, pointing her finger in his face. "You tell me the truth, or you get out!"

"The truth? Which truth is that?" He grabbed her roughly by the shoulders and shook her. His strength and power overwhelmed her. Astonished her. "How about this: I *hate* my brother now! I can't stand to be in the same room with him! I can't make myself look him in the face, because I'm so jealous that he's such good friends with you!"

She gaped at him, not daring to breathe.

His grip tightened. "What about this truth, Dara. Since the second I laid eyes on you, I haven't been able to think of anything else! I don't care that you're eleven years younger than I am! I don't care that my brother wants you, too! All I care about is being with you! And I can't even throw myself into my work, because there you are every single day, a thorn in my side!"

Dara's body sagged with relief, and she felt happy—happier than she'd ever been in her life. He cared for her. He'd admitted it. There was no going back after this. "What about this, Dara?" His voice lowered to a seductive, mesmerizing whisper. His arms dropped, and he came closer, until he was only an inch away. He bent his head to speak in her ear. Soft puffs of his hot breath singed her cheek. Her entire body tightened with need, and her knees weakened to the point of collapse. "I crave you." She strained to hear him over her own harsh breathing. "Did you know that? I crave you the same way I crave my next breath of air. When I touched you the other night, it felt a thousand times better than I ever could've thought. And when I'm with you—when I look at you—I don't care at all about Sean. Is that the truth you wanted to hear?"

"Oh, Mike."

He jerked away and threw his hands up as if he would turn to stone if she touched him. "And here's the biggest truth of all, Dara. When the police called and told me there'd been an accident, for one second, I was afraid you'd been killed, and I was more scared than I've ever been in my life."

Still, she couldn't completely let go of her anger. How could he have hurt her like that if he cared for her? And what was to stop him from doing it again? "You hurt me!" she screeched, pounding her chest with her fist. "Do you understand that? I was scared, but I was willing to take a chance with you, and you pushed—no, shoved—me away! *You hurt me!* Why did you do that?"

Sorrowful eyes held hers for a long moment. "Because I wasn't ready for this, Dara," he said hoarsely.

God, he was going to kill her; the pain felt unbearable. She looked down at the floor and pressed her hand over her mouth until she'd collected herself enough to speak again. Finally, she looked back up at him. "Neither was I, but I was willing to try, anyway. So now, I guess, there's nothing else to talk about."

"Nothing except this." A flush crept over his face until he looked . . . uncertain. Almost nervous. Her heart turned over hard. "Tonight I realized I will regret it the rest of my life if I don't try to figure out what this is between us."

Astonished, she stared at him and saw the vulnerability and hope in his eyes. An answering hope unfurled in her chest. "What are we going to do about this, Mike?" she whispered.

He stretched out a hand to her, beckoning. A warm half-smile crossed his lips. "Take a chance with me, angel."

Mesmerized, lost, and hopelessly in love, Dara stepped forward into his arms.

Chapter 14

They came together in a tightly wound tangle of arms and legs, like English ivy climbing an oak tree. Mike caught her sweet mouth beneath his, and she opened for him like a rose blooming in June. His hunger—his clawing need for her—roared to life. His arousal was sudden and violent. There was no way he could ignore it. Not tonight. Whimpering, she wrapped her arms around his neck, pulling him closer. And suddenly, whatever self-control he'd had—if he'd had any at all—shattered.

Without breaking the kiss, he backed her out of the lighted foyer and into the dark living room, toward the sofa, but forgot completely about the coffee table. "Oof!" she cried when the backs of her knees banged into it. He quickly reclaimed her mouth and maneuvered her around the stupid table until she tumbled backward onto the sofa and pulled him down, too. He tightened his hold and shifted his weight on top of her. Instantly, her legs wrapped firmly around his waist; he was nearly strangled by her strength and insistence. Clearly, she had no intention of letting him go. His hands found her bare knees—she was wearing that

black knit dress that always drove him to distraction—
and slid up her thighs, pressing closer to her yielding
softness.

But not close enough.

"More," Dara whispered, rocking her hips against his.

Yes, more. His lips slid down her neck, and her back
arched up to meet him. She was impossibly flexible.
Yoga, he remembered vaguely. His shaking fingers
found the bottom edge of her dress and pulled it up
over her head, with Dara wriggling her hips to help
him. Just as quickly, he undid the clasp of her lacy bra,
taking only half a second to notice the bra was black.
When he was done, he faltered for a second, his breath
harsh in the silence, studying her in the dim moonlight
filtering in from the blinds. She was exquisite. Her
heaving breasts were two perfect globes. Large, dark,
erect nipples strained toward him. "Touch me," she
said breathlessly, leaning back against the pillows to
offer herself in a seductive pose worthy of a courtesan.

"Oh, I intend to," he said, not moving.

"Hurry."

He stroked her, tracing the dark edge of her aureole,
teasing her. Dara groaned a protest. Leaning down, he
flicked his tongue over one nipple. Thrashing, she
reached up and clamped her hands around his head,
locking him in place. And with this unmistakable invitation, he gave up trying to torture her. He opened
his mouth and suckled hard. Dara cried out.

"Dara," he whispered. "I want you. God, I want you."
His fingers and mouth slid lower—her abs were toned
and flat, just like he'd imagined—until his hands anchored her hips. He plunged his tongue into her navel,
and she leapt and moaned. He could smell her now,
faint and musky, through the black satin of her teeny

tiny panties. She was wet, then. But how wet? He needed to know.

He slipped his fingers underneath the elastic edge of the panties and slid them past her hips, then down her legs, pausing only briefly to notice her luscious thighs as he went. The panties joined her dress and bra in a growing pile on the floor. Then he slid his fingers down her belly to the lush patch of wiry hair, and finally, lower, to the thick folds of flesh. She was hot and slick, more thrilling than he remembered. He pressed his face to her sex, rubbing it with his nose and mouth, reveling. Dara's thighs slid open, issuing another invitation. A sob escaped from deep in her throat. "Please. *Please*, Mike."

How could he refuse her—or himself? How could he come this far and not taste her? Sliding his hands to her hips, he anchored her and dove in. He found the hard little nub—his holy grail—and zeroed in on it. He flicked, he circled, and, finally, he sucked. Dara sobbed. Suddenly, her entire body went rigid. "Mike!" Just as suddenly she went limp.

Still between her thighs, he sat up and stared at her. She panted, sweating slightly. Slowly, her eyes opened halfway and looked at him. She seemed dazed—as if someone had wrung her out and hung her up to dry. He felt thrilled. "Oh, my God." Her voice was almost inaudible.

If he didn't know better, he'd almost think she'd never come before. Certainly, she'd never come like *this*— so strongly—before. But he didn't have time to dwell on that thought, because he was in agony. He needed relief, but he also didn't want to embarrass himself by losing control like some kid. He pulled away from her.

"We're not going to make love tonight, sweetheart. It's too soon. You're not ready yet."

"Oh, I'm ready," she said smugly.

Mike swallowed hard and tried to remember he wanted to do the right thing. "You weren't ready the other night," he reminded her.

Dara blinked and looked away; obviously, at this juncture, she was having a little trouble deciding whether she was ready or not. She roused herself a little, sitting up. "Come here." Her arms stretched out to him.

Need clawed away in his gut like a dog digging a hole. "No."

Dara rose to her knees and crept closer. "No?" Her voice was simultaneously innocent and seductive. A siren's call.

"No!" His voice was firm, even though his resolve wasn't.

She pressed her breasts against his arm, then reached out to rub his chest, her soft hand circling his nipple. Mike gasped, his entire body stiffening. "Don't!"

Her hand shifted lower, kneading his belly, then slipped up under the edge of his T-shirt. "I need you, Mike. I need to touch you."

"No." But he turned his head toward her, leaned his face down. He couldn't breathe anymore; it felt as if someone had cut off all the oxygen to the room. She tilted her face up, meeting his lips with her own. And her hand slid below the waistband of his sweatpants and briefs. He sucked in a strangled breath and grabbed her wrist, intending to jerk her hand away. But her fingers had already tightened around him, and he couldn't seem to think straight. Actually, he couldn't think at all, straight or otherwise. Slowly, but firmly, she began to stroke, up and down.

She broke the kiss and pressed her hot lips to his ear. "I want you, Mike." Her fingers tightened. "I need you inside me. Please. *Please*." And with that, he was lost. Her voice, her scent, her touch coalesced and gave him a pleasure so intense, it was almost painful. He clamped his hand over hers and rubbed it roughly up and down until, groaning loudly, he came with a violence that scorched his body from the inside out.

Slowly—very slowly—the room came back into focus. He saw the shadowy furniture, the moonlight at the edges of the windows, heard his own harsh breathing. Dara was still pressed to his side. He turned to look at her. Her eyes were glittering and warm. Pleased. "Let's go to bed, sweetheart."

"Okay." She laughed triumphantly, and he grinned back at her. "But I better clean this"—he gestured vaguely to his bodily fluids, which now graced the coffee table—"up first."

When he got to the bedroom, he watched as she turned back the fluffy comforter. The bed was the most inviting he'd ever seen, with about a thousand pillows heaped on it. Dara, still nude, straightened and smiled at him, with no evidence of self-consciousness whatsoever. That was a problem. He felt the first stirrings of renewed desire. They'd taken the edge off, sure, but in about another ten minutes, he'd be ready to go again. So a few parameters and ground rules were definitely in order, because he was absolutely determined to remember she was only twenty-three, with much less experience than he'd had. He would never press her to do anything she wasn't ready for. "Don't you own any underwear?" A couple of layers of clothing, preferably something in wool or flannel, seemed like a good idea. She rolled her eyes. "How about a nightgown?"

Her eyes widened innocently. "A nightgown?"

He didn't like her tone. He watched warily as she rummaged in one of her bureau drawers. From way in the back, she pulled out something white and filmy, with dangling price tags. She jerked off the tags and slipped it over her head. It slithered down her breasts, hips, and thighs until it reached her toes. His jaw dropped. The lousy nightgown—if you could call it a nightgown—had spaghetti straps and a deep V in the front that barely covered her breasts, not that it mattered, because the thing was entirely transparent. He could still see tantalizing images of her dark nipples and the triangle he so longed to explore. Fantasies of violently ripping the gown away from her body danced through his dazed brain. It'd been better when she was naked. "For goodness sake," he muttered. "Where'd you get that?"

"When we were seventeen, Monica and I wandered into the Victoria's Secret at the mall, and, well, one thing led to another. You should see the one *she* picked."

He stared at her. "And you haven't worn it until now?"

She ducked her head, looking suddenly shy and a little embarrassed. "No."

Something joyous and unprecedented unfurled in his chest. He caught her hand and pressed it hard to his lips. She sighed. "Then I'm the luckiest man in the world, aren't I?"

She laughed, the sound low and seductive, then climbed into the bed. He slipped under the covers behind her and, wrapping his arms around her waist, pulled her back against him. It was as if he'd been there thousands of nights before this one—as if he belonged there. One of his hands automatically went under her neck and cupped her breast, and the other went over one hip to her belly, pressing her to him. He felt more at home than he'd ever felt in any other bed—including his own—in his life.

Suddenly, his guilt knifed through him. He was scum. Because he wanted this time with her, and he wasn't thinking about what it would do to Sean if he found out. But then he shoved Sean far away and focused on Dara, and the fact that they would take this risk together. The familiar panic was there, but it seemed muted now, distant. Manageable.

He slept soundly for the first time in months.

Dara woke to the slide of the sateen sheet down her mostly bare back. Before the cool bedroom air could hit her skin, she felt the press of Mike's warm mouth and tongue in the hollow of her back, at her waist. "Good morning," she cooed, smiling into the pillows.

Mike's mouth slid up her spine and lodged between her shoulder blades, a very fine spot for it. "How are you, sweetheart?" His mouth and tongue swirled in languid circles.

"Wonderful," she sighed.

He kissed her nape, then scratched it with his rough cheek. Dara cried out, dazed with pleasure.

"I have to go. I've got early court, and I need to go home and change."

"Nooo!"

He sat on the bed beside her, and she forced herself to sit up and open her eyes. It was absolutely dark in the room, except for the red glow from her clock radio, which read 6:00. He smiled, amused by her disappointment, and pulled her into his arms. She held him tight, resting her head on his shoulder. He'd dressed again but had a wonderful, rumpled, clean linen smell. She doubted she'd be able to let go long enough for him to walk out the door. His hands caressed their way up her back, then filtered through her hair, letting it fall to her shoulders. Her sex swelled and ached painfully. "Why do you touch me like this when you have to leave?" she complained.

She felt him smile as he skinned his teeth along the curve of her neck. "Because I want you to think about me after I'm gone."

"Mmmm," she said, catching one of his hands and pulling it to her throbbing breast. "Well, maybe you should touch me some more. My memory's not what it used to be."

Mike rubbed the flat of his palm against the nipple, and she arched into him, moaning. "Can't," he said hoarsely. He took her hand and brought it to his lap, where the size of his rigid arousal made her mouth go dry. "I don't want Judge Smythe to think I'm overly glad to see him."

Laughing, she turned her face and flicked his ear with her tongue. "Later, then."

"What about your SUV?"

"The rental place will drop one off here for me, I think."

"And what time should I look for you at work?"

She pulled away and smiled coyly. "Why do you ask?"

He did not smile. "Because I need to know how

much time I'm going to waste daydreaming about you before I can see you again and settle down to work."

"Eight o'clock," she said, breathless.

He smiled. "Good."

It was nine-thirty before Mike got back to the office. He went directly to Dara's office, too far gone over her to worry about wearing his heart on his sleeve. She sat at her desk, with Laura leaning over her shoulder, both heads bent low over some document they were discussing. But the second he stepped into view, Dara's eyes looked up and widened. She smiled, a wide, glorious smile that made his chest ache with indefinable emotions. "Good morning," she said.

Laura looked up and saw him. "Hey, Mike."

He stared at Dara, barely aware that anyone else was present. One of Dara's brows rose slightly in amusement. Clearing his throat sharply, he tried to come to his senses, an impossible task. "Good morning."

Laura looked back and forth between them, comprehension dawning on her face. Very quickly, she gathered her papers from Dara's desk and scurried out, grinning all the way. "I'll see you later."

Slowly, as if mesmerized, Mike walked into the office, watching Dara the whole time. He'd always thought she radiated some sort of inner light or something, but today she seemed to glow, with her flushed skin, bright eyes, killer smile. Did anyone else see what he saw? And did it have anything to do with him? Did he make her this happy? He sat on the edge of her desk and, reaching out to cup her cheek, kissed her gently on the lips.

"I missed you," she sighed.

"Yeah," he said around the basketball-sized lump in his throat. "Dinner? Tonight?"

"I think I can manage that."

He took her to an Italian restaurant downtown where they could see the skyline's reflection shimmering on the river. Candles glittered inside on the white tablecloths. Normally, Dara would pause a minute or two to enjoy such a romantic scene, or at least to soak up the savory scents of basil and sausage, but not tonight. Mike had commandeered all of her five senses, and she was oblivious to almost everything else. She sat next to him at a secluded booth in the corner, and the distance was unbearable. She was a little annoyed to see women at other tables staring at Mike like they'd never seen a man before. As far as Dara was concerned, they hadn't; there was no one else as gorgeous as Mike. He exuded testosterone and energy and power.

And he only had eyes for her.

"I'll have the veal marsala." She handed the server her menu and smiled her thanks.

The server turned to Mike, waiting patiently. "And for you, sir?"

Mike didn't seem to hear him. His gaze remained fixed on Dara's face. Her lips, actually. Dara's skin felt hot, like when she fell asleep on her towel at the beach and woke to find the sun blazing down on her.

The server cleared his throat discretely. "Sir?"

Mike blinked and handed the server his menu. "I'll have the lasagna." He held the menu up in the man's general direction, without ever looking away from Dara. "Please."

Dara smiled. "You didn't even look at the menu."

He slid closer to her on the seat. "I have more interesting things to look at. Anyway, I always order the lasagna."

This gave Dara pause. "What do you mean, you always order the lasagna?"

"English *is* your first language, isn't it?"

"There's spaghetti, scampi, marsala, fra diavolo." She counted off on her fingers. "There's fettucine Alfredo and manicotti and ravioli."

"I'm aware of all that."

"So how can you always just order the lasagna, without looking at the menu?"

He shrugged. "It's my favorite meal."

"But what if there's a better meal out there? You'll never discover it!"

He laughed. "I guess I'll just have to learn to live with that tragic possibility."

"You're very set in your ways," she noted thoughtfully. "If we're going to be spending more time together, I think I'm probably going to drive you crazy."

"We *are* going to be spending more time together—in fact, the phrase 'glued at the hip' comes to mind—and I look forward to you driving me crazy. If you'll recall, I told you the night we met, I knew you would drive a man crazy."

"And I think I said maybe you should run while you have the chance."

"Dara," he said mildly, "you've got a better chance of being abducted by aliens in the next ten seconds than you do of getting rid of me."

She slipped her hand in his. "Good."

"This is our first meal together," she noted when the server brought their plates.

He made a face. "I know. We could've had dinner together that first night at the party."

She dug into her veal, which steamed with melted fontina cheese, just the way she loved it. "Yes, but I believe I told you I don't leave parties with strange men."

His eyes glimmered with mischief in the candlelight. "Clearly, a good policy." He took a bite of lasagna. "But I'm not a strange man."

"Hmmm. I'm not sure I'm willing to concede you're not a strange man—"

"Very funny."

"But even if you *are* entirely normal, I didn't know that then."

"Yes, you did." He stared at her, daring her to deny it. Every inch of her skin tingled. When he looked at her that way—like she was the most fascinating creature on the planet, those eyes focused on her to the exclusion of everyone else in the room—she felt like a moth drawn to a flame, unable and unwilling to fly away. Ready to throw herself into the fire.

He slid even closer to her in the booth until their hips touched and his thigh, impossibly muscular and long, pressed against hers. He slid one arm around her shoulders and lifted her hand with his free hand, twining his long, warm fingers with hers.

Dara immediately forgot all about her veal. She'd never known hand holding to be a sexual act as intimate as intercourse itself, but then she'd never held hands with Mike in the candlelight. He stroked her fingers, rubbing his thumb over her knuckles. If he kept it up, he'd have her moaning like Meg Ryan in the deli scene from *When Harry Met Sally,* only she, Dara, wouldn't be faking it. "I've been wondering something."

"Shoot."

"What attracted you to me?"

He'd released her hand long enough to take a quick sip of wine, and now he snorted and almost choked on his merlot. "Is this some kind of a joke?" he sputtered.

"Nooo," she said, embarrassed.

"Dara, you're beautiful. You're the most beautiful woman I've ever seen, in fact."

"Is that it?" she said, a little disappointed by the most lavish compliment she'd ever received. There was more to his attraction than that, wasn't there? Something to keep him interested when she turned old and gray, or if, God forbid, she had a terrible accident and was no longer pretty?

"No." He seemed sheepish, and she found that powerfully alluring.

"Tell me," she murmured.

He grinned and looked away. "I can't . . . I can't."

"Now you *have* to tell me."

He shook his head and opened and closed his mouth. Surely, this was the first time in recorded history the great Mike Baldwin was at a loss for words. He picked up her hand again, then slid his other hand from her shoulder to the nape of her neck, which he stroked until she nearly leapt out of her skin. "I don't think I can explain it." His face and voice softened at the memory. "When I saw you that night, I felt like I recognized you. And when I looked at your eyes . . ." He broke off, too embarrassed to continue.

But Dara was mesmerized. "Please tell me."

"When I saw you, all the other people in the room disappeared. And when I looked in your eyes, I thought, 'There she is.' I thought you were exactly what I needed, even though I hadn't realized I needed anything. And when we talked—before you started to run away—you confirmed all of my initial impressions. I knew you were smart and funny and strong and willful. I knew . . . I wanted you." He wanted her now; his smoldering eyes were a dead giveaway. He lifted his arm and half glanced at his watch. "It's getting late."

She nodded somberly. "I wouldn't want to stay out past my bedtime."

He pointed to their plates. "Maybe we should finish our food—"

"I'm stuffed," she said quickly.

His glittering eyes crinkled at the corners. "You hardly ate."

"Doggy bag, then. But . . . one thing."

"Anything."

"They have a wonderful carrot cake here. Can I get some to go?"

He laughed. "You can have anything you want."

"That's all I want—for now."

His eyes heated up again. "Well, then, let's go now that we've settled the crucial dessert issue."

On the way home, Mike was a little quiet, and by the time they'd climbed the stairs to her apartment, the silence was deafening. Dara slipped the key in the lock and opened the door, determined to ask him about it as soon as they went inside. But when she stepped over the threshold, juggling the shopping bag filled with their leftover dinners, he held back. Surprised, she turned to face him.

Mike eyed the interior of the apartment as if he feared a velociraptor crouched somewhere inside, waiting to dismember him at the first opportunity. "I, uh . . . I think I'll just go on home."

"What?" she cried, wounded and disappointed. "Why?"

He put one arm around her waist and, with the other hand, brushed her hair back from her face. "Well, I, uh," his eyes lingered on her lips, "I have, you know, some work I need to do tonight, and I need to get to the office early."

"But tomorrow's Saturday!"

"I know, but Saturday's like any other day for me. I've got a ton of work to do."

Dara felt like crying, but she was determined not to do anything idiotic, like bawl, just because the man had work to do. He *did* have work, didn't he? She was not going to turn into a clinging vine. No, sir. She was perfectly secure. "Okay," she said, leaning into him. "Kiss?"

His lips were on hers almost before the word was out of her mouth, leaving her no doubt he still wanted her, even if he did have to leave. Abruptly, he broke away, pushing her back a little. "I have to go," he croaked, his face strained.

"Well . . . good night," she said, smiling bravely.

He just nodded, then took off down the hall—as if he was running away from something.

Forty-five minutes later Mike was back, standing in the hall outside Dara's apartment, staring at her shut door. This was the story of his life, and it didn't look like it would change anytime soon: he couldn't stay away from Dara.

He couldn't explain what had happened to him between dinner and when they'd arrived at her apartment, even though he'd thought about it quite a bit. Sure, he had a mountain of work to do, and sure, he did need to be at the office at the crack of dawn. But neither of those excuses really explained his sudden feeling of claustrophobia. All he knew was the stupid—silly—panicky feeling had come back, stronger than ever. And he'd thought he needed to get away from Dara as quickly as possible.

But then he'd gotten home, and instead of feeling glad to be there, he'd felt like he'd arrived for a long stay in solitary confinement at Rikers Island. Dara's apartment—warm, cozy, with the added benefit of having Dara in it—flashed through his mind. So, without ever doing a lick of work, he'd hauled his tired butt back out to his car at nine-fifteen on a cold fall night and come back.

He just couldn't figure out how to get himself inside the apartment.

He raised his fist to knock, and the door suddenly swung open. He froze, arm suspended in midair. Dara stood there, watching him with coolly appraising eyes, and his heart began its familiar drumbeat. She'd changed out of her work clothes and wore a satiny navy blue robe with a belt around the middle. Her pretty feet were bare, her sweet face scrubbed free of make-up. She smelled delicious, powder fresh, like she'd just taken a shower. His body heated up as if he'd stepped, fully clothed, into a sauna.

Leaning against the door frame, she crossed her arms over her chest. Traces of amusement glinted in her eyes. Clearly, she planned to make him eat a little humble pie. "Were you going to stand out here all night?"

"Possibly."

"What are you doing here?"

"I have a very important question to ask you, and it couldn't wait till tomorrow."

Her eyes narrowed suspiciously. "What is it?"

"What kind of perfume do you wear?"

Her dewy mouth dropped open; her eyes softened. "I . . . what?"

He stared at her. "I smell it all the time, even when you're not with me." He stepped closer. "I need to know."

Unfortunately, she seemed to realize she was weakening. "Gardenias," she said briskly. Her hand found the door and started to swing it closed again. "So if that's all . . ."

Panicked, he flung out his arm, blocking her. "That's not all! I . . . thought maybe you needed a little help with your reading tonight. Con law, torts, civil procedure, contracts . . . I'm happy to do whatever I can to help out."

Her lips twitched up into a lopsided smile, but she pressed them firmly together until they disappeared in a thin line. Her chin lifted. "I thought you had important work to do."

He nodded earnestly. "I do. I'm a very important man with lots of important work to do. All kinds of criminals depend on me, and Laura and Amira and Jamal depend on me. And I need to get the firm in the black. It's all very . . . important." He cleared his throat. "I thought maybe I could do it here with you, while you study." On a sudden inspiration, he grabbed his laptop, which he'd propped against the wall outside her door, and brandished it.

Her head tilted thoughtfully. "Well, this certainly seems like a good plan, but unfortunately, you have to get to work early in the morning, so I guess you can't stay very long."

Without a word, he picked up his garment bag, filled with clothes for tomorrow and toiletries, but no pajamas, and showed it to her.

This time she gave him the full smile. She backed inside, holding the door open for him. He gratefully gathered his bags and followed her. But then Dara turned to face him, and her smile faded. "I'm not the enemy, you know."

He stared at her warm eyes for a long time, fighting the panic that wanted to creep back up his throat. Suddenly, his nameless fears seemed ridiculous, like being afraid of a kitten. "I know."

"Are you finished fighting me and running away?"

He let out a relieved laugh. "God, I hope so."

She turned to lead him into the living room, where he saw her books spread open on the coffee table and heard the low murmur of the television. A wave of contentment washed over him; he belonged here—or wherever she was. He thought of the work he needed to start on, but the swish of the silky robe against her legs and the sway of her hips quickly fogged his brain. Pausing to give him a sidelong glance over her shoulder, she untied her robe and let it slide off her arms to reveal a slinky little matching nightgown with spaghetti straps. Mike froze, gaping at her.

"Of course, you'll have to be punished," she said, smiling.

"What did you have in mind?" he asked, dropping his bags and lunging for her.

Chapter 15

Mike woke up slowly, stretching and feeling a strange but exciting combination of utter relaxation and boundless energy. He knew why: he and Dara had been having the best non-sex of his life. Her flexible, eager little body, clever hands, and sweet mouth had, in fact, reduced him to a quivering mass of flesh on more than one occasion. When was the last time he'd engaged in this much foreplay? He couldn't begin to remember. Generally, the women he dated were happy to jump in his bed at the end of the first date, which was, he supposed, the reason he dated them. Not that he wasn't anxious—desperate, actually—to make love with Dara. It was just that he absolutely did not want to rush her, nor did he want to hurt her. For now it was enough to revel in getting to know her, emotionally and physically.

Besides, he had the feeling the little siren was going to blow his mind when they finally did make love. Worse, he feared that when they made love—when she became his—he would never let her go. *Could* never let her go.

Smiling, his eyes still closed, he reached across the

rumpled pillows, but she wasn't there. Disappointed, he opened his eyes and sat up. Bright sunlight streamed through the closed blinds. At the foot of the bed, dressed in exactly the kind of skimpy little black yoga outfit he'd fantasized about, sat Dara on a purple mat.

Except she wasn't really sitting. She was balancing on her tailbone, her mostly bare legs straight and about three feet apart, her toes pointed toward the ceiling, with her hands gripping her ankles. She looked like a huge V. Never had he seen anything as erotic as Dara with her legs in the air; he had the sudden and nearly irresistible urge to leap out of bed and take her now, roughly. He watched, riveted, while, still holding onto her ankles and keeping her legs straight, she rolled onto her back, then back up into the original position.

Mike made a strangled sound, with a suddenly dry mouth.

Startled, Dara dropped her legs and twisted on the mat to face him. "Good morning," she chirped, smiling as brightly as the morning sun filtering through the window. "I hope I didn't wake you up. I was trying to be quiet."

Stalling for a moment in a vain attempt to collect his thoughts, he crept to the end of the bed, keeping the sheet at his waist to cover his violent arousal. "Wha"— he cleared his husky throat—"what are you doing?"

"Pilates work."

"Pi . . . what?"

"Pilates," she said, laughing. "Stretching. Toning. It's good for the abs. That was called the open-leg rocker."

Good Lord. Pilates was good for a whole lot more than abs. "I thought you did yoga," he said weakly.

"I do." She resumed her V position, causing his groin to ache painfully. "You slept through yoga."

She rocked back again, and he lost the last threads of his self-control. He leapt off the end of the bed, rolling on top of her; Dara squealed with surprised delight and wrapped her legs around his waist. He ground his erection against her, fitting himself to the place where he belonged. Dara cried out, clawing at his back, pulling him closer. "Tomorrow," he told her, burying his lips in her neck, "I'm setting the alarm clock."

"You look great!" Dara pulled away from hugging Jamal to survey him critically. He'd already removed the bandage from his forehead and therefore looked the same as he ever had. "How are you feeling?"

Jamal sauntered back around his desk and sank into his chair. "Fine." He picked up his steaming mug of coffee and took a big gulp. "Tried to get the doctor to excuse me from work for a few more days, but no dice."

Dara laughed and sat in the chair opposite him. "Too bad a major head trauma didn't improve your attitude at all."

"Yeah, well," he said, grinning. "And I'll have to wait a few more weeks before I take the GED exam, but I'm not cryin' about that. So what's up with you and Mike? He practically skipped off to court this morning, he looked so happy."

Dara flushed and tried unsuccessfully not to giggle. "Nothing! We just . . . well, you know." Fidgeting, she ran her fingers through her hair. "We talked. A little."

Jamal snorted. "Y'all been doin' a lot more than talkin'."

Before she could manage an outraged splutter, Amira's voice came over the intercom on Jamal's desk. "Dara? You in there?"

"Yeah," Dara said. "What do you need?"

"Sean's here."

"I'll come right down." Dara felt her shoulders droop guiltily. Sean had called several times over the last few days, and she, totally immersed in being with Mike, had blown him off. As she and Mike had agreed, they wouldn't tell Sean about their relationship. At least for now, she would have to act like everything in her life was the same as ever.

Jamal, of course, sensed what was going on. "You need to cut him loose, Dara."

"Cut him loose? Why would I do that to a good friend?"

"'Friend?'" Jamal's mouth twisted disdainfully. "Sean doesn't want to be your friend, and you know it. And you're sending him mixed messages by spending so much time with him."

"I don't know what you're talking about," she huffed, getting to her feet and walking to the door. "Sean knows what the deal is."

"Why don't you *think*," he said, tapping his temple with his index finger. "Sean thinks he can change your mind. And Mike doesn't like this 'friend' business, especially now. You mark my words. This 'friend' stuff is gonna blow up on you."

She waved a hand. "That's ridiculous. I'll see you later." She had a glimpse of Jamal shaking his head regretfully before she marched downstairs to the waiting area. Sean sat on the sofa, chatting with the woman sitting next to him. Dara took one look at the woman and immediately felt like an ugly duckling. She was exceptionally beautiful, with flawless toffee skin and gleaming wispy black hair, which framed her oval face and perfectly accentuated her sharp cheekbones and almond-shaped eyes. Just then the woman laughed at something Sean said, revealing a stunning, wide smile full of startlingly white teeth.

Dara's steps slowed; she couldn't take her eyes off this woman. She wore a pink and black plaid Chanel suit, and her long, shapely legs stretched out for miles before ending in spectator stiletto pumps that cost four hundred dollars if they cost a dime.

Sean saw Dara and leapt to his feet, smiling. "Hey, gorgeous," he said.

Dara approached slowly and tried to smile. "Hey." She turned to the woman, determined to find out who she was and what she wanted. "I don't believe we've met."

The woman's smile faded as she stood up to her full height—which was somewhere in giraffe territory—and eyed Dara speculatively. Her cool gaze slid over Dara's pretty but plain brown wool wrap dress and brown pumps, clearly assessing and dismissing her as competition. "Lisa Parker," she said, smiling politely but coolly. She extended her hand. "And you are . . . ?"

Dara took the witch's soft, freshly manicured hand. "Dara Williams. Are you a client of the firm?" she asked sweetly.

Lisa smirked. "I'm a *friend* of Mike's," she said, gripping Dara's hand tightly.

They stood like that for a tense moment, understanding each other perfectly, battle lines drawn, until they heard footsteps. As one, they all turned to see Mike approach from the stairs. His sharp eyes flickered to Dara, her hand still in Lisa's, then to Sean, where they narrowed. "What's up, man?" he said, shaking his hand. "What're you doing here?"

"Trying to take Dara to lunch," Sean told him, shooting a questioning look at Dara.

"Well, I don't—," she began.

"How *are* you, Mike?" Lisa cooed, sidling up to him and stopping only when she was well inside his personal space. She leaned in, kissing his cheek. Clearly surprised, Mike kissed her back, but his gaze immediately returned to Dara, then Sean. "Have you got a few minutes?" Lisa asked him.

"Uh . . . sure," he said. He turned to Dara. "Are you leaving for lunch?" he asked, his face looking a little strained.

Seething, Dara nodded. She certainly wasn't going to stick around while this slut tried to seduce Mike right under her nose. And if he wanted to spend time with a Stepford wife clone, then so be it. "Yeah."

Sean put a hand on the small of Dara's back to steer her toward the front door. "Let's go. Maybe we can try the bistro over on—"

"You *are* coming back this afternoon," Mike said to Dara through his tight jaw.

Dara did not for one second think it was anything other than a command. Well, she wasn't in a mood to be commanded—and certainly not by Mike, who still had that woman's hand on his arm. And she knew exactly what he was saying: he wanted her to know they were still on for dinner tonight, and he expected her to meet him back here at the office when her afternoon classes were over. Well, no, thank you. "Not today," she said pleasantly. "I finished my work this morning. I'll see you *tomorrow*."

His eyes narrowed into impotent slits of anger, but he didn't argue. As Dara ran to get her purse, she heard Lisa's sultry laughter in response to Mike's murmur and wanted to commit murder.

* * *

"Did you forget about me?" Lisa pouted.

Mike regarded her from the other side of his desk; he caught himself drumming his fingers impatiently on his blotter before he stopped and shoved his hands in his lap. She sat in the chair opposite him, with most of her crossed legs exposed. He was certain she'd hiked up her skirt a little before she sat down. Normally, when he had a visitor at work, he liked to sit with them on the sofa against the wall, or at least in the chair next to them, but he'd decided sitting behind his desk was the best way to keep himself away from Lisa's wandering hands.

Hands he used to quite enjoy.

"I've been really busy," he told her.

She smiled broadly. "Well, I've been busy, too. I've been working on a custody case and . . ."

Mike's mind shifted immediately back to Dara. He could safely zone out on Lisa for the next five minutes or so because she would talk nonstop—mostly about herself—and require him to make only periodic monosyllabic responses. Most likely, that was why he'd never spent much time with her outside of her bedroom.

Was Dara having a good lunch with Sean? he wondered bitterly. Was Sean confessing his undying love for the hundredth time? Was Dara laughing at all his little jokes and smiling up at him with those wondrous eyes?

"Don't you agree?" Lisa said.

His gaze shot back to her. "Umm-hmmm." She happily resumed chattering, a sound like the scraping of nails across a blackboard.

What had he ever seen in this woman? He could remember a time when he'd thought she was beautiful, and he supposed she was, but Dara was far more so.

Lisa wore way too much make-up. Her dark eyeliner made her look like a raccoon. Dara's make-up was much more subtle. Lisa's skin was pretty, sure, but Dara's glowed. Lisa was way too tall and thin. She did not have Dara's lush, toned figure at all. And what was the deal with Lisa's fake fingernails? Those chips of white plastic she had glued to the ends of her fingers looked like they could claw a person's eyes out.

But really, Lisa *was* attractive, even if she wasn't Dara, and her little defects would not previously have been enough for him to kick her out of bed. The real reason he found her unappealing was he could see—very clearly—that she wasn't *sweet*, that she had no real warmth, that she wasn't funny and open and engaging.

That she wasn't Dara.

God, when would she get to the point and stop yakking? He had a ton of work to do. Very discreetly, he twisted his left wrist in his lap and checked the time. Great. She'd already wasted ten minutes. How much longer was she planning to chatter?

His eyes caught a piece of paper on top of a stack of files, and he cringed inwardly. It was the latest estimate for replacing the roof on the brownstone: eighty-five hundred bones. And that was the lowest of the three estimates he'd had done. He snuck a glance out his window. Wonderful. Across the river, in Kentucky, he saw a huge patch of dark gray sky and roiling clouds headed this way. More rain. Just what he needed. At this rate, the storage closet would be five feet under water by Thanksgiving. If only he hadn't had to return Johnson's retainer! How was he going to . . .

"So can you come?" Lisa asked brightly.

Caught, Mike's guilty eyes darted back to her face. He had no idea what she'd asked him to come to—he

sincerely hoped it wasn't a free money giveaway somewhere—but it didn't matter, because he had no intention
of going anywhere with her. He managed a rueful smile.
"I'm really sorry. I'm just way too busy right now."

Lisa's smile disappeared; her eyes narrowed slightly.
Then she slid out of her seat and sashayed around to
perch on the corner of the desk, her skirt riding up
again. Had her thighs always been this skinny? Wary,
he slid his chair back a little.

Undeterred, Lisa leaned down and put her hand on
the inside of his thigh, where it immediately began to
roam upward. "But it's been so long since you came
over for dinner. And I can make *lasagna.* . . ."

Mildly irritated now—Dara would never throw herself
at a man like this—he caught her hand, stopping it right
before it reached his crotch, which was *not* straining for
her. "Thanks." He smiled tightly. "But no thanks."

"Mi-ike," she cried. Clearly, she'd never been turned
down flat before and did not intend to give up gracefully. And maybe he was out of his mind. He hadn't had
sex in months, and Lisa was only too happy to oblige,
no questions asked, just like always. But he could no
more have sex with her—or anyone else besides Dara—
than he could with a twelve-year-old boy. Mike picked
up her hand, kissed it, and just as quickly dropped it.
"Take care, Lisa. I need to get back to work."

Lisa huffed once, snatched her purse from the chair,
and swept out.

And Mike wondered whether Dara was now having
dessert with Sean.

"What's wrong with you, Dara?" Sean asked her as
they walked down the street to the little Chinese

restaurant. She'd been acting so strange the last few days. First, she'd lit up like Paul Brown Stadium during a night game, all smiley and giggly, practically floating through the halls at school—except when she saw him. Then her eyes darted away, and she got all quiet and subdued. He couldn't think when she'd last returned one of his phone calls. And then, today, she hadn't said two words to him since they left the office. She looked preoccupied, like she was trying to work out the theory of relativity in her head or something.

"Oh, I don't know," she said vaguely, keeping her eyes on the sidewalk in front of them. For the first time, she looked him directly in the face. She tried to smile. "What's been up with you?"

"Not too much," he said as they stopped at the corner and waited for the light to change. People hurried by them on all sides, hustling to and from lunch. "Well, my boss has really been sticking it to—"

"So, who was that woman? What was her name? Linda?" she interrupted, shooting a quick glance at his face. Something in her strained expression jolted him, and when the WALK light came on, he watched her march off for a few steps before it dawned on him he should be walking with her.

What was going on? Why on earth should Dara care—much less be upset about—who that woman was? He took a few long strides and caught up with her. "Her name's *Lisa*. She graduated with Mike."

"Graduated," she muttered under her breath. "Right."

Sean stared at her. "I think they hook up every now and then, too."

Her lips twisted, but she looked straight ahead. "I guess he does a lot of that. Hooking up."

Suddenly, he thought about all the time Dara spent at the office. She'd claimed Mike was working her rear off, and having worked for Mike himself, he didn't doubt it. But was there more to the story? Dara was beautiful. Mike was a man. A man who had dated some of the most beautiful women Sean had ever seen. A man who could pretty much sleep with whomever he wanted. Everyone knew Mike drew women the way an open flue draws smoke up a chimney.

Something ugly awakened and twisted inside his gut.

He stopped walking and grabbed her arm, oblivious to the people brushing past them on either side. Surprised, she stared up at him and pulled her arm away. "Yeah, he hooks up a lot. Why shouldn't he when he doesn't have a girlfriend and says he doesn't want to get married anytime soon? And what's all this to *you*?"

Her face closed off as if he'd flipped a switch. She whirled and resumed her march up the street. "Nothing," she said over her shoulder. "Nothing at all."

At seven-fifteen a loud knocking on her door startled Dara out of her deep concentration. She sat on the floor, with her back against the sofa; her contracts book and notebook lay open on the coffee table in front of her. The muted television was on CNN.

After lunch with Sean, she'd gone to class, then had come back home to wallow alone in her jealous misery. Of course, she'd known someone like Mike could have any beautiful woman he wanted, but it was something else again to be confronted with one of them. And here she was, too scared to even sleep with him! What on earth did he want with *her*—a nervous

Nelly and near virgin—when he could have a woman like *that*?

She stalked to the door and checked the peephole. Bracing herself, she opened it. Mike walked in, trench coat covering his suit, his face carefully neutral. "Let's go." He checked his watch. "Our reservation's at eight."

"Not tonight," she said, brushing past him to go back to the living room. She picked up the remote and clicked the TV off. "I really need to study."

Mike was right on her heels. "Is there a problem you'd like to discuss?"

She shoved her hands in the back pockets of her jeans and sulkily watched him. Had he gone to lunch with Lisa? Had they made plans for one night this week? Her heart twisted at the thought. Still, she had no intention of letting him know she was jealous. They had no claims on each other, and he'd certainly made her no promises. Her mother would cringe in horror at the thought of her wearing her heart on her sleeve like this. "No." She tried to smile. "No problem."

He snorted, yanking his arms out of his trench coat and throwing it across the overstuffed chair. "Cut the sullen, passive-aggressive crap, Dara," he snapped. "If we're going to be together, then we need to figure out a way to work these things out. We had plans for tonight, and I'm not gonna let you ruin them like this. Tell me what the problem is!"

"Oh, all right!" she exploded, marching up to stand in his face. "Who's your little friend? You sure you don't want to spend tonight with *her*?"

Mike stared at her. "Lisa is a classmate of mine from law school and a woman I occasionally have sex with," he said very quietly.

"'Occasionally?'" she cried, astonished he hadn't

bothered to deny it or at least sugarcoat it. "Well, when was the last *occasion*?"

His jaw tightened. "About a week before I laid eyes on you."

"Right," she said, glaring at him, wishing he would get out so she could cry like she wanted to.

He snatched her arm, pulling her up against him. "Yeah, *right*." He leaned down in her face. "I haven't had sex with her—or anybody else—in months, because the only person I want to have sex with is *you*."

Jerking her arm free, she screeched, "But you're not having sex with me!"

He shoved his hands in his pockets. "I intend to rectify that as soon as I think you're ready. In the meantime, I can wait."

Slightly mollified, Dara took a deep breath. "Why was she there today? Did you call her?"

Lips twisting, Mike leaned down in her face again. "No, I didn't call her! She just showed up, and I sent her on her way! What kind of a jerk do you take me for?"

Something in her heart soared, wild and free. Suddenly, she felt ridiculous for her little temper tantrum. Mike must think she was a raving lunatic. "Well . . . we just started dating, and we don't have any claims on each—"

"Bull." His harsh voice was like a slap across her face. She gaped at him, too stunned to argue. "I would never expect you to sleep with me if you thought there were other women, so let's clear this up right now. There's nobody else, and there won't be anybody else as long as we're together. Do you understand me?"

Somehow she nodded.

"In fact, I took an HIV test the other day. It was

negative, but we'll still use condoms to protect ourselves. Okay?"

"Okay," she said, her head spinning.

"Let's get something else straight." Muscles flexed in his jaw, and his eyes glinted dangerously. "I want you, and I don't share what's mine."

"Am I yours?" she asked breathlessly, thrilled.

He paused, his cheeks flushing. "Yes."

She moved to touch him, but he stepped back and threw his hands up. "Don't get too excited. I don't like you spending so much time with Sean."

"Why?" Why would Mike ever feel annoyed by something so harmless as her friendship with his brother? Surely, he didn't expect her to just dump Sean as a friend.

"Let me ask you something," he said calmly. "Would you want me spending a lot of time with Lisa when you know she wants to sleep with me?"

"Of course not," she snapped, bristling again at the thought.

"Exactly." He reached out a hand to stroke her cheek, smoothing her ruffled feathers. "And that's why I sent her packing today."

Comprehension dawned; she understood Mike completely. She would have to tone things way down with Sean. She stepped forward into his arms, clinging tightly to his neck. He held her close enough to hear his heart thundering. "I'm sorry," she whispered. "I'm sorry. I don't like to fight with you."

He pulled far enough away to kiss her temple, then her forehead. "Neither do I." Smoothing back her hair, he smiled a little. "But sometimes we'll have to fight; that's how it goes. We'll get through it. What I can't get through is you pushing me away or pretending nothing's wrong."

Out of nowhere, a surge of panic hit her, worse even than the panic she'd felt when she'd thought Mike preferred Lisa to her. Her feelings for him were so overwhelming, she felt absolutely helpless to control them. Stiffening, she shrank away from him; he let her go reluctantly. She backed up a couple of steps. "What is it?" he asked, his worried eyes wide and intent. "Tell me."

Her hand went to her chest as if she could force her heart to slow down to its normal rhythm. It was impossible to put the way she felt into words. Just as she'd feared, he'd taken over her every thought. At times he seemed to read her mind. She depended on his support at work and with school and with . . . everything. He made her laugh; he made her body sing.

And he could walk out on her tomorrow and blow her heart to smithereens.

The vast power he had over every aspect of her life terrified her. "Sometimes . . . I get so scared about . . . what's between us," she whispered.

His eyes softened a little, and he nodded as if he understood her perfectly. As if he felt the same way. "I know." He held his hand out to her. "Let's hang in there, anyway."

Nodding, relieved, she took his hand and held on for dear life.

That night Mike couldn't sleep, so at around two, after tossing and turning for a couple hours or more, he slipped on his pants and let himself out onto Dara's balcony, which overlooked a small woods. The full moon provided enough light to read by, and the air was frigid—just what he needed to clear his mind a little. Breathing deeply, he braced his hands on the railing.

He'd talked to Mama earlier. She sounded weak and dispirited, and she was allowed, of course. Her chemotherapy was generally going well, although she tired very easily. She was—big surprise—worried about Sean, who'd told her he didn't like his internship. He'd also apparently told her again about his unrequited love for Dara, so now she was worried about *that*, too. And Mike felt guiltier than ever because the last few days with Dara had been the best of his life, bar none.

And he had no intention of giving her up—not for his mother, not for Sean. Not for anyone.

The other reason he couldn't sleep was his continued money woes with the firm. He'd finally gone ahead and authorized the roofers to replace the roof. Little did they know, he had no idea how he'd pay for it once they finished. Most likely, he'd charge it on a credit card, same as always.

Maybe he'd overextended when he'd bought the brownstone so soon after opening the firm, but he didn't want to pay rent forever. The building had been a steal and was in one of the up-and-coming sections of downtown. No, it'd been a good investment of his inheritance. He'd just have to work a little harder, bill a few more hours here and there. That was another part of his life that was going exceedingly well now, thanks to Dara. They'd made it a habit to do their work together every night, and he'd discovered that when Dara was with him, he could settle down and work.

Shivering a little, he turned to go back inside, but the French door swung open, and Dara, looking deliciously tousled with her rumpled hair and loosely belted robe, appeared. She came to stand beside him and braced her own hands on the rail. "Brrr," she said, rubbing her hands up and down her arms. "The bed was too warm and comfortable for you, I take it?"

He stood behind her and pulled her back against him for warmth. She gratefully snuggled closer. "I couldn't sleep."

"Why?"

"I dunno. Worried about Mama. Worried about the firm."

"Oh, I see. And worrying about things at two in the morning will solve . . . what, exactly?"

"Nothing," he said, resigned. "Absolutely nothing."

"The doctors said your mother's prognosis is good. But you know she's got to go through the chemotherapy to come out the other side. That's all there is to it."

He nodded and pressed his lips to the top of her head. "I know. But I don't want her to suffer."

She slid her soft hands along his arms. "I know. But she was blessed to discover the cancer before it spread to other parts of her body, and she's blessed to have health insurance to pay for all this." She twisted around to face him. "And she's blessed to have you to lean on."

Whenever she was with him, he felt his worries shrink down to a manageable size. She was such a commonsense, practical person. And he didn't know what he would do without her. He kissed her forehead. "You take all the fun out of a good worry."

Smiling, she laid her head on his chest. "Yeah, well, there's always global warming." He was still laughing when she stepped away, tugging his hand toward the door. "Come to bed. You've got a full day of worrying tomorrow."

* * *

"Let's put them on the counter for now." Mike waved his hand at the stretch of the island in front of his refrigerator, and he and Dara each laid a small pumpkin down. Mike also set a large paper grocery bag on the counter and fished out a gallon jug of fresh apple cider, several large tart apples covered with homemade caramel, and a plastic mesh bag full of the weirdest squash they'd ever seen. All about the size of tomatoes, they were green, yellow, and orange—some striped, some nubbly, some with long necks, some oblong, some round. He raised the bag. "What's this stuff again?"

"Gourds," she said patiently. Another weekend had come and gone already. After spending most of the morning working and studying, they'd gone for a long ride in the country so they could enjoy the remainder of the fall colors in the trees. They'd stopped on the way back at one of the farms outside town and made a few minor purchases.

"What's a gourd?"

She took off her fleece jacket and laid it across the back of one of the chairs at the heavy oak table. "It's a decorative squash."

Mike dubiously studied the gourds. He ripped the bag open and removed one, sniffing it before he tapped it on the counter; it sounded about as soft as a bowling ball. "Can you eat them?"

"No," she said, laughing. "Hence the word 'decorative'"

"And I need gourds because . . . ?"

"Good grief!" she cried. "What are you going to be like at Christmas?" Opening the cabinet next to the dishwasher, she quickly found his fruit bowl and emptied the gourds into it. They'd been splitting their time evenly between her apartment and his house, so she knew his kitchen pretty well. Then she arranged the pumpkins and the gourds on the table. "*Voila*!" She held her hand out with a flourish. "Now you're ready for Thanksgiving!"

He raised one unenthusiastic eyebrow. "But I thought you were going to bake me a pumpkin pie with those," he said, a trace of a whine creeping into his voice.

"Awww, poor bay-bee," she murmured. His frown deepened, and she decided to take pity on him. "If I make you a pie with *real* pumpkins—the canned kind —do you promise not to cry?"

He nodded, clearly relieved. "Thank you, sweet-heart," he said, grinning.

"You're welcome."

She sat on one of the stools at the counter and watched, bemused, as, humming absently, he bustled around the kitchen and efficiently put away the gro-ceries. Just as efficiently, he went to the great room, which was connected to the kitchen, and started a fire with the logs he'd laid in the fireplace this morning.

It's time.

The thought popped into her head, and much to her surprise, there was no corresponding fear—only an absolute certainty. She knew he was as much in love with her as she was with him, even though they'd never said the words. She knew he wasn't seeing anyone else and wouldn't. She knew she could trust him.

"Where should we go for dinner?" he asked, strid-ing back into the kitchen.

It was dinnertime and completely dark outside al-ready. On their way home, a light rain had begun to fall, although now it sounded as if they needed to start building an ark. Going back outside was an unappealing thought. "Let's stay in," she told him.

"Yeah, good idea." He opened a drawer and removed a handful of take-out menus. "Chinese. Indian. Pizza." He sifted through them. "What do you have a taste for?"

"Oh, I don't—"

He opened the refrigerator door and leaned down inside, considering. "Or I could grill those steaks, or I make a pretty good omelet—"

"I don't think so," she said. Eating was the last thing on her mind right now.

Nonplussed, Mike stood up straight and looked over his shoulder at her, one hand still on the door. "Well, what do you want?"

Vaguely aware of the thunderous beat of her heart, Dara took a deep breath and leapt into the unknown. "I want to make love in front of the fire."

Mike froze. His amber eyes went dark; a muscle throbbed visibly in the strong column of his throat. Very deliberately, he closed the refrigerator door and turned to face her, the island between them. "Don't play, Dara," he said in a hoarse voice.

"I'm not playing."

He stared at her, with his hands braced on the counter, his shoulders rigid with tension. "You weren't ready before—"

"I'm ready now."

He looked away and ran a trembling hand through his hair. Finally, he looked back at her; the strain on his face had, if possible, grown even more intense. "I don't want to rush you, sweetheart. I can wait as long—"

"I'm tired of waiting," she said impatiently.

"Are you really sure? Because—"

Incredulous, she shook her head. "I really never thought it would be this hard to get you to have sex with me!"

He gave a snort of laughter as he walked around the counter toward her. "Neither did I." Taking her hand, he pulled her to her feet and led her to the great room, where the roaring fire crackled and danced. "Come here."

Chapter 16

After grabbing a condom from her purse—the clever girl knew they'd need them sooner or later and had started carrying them—Mike almost didn't know where to start. He'd dreamed and daydreamed of this moment so many times—so vividly—the choices nearly overwhelmed him. They'd never made love before. In theory, he should go slowly and gently. In reality, his frantic need for her would be difficult—very difficult—to control. What should he do first? Slide his fingers through her thick, glossy, fragrant hair? Dive for her breasts, her butt, her legs? Indecision paralyzed him. He stared down at Dara's sweet face for a long moment, and when his eyes found her lips—full, tender, dewy—he made his choice. He cupped her face and lowered his head, fusing his mouth to hers for a kiss that was hot and wet and deep. Frenzied.

Dara locked her arms around his neck. Her restless fingers ran through his hair, caressing his nape and massaging his shoulders. Then she found the buttons on the front of his heavy cotton shirt. She broke the kiss and looked down at the endless row. She fumbled with the first couple of buttons—her hands shook—then her accusatory gaze shot to his. "Don't you own any turtlenecks?"

He did not answer. Instead, he put one hand on each side of his collar, ripped the shirt open down the middle, and threw it on the floor. Buttons skittered across the carpet, and one or two plinked against the fireplace. Dara laughed triumphantly. Before he could blink, she slid his undershirt over his head. Gasping, she studied his chest in the firelight. The barest smile touched her lips. Her wide eyes flicked back to his. "You're so beautiful," she told him reverently.

Mike stared at her, stupefied. Her eagerness and her soft, warm hands stroking all over him—not hesitantly, either, but firmly, confidently, the way he'd taught her he liked—were almost too much to bear. "I want you, angel. God, I *want* you." His need for her clawed relentlessly at his gut. His mouth covered hers again; his hands found the edge of her fluffy blue sweater. Suddenly, he hated that soft sweater, because it was a barrier between them. He wanted to rip it off and drag her to the floor beneath him. He wanted to come inside her—to be part of her—and to love her until she sobbed with joy and begged for mercy, which he wouldn't give.

But he looked into her warm brown eyes, half-closed now with passion, and forced himself instead to go slowly. He slid the sweater up over her silky belly, brushing his fingers along her flesh, and her skin seemed to shiver to life beneath his fingertips. Obediently, she raised her hands over her head so he could slip it off. He dropped it to the floor, then looked at her.

He paused, panting. She was perfection in her black lace bra and jeans. Glowing brown skin, the ripe curves of her breasts and hips, the gentle curve of her belly, her endless legs. His body teetered on the edge of explosion, and he felt a fine sheen of perspiration on his forehead. "God, Dara."

She smiled a slow, seductive smile at him. Very deliberately, she reached up and unhooked her bra—it had a clasp in the front—and her lush breasts spilled free. Her large, dark, distended nipples seemed to strain for him. She bent and slid her jeans and panties off, then straightened, watching him.

He smelled her; the faintest trace of her intoxicating feminine scent washed over him. His heart seemed to have stopped beating because he knew she must be very wet—ready for him. He pulled her hard against his chest, and she moaned, rubbing herself against him. He clamped his hands on her rear, then pressed his fingers lower, between her legs. She gasped sharply. He trailed his fingers in her dew; she was soaking wet. "What have I gotten myself into with you, Dara?"

Her unfocused eyes found his. It seemed to take her a moment to process his words. She paused long enough to give him a half smile as she tossed her head. She pressed her breasts against his chest and slid her hands down his torso to his belt. She unbuckled it, unhooked his pants, and opened his zipper. Before he could protest, she put her hand inside his boxer briefs and rubbed firmly up and down his length. "Do you want me to stop?"

"God, no." His voice was a hoarse croak. "But I do want you to slow down, because if you keep up like this, I won't last another thirty seconds." He pulled her back into his arms and buried his lips in the sensitive hollow between her neck and shoulders until she cried out. "And that would be a shame," he continued, "because this is our first time." She laughed and rubbed him, anyway, torturing him. Then she closed her fingers around him and slowly but firmly moved her hand up and down.

"Don't!" Mike caught her hand, stopping her. Her smile was knowing and satisfied. "You little witch," he murmured. Impatiently, he shoved his pants and briefs down his legs and stepped out of them. When he straightened, he started to reach for her again, but the look on her face stopped him. She stared at his chest; then her eyes traveled down over his arousal and thighs, before they returned to his groin. Her obvious appreciation made him swell even more. She stared intently at him. "You're so amazing."

Mike was incapable of speech. He dropped to his knees in front of her and buried his face between her breasts, reveling. Catching a nipple between his lips, he rubbed his tongue across the swollen tip, then sucked hard, then nipped. She mewled like a kitten. He ran his hands from her shoulders to her wrists, massaging her, delighted when he felt her gooseflesh rise to his touch. He touched her everywhere, and everywhere he touched, she shivered helplessly.

She wrapped her arms around his neck and shoulders, while his hands moved from her waist to her hips, then lower, kneading her butt. His fingers slid along her shapely thighs and calves, his lips trailing behind. He pulled her down to lie beneath him on the plush carpet before the fireplace. To Mike's amazement, his hands trembled with anticipation. His hands hadn't shaken with a girl since he was in high school. Not one inch of her body escaped his attention; he couldn't stand the thought of missing anything or of leaving any part of her unclaimed tonight. He rolled her onto her stomach and straddled her, massaging her back and shoulders, then ran his mouth down her spine while she murmured unintelligibly. Then he rubbed his chin against her back, scratching and tickling her with his mustache and cheeks while she laughed and squealed and squirmed.

Suddenly, he gentled, gliding his lips across her nape until she crooned and purred. He turned her onto her back and anchored her hips with his hands. Her thighs opened, and her hips arched up to meet him. With a low growl, he put his head between her legs, teasing and tasting her. Tears streamed from the corners of her closed eyes, and she sobbed, the most thrilling sound he'd ever heard. Then her body went rigid, and she cried out his name.

He slid back up her body and stared down at her face, nuzzling her lips. "I need you, Dara." After he protected them, he held his penis and rubbed it insistently back and forth over her sex. She twisted and writhed, then clamped her strong legs around his waist and pulled him closer. His body throbbed on the edge between agony and rapture, but he paused and waited, shuddering. "God, you don't know how much I need you."

Slowly, she opened her dazed eyes. Tears still sparkled in them. "You're killing me."

"Die for me, then." Surrendering at last to his need, he thrust his hips forward, and with one sure stroke, he was inside of her. They both cried out. There was no way he could have anticipated how exquisitely tight she was, or how violently she would grip him. Her tight, hot, slick muscles clamped down around him, and his control—what little he'd had left—went up in flames. He circled his hips once, twice, and she cried out again, clutching and scratching his back. Her shuddering spasms went on and on, clenching and un-clenching around him until the pleasure blinded him. His mind was empty of every coherent thought but one: she was his now, and he couldn't ever give her up. "Don't you ever leave me, Dara," he said, panting, his voice hoarse. "Do you understand? I need you."

Her face was rapturous; she whimpered. He inched out of her—slowly, slowly, torturing himself far worse than he tortured her. Dara's eyes flew open, and she groaned a protest, thrashing beneath him. "*This* is what I've wanted since the second I saw you." Just as slowly, he eased back inside; Dara cried out. "*This* is what I want every time I look at you. Look at me," he commanded. Dara's eyes, dazed and unfocused, fluttered open. "I *need* you. Don't you ever leave me. You promise me?"

Tears streamed down her temples to fall onto the carpet; a sheen of perspiration covered her face and chest. She panted. "I promise," she whispered. "*I promise*."

That was what he needed. Easing back inside her, he picked up his rhythm. Dara's back arched, her legs wrapped tightly around his waist, and her hips rose up to meet him, thrust for powerful thrust. He stroked harder now, savagely, driving toward an ecstasy from which he knew he would never recover. Impaling her one last time, he shattered. He cried her name over and over again, astonished a man could experience such violent pleasure and live.

They'd done it, he thought wildly, tightening his arms around her.

There was no going back.

At some point during the night—dinner forgotten entirely—they made it upstairs to his tan and navy bedroom, which was one of four, and into his massive king-sized four-poster bed. She'd never been so happy or relaxed. Mike's lovemaking was the most addictive of drugs, and she felt as languid as a cat napping on a sunny porch. She lay propped up on the pillows, with his head nestled between her bare breasts, his hands absently stroking her skin while she ran her fingers through his wavy hair. Mike really had incredible taste, she thought drowsily. The bed, dresser, chest of drawers, and nightstands were all antique mahogany pieces with beautiful, intricate carvings. The navy duvet was exquisitely soft—400-count? 500?—and the rug covering the dark hardwood floor was Indian, like the one in the foyer, with vivid blues and greens and reds.

"Sean called me today," Mike said sleepily. "Actually, he's called several times. I've been dodging him."

"Yeah. Me, too." She propped herself up to sit beside him, and he stroked her cheek. "When will we tell him?"

His eyes wavered, and he looked away. "I don't know. That part's going to be hard."

"You don't want to hurt him any more than I do."

"No."

"Why don't you get along? You've never told me what happened between you and him."

"Sean was the greatest kid in the world." He smiled at some distant memory. "I *loved* him. I remember the day they brought him home from the hospital. I felt like he was *my* baby. I looked out for him. I taught him everything I knew. I stuck up for him. I took him everywhere with me."

Mike seemed so far away suddenly. He stared vacantly at the mirror over the dresser. Dara almost had the feeling he was talking to himself and she was an eavesdropper, but she had so many questions. "Did you fight?"

"Hardly ever. We got on each other's nerves, but never anything serious. He was so much fun, you know? He was funnier than any of my friends. And I was always serious, so I needed someone around like Sean." His face clouded over. "But he could never focus. He never studied, never did his chores, never stuck through a whole season of a sport—"

"And you focused enough for two or three people," she interjected.

He looked startled by her observation. "That's right. Things always seemed to come pretty easily to me—"

"Sports, school, girls."

His smile was slow and lazy. "Yeah. *Especially* the girls."

She could just imagine. Irritated by her irrational jealousy for those faceless teenage girls, she jabbed him in the ribs. He caught her hands and kissed her wrists. She froze immediately. "Do you want to hear this or not?"

Her sex throbbed again. Painfully. Still, she did want to hear this story. She snatched her hands away. "I'm trying to listen." She pulled the duvet up to cover her breasts and tried to focus.

Mike stared off in the distance again. "Sean always charmed my parents," he said softly. "He could talk his way out of anything. But he was always angry; it was always right there, below the surface. Angry at the coach for making him run harder, angry at his pet hamster when it died, angry at my parents because he thought they favored me. And, most of all, he was angry at me."

He snorted. "Whenever I had an accomplishment of any kind, he seemed to take it as a personal slight."

"How terrible."

"He could never find a purpose in life, and he seemed to think it was just bad luck that good things didn't happen to him, bad luck if he flunked a test even though he didn't study, bad luck if he got fired even though he'd been late every day. That kind of thing. Nothing in his life was ever his own responsibility. And the harder *I* worked, the more he seemed to hate me. And I would always cover for him. I couldn't stand to see him in trouble. I made excuses with my parents and with his friends and girlfriends. I don't know how he made it through college. I guess he had someone else there to enable him since I wasn't around."

She stroked his face. His jaw had turned to granite. "You did the best you could to be a good brother. It sounds like he never even met you halfway."

He winced. "Well, anyway," he continued, "when he graduated, he messed around with a couple of jobs, and then I hired him because he said he wanted to be a lawyer, but his grades alone weren't good enough to get him into law school. I'd done pretty well in law school, and I'm a big alumni donor. I knew a couple years as a paralegal, plus me putting in a good word for him, would probably get him in. And that's what happened. We'll see if he makes it through."

"How did he do when he worked for you?"

Mike threw up his hands. "It was terrible. He was late, or he wouldn't show up at all. He was disorganized. He lost files. He missed deadlines. The staff was resentful because it was the boss's brother who was messing up. It was two years of misery, but I couldn't bring myself to fire him. Finally, when he went back to school, I told him he'd had the last favor he would ever have from me."

"Wasn't he grateful?"

He looked at her as if she'd grown a second head. "Of course not. He said, 'Screw you!' He said he didn't need any help from me and to stay out of his life." She couldn't muster up any words of comfort. She laid her head on his shoulder and tightened her arms around him instead. "I've tried Dara." She could hear the frustration in his voice. She sat up to look at him. "I've tried so hard to understand. To help him. But nothing ever helps Sean. Nothing's ever enough. And he never tries to help himself. What else am I supposed to do?"

"There's nothing else you can do."

He pulled her into his arms and held her tightly, his chin resting on her shoulder. He threaded his hands through her hair. "So you see," he murmured, "our relationship was all screwed up long before you came along."

It was very late, probably well past two. The scented candles he'd lit hours ago and put on the nightstand had long since burned down. Even though he'd achieved a state of supreme relaxation and contentment, Mike couldn't seem to let himself—or Dara—drift off to sleep. He didn't want to let go of tonight. Dara laid her head on Mike's chest, stroking the tiny hairs around his nipples. "We need to go to sleep. Otherwise, Jamal will take one look at our bleary eyes tomorrow and know what we've been up to."

"Yeah. And tomorrow's a busy day. We've got

Aidan Sullivan coming in to go over his testimony for trial."

"I'm looking forward to meeting him. I've read so much about his accident and his medical history and his life in the wheelchair, I feel like I know him already." She slipped out of his arms and off the edge of the bed. "When I get back, it's time to go to sleep."

He scowled and reached for her arm, pulling her back. The sight of her naked body diverted him entirely from any thoughts of the Sullivan case. "Where do you think you're going?"

"To the bathroom." She laughed and twisted out of his reach. "Do you mind?"

What had gotten into him? He'd become such a possessive freak, he couldn't even let the poor woman go to the bathroom in peace. "No," he said unhappily. "Hurry back."

She threw her head back and laughed, as if this was the funniest thing she'd ever heard. "Mike." She wiped the tears from the outside corners of her eyes. "I'm not going anywhere. You're going to have to pace yourself. At this rate, you'll be sick of me by Friday."

He tried to laugh, but that gnawing uncertainty was still there. "You'll have to give me some time to adjust to us actually being lovers," he told her. "I'm a little out of control. I feel like a kid in a candy store."

Her smile slowly vanished. Her stare grew intent and heated. His eyes slipped to her breasts, which were heaving now, and her nipples hardened and darkened instantly. And his body stiffened urgently—and completely—in response. Suddenly, the space between them felt like a canyon. He got up on his knees and scooted to the edge of the bed. The sheet slid away, and the second it did, her eyes shot to his groin.

She let out a long, serrated breath. He held his hand out to her. "Come here."

With a cry, she stepped back to the bed and into his arms. Mike lost all control. He needed her the way a drowning man needs a breath of air. He couldn't possibly be gentle now. His fingers twisted in her hair, pulling her head back so he could bury his lips in the hollow of her neck. She shuddered and moaned loudly. He grabbed her face and kissed her roughly and deeply.

His voice was low and harsh. "I never thought I would have you, Dara. There were days in the office when I saw you and I felt like my skin was on fire because I wanted you so much." Mike felt that same frustration, that helpless gnawing in his gut, right now. He had to have her, and it had to be hard and fast. He couldn't help himself. Not this time.

"And now?" she said, gasping.

He gave a hoarse, bewildered laugh. They were part of each other now. He couldn't be happy if she was unhappy and couldn't be happy without her. It was thrilling and terrifying. "And now it's worse. I don't want to let you out of my sight. You're my obsession, Dara."

"No. Obsessions are bad."

"No, sweetheart." He pulled her back beneath him, flipping her over onto her stomach. "Not this one." After slipping on a condom, he slid over her and used his knee to spread her legs wide. Her hips lifted automatically, and he entered her with one hard stroke. Dara bucked beneath him, squeezing her legs and butt together around him. She drove him wild, and he used her mercilessly—pounding them both into oblivion.

* * *

Dara woke up, face down, the tangled sheets and blankets wrapped around her waist, and immediately reached across the bed for Mike. He wasn't there. Frowning, she sat up and forced her tired eyes open. It was still dark, although a thin sliver of light shone from underneath the closed master bathroom door, and she heard the faint sound of water running. The alarm clock on the night stand read five-thirty. She'd gotten two hours of sleep, if that.

She stretched her arms over her head, reveling in the delicious ache that seemed to permeate every part of her body. Mike had worked parts of her anatomy that yoga and Pilates could never hope to reach; the soreness between her thighs was an exquisite pain she hoped would not go away anytime soon.

Creeping over to the bathroom, she cracked open the door, squinting her eyes against the sudden infusion of bright light. The steamy air felt wonderful after the slight chill of the bedroom, and she slipped inside. Mike stood in the large, square, clear shower, in the far corner, his back to her. Bracing himself against the sand-colored tiles in front of him, he leaned down to let the powerful spray soak his head.

Technically, after the night they'd just had, sex should be the last thing on her mind, but she shuddered with desire, anyway. Her nipples hardened, and the sweet, tight ache in her loins began to throb insistently. He was the most stunning man she'd ever seen or could ever hope to see. Fascinated, she watched the ripple and play of muscles in his sculpted arms, shoulders, and back as he straightened and began to wash his hair. His butt was a perfect basketball—high, round, solid as a slab of marble. Long, powerful thighs tapered to shapely calves. The water splashing over him, running in various and thrilling channels and grooves down his body, only highlighted his perfection.

She opened the shower door and stepped inside behind him, sliding her hands up his back and pressing her body full against his. He froze. "I thought you might need some help with the hard spots," she murmured in his ear.

Mike faced her, smiling. "Good thought." He took a washcloth from the rack and lathered it with soap, his glittering eyes never leaving hers. She took it, and he turned back around while she rubbed his back in languid circles, which left him murmuring unintelligibly with pleasure.

"Now you." He took the cloth back, reached over her shoulder, and trailed it down between her breasts to her belly button, where he increased the pressure. Her body jerked. She pressed herself closer to him, whimpering, but he gently pushed her away. "Not yet."

He circled the rag on her breasts, deliberately keeping his touch light and teasing. She arched her back, thrusting her breasts into his hands, but he retreated again. "Please," she begged.

His hand moved lower, to the thick thatch of hair at the top of her thighs. He let his fingers dip, for one second, to her engorged sex. She cried out. He pressed his lips to her ear. Helplessly, she turned her head, moving closer. "Please what, Dara?"

Her eyes closed, and she slumped against the glass stall. Her head fell back. She caught his hand and tried to pull his fingers back against the heavy folds of her lips, but he circled around her core, as if he didn't quite understand what she wanted. "Please, Mike." She moaned loudly. "Please . . ." He stroked her firmly, once. She writhed. He lowered his head and bit

the tender hollow between her neck and shoulder.
"God!" she gasped.

He stroked her again. "What is it you want, Dara?"

"I want you—"

"You want me to what?"

She opened her eyes and tried to speak, but no
words came out. She swallowed convulsively. "I want
you to touch me. I want you inside me. I'm begging
you." She tightened her grip on his wrist, shoving his
hand at her sex. "Please."

He gave her an amused—though strained—smile.
"Since you asked so nicely." His fingers found her
bud, and he circled it, stroking, and then he thrust two
fingers inside. Dara went rigid, crying out. He palmed
her, hard. It took her a long minute to recover. When
she opened her eyes, she focused immediately on his
rampant erection.

Mike froze.

She smiled slowly. "You're going to pay for that."

"What did you have in mind?" His voice had grown
husky. Her smile widened. She reached down and
took him gently in her hands. Mike's harsh breath reverberated off the glass stall as she knelt. Mike's
knees sagged, and he slumped against the wall. Dara
looked up in time to see his eyes roll closed and his
head fall back.

She smiled, thrilled with herself, and lowered her
head.

Eventually, he left her to finish her shower while he
dressed. By the time he came back in the bathroom,
suit on, briefcase in hand, she'd wrapped a towel
around her hair and her body and had begun fishing
around in her overnight bag for her make-up case. He
came up behind her, circled her waist with his free

arm, and kissed her nape, catching her gaze in the mirror. "Sullivan's coming at nine. You'll be there?"

"I'll be there. The trial's in two weeks. Are you ready?"

"Getting there. I'm way ahead of the game with the question outlines you've put together for me. I pretty much know what I'll ask Aidan on direct and the truck driver on cross."

"Good," she said, enormously pleased.

"And then you have finals right after Thanksgiving."

She made a face. "Don't remind me. The only good thing about finals is that I have the world's greatest tutor on twenty-four-hour standby."

His flat hand slid up her waist to her breasts, where he rubbed his palm over one nipple, then the other. She gasped; the nubbly, fluffy towel abraded her skin in the most delicious way. "I'm glad to hear I'm the world's greatest at *something*." His glittering eyes held her gaze in the mirror.

She flushed deeply. "Oh, you're the world's greatest at a couple of things I can think of."

"Good." His grin was knowing and satisfied. "We make a good team, don't we, Dara?"

"A very good team."

Mike didn't seem to be in any particular hurry to let her go and head to work; he continued to stare at her in the mirror, a contented smile on his face. Her heart swelled. "I left an extra key and the security code on the nightstand for you," he told her, skimming his lips over her nape again. "Lock up when you leave."

"Okay."

"Dinner tonight?"

She raised her eyebrows. "Dinner?"

He grazed her earlobe with his teeth; she whimpered. "Dinner . . . and other things."

An idiotic grin split her face. "Okay."

Turning her around to face him, he kissed her thoroughly, then slowly let her go. "I'll see you soon, angel."

A vast emptiness opened up inside her the second she heard the front door shut after him. Close on its heels came doubts. She'd done something profound and irrevocable: she'd given herself completely to Mike. He'd already had her love, and now she'd given him her body, too, and he'd made it his own. And she'd given it to him without any proclamations that he loved her or promises about their future. She'd shamelessly held nothing back, and now he knew all her secrets. She was addicted to Mike in every possible way, and if he wanted to make her his slave, she was helpless to do anything about it.

Groping in her make-up bag, she pulled out her compact and snapped it open with trembling hands. Unbidden, Lisa's image flashed through her mind. Mike had made love to Lisa once, too, and look where it had gotten *her*—tossed aside for someone new. Surely, everyone who slept with Mike came out of the experience ruined for other men. She had precious little experience, but enough to know Mike's skilled lovemaking was a rare and wondrous thing. It certainly bore no resemblance to the awkward, unsatisfying fumbling she'd experienced with Antonio. She'd taken Lisa's place, and maybe, all too soon, someone else would take *her* place.

Stop it.

Disgusted with herself, Dara shoved all doubts and images of Lisa and Antonio far away. She stared in the mirror. Mike *loved* her. She knew it even if he'd never said it. Their relationship was about much more than the thrill of the conquest, and her worries were just a sign of her pathetic—and groundless—insecurities. Mike had given her no reason to doubt him, and she needed to pull herself together and get to the office.

As soon as she saw him again, she would realize how ridiculous her fears were.

Mike sat at his desk, flipping idly through his notes for the meeting with Sullivan, his mind on Dara. His panic was back, full-blown, and he knew why: he was whipped. Just as he'd feared, she'd done a number on him last night, and he knew absolutely that he could not live without her. Certainly not now, or next month. Probably not ever. Leaving her this morning to come to work had been, quite possibly, the hardest thing he'd ever done. Voluntarily giving her the extra key— the *only* extra key—to his house had been the easiest.

He pressed his eyes shut, dropped his head, and ran his hands roughly over his forehead and temples. What was he going to do? This kind of romantic entanglement was the last thing—the *very* last thing—he needed. He should be spending all of his time, including the time he'd spent mooning over Dara, developing his practice, finding clients, billing hours, and figuring out how he'd make payroll this month and pay for the new roof. He needed to be worrying about his cancer-stricken mother and his dope of a brother, not wondering when Dara would arrive at the office.

Before he'd had sex with her, he'd deluded himself into thinking he wanted her so badly because he hadn't had her yet. Well, now he'd had her, and he wanted her more than ever. He'd always had plenty of sexual stamina, but with Dara last night, he'd ventured into uncharted territory.

Worse, he wanted to be in the room with her, to see her smile, to make her laugh, to watch her sleep.

He heard voices coming from downstairs and glanced at the clock. Nine already. He started down the stairs to the reception area and froze. Dara, still in her jacket, smiled down at Aidan Sullivan, their client, in his high-tech, sturdy wheelchair. She did not seem at all daunted at the sight of a man, not that much older than herself, struck down in the prime of his life, or of the heavily padded headrest, or the breathing tube protruding from his throat, or the lifeless hands that lay across armrests. "Mr. Sullivan." She smiled warmly and reached down to touch his arm, without a hint of condescension. "I'm Dara Williams, Mike's intern. I've been working on your case. It's so nice to meet you."

Mike watched, mesmerized, as Dara similarly greeted Sullivan's wife, Audrey, and relieved Audrey of her bundle, a smiling, cooing baby of about six months, while Audrey took off her coat and turned to help Aidan. Dara happily took the baby and held him high over her head, laughing. "Hi, precious boy!" she sang. The baby gurgled at her. "How are you? How *are* you, sweet thing?"

Mike blindly reached for the rail and held on for dear life as some overwhelming, undeniable, and unwanted primitive instinct unfurled in his chest: he wanted to make love with Dara, he wanted to get her pregnant, and he wanted to see her holding *his* son—*their* son.

And he wanted it desperately.

Chapter 17

Dara grabbed her coat from the hook on the back of her office door and hustled down the hall, pausing outside Mike's office long enough to see he wasn't there. They'd been so busy with Aidan Sullivan all morning, they hadn't had a word alone together, and now she needed to grab a quick lunch and get to class. She really hoped she wasn't forgetting something; her thoughts were so scattered today. Maybe Mike was in the kitchen, she thought as she trotted down the stairs. Halfway down, she slowed to a more decorous pace. Mike stood in the reception area, talking to an older woman, who was, quite clearly, his mother.

She was petite—Mike must have gotten his height from his father—with her salt-and-pepper hair styled in a short, smart cut. She wore a beautiful royal blue suit of raw silk, along with black pumps. Laughing up at Mike, she looked the picture of health, and her eyes sparkled. Clearly, she felt better.

Dara's heart kicked up its pace a little. Here was Mike's mother, and there was no way she could avoid meeting her. She desperately wanted to make a good impression on the woman. Smiling bravely, she walked down the last couple of steps. They both turned toward her; Mike smiled broadly.

"Leaving already?" he asked her.

"Yes," she said, nodding. "Time for class." She looked expectantly at Mike's mother, who regarded her with warm, speculative eyes.

Mike touched his mother's arm. "Mama, this is . . ."

Dara held her breath, wondering what label Mike would possibly give her.

"My wonderful intern, Dara Williams."

Somehow Dara kept her smile from slipping even though a sharp pain sliced through her chest in the vicinity of her heart. She extended her hand. "How are you?"

Mrs. Baldwin wrapped Dara's hands in both of hers. "Dara! Sean has mentioned you so often! I didn't realize you worked for Mike!"

The pain in her chest intensified. So Sean had thought to mention her to his mother, but Mike hadn't. She darted a glance at Mike and saw his face had darkened perceptibly at the mention of Sean's name. "Yes," she managed. "It's a pleasure to meet you. You'll have to excuse me." She slid her arms into her coat. "I need to get to class."

Mike turned to her. "I'll talk to you later."

It was a statement, but Dara saw the question in Mike's eyes. She also saw Mrs. Baldwin looking intently back and forth between them. Somehow she summoned another smile. "Bye."

She made it all the way out to her car before she realized she'd forgotten her keys.

* * *

Mike watched Mama settle herself in the chair opposite his desk. "You look like you feel pretty good today," he told her.

Mama waved her hand. "Forget about me. That was *her*, wasn't it, Michael? Dara?"

He should have known she'd figure it out; his entire life he'd never gotten away with so much as a filched chocolate chip cookie without his mother discovering it. He smiled wryly. "That was her."

"She's beautiful!"

"I know."

Mama beamed at him as if he'd told her he'd been invited to the White House for dinner. He half expected her to start clapping. "Are you in love with her? Do you want to marry her?"

Mike leapt from his chair as if the seat had caught fire. "Marry?" he sputtered, pacing around his desk to the window. Mama's questions cut a little too close to the bizarre thoughts that had been running through his own head today, especially since he'd seen Dara with the baby. "I don't even know what I'm going to have for dinner, much less who I'm going to marry. And you know very well, I don't plan to get married anytime soon—if ever."

Mama's face fell slightly. "But you love her . . . I could tell by the way you smiled at her."

You love her.

Panic bubbled up in his throat, making all speech impossible. Stalling for time, he reshelved several books, all in the wrong places. "There you go with your fairy tales again," he said. Mama's smile finally evaporated. "Why can't I just enjoy a relationship with a beautiful woman for as long as it lasts without you"—he waved his arms ineffectually—"booking a church and picking out china patterns?"

"Michael—"

"And, anyway," he huffed, pulling on his jacket. "My private life is not up for discussion. Are we going to lunch, or not?" He heard a noise in the hall—it sounded like the scuffle of feet—and wondered if it was Jamal returning from his courthouse run. He poked his head out the door and looked up and down the hall, but saw nothing.

"Because if this is about Sean—"

Mike stopped pacing long enough to look down at her. "Yeah, what about Sean? Did you forget he's crazy about Dara? What do you think he'd do if he knew I was involved with her? That would kind of ruin your whole little family reconciliation setup, wouldn't it?"

Mama got slowly to her feet, her eyes sad. "If you love that girl, you shouldn't let anything stand in your way—not even your brother." She picked up her purse and turned toward the door, but then paused to look back at him. "And I'll tell you this: I know by the way she looked at you. She's not thinking about Sean."

Mike nodded curtly, then pressed his hand to her back to lead her out of the office.

Mike strode down the crowded sidewalk at dusk and marveled at how different the beaten path looked when the sun was still up. Normally, he only saw the world in the black predawn and postsunset hours, unless he had to run to court or remembered to take time during the day to look out the window. Twilight over the city, with the lights beginning to twinkle on the river and the setting sun a fiery pink confection against the graying sky, was actually quite pretty. It was five o'clock, quite possibly the earliest he'd ever left the office. He'd stunned Jamal, Amira, and Laura into speechlessness when he'd announced he planned to go home early, and they could therefore also go home. And he did plan to go home—to Dara's.

His ridiculous bout of panic had ended during lunch with Mama. Over his turkey club sandwich and iced tea, he'd had an epiphany that had calmed him right down and put things into perspective. It'd dawned on him that he didn't have to figure everything out *today*. There was no emergency, and Mama's desperate desire for a grandchild notwithstanding, there wasn't even a rush. He and Dara had plenty of time to explore their relationship; they'd barely just started dating. And if they fell in love—if they *were* in love—it would certainly not be the end of the known world. And—he gave a mental gulp—if he decided she was the woman he wanted to marry, well, he could think of worse fates than spending the rest of his life with the most fantastic, sexiest woman he'd ever met.

He turned the corner, picking up his step. He just had the one errand, and then he was very anxious to get to Dara's and touch her again. Keeping his hands off her all day at the office—after last night's orgy of feeling and exploration—had been a special agony. He'd meant it when he'd told her he could wait to make love to her, but now that the waiting was over, he felt profound gratitude. He needed to touch her the way he needed sunshine on his face.

Veering around a woman pushing twins in a stroller, he caught sight of a Christmas display in the window of a clothing store. The holidays were almost here, and he had no idea how they would spend them, although he suspected they would *not* be at his mother's house, sharing turkey with Sean. Most likely, Dara would want to go home to Chicago. He hated the thought of not seeing her for a couple weeks, and he'd had an inspiration: he would surprise Dara by taking her to Miami with him the week after Christmas. He had to attend a conference for criminal defense attorneys; he'd made the reservation months ago. He could buy an airline ticket for her as her Christmas present, and they could have several relaxing days alone together.

The thought was his idea of heaven. He turned one last corner and hustled into his travel agent's office to pick up the tickets. He would surprise her with the trip tonight. He could hardly wait to see the glee on her face.

"Now really isn't a good time, Sean," Dara told him.

I don't even know what I'm going to have for dinner, much less who I'm going to marry . . . I don't plan to get married anytime soon—if ever.

Somehow she'd made it through her afternoon classes when what she'd really wanted to do was curl up in the fetal position and die. Miraculously, she'd driven home without killing herself or anyone else, and now she needed to drink her way through the bottle of Riesling she had chilling in the refrigerator, or, at the very least, take a hot shower and try to numb her body, if not her brain. Sean was a complication she did not need at this juncture.

Sean nodded morosely, then leaned against her door

frame and shoved his hands in his back pockets. "I thought we could talk for a minute. You didn't stick around after class, and I had a really rough morning."

Rough mornings. Well, now, that was something they had in common, wasn't it?

Why can't I just enjoy a relationship with a beautiful woman for as long as it lasts?

The room swirled in and out of focus, and she pressed her hand to her temple, trying to pretend everything was fine when really nothing was.

"Dara?" Sean's worried eyes skimmed over her face. "Are you okay? You look a little . . . pale."

This is my wonderful intern.

Nodding, she motioned him inside. After she shut the door, she followed him into the living room and sat beside him on the sofa. "What's happened?" she said faintly.

"I got fired from my internship today." He shook his head in a gesture of absolute disbelief. "My boss said my latest memo wasn't up to par and he'd counseled me enough. He said we were wasting each other's time. That racist bastard never did like me."

Dara gaped at him, surprised out of her own misery. "Sean, your boss has several black lawyers working for him. I don't see how you can call him a racist."

"Well, you didn't know him," Sean snapped irritably. "He's been trying to get rid of me from the beginning."

Something told Dara to just keep her mouth shut, but she couldn't sit silently by when Sean seemed so determined to mangle the truth. He didn't really believe what he'd been saying, did he? "Sean, you said he's been counseling you. He's invested a lot of time in you. I don't think—"

"I thought you were on my side," he said, incredulous.

She threw her hands up. "This isn't third grade, where you have to pick sides, Sean." Her voice rose. "I'm just pointing out your boss isn't the Antichrist."

Sean sprang to his feet. "Yeah? Well, what am I going to do now? I'm probably going to get an incomplete on my transcript. I'll have to do another whole internship." He thumped his fist on the wall. "I can't believe this crap."

Dara watched him dispassionately. She felt bad for him, but his little firing seemed like a walk in the park compared to the mess her own life had become in the last few hours. Once again, she'd foolishly slept with a man who cared nothing for her. Once again, she'd given her body to someone to whom she was just another notch on the bedpost. Once again, she'd trusted her heart only to have her heart betray her.

And, God, how it hurt.

Just as she'd feared, Mike had blown her life to smithereens, and all it had taken was a few careless words. She'd loved him and given him everything—*everything*—and all he was doing was enjoying time with a beautiful woman. Well, at least she'd found out now, she told herself pathetically. As if it made any difference. At least she'd found out before she'd invested any more time and energy in him. Before she'd spent another unspeakably tender night in his arms. Yes, she needed to look on the bright side. She'd been a fool last night.

She wouldn't be a fool tonight.

"So I think that's what I'll do," Sean said.

Dara blinked up at him, with no idea what he'd said. For a second, she thought about asking him to repeat it, but she really didn't care, and she wanted him to leave. "Okay."

He smiled slightly. "What would I do without you?"
She shrugged, dropping her eyes. "By the way, I'm
finished with the con law notes I borrowed. I forgot to
bring them with me. They're in the car. Do you want
to come down and get them?"

She stared at him. Life as she'd known it had just
ended, and he wanted to know about some notes?
Hysterical laughter bubbled up in her throat, but she
swallowed it. "Sure. Let me get my keys."

A little of Mike's euphoria evaporated when he
pulled into Dara's parking lot and saw, in the rapidly
dimming light, Dara standing by Sean's car. As he
drove by, he had a quick glimpse of Sean handing Dara
some papers or something, before he pulled her into—
big surprise—a hug. This time, instead of a full-blown
jealous snit, he felt only mild annoyance. What was
Sean doing here? Had he been in her apartment?

By the time Mike finished parking, Sean was gone.
Dara took an unaccountably long time to answer the
door after he knocked. He'd just started to wonder
whether she'd jumped in the shower—although he
didn't think she'd had enough time to do that—when
the door swung slowly open. He reached out to pull
her into his arms like he always did, but she flinched
away from him. Bewildered, he took a good look at
her face and froze. She didn't look like she'd been
crying, but a bottomless sadness filled her flat eyes,
and she seemed deathly calm, almost like she was in
shock. Two jumbled thoughts formed in his worried
brain: someone must have died, and she must have
taken a sedative.

"What is it?" he cried, shutting the door behind him.

She turned to lead him into the dimly lit living room, where the blinds were still open even though it was now mostly dark outside. Only the light from the foyer table kept the room from complete darkness. Hadn't she noticed how dark it was? He strode to the French doors to close the blinds, then switched on the floor lamp next to the sofa. He moved toward her again, but she went rigid, as if her feet were now rooted to the floor, and he stopped four feet away from her. Apparently, they were not going to sit on the sofa for this discussion.

She stared at him, wringing her hands. "I forgot my keys," she said finally.

"Well . . . okay," he said, more puzzled than before. Surely, a set of lost keys would not account for her obvious upset. And how had she gotten inside her apartment if she'd lost her keys? "Do you need some help or—"

"And so I went back to get them. To my office."

"Okay," he said, nodding encouragingly, wondering when she'd get to the part about who had died.

"And I overheard . . . you talking to your mother."

Mike stared at her, his mind racing. It took a long minute for the words to sink in, although he knew immediately he'd done something terribly wrong. What had he said that was so bad? He struggled to remember exactly what they'd discussed. They'd talked a little about Sean, she'd claimed he was in love with Dara and asked if he didn't want to marry her, he'd dodged the question, and . . . oh, dear God. No wonder she looked so upset. He'd made some stupid comment about enjoying her while it lasted. Now she probably thought he was just seeing her for the sex.

He realized this was a very high-stakes conversation, one that would require all his debating and quick-thinking skills. Energized, now that he knew what he was dealing with and what he had to overcome, he reached out a conciliatory hand. "Dara—"

She backed away as if he'd approached her with a red-hot poker, her wide, miserable eyes riveted on his face. "It's okay." Her voice was oddly soothing, as if she wanted to reassure *him*. "You don't have to explain."

"Of course, I have to explain." He jammed his hand through his hair, wildly grasping for an explanation that would make sense. "I know how it must have sounded, but—"

"It's not your fault," she said, very reasonably, and he wondered suddenly why she wasn't furious with him. What had happened to her firecracker temper? Where was the woman who'd never hesitated to read him the riot act when she thought he deserved it? "You never made me any promises," she continued, "and I guess I . . . I just assumed things and saw things that weren't really there."

Stupid, stupid, stupid, Mike thought, infuriated at himself. How could he have been so stupid as to say such things when there was even the slightest possibility Dara could overhear him? Now she'd jumped to the wrong conclusion—that he didn't care about her. But he could explain. He could tell her how much he *did* care. And she was the most reasonable person he knew. They would have this mess cleared up in no time, and one day, a long, long time from now, they'd laugh about this whole ridiculous incident. "Dara, I do care about you. You know that. You *know* that." He touched her arm—maybe if he touched her he could bridge the gap between them, just a little—but she twisted away, out of reach, and wrapped her arms around herself.

"Don't make it worse," she said, her voice shaking, "by saying things you don't mean."

He held his hands out, palms up. "I do mean it! Dara, I'm sorry I said something so stupid, but *think*! Think about all the time we've spent together. You can't doubt how I feel about you!"

For the first time, her eyes wavered a little, as if maybe she wanted to believe what he said, but then her chin firmed and her eyes narrowed. "You called me your intern."

Frustrated, Mike struggled to keep up with the flow of her thoughts. "*What*?"

"When you introduced me to your mother today, you called me your *intern*," she said impatiently.

"You are my intern!" he snapped.

Her face tightened, and she looked heavenward, as if to ask for deliverance from having to explain something so obvious. "The day after we made love for the first time, you told your mother I was your intern. Not your girlfriend or even your good friend. You said I was your *intern*."

She spat the word out as if he'd called her a cannibal; clearly, he'd deeply offended her somehow. His mind spun in endless circles, but he latched onto the truth—the logical explanation for why he'd said what he did. "Dara, I called you my intern because I hadn't had the chance to tell my mother about you yet. I needed to explain to her about you and me, and Sean—"

"Exactly." She nodded, looking very satisfied, as if he'd just proved her point for her. "And when you had the chance to explain, you told her I was the beautiful woman you were enjoying. That you didn't love me," she said tonelessly, nostrils flaring.

He stared at her, stunned by her logic. He wondered wildly where the real Dara had gone, the passionate Dara who would happily kick his rear for being so stupid. What had happened to her? When would he see her again? "Dara—"

A hand came up, silencing him. "Maybe you do care for me, but not the way I thought you did. Not enough."

The fear began then. Deep in the pit of his belly, a tiny spark of fear appeared and quickly burst into flame because all of his skills were failing him. He'd argued before judges and juries and courts of appeal, and more often than not—almost always—he brought them around to his way of thinking. But this time, in the conversation that was, he suddenly realized, the most important of his life, he wasn't getting through. "What are you saying?" he asked, filled with dread.

She blinked once, twice, her mouth turning down a little at the edges. "I'm saying sex isn't a casual thing to me, and I can't . . . I can't handle sleeping with someone who's just in it to have a little fun while it lasts."

Mike went absolutely still, waiting for the ax to fall, incapable of speech.

This time her mouth twisted with something that looked like pain, but she pressed her lips tightly together, recovering. "I'm saying good-bye."

"Good-bye," he repeated softly. She nodded miserably, her eyes still on his face.

I need you, Dara. Don't you ever leave me. You promise me?

I promise.

Good-bye. She didn't want to see him anymore. Last

night they had made love, and he had been part of her and said how much he needed her, and she had cried in his arms and sworn she would never leave him.

And today—less than twenty-four hours later—she was breaking her promise.

A red haze of panic and anger swirled around his brain; his stomach knotted painfully. "You're breaking up with me . . . over a misunderstanding?" he managed to ask, his voice deathly quiet.

"There's no misunderstanding."

Suddenly, her calmness enraged him more than anything else, and he cried out in anger and frustration. What kind of woman would break her promise and do this to him—rip his guts out and stomp them into the floor—without listening to reason? Without even giving him a chance to explain? "There *is* a misunderstanding!" he shouted, pacing around the coffee table, waving his arms. "You think I don't care about you, and I'm telling you I do!"

"Not enough," she whispered.

Tell her you love her.

He lunged forward, grabbing her upper arms and shaking her once, hard. Leaning down until they were nose to nose, he tried to stare her down, but she lowered her eyes and turned her head away. "Enough? What's enough?"

She tried unsuccessfully to shove him away. "Please let me go," she said calmly, as if trying to talk a jumper down from a ledge. "You won't change my mind."

His mind veered to Dara and Sean hugging in the parking lot. Ugly thoughts crowded his brain; maybe there was something else going on here that had nothing to do with what she'd overheard him tell Mama. "What's this got to do with Sean?"

Her eyes flew open in outraged surprise; her sudden animation—at the mention of Sean's name—only added fuel to his fire. "Sean? What are you talking about?"

Of course, she didn't know he'd seen them in the parking lot. Would she lie about it? "I saw you with Sean outside," he yelled, tightening his grip. "I saw you in his arms! Did you think I didn't know?"

Her voice rose to a shriek. "What are you talking about?"

"Maybe you've decided you want the other brother, after all." He shoved her away, unwilling to touch the body Sean had just touched. "Hmmm? Is that it? You thought maybe you'd compare us, see which one you like better? Is that it?"

A choked sob escaped her lips. "Get out! Don't you dare talk to me like that! You get out of my apartment!" Planting her hands on his chest, she shoved hard, like she meant to physically remove him, but he didn't budge.

"No. I'm not going anywhere until you tell me the truth."

Crying now, she threw her hand over her mouth and struggled to pull herself together enough to speak. Finally, she dropped her hand. "This is about you not caring about—"

Something inside him came unglued. How dare she tell him he didn't care for her! How dare she tell him how he felt! How dare she refuse to listen to reason! How dare she break her promise! "Stop the bull, Dara!" He clenched and unclenched his hands at his sides and somehow resisted the urge to smash his fist through her wall. "I don't know how many different ways I can prove that I do care about you! I waited to have sex with you! I spent every waking moment with you! For God's sake, I gave you a key to my house—"

"Because it was convenient this morning," she said quietly.

"I gave you the key to my house!" he roared, thinking of Lisa and countless others who would have thanked God on bended knee if he'd ever given them such access.

Swiping at her eyes, she walked very slowly to the hall table, picked something up, and came back again. She held out her hand, and there was his key, shining on her steady palm. "I don't want it."

"I gave it to you—"

"I don't want it."

"I gave it to you!" He snatched the key out of her hand and threw it as hard as he could across the room. It hit the wall to one side of the TV with a hard thunk, then fell to the carpet along with a plum-sized chunk of paint and drywall. Before he could stop himself, he reached into his inside jacket pocket and pulled out the envelope with her airline ticket, which he'd foolishly had his travel agent tie with a red satin ribbon. "Here's how much I don't care about you!" He hurled it at her; it hit her in the chest, then ricocheted and landed on the coffee table. She flinched. "I don't care about you so much, I bought a plane ticket for you today so we could go to Miami together after Christmas! I don't care about you so much, I couldn't stand the thought of you going home to Chicago and me not seeing you until after New Year's!"

Her shoulders shook as she cried again; she ran her hand through her hair, shoving it away from her face, messing it up. "I . . . I'm sorry," she began. She bent over the table and reached for the envelope. "I can write you a check and—"

He stared at her, stupefied. "I don't want the money! I want you to tell me what I have to do to convince you—"

"Nothing." She straightened, leaving the envelope on the table.

Mike gaped at her. Once again, that calm, flat mask had descended over her features, and once again, her voice sounded wooden, as if they were discussing whether to have Rice Krispies or Frosted Flakes for breakfast. Some modicum of control returned to him. Good God, what was he doing? Dara—the most important person in his life—was trying to dump him, and here he was, throwing things at her! What was the matter with him?

"Dara, please." He caught both of her hands—they felt stiff and icy—and held tightly, refusing to allow her to pull away. Very quickly, he pressed first one, then the other, to his lips. She gasped, then gripped his hands. "Please, angel." Her teary eyes softened, and when he eased his grip a little, her hands went to the sides of his face, cupping them. Overwhelming relief swamped him. She did care! She would never leave him! Dizzy with gratitude, he turned his head into her palm and kissed it. "We're building something here, angel. Don't throw it away. Please." Covering her hands with his, he stepped closer and, when she didn't protest, lowered his mouth to hers.

Moaning, she kissed him hungrily, deeply; her trembling mouth tasted salty from her tears. Thrilled by her eager response, he put his hands on her hips, pulling them against his own.

She stiffened immediately and pulled away, but he

did not drop his hands from her hips. "I can't do this," she told him. Hastily, she backed away, out of arm's reach. "I can't make love to you and wait around for you to feel something you don't feel."

Pain shrieked through his chest as he watched her turn and walk to the door, opening it silently. She stood, waiting, tears streaming down her face. The full realization hit him then: they were over. Nothing he could say would make Dara change her mind, ever. With a clinical detachment, she had just sliced him from her life, the way a surgeon slices open an abdomen to remove an appendix. He, Mike Baldwin, had just begged a woman not to dump him, and she had refused. Dara had promised she wouldn't leave him, but she hadn't kept her word. She'd betrayed him.

Hatred twisted in his gut.

Very slowly, he walked to the door, pausing to glare down at her as he passed, reveling in the anguish he saw in her shimmering eyes. Without another word, he walked out, and she immediately shut the door behind him. He heard a slight thump, along with a sliding sound—he had the image of her slumping against the door, then sinking to the floor—before he heard her loud, tortured sobs, muffled only slightly by the wall between them.

And as he turned and walked away, he felt a savage satisfaction because she felt some small fraction of the misery she'd just inflicted upon him.

Chapter 18

Dara got to the still-dark office in the morning, at about seven-thirty, having slept for a scant three hours. She'd cried and cried, more tears than she'd shed in her entire life up until now. Exhaustion covered her with numbness. She'd passed two nights with little sleep, and she had more long, sleepless nights—weeks—ahead of her, what with trial prep immediately followed by finals. She hoped she'd make it.

Mike was there. She knew because some of the lights were already on, and she could smell the strong Colombian coffee he loved brewing in the kitchen. Steeling herself to face him, she'd just slipped off her jacket when she heard a key in the door. Turning, she saw Jamal come in.

"Hey, Dara," he said, shutting the door behind him.

"Good morning." She moved toward the steps to go to her office, but something in her voice made Jamal swing around and catch her arm.

He took a good look at her face. "What's going on, Dara?" he cried. "What's happened to you?"

Bristling a little, she raised her chin. She looked a little tired, sure, and her eyes were a little puffy, her nose a little red. But Jamal stared at her like she was death warmed over, which she definitely was *not*. She pulled her arm free. "I'm fine. Nothing's wrong."

"Bull." He caught her arm again. "What's going . . ."

They heard footsteps and turned to see Mike, in his shirtsleeves, emerge from the kitchen, steaming coffee mug in hand. Dara tensed. He came to within five feet of them, then stopped, staring at Dara. From where he stood under one of the fluorescent lights, Dara saw that his glinting amber eyes had gone black and had large, dark circles under them. His slashing cheekbones and jawline stood out more starkly than usual, throbbing, and she realized that he must be clenching his back teeth together. His sensual lips were set in a tight, cruel line; his posture and shoulders were rigid.

Their eyes locked, and she flinched helplessly. His hostility washed over her in waves, as if he'd dumped a barrel of ice water over her head. He didn't bother trying to hide it. Tears immediately came to her eyes, but she didn't look away. From a great distance, she was aware of Jamal looking back and forth between them.

After a long, volatile moment, he started walking again, stalking by them. He reached the stairs and took them two at a time. "Jamal, I need you in my office," he said, not bothering to look over his shoulder.

Jamal and Dara stared after him, then at each other; all the air had left the room, as if a tornado had swept through. At the look of horrified pity on Jamal's face, Dara quickly turned away, embarrassed.

"Dara," Jamal began, reaching for her.

She quickly threw her arms up, holding him at bay. The last thing she needed now was pity; if he gave her a sympathetic shoulder to cry on, they'd be standing there all day. "I'm okay," she said, sniffling, willing herself not to cry.

Jamal steered her into the reception area and pushed her shoulders so she had no choice but to sit on the sofa. He quickly sat next to her. "What's going on?"

Denials at this point seemed ridiculous. "Mike and I aren't seeing each other anymore."

Jamal's mouth dropped open. "You barely started seeing each other!"

"Yeah, well, now it's over."

"Yeah, well, you need to fix it," he said vehemently.

Very tiredly, she got to her feet. "I can't. And I don't want to talk about it. Okay?"

Jamal leapt up. "Dara—"

"Okay?" she repeated firmly.

His lips compressed into a disapproving line. "Whatever."

After their two-hour trial preparation session with Aidan Sullivan had finished, Dara crept to the door to Mike's office. They'd somehow both been professionals during the meeting, with Mike frequently referencing the outline of questions she'd drafted to help develop Sullivan's testimony, but it had occurred to Dara that the situation was intolerable—unhealthy—and the best thing for both of them would be for her to end her internship and leave the firm. Her stomach had been in knots all morning, and by the looks of things, he wasn't doing much better.

She stood in the doorway, watching him. His dark head was bent low over a stack of letters on his desk, and he didn't acknowledge her, although he had to know she was there.

"Can I help you?" he said finally, coolly, as if she were a telemarketer interrupting his dinner. He didn't look up, instead picking up his pen and scrawling his name on the top letter with a scratching sound. He efficiently slid the letter aside and signed the next one.

Slowly, she approached his desk. "Do you have a minute?"

"Not really."

Well, she hadn't expected a warm reception, and she certainly wasn't getting one. Still, the obvious depth of his hard feelings surprised her, given what he'd told his mother about the casual nature of their relationship. Maybe he was so angry with her because she'd pricked his ego a little; certainly, he was not used to being dumped by women. Shifting nervously, she fumbled with her shirt cuffs, then ran her hand through her hair. When she realized what she was doing, she clutched her hands together in the front. "I thought maybe it would be best if I finished my internship now."

He froze; the pen, still poised over the page, stopped scratching.

"Finals are coming up, and lots of my classmates have already finished their internships," she continued quickly. "I just thought—"

"No."

Her heart fell; she started wringing her hands together. "But—"

Dropping his pen, he finally looked up at her, glinting eyes narrowed. One side of his upper lip lifted slightly until it formed an unmistakable sneer of contempt. She winced. "I realize you're not big on honoring the commitments you make to people, Dara," he said quietly, "but you might remember that your internship is for the full first semester of school. The first semester—last time I checked—is not over yet."

"Mike—"

"You might also remember that I have a big trial coming up very soon, and I have a ton of work that needs to be done. . . ."

She dropped her head and took a deep, steadying breath.

"So, no, we will not be ending your internship yet." He stared at her, waiting.

She brushed a tear from her eye and looked up at him again, trying to smile. "Well," she said in the most professional voice she could muster. "I guess I'll see you tomorrow, then." Turning on her heels, she walked out of his office as quickly as she could without breaking into an actual run, grabbed her coat and purse, then fled down the steps and out the door, brushing past Jamal as she went.

Mike watched her go, then sprang from his chair to pace in useless loops in front of his windows. He'd never felt so dangerously unhinged, like he was one broken shoelace away from committing some heinous act of violence or destruction. One thought ran endlessly through his tortured brain.

Why would she do this to me?

With one fell swoop, his sweet angel had ruined his life; he didn't delude himself into thinking anything could ever be the same again after this. If he'd been in purgatory before they'd started dating, he'd gone straight to hell when she'd broken up with him. He couldn't imagine how much worse he'd feel when her internship actually ended, but he certainly wasn't about to speed up the arrival of that inevitable day.

He leaned into the window, resting his elbow on the

glass above his head. He could understand her pain, of course. She'd overheard him minimize their relationship—although for the life of him, he didn't think he'd come right out and said he didn't love her—and she was deeply hurt. But surely, she didn't really think he didn't care for her! Hadn't she been there these last few weeks? Couldn't she see how crazy he was about her? Surely, he didn't deserve to be frozen out of her life like this!

Was it true that this all had nothing to do with Sean? Could it really just be a coincidence that he'd seen them hugging just moments before she'd broken up with him?

For some odd reason, his girlfriend from college, Debbie—the one who'd slept with his roommate—was very much on his mind, not that he wanted her back, and not that Dara was anything like her. But still, they'd both betrayed him, hadn't they? Neither one had lived up to her side of the relationship. And somehow he'd really thought—he'd hoped—Dara would.

He should have known better.

Furious again, he turned to sit back at his desk and try to do some modicum of work to get ready for the trial, but Jamal stood in the doorway, watching him silently. "Don't kill me, Pops," he said when Mike saw him.

Mike frowned. "What is it?"

Jamal marched in and stood up to his full height. "What did you do to Dara?"

Mike crossed his arms over his chest and felt his blood pressure begin its slow rise. "Why do you assume *I* did anything to *her*? Did she say something to you?"

Jamal snorted; he looked like he'd happily kick

Mike's butt. "No. She was too busy trying not to cry to say anything."

Mike dropped into his chair and picked up his pen. It'd crossed his mind that Dara's breaking up with him was some sort of ploy designed to get a commitment out of him, but her obvious—and continued—upset told him that wasn't the case, not that he'd thought Dara was capable of being so manipulative, anyway. "I can't get into it," he told Jamal.

Jamal flapped his arms, clearly exasperated. "Man, that's *bull*—"

"Mike?" Amira's voice came over the speakerphone on Mike's desk, interrupting them.

"Yeah?" Mike barked.

"Randall Jackson is on line two."

Great. All he needed right now to make his day even worse was to deal with the idiot lawyer for the trucking company responsible for Aidan Sullivan's accident. Now that the trial was days away, they'd started making noises about wanting to settle. "Fine. I'll take it." He glanced up at Jamal. "You can get back to work now, junior," he said, relieved he had an excuse to abort their conversation about Dara.

Jamal squared his shoulders and sank into a chair. "I wasn't finished. I'll wait."

"Wonderful." Mike snatched up the phone. "What's up, Randy? I don't have much time."

"Mike, I told you my client wants you to send over a settlement demand. Where is it?"

"We want four million, same as before."

Jackson let out an exasperated sigh. "You're not going to get four million."

"Yeah, well, that's what we want." Mike eyed the

drafts of two motions he needed to edit and get back to Laura within the hour. "So if there's nothing else—"

"Look, Mike," Jackson said quickly, as if he was afraid Mike would hang up. "My client's willing to go up to half a million."

Mike stared, disbelieving, at Jamal; Jamal's eyebrows shot up in a silent question. "Half a million? With these kinds of medicals? Are you kidding me?"

A long silence ensued. Mike picked up the first motion, balancing his phone on his shoulder. "I may be able to get my client to move a little, but I'm not going to negotiate against myself," Randy said. "You need to name a figure—something less than four mil."

Mike snorted. The whole world had obviously gone insane. Dara thought he didn't care about her, and this clown actually thought he could settle this case for half a million dollars, never mind the fact that Sullivan, a thirty-something father of three, was confined to a wheelchair for the rest of what was sure to be his shortened life, unable to breathe unaided. Well, he didn't have time for this mess. He had work to do, and if and when he ever got done with that, he had sulking to do. "You want a lower figure? How about this: $3,999,999.00. I gotta go." He hung up before Jackson tried to argue with him.

Jamal gaped at him as if he'd suddenly flapped his arms and started to fly. "What are you doing?"

"What do you mean, what am I doing?" Mike asked impatiently, screwing his face up. What did he have to do to get people to just leave him alone today?

"You've been saying all along this case needs to settle. Why don't you negotiate with the man?"

"Because I don't have time for this, Jamal!" he shouted. "And I don't have time for this discussion."

He looked back down at his paperwork. "You need to leave me alone." He tried to read the first couple of paragraphs but couldn't concentrate. After a minute it dawned on him that Jamal hadn't moved. He glanced up to see Jamal staring at him, openmouthed, as if he'd never seen him before and didn't like what he was seeing now. Very slowly, Jamal got to his feet and crept out of his office, head hanging.

When Dara let herself into the office in the morning, the sight of Mike standing in the reception area, talking to a middle-aged, white-haired man in a well-cut dark suit, carrying a briefcase, greeted her. The stranger barely registered with her brain because her eyes were drawn—as always—to Mike. He looked, if possible, even worse than he'd looked yesterday. The circles under his eyes had deepened, and unbelievably, he had a five o'clock shadow; she'd never, *never*, known him to appear even the least bit unkempt in the office during the week. For one second, she thought maybe he'd slept there last night, but that was ridiculous. Anyway, his tie was different than the one he'd worn yesterday.

Mike pointed the man to the conference room, then turned his frigid eyes to her.

"Hi," she said. "What's going on?"

Mike's mouth tightened. "That's the lawyer for the trucking company. He called a couple of times yesterday. He insisted on having a settlement conference."

"Oh!" she said, excited. She'd never seen Mike—or anyone—in negotiations, although she suspected he must be very tough. "Would you mind if I sat in?"

One side of his mouth twisted up; he made a sound

that could have been a laugh but sounded more like a
bark. "Why bother asking? We both know you don't
give a damn about what I want." Feeling her lower
lip start to quiver, Dara clamped her lips together. She
stared reproachfully at him, determined to remain
civil no matter how he behaved. His hostile gaze wavered and fell. He stalked toward the steps, speaking
to her over his shoulder. "Do what you want. You
always do."

Undaunted, Dara took her jacket off and hurried
into the large, sunny conference room, where she introduced herself to Randall Jackson. Mike reappeared
a few moments later and settled at the head of the conference table. He stretched out his long legs, crossed
them at the ankles, and then folded his hands across
his lap. He turned his head to Jackson, looking like a
haughty, bored king deigning to listen to a peasant.
"So, what've you got?"

Jackson took a deep breath. "I can offer one million."

Dara kept her eyes lowered, but her heart leapt at
the figure. A million dollars was real money, and it
would make a big difference in the lives of the Sullivan family.

Mike didn't seem impressed. In fact, he seemed irritated. "I thought you were serious," he said impatiently.
"Why did you even bother coming over here?"

Jackson shifted in his chair; he looked distinctly uncomfortable. "You need to work with me, Mike."

Mike leaned forward, drumming his fingers on the
table for emphasis. "I don't understand you, Randy,"
he said. "You've read the files and the medical records.
You were at all the depositions. My client is in his thirties, and he'll never walk again. He can't use his hands.
He's hooked up to all kinds of tubes and wires. He'll

never be able to work as a physical therapist again, and he can't support his family. He can't touch his kids or make love to his wife."

"Mike—"

"Your client was driving an eighteen-wheeler and had been driving in the middle of the night for eight hours without a stop. We all know he probably fell asleep at the wheel. This was his second accident on the job in six months. He was cited. The company knew all about his poor driving record and put him back out on the road. And his nickname—which the company knew about!—was Gonzales because the other truckers thought he was too speedy."

"Mike—" Jackson's voice rose. Dara held her breath.

Mike shrugged. "If you think you can convince the judge your client isn't liable on that set of facts, you're a much better lawyer than I am." He slumped back in his chair, looking annoyed.

Jackson clutched his pen in his hands and pursed his lips. After a minute he rose from his chair. "Let me just give my client a call." He slunk out of the room, shutting the door behind him.

Dara stared at Mike, awestruck. He was such a great lawyer. If only she could be as good as he was one day. If only she could make a difference in her clients' lives, the way he did. "That was wonderful," she whispered. "I really think—"

His eyes narrowed; his hand came up, silencing her. "Don't bother." He flipped open the folder and leafed through it.

Wounded, Dara looked away. They sat in awkward silence for a few moments, until Jackson reappeared. He sat back down in his chair and scooted it to the table. Clasping his hands on top of his folder, he smiled at them. "Let's sharpen our pencils and see what we can do."

Dara reluctantly left Mike and Jackson, still haggling, to go to class at ten. She hurried through the crowded hall at the law school, her backpack clutched to her back. Contracts class started in about five minutes, but she had no idea what she was doing there. Why go to classes and learn about negligence and third-party beneficiaries when her heart was broken? Well, she'd go, anyway. School was the only normal thing left in her life; she needed to stick to her disciplined routine or go crazy.

"Dara?"

Dara stopped and glanced impatiently at her watch. She didn't have time for this, whatever it was. But then she looked over and saw a grim-faced Professor Stallworth marching up to her. Dara braced herself.

"I know you need to get to class, Dara, so I'll make this quick. Where's Sean? Two of his other professors have told me he hasn't been to their classes in weeks. I've called and e-mailed him, but he doesn't answer. Is he okay? Finals are in three weeks, and he really needs a good showing."

The unspoken words hung in the air: Sean needed to do well on his finals because he'd be getting an incomplete for his internship. Still, Dara pretended she was surprised. "Really? He seems fine to me." The urge to protect Sean was reflexive. The last thing he needed right now was trouble at school on top of his recent firing. "I think a lot of the material is a review to him because he was a paralegal. But I'll tell him he should call you."

Stallworth's eyes narrowed, and Dara's heart gave a hard lurch. Stallworth looked like she didn't believe a word Dara had just said. "Tell him to call me *immediately*." Her voice dripped ice. Dara couldn't possibly mistake her meaning. *Tell Sean to get it in gear before he screws up*.

"Okay."

Smiling, Stallworth rubbed her arm. "You, on the other hand, are doing great! Your scores on the practice finals the other week were through the roof! If you keep up the good work, you'll make law review in the spring, no problem."

Dara smiled weakly, and Stallworth swept off. Dara figured she'd do really well on her finals; Mike had taught her more about the law than any professor had. She should feel relaxed and confident. But all she felt was detached. When had her most cherished goal lost all its meaning for her? She didn't much care how she did on her finals, and if Stallworth came back and said they'd revoked her scholarship and she'd have to leave school immediately, she didn't think she'd care about that, either.

The only thing she cared about was Mike Baldwin. The man who didn't care about her.

Dara hustled back to the office the second class was over, desperate to hear whether Mike had settled the case. In the past she would've just called, but with the way Mike had been treating her lately, she thought that was a pretty bad idea. Of course, she'd die rather than admit why she'd come back. Luckily, she'd planned ahead and "forgotten" her constitutional law book on her desk, so she had a ready excuse in case anyone asked what she was doing there.

When she stepped into the foyer, she saw Jamal, Amira, and Laura standing in a circle, talking in hushed, worried tones. They looked like someone had died. "What's going on?" Dara cried, alarmed.

Jamal regarded her with a tragic look. "Mike settled the case."

"That's wonderful! Why do you all look like someone died?"

"We're going to kill Mike soon if he doesn't stop biting our heads off every time we look at him," Laura said grimly.

"Oh." Dara nervously rubbed the back of her neck, wondering who besides Jamal knew she was the cause of Mike's black mood. "Where is he?"

Jamal scowled and jerked his thumb in the direction of Mike's office. "Up there. And if you're not back in five minutes, don't think any of us are gonna come and rescue you. You're on your own."

Dara rolled her eyes, squared her shoulders, and marched up the steps, pausing outside Mike's office.

Chapter 19

Mike stood with his back to her by one of his bookshelves, with his shirt untucked and his sleeves rolled up. She watched while he turned to his antique drink cart—she'd scarcely noticed it before, but now she realized it held tumblers and snifters and the requisite scotch, gin, whiskey, and brandy—and selected a snifter. He splashed a healthy amount of brandy into it. "Dara," he said, thunking the snifter back down on the cart. "You're just in time."

She jumped; she hadn't realized he knew she was there. "You settled the case," she said brightly, trying to remain pleasant despite her alarm. She'd never known Mike to drink much at all, and certainly nothing stronger than a glass or two of wine, and certainly not at work.

He turned to face her, a dark, menacing gleam in his eyes, and raised the brandy bottle. "Would you like a drink to celebrate?"

"No."

He walked back to his desk and, putting the snifter down, picked up a check. "See this?" He waggled the check back and forth, and it made a flapping sound. "They just messengered this over. It's a check for my fees. Did I mention it was a contingency case? You know what that means. I get one-third of the settlement. Would you like to see it?" He held it out for her.

Wary, Dara took the check. He looked so dangerous, she was half afraid to come within striking distance. She did notice there was no alcohol on his breath, which was a good sign. She held his glittering gaze over the top of the check, then glanced down at it and gasped. It was a check for 1.1 million dollars and some change. It was like Mike had won the lotto. Here, in her hand, was the answer to all his financial woes. After taxes, he could pay cash for the roof, and he could pay off the mortgage on the brownstone! He could buy a new building! He could build up his slush fund for times when work was slow, although, after this, she didn't think work would ever be slow. "Mike!" she cried, beaming at him. "This is wonderful! I'm so proud of you! You must be so thrilled!"

He stared at her. For one second she thought she saw some warmth, some soft emotion deep in his eyes, underneath the anger and sarcasm, but then his mouth twisted down. "Why wouldn't I be thrilled?" His tone and the glint in his eyes were malevolent. Her heart started to race. He held out his hand, and she gave the check back to him. He walked to his desk and flicked the check onto it as if it were a worthless receipt. Then he picked up the snifter. Turning, he leaned his hip against the desk and watched her. "I have my health and my house and my career." His voice rose steadily, along with the alarm in her throat. "I'll be thirty-five next week, and I'm financially independent. I have a check for a million dollars in my hand. Hell, I could take off for Tahiti tomorrow and live there for a year. I have everything I always thought I wanted."

A muscle ticked in his forehead; cords stood out in his neck. Dara involuntarily staggered back a step at the raw pain she saw on his face. He slammed the snifter down on the desk, and she heard the stem break off with a sharp snap. Brandy spilled over his blotter but luckily missed the check. Crying out, afraid he'd cut himself, she reached for him, but he stood up straight now, feet wide in a fighting stance, trembling with anger. "I can't think of a single reason why this shouldn't be the happiest day in my life, Dara," he roared. "Can you?"

He didn't wait for her to answer but swung around and returned to the drink cart and selected a fresh snifter. Shaking, she cleared her throat. "Please don't do this, Mike."

"Do what?" His voice sounded conversational now, although his broad shoulders were rigid. "Have a little drink to celebrate?" He shrugged, then set the snifter back down. "You're right. You're not worth it." Dara flinched but was at a loss for words. "You can go now," he told her quietly.

"Well . . . okay," she said reluctantly, almost afraid to leave him alone. "I'll see you tomorrow." She turned to leave.

"No. I mean clean out your desk."

Dara whirled back, gaping. He looked suddenly haggard and sad. "I don't want to see your face again."

She blinked furiously, but holding back her tears was impossible. "How long are you going to be this cruel to me?" she asked him, her voice breaking.

His face tightened, and animosity replaced the sadness. "I don't think you want to get into a discussion about which one of us is the cruelest, Dara."

Clapping a hand over her mouth to muffle a sob, Dara fled.

Somehow Dara survived the worst Thanksgiving of her life at home in Chicago with her parents, then immediately returned to Cincinnati for the moment of truth. Finals were only a few days away. There'd been no midterms, no tests, no pop quizzes. A three-hour final exam would constitute Dara's entire grade for each class. She'd have no second chances and no redemption if she screwed up. This was it.

She and Monica flew into a frenzy of activity when the reading week began. They met by eight-thirty every morning at the library and studied most days until ten or eleven at night, breaking only for meals. They quizzed each other, took practice exams, worked with flash cards and study guides, and reviewed their endless class notes. They guzzled coffee until they were bleary-eyed and jittery. "We know this stuff cold!" crowed Monica one night at eleven-thirty, when they sat at their table in the packed library, huddled over their books, reading as if they could discover the way to end world hunger if only they worked hard enough.

Dara glowered at Monica, with eyes so gritty and tired they felt like they had sand in them. "Would you hush before you jinx us?" Technically, Monica was right. They had taken several practice exams, and they'd both done remarkably well. Still, Dara didn't want to count any of her chickens before they hatched.

"You oughta relax a little."

"Well, you need to keep quiet. You know how superstitious I am." Dara worried something would happen to screw up finals. She was maxed out already and couldn't handle one more problem of any sort. She couldn't ever remember being this exhausted or this miserable; she was doing good just to get through each day. She wondered idly what would kill her first: law school or her longing for Mike.

Or her frustration with Sean.

When Dara told him the study schedule, she had no real hopes of seeing him, but he surprised her by showing up by ten a.m. the first couple of days. "Look, Sean," said Monica, who'd shifted into a sort of combat mode, as Sean unpacked his books the first morning, "I don't want any of your mess. It's time for finals. We're here to study. So if you're going to start talking and goofing off, then you can get out." Her smiling mouth softened her words, but Dara knew she was serious and felt secretly grateful Monica had laid down the law.

Sean saluted her. "Ooh, yah, master chief." He winked at Dara and slid into his chair.

Dara studied him for a moment, taking inventory. His eyes looked bright and clear, and he seemed cheerful and well rested. And serious. She felt a glimmer of hope; maybe Sean would pull his act together and make a decent showing of finals even though he'd blown school off for the last several weeks.

Unfortunately, her hope died a quick death. They all immediately realized Sean was in a world of hurt. His study outlines were useless because he'd skipped so many classes, so Dara let him copy hers. It annoyed her to share the fruits of her labor with him when she'd worked hard all semester and he hadn't. Why should she reward him for being a lazy slug when she'd dragged herself out of bed to get to class most of the time? But she knew he was fighting an uphill battle, and she wanted to do whatever she could to help him.

They tried to discuss the materials with Sean, but that was impossible. He tried to bluff his way through, but he usually had no idea what he was talking about. They teased him when he gave wrong answers, but Dara's heart was broken. She couldn't begin to imagine how embarrassed and overwhelmed he must be. In civil procedure alone, they'd covered nearly all of a six-hundred-page textbook. How on earth could Sean possibly tackle that at the eleventh hour?

She wondered how long he would stick with the studying. Sure enough, on the third and fourth days, he didn't appear until noon and left at six. After that, he didn't show at all.

She tracked him down at his apartment, determined to see how he was doing with her own eyes. "I'm studying here now," he said when he let her in. His living room looked like the recent site of a minor tornado. His closet or dresser had obviously exploded, trailing clothing across the floor, and several of his law books and CDs and DVDs littered the sofa and chairs. She was not surprised to see that the one thing conspicuously absent from this cavalcade of junk was an open contracts book or notebook; contracts was the first final Monday morning. She watched him scoop several items off the sofa to make a place for her to sit. "The library was too distracting for me."

This statement was patently ridiculous. The library, crammed to the gills with anxious first-year students, was as solemn and silent as a crypt, but Dara didn't push.

"How are things coming?" Sean asked.

"Good," she said, worried. Sean was going to screw up his finals. It was inevitable. Still, she couldn't quite let it go. "Sean, I really think if you gave it a hard push and pulled a couple of all-nighters, you'd do really well. You're so smart." *If only you weren't so lazy.*

"I've got things under control." A new layer of tension overlaid his voice. "Why don't you get off my back? What kind of a friend are you?"

She raised her chin, truly annoyed now. "One who cares enough about you to tell you the truth even when you don't want to hear it." Dara felt much better for having told him what she thought, even though it looked like he was determined to ignore her. "Anyway," she told him, "that's the end of my speech."

"Let me ask you something," he said coolly, looking out the window, "since you're in such an honest mood this morning. What's going on with you and my brother?" He swung around to gauge her reaction; his sharp eyes focused intently on her face.

Astonished and horrified by the question, Dara could not stop her jaw from dropping. "My personal life is none of your business."

He scowled. "Well, whatever's been going on with you lately, you look terrible."

Unfortunately, she knew exactly what he meant. Deep hollows had carved their way under her eyes, and she suspected she'd lost a pound or two in the last couple weeks because she wasn't eating much. "I'll be a lot better when finals are over," she told him, the biggest lie she'd ever uttered.

Mike sat in his SUV in the parking lot of Dara's apartment building, staring at the door, willing her to appear. He needed to see her, even if it was only for a second, and even if it was from fifty or sixty feet away. His life seemed to depend on it.

Suddenly, the door opened, and Dara came out with her backpack. His heart lurched hard. She went down the steps, with her typical brisk, purposeful walk, and headed toward her new car. Her head was down, but she looked grim and determined. And tired. He wished he'd brought his binoculars so he could see her better. It didn't matter. She was ready, and she was going to ace her finals. He didn't have a single doubt about it.

At the door to her car, she stopped. For no apparent reason, her head turned over her shoulder, and she looked directly at him, or, rather, directly at his SUV. He sat up straight, agitated. He didn't want her to see him; he didn't want to distract her from her finals. She stared in his direction for several seconds, then shook her head as if to clear her thoughts. He relaxed a little. Of course, she couldn't have seen him. He was several rows back, much too far away.

When she drove away, the searing pain came. He'd known there'd be a reckoning; the price for the pleasure of seeing her was the agony of loss he felt now. He didn't know when—or if—he'd ever see or talk to her again. He would have to wonder how she did on her finals.

But for now he knew she was okay, and that was enough.

That had to be enough.

Dara sailed through her finals.

Sean didn't.

During the first two, on Monday and Tuesday, he sat

near her, close enough for her to see his entire body clench as he read the questions. He seemed to take hours before beginning to write his essay answers. For both finals, he handed in his blue booklets well before the allotted three hours had passed, when all the other students still scribbled furiously.

During the third final, torts, she saw him writing thoughtfully for the entire time period. In the hall afterwards, he radiated triumphant excitement. "Well?" She felt thrilled for him. He was past due for a stroke of good luck.

"I really nailed that second negligence question about duty."

Monica strolled over in time to hear Sean, and she caught Dara's eye. The women exchanged a perplexed look; Dara's heart fell. Sean caught their look. Immediately, his face darkened. "What?" he demanded.

"Sean," Monica said gently, "that question wasn't about duty. It was about standard of care and damages."

Sean's mouth hit the floor. "No, it wasn't." He seemed to be talking to himself. He was obviously shocked, almost dazed. Why couldn't Sean get a break, just this one time? Finally, he turned to her, his face stricken. "Dara?"

It was a plea. Dara hated to do it, but she told him the truth. "Monica's right, Sean."

He glared at them suddenly, as if they'd rigged the exam to make him fail. "You two don't know what you're talking about." His voice sounded ugly— malevolent. Sean held Dara's gaze for a long moment— she had the feeling he meant to stare her down—then turned and stalked off.

Dara was too stunned to speak. "It's not your fault,

girl," Monica murmured. "We did everything we could to help him."

"I know," Dara said. She was not, surprisingly, angry with Sean for talking to them that way. All she could feel was a desperate sadness. "But he's ruining his life. I know he's going to flunk out of school. Why didn't he quit when he had the chance? What's going to happen to him?"

Monica just shook her head.

When she stepped, exhausted and crabby, out of her last final and into the crowded hallway filled with her relieved comrades, Dara's eyes immediately fell on a figure standing alone, looking back and forth in the crowd with long, sweeping glances. She blinked hard, certain her bleary eyes were playing tricks on her, but he was still there. Seeing him there, out of context, was disorienting—as if she'd been riding on a roller coaster and looked over to see a dolphin in the seat next to her. "Jamal!" she cried, delighted. "Is that you?"

A wide grin split his face, and he sauntered through the crowd, arms open wide. "Come here, girl!"

Dara threw herself at him, hugging tight. "I'm so glad to see you," she said over and over. "What are you doing here?"

Jamal extracted himself from her arms and tugged her hand until she followed him over to a small seating area surrounded by potted palm trees. They settled onto a pleather love seat. The crowd around them thinned rapidly; her classmates, finished with their first set of finals, couldn't leave the building fast enough.

"How are you?" he asked her. "You look terrible."

She smacked him hard on the arm. "Of course, I look terrible. I just finished up with finals."

His eyes narrowed. "You looked terrible before that. So how'd it go? You get all As?"

"I'm not counting my chickens—"

"You got all As," he said flatly. He leaned back and looked around, sprawling his long legs out in front of him. "So this is law school, eh?"

"This is law school."

Nodding thoughtfully, he caught her gaze and stared at her. "You been gone three weeks. I got lots of stuff to tell you."

The perpetual knot in her stomach tightened, but she managed a smile. "So what's new?"

"Well, I got my GED," he said, grinning.

She shrieked, wrapping her arms around him again. "That's wonderful! I'm so proud of you!"

He submitted for about three seconds, then pulled away. "And Mike gave all of us a bonus—me and Laura and Amira. A whole year's salary." Dara gasped; Jamal nodded wryly. "He said we needed to share the settlement because we'd all helped him get it. Can you believe it?"

Dara's heart constricted painfully. "Yeah," she said quietly. "I can believe it."

"So I think I'm gonna use that money and maybe see about getting into college. You know, maybe I could get a little two-year degree or—"

She squeezed his arm, horrified to hear him diminish his accomplishments. "Oh no! As smart as you are, you need to sign up right away for a bachelor's program." She swept her arm wide. "And in four years, you could be right here in this building, getting your JD. If that's what you want, I mean."

He stared at her. "That's the same thing Mike said."

She bent her head, looking down in her lap. She wondered if she should just go ahead and ask Jamal to stop mentioning that name, because it felt like a pitchfork to her heart every time she heard it.

"You wanna know how he's doin'?"

"No," she said quickly.

"Terrible!" Jamal grabbed her chin, jerking her face up to meet his eyes. "He looks awful! I think he's lost, I dunno, ten pounds or something. And he's sleeping at the freakin' office—on his sofa! He thinks no one notices, but everyone knows!"

"I'm really sorry to hear that."

"*Sorry*?" Jamal's eyes grew to the size of saucers. "Is that all you got to—"

"He doesn't love me."

Jamal faltered, his mouth hanging open. "Say what?"

She looked around quickly, making sure no one was within earshot to hear her blurt out her most painful secret. "I overheard him telling his mother he doesn't love me. Doesn't want to ever get married"—she grabbed his arm, squeezing hard—"and I will *kill you* if you repeat any of this to anyone, especially *him!*"

He covered her hand with his own. "Dara," he said soothingly, "I don't know what you think you heard, but Mike is crazy in love with you. He misses you so much, he's gonna make himself sick pretty soon."

Hope did not flare in her heart. "I heard what I heard. Why would he lie to his sick mother? And why didn't he deny it when I confronted him? He kept saying he cared about me." She snorted. "Cares about me! That's like saying he cares about world peace! What does it mean? Nothing! That's what it means!"

Jamal caught both of her hands in his, then hunched down until his piercing eyes were all she could see. "Read my lips, Dara. I am telling you, Mike loves you. You gotta believe—"

Agitated now, she jerked free. "Why would he lie to his mother? Huh? Explain that to me!"

"Maybe he's only lying to himself, Dara."

Stunned, she could only stare at him. "Why would I want to be with a man who can't—or won't—recognize he loves me?"

A faint smile softened the intensity of his expression. "Because it's *Mike*. The greatest guy we know. And he's worth a little extra trouble, Dara." She gasped and looked away, her mind spinning in useless circles. Jamal got to his feet. "I think his mother's having a late birthday party for him or something. She called today and asked me for your phone number."

Jolted at the thought of seeing Mike again, she shook her head in a blind panic. "I can't! There's no way I could—"

Leaning down, he kissed her on the cheek. "Think about it," he said before he turned and walked away.

The phone was ringing half an hour later, when Dara walked into her apartment, juggling the weight of her twenty-pound backpack crammed full of books. Slamming the door shut behind her, she dumped the backpack in an unceremonious heap on the foyer floor and snatched up the phone. "Hello?" She held her arm over the basket on the hall table, ready to drop her keys inside.

"Dara?" said a warm, crisp, vaguely familiar female voice with a trace of a southern accent. "It's Serena Baldwin, Sean and Mike's mother. How are you?"

Dara froze, with her arm suspended. "I-I'm good," she stammered. Her mind fumbled about, trying to think of a good excuse to get out of whatever social event the woman was about to invite her to. "How are you feeling?" Her arm began to throb, and she remembered to let go of the keys.

"Pretty good today," Mrs. Baldwin said airily. "That's why I'm calling. You know Michael just settled that big case the other week—"

"Right."

"And he just had his thirty-fifth birthday. I have a little time off this week between my chemotherapy treatments, so I thought I'd go ahead and throw him a little get-together. Nothing big. Just a few friends and family and everyone from the office, of course."

"Wow. That sounds really wonderful, and I'd love to come. But I, uh"—she swallowed hard—"am going home to Chicago for the holidays, and I can't make it." Pleased with the relatively smooth delivery of her excuse, Dara kicked her shoes into the hall basket.

"Oh, dear," Mrs. Baldwin said worriedly, "are you leaving tonight?"

Dara's essentially honest nature caught up with her. "Well . . . no, but—"

"Good!" Mrs. Baldwin's voice brimmed with triumph. "Then we'll see you at eight. Sean can bring you."

Dara gave up trying to be diplomatic. The woman was trying to be polite, but she obviously had no idea what kind of hornet's nest she was poking with her stick. "Mrs. Baldwin, I really appreciate what you're doing, but Mike doesn't want me there. Trust me."

"You leave Michael to me."

Dara collapsed on the sofa and smacked her hand

to her forehead. Well, now she knew where Mike's tenacity came from. She looked heavenward for help, but none was forthcoming. "I just don't think—"

"You're not arguing with a sick woman, are you, Dara?"

"Mrs. Baldwin," Dara said tiredly, "please don't do this to me."

Mrs. Baldwin laughed. "Eight o'clock, dear."

Dara, balancing the two-foot-tall box containing Mike's present—she couldn't very well show up empty-handed to a birthday party, after all—ran into Sean while walking up the sidewalk in front of his mother's house at eight-fifteen. Mrs. Baldwin lived on a lovely street lined with huge oak trees and gaslights. Her house was a beautiful two-story white brick colonial with black shutters. The shades were drawn, but Dara could see that the inside of the house was well lit. Smoke wafted from the chimney, and its woodsy smell filled the cold air.

Sean hurried up to her from the other end of the sidewalk, and she could have sworn she saw him weave slightly on his feet. "Hey," he said, kissing her on the cheek. His yeasty breath confirmed her impression. "I don't see why we didn't just come together," he complained.

"Well," she said uneasily, "you know I always leave these things early." That was only her excuse, of course. The real reason she'd insisted on driving herself tonight was she didn't want Mike to see her arrive with Sean and jump to the wrong conclusions—not that it mattered now. But it looked like her efforts had been in vain. Still, if she'd known Sean had been drinking, she would have insisted on driving him. "What did you do?" she said, taking his arm and turning up the front walk. "Start the party early?"

He snorted; there was an ugly gleam in his eye, which she did not care for. "It's the end of finals. We both know I probably flunked out of school, so this was probably the last set of finals I'll ever take. Why shouldn't I celebrate?"

They reached the porch, and after ringing the bell, Dara turned to face him, keeping her hand on his arm. "It wasn't that bad, was it? How did things go today?"

His face closed off. "I don't want to talk about it. Let's talk about you." He leaned a little closer, and one corner of his mouth turned down. "Aren't you glad to be seeing Mike?"

Just then the door swung open, and Mrs. Baldwin appeared. She favored Sean with a quick smile and kiss, then turned her complete attention to Dara. "Thank you *so much* for coming," she told her, wrapping her arm firmly around her waist and steering her into the foyer. Without missing a beat, she passed Mike's present to Sean while she divested Dara of her coat. "Sean, you go in the kitchen and get Dara a drink. Merlot okay, Dara?" She did not wait for any response, instead snatching the gift back from Sean and handing it to Dara. She propelled Dara through the foyer and kitchen, where several people she didn't know had congregated, and into the living room, where Mike—Dara saw him immediately, even though he had his back to her—stood talking to Jamal by the roaring fire. He wore a black cable-knit turtleneck sweater along with faded jeans that lovingly covered his tight rear and powerful thighs.

Dara's mouth went dry, her heart thundered uncontrollably, and her feet froze into two blocks of granite, unwilling to carry her another step. Mrs. Baldwin followed the path of Dara's gaze and squeezed her arm reassuringly. "He's just a man, Dara," she murmured. "Sometimes we have to help them along a little." She disappeared before Dara could think of any response.

Jamal's eyes locked with hers, and beaming, he abruptly abandoned Mike and rocketed to her side. She had a brief impression of Mike looking over his shoulder to see where Jamal was going before Jamal blocked him from view. "Good girl," Jamal said warmly, kissing her on the cheek. He discretely tilted his head in Mike's direction. "Why don't you go say hi to the birthday boy." He took off for the kitchen, leaving her alone in the living room with Mike.

Chapter 20

A stunning jolt of energy leapt between them the second Jamal moved out of the way and their gazes locked. Stupefaction did not seem like a strong enough word for the way Mike stared at her. A vivid flush crept from under his turtleneck and up his cheeks; his lips remained open in a gape. After a long moment, he seemed to recover himself, which was fortunate because she still felt paralyzed. She watched as he approached slowly. He stopped when he came within four feet of her.

"Hi," he said hoarsely, his piercing gaze riveted to her face.

Smiling was out of the question; her muscles felt much too rigid for such a maneuver. "Hi."

"What are you doing here?"

Dara's heart fell. This was not the reaction of a man who was thrilled to see her, or even of a man who had missed her a little bit. "It wasn't my idea," she quickly told him, before he had the chance to get angry and throw her out. "Your mother insisted."

For the first time, he blinked; his expression darkened perceptibly.

"Well, well, well," said Sean on her right. His tone was biting. "Look who it is." Dara turned to see him watching Mike, eyes narrowed, a goblet of red wine in each hand. He handed one off to her, then turned back to Mike. "Dara's here, man." His eyes were cool and calculating. "You must be pretty happy about that."

Dara's stomach lurched sickeningly, but she raised her chin. The best defense was always a good offense. "Is that all you have to say to your brother?"

Sean gave her a twisted, mocking little smile. "Sorry, man," he told Mike. "I just flunked my fourth and last final today." He took a generous swig from his goblet. "My manners aren't what they should be. Congratulations on another glorious victory. A million dollars. You must be thrilled."

Mike rolled his eyes and grunted. Dara flinched. Sean's flashing eyes locked with Mike's in open hostility. Sean turned to Dara. "Did I ever tell you what it was like growing up with a perfect brother, Dara?" He drank deeply from his goblet. "Did I mention how much fun that was? And did I tell you Mike can do anything?"

"Shut up, Sean," Mike interjected. "You're only embarrassing yourself."

"Mike can speak—what is it?—Spanish and French and Latin. Well, maybe Latin doesn't count, because nobody *speaks* it—"

"Sean—," Dara tried.

"I flunked Latin. But I guess you probably figured that out already. Maybe if I hadn't flunked it, I'd be doing a little better with all those stupid Latin legal terms in law school, huh?" He drank again. "And Mike plays basketball. The team won the state semifinals his senior year. I got cut. What else? Oh yeah.

Mike went to Harvard. Mike's an engineer. Mike was a Boy Scout. Mike's kind to orphans. Mike's Johnnie Cochran—"

"I'm not listening to this." Dara started for the kitchen.

"And everyone loves Mike best."

Dara froze, then whirled around. Rage glittered in Sean's eyes, but despair was right underneath it. "That's not—"

"Dad loved him best. Mom loves him best." Sean stared at her. "*You* love him best."

Dara could not move, nor could she think of anything to say.

"You've got an excuse for everything, don't you, Sean?" Mike asked calmly. "Which part of your life is *your* responsibility?"

Sean winced. "Screw you, man." He stormed out through the kitchen, brushing past Mrs. Baldwin, who stood next to the back door, watching them.

Dara looked helplessly at Mike, still gripping his brightly wrapped present. She felt horrified to have been part of such an ugly scene while a guest in someone's house. "I-I shouldn't have come. I'm going to go."

She whirled, thunked her wine on the nearest table, and rushed back through the kitchen to the foyer, raising a hand to stop a visibly alarmed Mrs. Baldwin from approaching her now. She hated to be rude, but she would call the woman tomorrow to apologize. Jerking the hall closet open, Dara rummaged inside until she found her coat. She yanked it off the hanger, ignoring a loud ripping sound. Slinging it over her arm, she reached for the heavy brass doorknob on the front door.

"Dara!"

She hesitated, then turned the knob. "I have to go," she said over her shoulder. A blast of frigid air hit her face.

"Wait." Mike's hand touched her arm. "Please."

Disregarding the trembling in her hand, Dara pushed the door shut and turned to Mike. This time he'd come much too close, right up to her. If she took one step forward, her entire body would press against him. She felt a desperate urge to run away—far away, where she couldn't smell the crisp scent of his cologne or see the intensity in his eyes—but she was trapped between him and the door.

He stared hungrily at her, as if she were the first woman he'd seen after being marooned on a deserted island for thirty years. Finally, he smiled a little. "How were your finals? Did you kick butt?"

She had to laugh. "I think so."

"I know so."

His tone was absolute, as if he was describing the sun's tendency to rise in the morning, and for the first time, she felt the thrill of accomplishment. Prior to this, she'd felt only relief that finals were over. How strange. She'd done what she'd set out to do, what she'd worked so hard for—nailed her finals—but without Mike to share it with, it hadn't meant much of anything. Until now. Flustered by the realization, she tried to think of another, safer topic to discuss. "Jamal told me about his bonus," she told him. "That was a wonderful thing to do."

"Yeah, well." He dropped his head, rubbing the back of his neck; she had almost forgotten how uncomfortable he was with this kind of flattery. After a minute, he straightened and looked pointedly at the

brightly wrapped box. "Is that for me, or is it an ap-
pendage you've grown in the last three weeks?"

"Oh!" Surprised she still held the thing in her hand,
she thrust it at him, thoroughly disconcerted now. "It's
for you." He took it and put it on the foyer table, tugging at the ribbon. "What are you doing?" she cried. He
wouldn't open it *right now*, would he? She'd thought
he'd take it home and open it later. The last thing they
needed was another awkward moment.

Amused, he spared her a quick glance. "It's custom-
ary to unwrap gifts people give you."

"Oh no!" She reached for the box—he'd peeled off
all the wrapping by now—prepared to snatch it away
from him, but then she realized she could hardly do
that. "It's really nothing," she said hurriedly. "And I
left the gift receipt inside, so you can always exchange
it." She wrung her hands as he peeled the tape off and
opened it. "You'll probably want to exchange it. It's no
big deal. Really."

Mike peered into the box and gasped. His astonished gaze shot to hers, then back to his present. Very
gingerly, he reached inside and lifted out a ceramic
Christmas tree studded with colored lightbulbs. An
electric cord dangled from its base. Mike carefully
held it up and stared at it as if it were something im-
measurably precious—like the chalice Jesus used at
the Last Supper.

Dara didn't know what to make of his reaction. "It's
a Christmas tree," she said ridiculously. "When I was
a little girl, my grandmother gave me one just like this,
and I kept it on my nightstand." Mike did not answer
her. She grabbed the cord and held it up. "See?" she
babbled. "You plug it in, and it lights up." Mike's jaw
tightened; he didn't say anything. Dara felt a trickle of

sweat slide down the valley between her breasts. If only he would say something! "Anyway . . ." She faltered. "I know you're not big on decorating for the holidays, and I wanted you to have one little . . ."

He turned his head and stared at her in utter disbelief, as if he'd never seen her—or any of her species—before. A muscle ticked in his temple; indefinable emotions burned behind his eyes. "You bought this for me?" he whispered.

"Well . . . yes."

A slight frown creased his forehead, his nostrils flared, and his mouth opened and closed. "Thank you."

Dara stared at him, puzzled. Did he like it, then? "You're welcome."

Mike hastily looked away. Very carefully, he lowered the tree back into its box.

"Well . . . I should go now," she told him.

He nodded once. "When"—he cleared his throat—"when do you leave for Chicago?"

"In a few days. I hope you have a good . . ." She trailed off because it occurred to her suddenly and painfully that when she left this house, she wouldn't see him again anytime soon, and certainly not for Christmas. "Merry Christmas, Mike."

One corner of his mouth turned up in a Mona Lisa smile. Intrigued, she wondered what he knew that she didn't—and when she would find out. But all he said was, "Merry Christmas, Dara."

Dazed, Mike watched her leave, then stared after her long after she'd gone. The voices and music in the other rooms did not register with his brain, and he felt no obligation to mingle with the guests, who were, after all, there to be with him. Finally, he sprawled on the bottom few stairs, the better to process his thoughts. He stretched his legs out in front of him, leaned his elbows on his knees, and dropped his head into his hands.

He was in love with her, of course; he'd stupidly been the last person on the planet to recognize the emotion for what it was. In the past, whenever his brain had accidentally wandered in that direction, he'd immediately felt that roiling panic in his gut—as if he couldn't simultaneously love Dara and live a normal life, as if any love for her would somehow suck the essence out of his soul until he became some new, unrecognizable, and lesser Mike. And the prospect of marriage had practically caused him to hyperventilate.

But *tonight*, tonight everything was different. He'd taken one look at her and frozen. He'd felt like he'd been hit by one of those curare-filled darts South American Indians used to immobilize people. After the torture of not seeing her for three weeks, he'd known—*known*—three things: he loved her, couldn't live without her, and wanted to marry her. Just like that, he'd known. Instead of endings, he'd envisioned a wonderful life with her, filled with endless possibilities: Dara moving into the house with him, them cooking together at the granite island, bickering over whose turn it was to wash the dishes, Dara decorating the house for Christmas and Easter and every other conceivable holiday, Dara pregnant with their first child, Dara in the hospital smiling at him over the downy head of their sleeping baby. Each possibility was unspeakably thrilling, and he couldn't wait for any of it.

And when he'd stared into her sweet brown eyes,

which miraculously still glowed warm when she looked at him, it'd been equally clear she loved him—*still* loved him—even after the nonsense she'd overheard him spouting to his mother, even after he'd been so cruel to her. How was it possible he could be so blessed? And how could he have not realized it before? Of course, she loved him. Hadn't she told him as much the day she'd broken up with him? Why else would she have been so upset? He'd been so focused on his own broken heart, he hadn't noticed hers.

Mama poked her head around the corner from the kitchen, surveyed the scene, and approached cautiously. Mike met her concerned gaze and gave her a wry half smile. At the foot of the stairs, she silently smacked his knee, and he drew up his limbs so she had room to sit on the step next to him. They both stared at the closed front door, as if something infinitely entertaining danced across its panels.

"Scared her off, huh?" Mama asked him.

"Yeah," he grunted. "I'm pretty good at it."

"You should stop."

"I know."

Mama pursed her lips thoughtfully. "I like that girl. She's got a lot of sense."

Mike turned to face her. "Good. That's your future daughter-in-law, if she'll have me. It's not looking too good at the moment, though."

Mama smiled, her eyes still on the front door. "I know. Why else do you think I threw this party for you to try to get her back?"

Mike heaved a harsh sigh, then had to laugh. He should have known. He wondered how much misery he could have avoided in his thirty-five years if only he'd listened the first time Mama told him something.

"Well, tell me this, Ms. Smarty Woman," he told her. "If you know so much, tell me why I pushed her away the other week and put myself through this misery."

"The real reason?" Mama gave him a sideways look, her lips twisting with amusement. "It's because I raised a fool for a son."

Grinning, Mike dropped his head and shook it.

She slid a hand across his shoulders, stroking them. "I think it's because of that girl from college. What's her name?"

Mike's head shot up; his smile vanished. "Debbie? What the hell's she got to do with this?"

Mama pinched his arm; he winced and rubbed the spot. "Language, Michael." She sighed thoughtfully. "I told you months ago. She taught you that nothing is the way it seems, that you can't trust women, and that you can't have faith in the future. She taught you that relationships hurt." She shrugged. "Why wouldn't you have run away from Dara?"

Pieces of the thousand-piece, three-dimensional puzzle his life had become clicked steadily into place at Mama's words, but at her last comment, Mike gave her a dark look. "I didn't run away."

Mama very tactfully ignored this blatant lie. "Look here." At her sharp tone, Mike's gaze flew to her face; he had enough sense to know he'd best not argue with whatever she said next. "I want you to go talk to your brother—right now. He deserves to know what's coming because he cares for that girl, too. And we both know he's having a hard time."

Mike watched Mama get to her feet and smooth her slacks. "I know. I will."

Mama headed toward the kitchen. "And I expect my first grandchild by this time next year," she said, without pausing to look back. "None of us is getting any younger."

Mike was pacing the foyer a few minutes later, when Sean came in, eyes glazed, a slight sheen of perspiration on his face. Mike felt certain he'd been drinking heavily this whole time. Luckily, he could stay in his old room tonight and sleep it off. Mike would have to remember to take his brother's keys. Sean stopped and eyed him warily.

"We need to talk, man," Mike told him. "I've got something to tell you."

Sean stiffened as if to brace for a blow to the ribs.

Mike's brain thrashed around for the right words; he took a deep breath. "I've . . . been seeing Dara." He cleared his throat. "It's . . . serious."

Sean glared at him with absolute revulsion and trembled with rage. "You rotten punk!" he spat. He took a couple of hasty steps forward, then stopped, clenching and unclenching his fists impotently. He probably wanted to hit him, but Mike was much bigger than he was, and Sean wasn't stupid.

"I'm sorry, Sean," Mike told him sincerely. "I didn't want this to happen."

"Don't give me that bull!" Sean jabbed two fingers in Mike's face. "You wanted her! Don't deny it! What man in his right mind wouldn't want to sleep with Dara?"

Anger speared through Mike; suddenly, his hands itched to shut Sean up. He balled his fists at his sides. "Careful, Sean," he warned.

Sean marched up until he stood in his brother's face. "You can have anyone!" he roared, throwing his hands open wide, spittle flying from his mouth. "*Anyone*! Why do you need the one woman I want?"

Mike blinked against the stench of alcohol on Sean's breath but stood his ground. His hands still wanted to pummel Sean, but he realized this was a fair question. "You know why," he said quietly. "She's special. There's no one else like her."

Sean's eyes bulged to the point of apoplexy. "*I* know that! But *you* just want to sleep with her! You've never had a relationship with a woman in your life! You're just going to break her heart!"

Mike froze. "No." He said it very quietly, a vow to Dara and their future together. "I'm going to treat her like a queen. I promise you that."

Mike turned for the kitchen without another word, leaving Sean gaping behind him.

Two days later Dara trotted down the steps outside her apartment building, pulling on her leather gloves as she went. She held her rolled-up purple yoga mat under her arm. A fresh layer of snow shimmered on the grass and the ground; she would have to spend a minute or two scraping her windshield before she could leave. The weak early morning light matched her gloomy mood, which was one of the reasons she was going to yoga class. She needed something to lift her spirits and keep them off Mike and the fact that she would not see him anytime soon—if ever.

It was time to think about packing to go home to Chicago for Christmas, she thought as she crossed the parking lot to her car. She couldn't muster up any enthusiasm for the whole exercise, although she'd be glad to see her parents and other relatives. Chicago was still—always—blanketed with snow, so she'd need to make sure she packed her wool socks and her . . .

A tall man moved to stand in front of the driver's side door of her car, startling her out of her thoughts. She'd been so absorbed, she hadn't seen anyone there. She took one look at him, and her knees locked up. She froze, several feet away. It was Mike.

Chapter 21

He stared at her, as powerful and unmoving as a mountain. He wore his black wool topcoat over a dark suit, with his black leather gloves on and a black and red plaid scarf crossed at his neck. He was astonishingly handsome. Agony twisted in her chest, with longing hot on its heels. What right did he have to show up unannounced here—*here*—at her car, where it should be safe? Why would he do this to her, especially after the other night, when they'd talked like civilized people, and she could almost delude herself into thinking he still cared something for her?

Slowly, he stepped toward her, never taking his eyes from hers. Her instinct was to drop the yoga mat and sprint back to the apartment, where he couldn't follow her, but she couldn't move. When he came within four feet of her, he stopped, as if he sensed she wanted to run away. At this distance she could see the strain on his face and the dark circles under his eyes. And she could see his amber eyes were very dark, almost black, with intensity. He did not look away and did not smile. She stared at him, waiting.

"There were some things I should have told you the

other night, but the time wasn't right. So I took a chance." His breath formed white puffs of steam; his deep, husky voice danced up her spine, music to her ears. "I thought maybe you couldn't sleep any better than I could. And maybe you'd be up early to go somewhere and keep busy so you wouldn't think about me. Just like I've been doing. Last night I worked until two-thirty, and then I fell asleep on the sofa in my office because I couldn't stand the thought of going home without you there. I went home a little while ago to change. It's been like that every day since you stopped working."

Her throat constricted much too tightly for her to answer. He took another half step toward her, and she went rigid. He was too close now—much, much too close.

His face softened; that flush she'd seen the other night crept over his cheeks again. "I can't go on like this. This has been the worst three weeks of my life."

"Oh," she said faintly. She would not allow herself to wonder where he was leading or what he would say next.

"I want you back. I was stupid to let you get away in the first place. I don't deserve a woman like you, but I'm going to try, anyway." His gaze did not waver, not once. She saw absolute resolve there, absolute determination. And suddenly, she felt absolute terror. She blinked and turned away, unable to look at him now. "So I have something to tell you." His voice dropped to a whisper. "I *do* love you. I need you in my life."

Hesitantly, he touched her face with his gloved hand. She stiffened and closed her eyes. But she couldn't bring herself to move away. "I need to know how you are, sweetheart," he continued. "I need to know how your Thanksgiving was and what you had for breakfast. I need to know what you want for Christmas. There's a new Indian restaurant downtown, and I need to take you there." She forced herself to open her eyes, but she still couldn't look him in the face. "I need to make love to you."

"Don't," she said sharply. She wanted to snarl at him like a lioness. She hated him in that moment. Hated him with an intensity and purity that demolished everything else in her life—except her body's desperate, throbbing response to him. How could he do this to her? She wanted to kill him.

He winced at her murderous expression. Infinite sadness appeared in his eyes. "I need you to smile at me again." His voice broke. To her utter astonishment, a tear rolled down his cheek. Her mind spun in endless circles, like the cars on the speedway at the Daytona 500. She couldn't make sense of anything, least of all Mike's tears. She'd never seen him cry before; she'd thought he was one of those men who never cried, no matter what.

He dropped his hand. "I don't expect you to forgive me for what I said to my mother and for letting you go without telling you how I feel. But I'll love you whether you do or not."

Mike reached for his throat and fished around under his scarf, tie, and collar. Then he hooked his gloved thumb through a thick, shining gold necklace and held it up for her to see. A strange charm flashed there, but then she did a double take and gasped. It was a ring. An engagement ring—a large oval diamond set in white gold or platinum. She'd never seen anything so glorious. "Oh, my God," she cried, clapping her hand over her mouth.

"I'm going to wear this, for now," Mike told her. "I know it's the closest to you I'm going to get. I know you need to think about whether you want to take another chance with me." She stared at the ring, hypnotized by his words and by the dazzling shimmer of sunlight on the diamond. The sun's rays splintered into a thousand rainbows. "But this is *your* ring, Dara."

Dara's eyes flew back to his face, and she waited breathlessly.

"And I intend to do whatever it takes to put it on your finger." His expression hardened into fierce resolve. "I want your love back, and your trust. And I'm going to get them. I don't care how long it takes." Without looking away from her, he lifted the ring and kissed it gently, reverently. She did not need to be a psychologist to know he wished he could kiss her instead. Finally, he lowered his hand and tucked the ring back inside his collar. "I just thought you should know." Mike turned and walked off across the parking lot, his feet crunching on the snow, leaving Dara to stare helplessly after him.

Dara, still in her yoga gear, opened the door to her apartment, balancing a small bag of groceries on her hip; she'd needed some fresh produce and a few toiletries. Grocery shopping was part of her routine, and she might as well stick with it. Mindless activities seemed to help keep her mind off Mike, if only for thirty seconds here and there. Of course, Mike hadn't helped matters any when he showed up out of the blue this morning, muddying the waters and throwing her life upside down—again.

She tossed her keys in the basket and set the groceries on the counter, pausing to glance at today's paper. Trying to keep up with the news during finals would have been an exercise in futility, but now she at least had time to glance at the headlines. One of the stories on the front page, below the fold, mentioned that Mark Johnson—Johnson! She hadn't thought of him in eons—had rested his defense at trial, without testifying. Experts predicted a conviction. She smiled inwardly. Good. The jerk deserved it.

Dropping the paper, she turned toward the refrigerator to put the groceries away; a strange, thrilling new smell wafted through her nostrils. She froze in place. After a minute, realizing she was being ridiculous, she followed her nose, crept over to the breakfast nook, and peeked around the corner at it. She knew what it was, even before she saw it, boxed and wrapped in green tissue paper, sitting on the kitchen table. The apartment manager had apparently let the delivery man in earlier, while she was gone. Dara circled the table, staring at the box as if it were a terrorist with a bomb strapped to his chest. If she had any sense whatsoever, she would throw it away without ever opening it. Before it could infect her brain, the way Mike's visit this morning had. But, of course, she'd never had any sense where Mike was concerned.

Her hands trembled as she gently turned the tissue back and lifted out the lush gardenia plant. Dara couldn't believe her eyes. She'd forgotten how creamy and white the petals were, how deeply green and waxy the leaves were, how intoxicating the fragrance was, or how strong. She lifted it to her nose and breathed deeply. This was obviously what it smelled like in heaven.

Mike. She cursed him again, for the three thousandth

time today. How could he do this to her—throw her into this kind of confusion when things had seemed so clear? There was a card in the box, she realized. She'd been weak and opened the box, true, but she could be strong now and just throw the card away. Better yet, she could throw both the card and the flower away and start packing. Yes. That was exactly what she should do.

She ripped the envelope open. Mike's scrawl filled the plain card:

Forgive me.

For one second her heart melted. For one pathetic, misguided second, she thought she would call and ask him to come back. For one blink of an eye, she thought she could forgive him, and they could start over again. But then the pain surged back.

Did he think it was this easy, that all he had to do was cry a few tears and send her one lousy plant, and she'd forgive him for breaking her heart for the second time? Well, she couldn't. She was woman enough to recognize her weakness where he was concerned; that was why she was so scared. She knew very well that once Mike set his mind to something, he didn't stop until he got it. And now he wanted her—probably only because the sex had been good, and he'd missed her a little for a couple of weeks. And she was too weak—much, much too weak—to withstand a full frontal assault. Just the sight of him destroyed her resolve and turned her body to Jell-O. She'd barely stopped herself from falling into his arms this morning. Maybe next time he'd catch her in a weaker moment, and then who could say what would happen?

No, this had to stop. Right now. No flowers, no tears, no begging—would *Mike* really beg?—would make her change her mind. She would never give him another chance to break her heart. They were over; he'd said he didn't love her, and he couldn't have suddenly changed his mind. He needed to stop toying with her emotions. And tonight she would march down to his office and tell him.

All at once, there was a loud, insistent knock on the door. Startled, she dropped the card and hurried to peek out the peephole. It was Sean. She swung open the door. "Hi," she said warily, remembering his ugly mood the other night. "How are you?"

Sean's cold, assessing gaze flickered to her, then away, as he stalked inside, into the living room. Bewildered, Dara shut the door and trailed after him. He sat on the edge of the sofa, his jaw tight. "Mike told me."

Dara's stomach lurched; her heart pounded. She pressed the palm of one of her suddenly clammy hands to her stomach in what she hoped was a casual manner. "Told you what?"

His lips thinned down to nothing. "That you've been"—he swallowed hard, as if to force himself to say the hateful words—"seeing him."

"Oh," she said faintly. Her knees weakened, and she sank into the overstuffed chair next to the sofa. "It's over now, though."

His lips twisted. "That's not the way it sounded to me."

Dara's thoughts churned aimlessly. She couldn't tell whether Sean was mostly angry or mostly hurt, and therefore, she had no idea what to say. Worse, she didn't know what to make of the fact that Mike had confessed to Sean. What did that mean? Could he possibly be serious about wanting to marry her?

Wouldn't he have to be before he told Sean about their relationship? She stared helplessly at Sean.

"Did you ever stop to think," he said, his voice low and harsh, "how I would feel about this? Did that ever cross your mind?"

"Yes," she whispered, trying not to flinch before the misery in his eyes. She felt terrible—every bit as bad as she'd thought she'd feel if Sean ever found out. But she couldn't find it in herself to apologize for loving Mike. That was something she couldn't change and didn't regret.

"But you did it, anyway."

She raised her chin, determined not to be cowed. "We didn't do it on purpose," she told him.

A single shoulder shrugged. "I know. But what difference does that make?"

None, of course. "I'm sorry we hurt you, Sean," she said uselessly. "*I'm sorry.*"

Sean's eyes, flat and expressionless now, stared at her; he seemed to be too angry—or hurt—to speak. After a moment, he stood up and walked to the door. She followed. She thought he would leave without saying anything else, but then he wheeled around. "Why, Dara?" he cried, animated now. "You know how I felt about you! Why couldn't it have been me?"

"Oh, Sean. The question isn't why it wasn't you. The question is why it only could have ever been Mike." She heard the sharp hiss of his startled breath before he turned, jerked the door open, and stalked out.

Mark Johnson sat in his dark SUV, waiting patiently. Some things were worth waiting for, and revenge was one of them. He glanced at the clock on the dashboard:

nine-thirty. He'd been there an hour already, but he didn't care. He'd stay all night if he needed to; Alicia—that witch—certainly wasn't waiting up for him at home. Who would have ever thought she'd have the guts to change the locks on the house. His house! The one he paid the mortgage on! That had been a kick in the teeth the day he'd tried to go home and his key didn't fit. He'd have kicked down the door if she hadn't threatened to call the police. That was the last thing he needed—another arrest. So he'd let Alicia's insult pass, for now. He'd deal with her later—financially.

He'd deal with Baldwin now.

The jury was out, but he knew they'd convict him. It was just a matter of time. The trial had been a joke from start to finish; the prosecutor had trotted out all those punks who'd claimed they saw him threaten Dante before the shooting. Then his replacement lawyer—the one he'd been forced to hire after Baldwin gave him the boot—had thrown a hissy fit and threatened to withdraw if he insisted on testifying in his own defense. The lawyer had said some nonsense about him not being a good witness—that he'd do more harm to his case than good. So he hadn't even had the chance to tell the jury his side of the story. And they hated him. Any fool could see it, the way they glared at him and rolled their eyes whenever his stupid lawyer made an objection. And when they returned the verdict, they'd revoke his bail and throw him right in jail.

So tonight could very well be his last night of freedom for a long, long time.

And he wasn't about to miss the chance to even the score with Baldwin.

He flexed his gloved hands. Luckily, he'd thought to

bring the leather gloves with the cashmere lining. It was pretty chilly in the car without the heat on. He reached for the gleaming pistol on the passenger's seat and ran his fingers along the butt, smoothing a smudge. Old Faithful. They'd seen a lot of action together, the two of them. She'd never let him down. That was all a man could count on, really. Himself and his gun. He couldn't count on anything else. Certainly not a woman. Or a business partner.

Or a lawyer.

He'd parked in the narrow alley behind Mike Baldwin's building. He hated to try to pull off something like this downtown—the getaway would be that much harder—but what else could he do? He'd watched Baldwin's house all week, but he was never there. The alley, actually, wasn't that bad a spot. He had a clear view of the brownstone's back door. There were also some trash cans lined up along the curb, but that was no problem. Baldwin had parked his own SUV out there, and when he was ready to leave the office, he'd probably go out the brownstone's kitchen door. Then, bam! He'd pop him, and it'd be all over for that arrogant jerk. He wouldn't even have to get out of the car.

A quick shot to the head was better than Baldwin deserved. It still pissed him off when he thought about how Baldwin had dropped him. Just like that. Didn't that jerk know who he was? Didn't he know he'd be a Hall of Famer as soon as he was eligible? And that he was worth a cool seventy million? Hadn't he heard that on the streets back in L.A., his nickname had been Killa? Didn't that entitle him to a certain amount of respect?

And who was Baldwin? Some lawyer who thought he could jerk him around. Some idiot who thought he was better than he was. Well, what had Baldwin ever done? How many dead presidents was *he* worth? What made him think he could treat him that way and get away with it?

He kept his eyes on the back door but flexed his legs a little. They weren't too happy about sitting in this cold car for so long; his bad knee was really starting to talk to him. Well, it'd all be over soon. When he was finished here, he could head over to Cheryl's crib. Cheryl had been only too happy to pick up where Desiree had left off. He'd kicked Desiree out of his apartment once she'd talked to Baldwin. Then she'd had the nerve to call his wife and tell her he'd been doing her. Well, now Desiree could try to make it on her own in the world. Let her try to make it on her back in someone else's bed. Let her run up someone else's titanium card. It was no skin off his back. Cheryl could work him better than Desiree any day of the week, anyway.

His thoughts shifted back to Baldwin. The disrespect was one thing. He could almost—*almost*—deal with that. No, the reason Baldwin had a date with his gun was he'd thrown him to the wolves. He'd had to find another lawyer, some chump who didn't know his head from a hole in the ground. Baldwin was the best, and now his new lawyer had blown it. Plus, Baldwin had encouraged Desiree to tell the truth, so he'd had no alibi to give the jury.

And Baldwin had to answer for that.

Soon Baldwin would come through the screen door, and he would pop him before he got to within ten feet of his own car. He thought of how Baldwin would look with his brains blown out all over the street and could feel himself getting hard. Yeah, he'd need Cheryl tonight.

Johnson picked up his gun and pressed it to his lips for a good-luck kiss.

Dara arrived at Mike's office after ten, and the dark alley made her jittery in a way she hadn't been since she was twelve and watched *The Exorcist* without her parents' permission. The street was so narrow back here, and the buildings seemed to crowd in on it, blocking out the sun, not that there was any sun right now. She figured it was as good a time as any to catch Mike. But even though the floodlights at the back door lit the immediate area, she was not anxious to get out of the car. Shadows crept along the walls, and the doorways of other buildings provided endless and varied hiding spaces for any thug who might happen by. Plus, it was cold and damp, and the moon was hidden by clouds and showed no signs of coming out anytime soon.

She got out of her car and kept her key ring at the ready. But when she climbed to the top of the three steps leading to the door, she stopped and cursed. How could she have forgotten she'd returned the key when she cleaned out her desk? She'd hoped to surprise Mike—like he was so fond of doing to her—but there was nothing else she could do but call on her cell phone and ask him to let her in.

Her heart thundered at the thought of talking to him again, by phone or otherwise. She fished the phone out of her purse and dialed with a shaky hand. Maybe she should just go back home right now and forget this whole stupid idea. She was way too nervous to have any sort of a coherent conversation, and he would twist it all around on her. Maybe she should sleep on it and rethink her confrontation plan tomorrow. Maybe . . .

"Mike Baldwin." He used his cool, efficient phone voice, with a hint of concern that anyone would call the office so late. Her stomach fell through the ground, and she gulped loudly. Jerking the phone away from her ear as if it had become a live wire, she started to hang up. She couldn't possibly do this, not now, and . . .

The sound of a loud crash came from the phone. She had the image of Mike, sitting with his feet propped on his desk, swinging his feet to the floor and knocking over several files. "Dara!" he cried. "I know it's you! Don't hang up!" Dara silently cursed the advent of technology that made the basic anonymous hang-up impossible. She'd forgotten that the firm's phones identified the caller. "Dara? Are you there?"

She took a deep breath and strove for cool detachment. "We need to talk."

"Whatever you want." She'd never heard him sound so excited, so anxious. "I can come to your apartment right now, or I could meet—"

"No, I-I'm here. You just need to open the back door for me and—"

"I'm coming." The line went dead, and she immediately heard his footsteps thundering through the brownstone and up to the door, which he snatched open. He stared down at her. Her heart contracted so sharply, she almost gasped. She'd thought she was ready to face him—he looked devastating in his shirtsleeves, with his tie loosened—but she wasn't. She wasn't ready to see his hopeful but strained expression, or those flashing dark eyes.

She wasn't ready for *this*.

Mike looked at Dara's wary face, ready to weep with gratitude. He'd prepared himself for a long persuasion campaign; not for one minute had he thought she'd show up so soon. "Come in," he said, shutting and locking the door after her. "No one's here. We can go up to my off—"

She shook her head vehemently, as if he'd suggested she needed to jump off the Brooklyn Bridge. "I'm not staying. I need to go."

His heart fell through the floor; he couldn't let her walk back out that door any more than he could flap his arms and fly to the moon. "I don't think so," he said quickly. He kept his voice soft, but he would not negotiate. She wouldn't leave until they'd worked things out or at least given it their best effort. No, scratch that. She was not leaving. Dara shifted restlessly. Her eyes panned the kitchen, and he knew she was considering alternate escape routes, wondering if she could make a break for the front door. Well, she could plot all she wanted. He stepped closer. "Why did you come?"

"I want you to stop. You need to stop."

For the first time there was an edge to her voice. Her anger had finally churned its way to the surface. He felt a tremendous satisfaction. "I can't."

Her eyes narrowed dangerously, then shifted away; she seemed unwilling—or unable—to hold his gaze. "Of course you can."

"I need you. I can't let go of something I need as much as I need you." He stepped closer and stooped down in her face so they were at eye level. For one second she looked him directly in the eye and he felt a terrible jolt of her abject misery. Then she jumped and scurried away until she backed up against the counter.

"Do you think you'll be able to look me in the face again anytime soon, Dara?" She was killing him. He knew he didn't deserve to look her in the eye, not after the way he'd hurt her, but he felt like a trash can full of garbage, left out on the curb for pickup.

She shrugged, but didn't lift her eyes from the floor. "I don't know. I don't know how long it's going to hurt when I look at you."

"You don't know?" he said savagely. "Well, here's what I *do* know." He stalked toward her. "I told you I love you and you didn't say *anything*."

Finally she looked him in the face, her eyes icier than an Alaskan glacier. "Right."

He winced. "'Right?' What's that supposed to mean?"

She laughed bitterly. "Well, I mean, let's review the facts." She counted off on her fingers. "After the night of the dinner you told me you just wanted to screw me. Then you retract that statement, tell me it's *not* just about sex, and eventually make love to me. Then you tell your sick mother you don't love me—basically that it *is* about the sex. Then when I ask you about what you said you don't even bother to deny it. You give me the worthless consolation prize of telling me you *care about me*." She flung the words in his face like she was throwing down a gauntlet. "But, wait! Now you *do* love me! You suddenly want to *marry* me, even though I've heard you say on at least two occasions that you don't want to get married. Well, my mistake!" She laughed that same ugly laugh again. "I guess we've got it all worked out now, huh? How silly of me!"

Mike stared at her, wounded and bleeding from the

verbal beating she'd just given him. He tried to re-group. "Do you want me to tell you the truth?"

"That would be a refreshing change."

"Well, here it is." He grabbed her upper arms and leaned down in her face so the only place she could look was in his eyes. "I *do* love you." She went rigid and tried to jerk away, but he tightened his hold. Her face twisted disgustedly, as if she'd just caught a whiff of a fresh load of manure; he plowed ahead anyway. "I've been in love with you since that first night we talked at the party."

"Bull." With one great jerk Dara threw off his hands and wrenched free, pushing him away from her. "You wanted me. End of story. I'm leaving." She marched to the door.

"No." He caught her arm and whirled her back around, ignoring her outraged splutter. "You are *not* leaving." This was going very badly, worse than he'd thought. He paced back and forth, frustrated. "You turned my life upside down, Dara. I thought I should be building my career now. I wasn't ready for this kind of relationship."

"That's all you've got?" she cried, clearly agitated. With one hand she clutched the edges of her coat to-gether again; with the other she swiped at her hair. Her whole body seemed to vibrate with adrenaline, like a cocaine addict desperate for her next fix. "You need to give me something I can work with. Because *I* was scared, too. And I thought I should be focusing on school—but I was willing to take a chance with you because I—"

He jerked. Now they were getting somewhere. "Be-cause you loved me."

She hastily turned her back to him, facing the refrigerator. "I didn't say that."

He circled around her so he could see her face. "So you don't love me?"

Her lip curled up in a sneer, but her eyes shimmered with tears. "Why would I be stupid enough to fall for a man who thinks loving me will ruin his life?"

He held his hands out, palms up. "I'm sorry, Dara," he said helplessly.

"This is so funny." Her mouth twisted into something that may have been an attempt at a smile but only made her look like a caricature of herself. "Jamal told me I was blind because I couldn't see how much you loved me. But you know what? *You're* the blind one. Because you didn't even see how much I worshipped you. That I would have done anything for you. That I was the best thing that ever happened to you and we could have been so happy together."

His heart thundered to a stop; they stared at each other for a long, pregnant moment. Desperate to touch her, he took one step forward, but her entire body went rigid, as if someone had shoved a telephone pole up her spine. He reached for her. "I see all that now. I want to marry you."

She jumped away and hurried to the door, which he'd foolishly left unguarded. "You don't get it, do you? I'm not trying to force you into anything. I'm not trying to manipulate you into a marriage you don't want. And I—I've started to accept that you don't return my feelings." Her eyes wavered a little. "I'll be o—"

"'Don't return your feelings?'" he yelled, incredulous. "Are you insane? After you broke things off with me it was like the sun stopped shining on my face! I wanted to kill myself and everyone else around me! I didn't eat, I didn't sleep—I spent all my nights on the office sofa! I even stalked you a little—the day your finals started I spied on you from the parking lot just to see if you were okay! And when I saw you at my party I realized how much I need you! For the first time in weeks I could breathe again." He grabbed her shoulders again, stooping down in her face. "And I am telling you we belong together and I am sorry I hurt you but I want to marry you!"

Dara fell apart.

She shoved him, hard, on his chest. "You get away from me!" she shrieked. "Do you think you can just tell me you're sorry and that's it?" He tried to grab her arms again, but she swatted him away. "I don't believe anything you say to me! I don't trust you! And I don't forgive you! *I don't forgive you*! I will never give you the chance to hurt me again! Never!"

Mike wrapped his arms around her, trapping her arms at her sides. She struggled furiously but he held her tighter, pressing her head against his chest. "Let me go!"

He leaned his head down to whisper in her ear. "I'm sorry, sweetheart," he murmured over and over, his voice cracking. "I love you and I'm sorry. *I'm sorry*." He told her he was sorry until finally his words ran out.

Eventually Dara stopped fighting him; he eased his grip a little and tipped her chin up so he could see what she was thinking. He did not expect to see her flushed face and deliriously bright eyes, nor did he expect to hear her breath turn ragged. She was clearly aroused. Did she forgive him, then? "Dara." Before he thought about what he was doing he bent and pressed his lips to her cheek, right at the corner of her mouth. She moaned. Slowly he pulled away as a new awareness shivered through his body. Suddenly he felt the sweetness and heat of her breath on his lips, the soft but firm pressure of her breasts against his chest and the flame of desire in her eyes; her face seemed to burn with fever.

Her glittering gaze locked with his, then slipped to his lips. He heard a harsh, rasping sound and distantly realized it was his own breathing; he was surprised he could hear it over the roar of blood in his veins. She stepped closer and her hands found his waist and slid up his sides. At the same time her hips shifted and pressed her into contact with his rigid arousal. Mike groaned roughly, jerked her all the way into his arms and lowered his head.

Chapter 22

Dara's need for Mike—her need to feel him thrusting violently, hotly, endlessly within her—spiraled out of control, like an avalanche thundering down a mountainside, obliterating everything in its path. There was no time for words or thoughts. This man was like a drug to her. A living, breathing, walking vial of heroin that could make her palms sweat and her heart race and her breath stop with just a look, a touch. She had to have him. Now.

Mike planted his hands in her hair and pulled her head back, deepening the angle of his kiss so they could feast on each other's mouths. He backed her up against the kitchen door—luckily the curtains were drawn—and ran his hands over her butt and hips, then up to her breasts. His hands couldn't seem to decide where they needed to be and so were everywhere at once. She did not expect—or want—him to be gentle, and he wasn't. He seemed desperate to touch her face, her breasts, her hair, her hips and her butt—desperate to make sure she was still the same, that nothing had changed.

Nothing had changed. Everything had changed. Mike tasted and felt sweeter than ever before. He broke the kiss for one second, long enough for him to sweep her jacket off and her sweater up over her head. His hot hands rubbed over her back, then squeezed her breasts together in the front. With a low growl he stooped to bury his head between them. Dara threw her head back and arched herself, clutching his head. He ran the heels of his hands over her nipples. "Harder," she begged. "*Harder*." Through her black bra he found her nipple with his thumb and rubbed it. He lifted his head, watching her, then stooped again and caught it with his teeth, biting.

Jolts of unbearable pleasure shot through Dara's belly to her loins until her knees gave out. Mike seemed to anticipate this; he shoved one of his long, hard thighs between her legs and she rode him, straining toward the relief she needed. Mike straightened and their gazes locked. She stared at him, panting. His eyes were so hot and intent she felt pinned to the door, not that she had any thought of escaping. The pulsing in her body grew almost painful. She needed to touch him and feel his bare skin. She hastily unbuttoned and removed his starched cotton dress shirt, then pulled his undershirt up and off his head, pausing to gape. She'd never thought she'd be with such a beautiful, masculine creature. He was all broad chest and shoulders, chiseled belly, long legs, sinewy muscles—more stunning than she'd remembered. She felt lightheaded with desire.

He seemed to know it. Deep in his dark eyes, beneath the fire and the lust, glimmered a hint of amusement. She didn't care. Dara leaned forward and pressed her breasts against his chest. Her hips undulated against his thigh, having apparently developed a mind of their own. She tightened her hands on the nape of his neck and pulled him down, kissing him deeply and frantically. When she couldn't get close enough that way, she arched into him and scratched his back.

That seemed to be more than Mike could take. He moaned and broke away, fumbling with the waistband of her low-riding jeans. Frowning, he looked down at her belt. He cursed viciously, then unbuckled it and slid it free. "Don't ever wear a belt again."

He unzipped her jeans and, stooping, yanked them down over her hips. Dara stepped out of her shoes then kicked the jeans off her feet. Mike started to stand, but paused to press his face into her belly. He rubbed his scratchy face—he hadn't shaved this morning—back and forth over her stomach, then down to the insides of her thighs. Suddenly he grabbed the edges of her black thong underwear with both of his hands and with one great jerk ripped them apart and out from between her legs. Dara cried out; her soaking wet sex tightened and quivered on the verge of a staggering climax.

Mike unzipped his own pants and freed himself, but then froze. "Wait," he said, looking wildly around. "I need—"

She'd just thought of condoms herself. "My purse." Panting, she pointed to where she'd dropped it on the floor.

He snatched it up, emptied it on the counter, and found what he needed. He put it on in a flash. There was no time for any other niceties. He planted his hands on her butt and lifted her off her feet as if she weighed five pounds. The power she felt pulsing through his arms— his body—was astonishing. He shifted his weight, using the door as leverage. Instinctively, she wrapped her legs tight around his waist and rubbed her aching loins against his rock hard arousal. With one hand, he grabbed his penis and poised himself at her core. Ecstasy shimmered on the horizon. *Yes. Now.* She needed him, and she needed him right now.

With one violent thrust, he was inside her. She felt as if she were hurtled through the air, her body spasming wildly, endlessly. The brightness of her climax stunned her; excruciating pleasure pierced through her womb and spread from there. She doubted she'd ever recover from it. "Oh, God!"

"God, I missed you, Dara." Mike's hips sped up, pounding her ruthlessly into the door. She tightened her arms and held on for the ride. *"I missed you."*

"I missed you, too."

His hips circled and drummed, every stroke driving him harder and deeper into her body. She couldn't bear the pleasure. It radiated up her spine and danced over her skin until she thought she would leap out of it. "Please stop," she begged. *"Please.* Please stop. I can't take this."

"No."

Impossibly, she felt the tension building again, rawer and a thousand times more intense than before. "Please," she cried, bucking against him, no longer sure of her name, desperate and insensible. "Please. Oh, God, Mike. *Please."*

His face was strained; his eyes locked with hers. "I love you, angel. More than anything else in the world."

She looked away, frightened by his intensity and the intimacy of the moment.

He grabbed her chin and jerked her face back around. "I love you, Dara. You can't hide from it."

"Don't," she cried, turning away again, unwilling to believe or forgive.

"I love you," he whispered. "I always have. I always

will." He held her even tighter. "I'm never letting you go again," he told her, his voice cracking. *"Never."* He kissed her, deep and wet and hot. She couldn't handle it. She exploded again, straining against him, screaming his name.

She saw the brief flash of a satisfied smile and the glimmering of his eyes. He circled one last time, then threw his head back and surged ahead, groaning and shuddering as he emptied himself into her.

They leaned against the door, panting, for one delicious second. But then Dara realized what had happened—what she'd just done—and she struggled against him, more disgusted with herself than she'd ever been. "Put me down," she said sharply. "Let me go."

Mike stiffened. Disbelieving, he raised his head from her shoulder to stare at her; in his eyes, she saw stark fear slowly replace the happiness. Very reluctantly, he loosened his grip enough for her to wriggle free and stand up. Horrified, she scurried away from him, looking down at the floor for her clothes so she wouldn't have to meet his gaze. "What's wrong?"

She did not answer. What had she done? What in God's name had she done? She'd come to tell him to leave her alone, and she'd let—no, encouraged!—him make love to her against the door, like some slut. He'd said he only wanted her for sex, and here she'd let him use her for sex. What was wrong with her? When would she ever stop being to stupid? When would she learn she shouldn't trust Mike, no matter how much she might want to? What cataclysmic event would have to happen before she could go thirty seconds without thinking about him or wanting him? Would a lobotomy do it? She found her ruined underwear on the floor; with a frustrated cry, she threw it back down again.

"What are you doing?" he asked dully, his voice filled with dread, as if he needed to ask but couldn't bear to hear the answer. He watched as she shoved her feet into her jeans, gripping the counter for balance. "Where are you going?"

"Home." Turning her back to him, she slipped her bra on and her sweater over her head.

He grabbed her arm roughly and swung her back around. "Why?"

Jerking her arm away, she found her shoes and slipped them on. "Because nothing's changed."

Mike's entire body sagged; for a long moment, he stared at her, aghast. "Everything's changed," he whispered, reaching up to catch the diamond ring still sparkling on its chain around his neck. "I love you. In my heart, I think of you as my *wife*. As far as I'm concerned, I just made love to my *wife*."

"No."

"Dara, please," he said, so softly she had to strain to hear. "You have to stop punishing me."

"I'm not punishing you," she said, swallowing convulsively, wondering if maybe she was lying to herself. "I just don't trust you." Ignoring the despair in his eyes and the corresponding pain in her own gut, she turned on her heels, snatched her jacket from the floor, shoveled most of the contents back into her purse, unlocked the door, and swung it open. The cold, fresh night air felt good on her hot face as she trotted down the steps.

"Dara, wait!" Mike stooped down to grab his undershirt and yank it back over his head, then followed her. Dara hurried toward her car, desperate to get away from him.

And screamed.

Chapter 23

A hulking figure of a man stood four feet away, by the trash cans, a gun pointed at her, blocking her only means of escape. He wore a black sweat suit, with the hood covering part of his face. Then he pushed the hood off, and she realized it was Johnson. The charming womanizer was gone, as if he'd never existed. His eyes looked flat and malevolent tonight—soulless. Instantly, she knew she was staring into the face of a murderer, and her blood turned to ice because he'd come for Mike. His beefy, rubber glove–covered hand, which, by rights, shouldn't have been so quick, shot out and grabbed her. She tried to jerk away but couldn't.

The door flew open, and Mike charged out, eyes wild with alarm. With one sweep, he surveyed the scene and shot Dara a warning look. *Hang on, sweetheart.* She could hear him as if he'd actually spoken the words. *Hang on.*

But then Mike turned to Johnson, and his face was black with rage. "What are you doing, man?" He stepped all the way out onto the stoop.

"I'm going to kill you. You told Desiree to cut a

deal so I didn't have an alibi. My new lawyer cain't chew gum and think at the same time. The jury hates me, and tomorrow they're prolly gonna convict me." Johnson's voice brimmed with triumph. "Only thing kept me goin' the last few weeks through the trial was the thought of killin' you first chance I got. Any other questions?"

Dara could all but see the hatred dripping from his mouth, like venom from the fangs of a snake. Worse, she could taste the bile in her own mouth. He really meant to do it, then. Of course, he'd also kill her. His plan wouldn't work otherwise.

"That's fine." Mike nodded as if this were a perfectly reasonable proposition. "But let Dara go first."

Johnson snorted. "I'm gonna kill both of you."

Mike's expression didn't change, but Dara felt him absorb this information like he would absorb a blow with a two-by-four to the ribs. "What about your wife and kids?"

Johnson shrugged impatiently. "She don't give a damn about me. And the kids'll never know. I'm goin' to jail, anyway. Got nothin' to lose."

Hatred, hard and icy and overwhelming, gripped Dara. If hell existed, this man would surely find it yawning before him when he died.

"Well, if you're going to kill us," Mike said, sidling down the steps toward Dara, "at least give us the chance to say good-bye and say a prayer."

Johnson shook his head with the detachment of an exterminator spraying roaches. "You been watching too much TV. I'm gonna cap botha you right now."

Everything happened at once. Johnson raised his gun and, taking a step away from her, pointed it at Dara. Mike took a flying leap off the steps toward her.

A shot rang out.

At first, Dara didn't know what the sound was; for one confused second, she wondered who would light firecrackers at a time like this. Mike knocked her to the ground, covering her with his body. He was on his feet again in an instant, lunging for Johnson. For a tense second, the men struggled with the gun between them—a clash of the titans. Sweat poured off Johnson's bald head, and blood vessels strained in his forehead. Frantically, Dara looked around for something she could use to smash Johnson over the head, but then she heard another shot and felt the instantaneous, sickening thud of three hundred pounds of animal tissue hit the ground.

And then everything was quiet.

"Mike!" Dara screamed. Swaying on his feet, Johnson's gun dangling from his hand, Mike stared at her. He staggered back a step, a strange smudge on his shirt, then crumpled to his knees.

"No!" she cried, running to him. She looked around wildly, assessing the danger. She saw Johnson immediately. He was a mound of flesh lying in front of Mike like a sperm whale run aground. He was dead, a gaping hole in his massive chest.

But Mike . . . Something was wrong with Mike. Now lying on his back, he opened his eyes and blinked, but something had happened to him. He couldn't have been shot. "Mike." She leaned over him and saw the flaming red stain, obscene against the crisp white of his undershirt, spreading over his chest. She'd never seen so much blood before in her life; surely, even a slaughterhouse didn't have so much. "No," she said faintly, frozen by an unspeakable terror.

Had he been shot in the heart?

Mike stirred and moved his hand weakly. Recovering slightly, Dara struggled to keep her face upbeat. Somehow she knew she had to stop Mike from bleeding to death and keep him warm, so she covered him with her jacket, pressing down hard on the wound. Was it her imagination, or was the blood stain twice as big now as it had been just a second ago? Immediately, the blood soaked through her jacket. Mike cried out in pain and clutched his hand to his chest, which heaved a couple of times before he seemed to have enough breath to talk. "You okay, sweetheart?" His voice was weak and raspy.

Her mouth sagged. "Am *I* okay? *You're* the one who's been shot." To her horror, she felt a warm, wet spot through the knee of her jeans where she knelt on the ground. It wasn't his blood, was it?

"Better me than you." Suddenly, his eyes closed, his head rolled back, and he made an obscene gurgling sound as he gasped for breath. Dara, who'd always imagined she'd be the soul of calm in a crisis, shrieked hysterically for several seconds before she got herself together, found her cell phone, and called 911.

After that, she uselessly watched his labored breathing and rubbed his arms to keep him from freezing. Her only hope was that the EMTs would come quickly so Mike could die in the comfort of the hospital or at least the ambulance, rather than here on the street like a dog. Because any five-year-old could see that someone bleeding like this had been shot in the heart and could not possibly survive.

Mike was going to die. It was only a matter of time.

* * *

"Let's talk in here."

The grim-faced surgeon pulled off his sweat-soaked green cap and ushered Dara and Mrs. Baldwin into one of the tiny conference rooms adjacent to the waiting area. Mrs. Baldwin, looking suddenly much older and haggard, leaned heavily on Dara's arm. Despite her own exhaustion and fear, Dara had spent the last several hours hovering over her, determined that nothing would happen to Mike's mother on her watch.

They sat at a small, cramped table, and the surgeon, clearly tired, rubbed the back of his neck as if to relieve the tension. What was his name again? Dr. Smitson? Smithers? With his fresh face, curly red hair, and sprinkling of freckles over his nose, he looked barely out of diapers, whoever he was. Dara stared dully at him through the protective shell of numbness that had thankfully descended over her. He couldn't tell her anything she didn't already know. There were, in fact, only two things he could say: that Mike had died on the operating table, or that he would die before the night was out. And she didn't want to hear either one.

"He came out of the surgery about as well as we could have expected," he told them. Mrs. Baldwin grabbed Dara's hand in her lap and squeezed tightly. "The bullet nicked his pulmonary artery. That's why he had such a massive bleed. We had to give him four units."

Behind the tissue clutched to her mouth, Mrs. Baldwin let out a muffled cry; Dara automatically reached up to rub her shoulder reassuringly.

"He's in the ICU, on a ventilator," the surgeon continued. "You can see him there."

"Is he going to be okay?" Mrs. Baldwin asked.

The surgeon paused to gather his thoughts before he spoke. "We need to see how he does in the next several hours," he said gently, his gaze wavering. "He's young and strong, so that's good."

A tiny flicker of hope sprang to life in Dara's breast. He hadn't died—yet. Was there a possibility that he wouldn't? She stared at the surgeon for some clue about what he really thought; doctors never told the whole story. But the second he saw her looking at him, his gaze darted away, and she knew the awful truth: while the surgeon would do all he could and would put the best face on the situation, he fully expected Mike to die.

Dara wondered if she wouldn't just shrivel up and die along with him.

Mrs. Baldwin turned to her, beaming. "This is good news, isn't it, sweetheart?"

Somehow Dara forced her lips to turn up into what was, she was certain, a sickly smile. "Yes."

Mrs. Baldwin, clearly pleased with her answer, smiled even more brightly.

Toward dawn of the longest night of Dara's life, they let them see Mike in one of the dimly lit, glass-encased rooms of the ICU. He looked awful; his skin had turned a terrible ghostly pale brown, the result of his blood loss. Some sort of tube, which looked like it rightfully belonged to a set of scuba gear, was taped to the side of his slightly open mouth. The IV lines taped to his arms now made it almost impossible for her to believe those same arms had lifted and held her so easily last night. Various monitors and pumps hummed and beeped. Kindly nurses bustled in and out.

Mike did not move.

Numb exhaustion set in, and Dara's legs gave out. She collapsed in a chair by Mike's bed and stared, dazed, at the sleeping man who was everything in the world to her. Staring at his sleeping face, she leaned closer to the bed and took his hand—it was cool despite all the blankets they'd heaped on him—in her own. He'd almost gotten himself killed—could still die—protecting her.

And she'd questioned his love for her?

They sat there for hours. From a great distance, Dara noticed that the sun had come up and the shift of nurses had changed. Her thoughts swirled like water in a vortex. Mike had risked his life for her, and she knew if she could somehow wake him up and ask, he'd tell her he'd do it all over again. Because he loved her.

"Dara?"

Hadn't she always known he loved her, even when he'd refused to admit it? Deep inside, hadn't she always known? But she'd been so hurt and angry, she'd wanted to punish him for what he'd put her through. He'd been right about that. She'd wanted to make him suffer the way she'd suffered.

He was certainly suffering now.

"Dara?"

Dara started and looked up, still clutching Mike's hand. Mrs. Baldwin smiled weakly at her. "I'm going to try calling Sean again. Then I think I'll walk down the hall and stretch my legs a little. I'll bring back some coffee."

Nodding, Dara watched as she left. Her bottomless misery threatened to kill her. Would Mrs. Baldwin be so nice to her if she knew how cruelly she'd rejected

Mike last night? How she'd been so determined to extract her pound of flesh, no matter how much she hurt him? How she'd done just about everything except laugh in his face after he'd bared his soul to her? How she'd refused to tell him the one thing he needed to hear—that she loved him?

How could she have been so foolish? Now God was punishing her for her pride and stubbornness, and rightfully so. Wouldn't that be the perfect punishment for her? To never have the chance to tell Mike she loved him?

If he died, she would never—*never*—forgive herself for not telling Mike how much she loved him when she had the chance; her life would be one of guilt and regret—nothing more.

"I love you," she whispered, rubbing his head. "I *love* you." His lids fluttered a little—could he hear her?—and she thought he might wake up, but then he went still again. Bitterly disappointed, she started to tremble, then gripped her arms and rocked herself in the chair. Trying to be quiet so she wouldn't wake him, she clamped her hand over her mouth and muffled a wail. Great, wracking sobs erupted from her throat, and she buried her face in Mike's blankets. She cried and cried, nausea overwhelming her until she thought she'd vomit. "Please don't die. *Please.*"

Finally, she drifted off into a troubled sleep.

"Ahhh."

Dara struggled to swim to the top of the brackish black water, but the seaweed, swaying gently back and forth with her kicks, reached out and clutched at her hands and feet. She kicked harder, her lungs bursting with the need for air, but she couldn't break free . . .

"Ahhh."

Dara woke suddenly, sitting bolt upright in the uncomfortable chair. Something had latched onto her hand. She looked around wildly, with no idea where she was. Then she saw Mike.

Staring at her.

Chapter 24

"Ahhh," he said again, his free hand going to the tubing still taped to his mouth.

Crying out, Dara leapt from her chair, overjoyed to see those amber eyes again, even if his lids did droop heavily over them. "You're awake!" She whirled away from the bed, intending to run to the door and call the nurse in to take that stupid tube out so he could talk, but his hand tightened around hers, pulling her closer.

She raised his hand to her lips and kissed it, resisting the urge to jump up and down with excitement. His thumb ran gently over her knuckles. "I need to get the nurse, Mike. She needs to take out your breathing tube so you can talk."

He stared at her, his lids sagging, then shook his head in a firm no.

Dara pursed her lips but had to smile through her relieved tears; she didn't want to leave him, anyway. "God, you're so stubborn," she muttered, fumbling around under his blankets to find the call button. "I should just let the tube stay in. That would serve you right, wouldn't it?"

His lips curved ever so slightly around the tube.

The nurse appeared instantly. "Well, look at you," she cried, smiling at Mike as if they were old friends recently reunited. "We didn't expect to see your pretty eyes for a while yet. Can you breathe okay, do you think? Let's see."

Mike grunted, then submitted while she peeled the tape away from his face and carefully withdrew the long tube. "Cough for me," she told him.

Mike coughed, then winced, clutching his side. His breathing remained steady and even.

The nurse smiled, satisfied with her work. "I'll get you some ice water and page the doctor. He'll want to see you right away." She bustled out.

Dara swiped her tears away and frowned down at Mike, who struggled to keep his eyes open. "I-If you ever pull another stunt like that, I'll kill you myself! Do you understand me?"

One eyebrow raised in that familiar sardonic expression. "Be . . ." he began hoarsely, then broke off, coughing again. His face twisted in pain, although she couldn't tell whether it was because of his side or his throat, which must be very sore. "Believe me . . . now?" His voice was no more than a gravelly whisper.

Sitting on the edge of his bed, she leaned down to press a lingering kiss on his forehead. When she drew back, he cupped her face in his hands, staring up at her. Her throat choked with emotion. "I believe you," she said softly, her voice breaking. "And I love you. So much. *So much.*"

A faint smile drifted across his face before his eyes fluttered closed. "I . . ." His chest heaved as he drew a breath. "I know."

"Still arrogant, I see." She pressed a gentle kiss to his lips, then tried to sit up again.

Mike's eyes opened, and his hands tightened around her cheeks. He blinked furiously, and his intent, determined gaze widened slightly. "Anything . . . else?" he asked her, his voice mostly gone now.

Unable to believe God would bless her with another chance like this, Dara made a strange, choked sound that was half laugh, half sob. She reached into her pocket to retrieve Mike's gold necklace, with her engagement ring still attached. The nurse had given it to her, along with Mike's watch, before they took him to surgery. She held it up for him to see. "And if you promise not to die, I'd like to marry you—if you'll still have me."

Mike smiled tiredly, a wide, glorious smile—as beautiful as ever. "Not dying, angel." He reached for the ring, and laughing and crying with relief, she hastened to undo the clasp so he could slip it on her finger.